MURDER BY ACCIDENT

A completely unputdownable cozy mystery

VERONICA HELEY

The Ellie Quicke Mysteries Book 4

JOFFE
Ostara
CLASSICS

Revised edition 2023
Joffe Books, London
www.joffebooks.com

First published by Severn House in Great Britain in 2003

This paperback edition was first published
in Great Britain in 2023

Cover art by Dee Dee Book Covers

ISBN: 978-1-83526-079-1

CHAPTER ONE

'I wouldn't try to get out, if I were you. The handle on the front door's been wired to the mains. Other things, too, so be careful what you touch! Ha! Ha!'

The front door slammed shut.

Was it a bluff, or was the handle electrified? Ellie backed away from the door.

'Be careful what you touch . . .'

She put her hands down at her sides, and looked around her. She wouldn't touch anything — no, not anything — till she was sure it was safe.

She spotted the phone by the overturned table.

Dare she try it? Would that be electrified, too?

They couldn't afford to let her go. She would have to die, preferably in another 'accident'. Sooner or later she would make a mistake and come into contact with one of their little surprises.

If she touched anything which had been booby-trapped, she wouldn't just get a mild shock; it would kill her.

* * *

Ellie Quicke was worried. Recently widowed in her early fifties, she was adjusting well to the change in her lifestyle.

But like most women, she could worry about several things at once.

She worried most of all about her daughter Diana, who had just got the sack. Diana would want Ellie to rescue her and Ellie really didn't know how. If she refused to help her daughter . . . Ellie dreaded to think what Diana would do. Ellie loved her only daughter — of course she did — but she had to admit that Diana could intimidate for Britain and was capable of doing, well, almost anything, to get her own way.

Ellie tried to think about something else.

The recent gale had loosened a gutter at the front of the house and the toilet in the bathroom was not always flushing properly. Well, those were two problems that she could fix. The builders she always used were working next door, so she went into her garden and had a word with them across the hedge. The boss man wasn't there, but one of his men — he was doing well and had taken on a couple of part-timers recently — said they'd try to fit her in, sure, no problem. She said she'd leave a key where they could find it. That was one worry the less — except that her builders were always busy and now she worried that they might forget her little jobs, which after all couldn't compare with the money they'd get from building the conservatory next door, or replacing windows or . . . well, almost anything, really.

She waved to her neighbour's son and a friend, as they walked along the alley at the bottom of her garden. They waved back. The two lads turned out of the alley into the Green around the church, cutting across it on their way to school.

It was good to see young people around. She only hoped her own dear little grandson would grow up as fine as those two boys, though Diana did tend to spoil him. Don't think about Diana.

Ellie looked down her garden and up to the Green, where the spire of the church was surrounded by mature trees just bursting into leaf. She sent up a short prayer, Please Lord, look after those two boys today. And be with me when

I talk to Diana. I'm worried about her, and don't know what to say or do to help.

She cut that worry off short and thought of another one.

She could do with a haircut. Her short silvery hair had grown long enough to try to curl again. She must make an appointment at the hairdresser's in the Avenue. She needed to look neat for the weekend as on Friday night there was to be a party in the church hall to welcome their new vicar, while on Saturday there was a local wedding to look forward to. Dear Rose McNally's only daughter was being married and of course Ellie was invited.

She must get out her best blue suit to see if it needed cleaning. She'd spilt a drop of coffee on it, and wasn't sure whether it showed or not. Did she have time to get it cleaned? This was Wednesday. Yes, there was time, just about.

Something was eating the geraniums she was overwintering in her newly built conservatory. There were semicircular bites being taken out of most of the leaves. Was it a caterpillar? And if so, where had it come from? Ought she to spray, and if so, what with? It was not politically correct to spray in the old-fashioned way with something that was bound to kill the caterpillars but might also damage the ozone or the plants or give her a rash. But what else would work?

On a deeper level she continued to worry about her difficult daughter. Diana had been sacked for defrauding her employer. Diana didn't think she'd been guilty of any wrongdoing, of course. Diana thought it was business as usual. A bit on the side wouldn't hurt anyone if they didn't know about it, she'd say.

Unfortunately, when you were managing a block of flats for someone as bright as Diana's aged but extremely intelligent Great-Aunt Drusilla, you had to get up very early in the morning to cheat and get away with it. Diana had never been that good at getting up in the morning.

Ellie plunged back into misery. Every time the phone rang nowadays it seemed to be bad news. Aunt Drusilla's phone call the previous evening had been typical. 'I suppose I should warn you. I've sacked Diana. She's had enough warnings, for heavens' sake. Don't try to make me change my mind because I won't. Oh yes, and I'm also thinking about getting rid of Stewart, Diana's husband. He's a nice enough lad and I don't think he's as corrupt as Diana, but he's simply not up to the job of managing my flats and bedsits. You haven't told him I own them, have you? You know I don't like everyone knowing how much property I have.'

'No, Aunt Drusilla. Diana knows you own the block of flats she's been managing, but Stewart has no idea that you also own the older houses. But . . .'

'That's all right, then. I'll be sending him a warning letter tomorrow.' The phone went dead, leaving Ellie to face an uncomfortable future.

Diana's temper at best was unreliable, and Ellie didn't like to think what it was going to be like when she heard that Stewart was under notice to quit, too. Diana ought to have been a rocket scientist; with her explosive temper, she'd have been able to send a space shuttle to Mars without any trouble. She might even turn violent.

No, she wouldn't really. Would she?

Which was a good reason for Ellie to concentrate on the geraniums. She broke off a couple of affected leaves and held them up to the light to see if she could discover a caterpillar at work. No caterpillar to be seen.

Was it dry enough for her to take a turn round the garden, see how the multicoloured polyanthus were doing? Or even stray across the alley into the Green around St Thomas' Church? The daffodils under the trees were at their very best, burning drifts of yellow. It would be pleasant to linger there for a while . . . even though the breeze was brisk in March. No, she'd stay cosily in her conservatory and look out upon the beauties of the day. There was much to be thankful for, if you looked for it. And Ellie did.

Dear Lord, thank you for the sun and the spring and the beauty they bring. And please help me with Diana . . .

The builders at work next door started up some machinery or other which rattled the windows and deafened everyone in the neighbourhood. That broke Ellie's concentration.

Ellie's marauding cat didn't like the noise of the concrete mixer, either. He plopped through the cat flap into the conservatory and through the open kitchen door to see what was in his food bowl. Ellie hastened to feed him, knowing that otherwise her life wouldn't be worth living. Midge knew how to get his own way.

Ellie had a mental picture of herself being battered from all sides by strong personalities and going down for the count. Perhaps she should pack a small bag, take a taxi to the airport and get on the first plane going to a warm climate. She could afford it.

She could just about hear the phone ringing over the noise the builders were making. She wondered if she had the nerve to walk out of the house and leave them all to it.

But of course she didn't.

A male voice that she felt she ought to be able to place. 'Mrs Quicke? That you?'

'Yes. It's Jimbo, isn't it?' It wasn't Diana. What a relief. Jimbo ran a very efficient plumbing and central-heating firm which she often used. Jimbo was a rough diamond, but reliable.

'Thing is, bit of a shock. You sitting down?'

'Yes?' Something had happened to Diana?

'It's Miss Quicke, your aunt. She rang us yesterday, said she'd heard about us from you, that she had this great big house, nothing been done to it for yonks, repairs to roof and gutters just been completed but new central heating and wiring needed, then plumbing, right? Well, she said she'd had to sack the people were putting in the plumbing. Tried to use the wrong gauge, stupid so-and-sos, bound to be picked up by the inspectors. Miss Quicke wanted me to quote. So I said, Fine. Be round half nine for a decko, right?'

'Right,' said Ellie, switching her worry to Aunt Drusilla. 'Something's happened to my aunt?'

Heavy breathing. ''Fraid so. You knew the wiring here was dud, din't you? Same as everything, in my opinion. What a shambles. Well, I come in just after ten, maybe, bit late . . . and she lets me in but don't say nothing and leaves me and my mate standing there in the hall like lemons. And after a bit, I say, Yoohoo! You haven't forgotten us, have you? 'Cause it's a big place and there's no one about but she don't answer. And I said to Tom — my mate, you know — That's funny, I said.'

'Yes,' said Ellie, sitting down on the hall chair with a bump. 'My aunt?'

'It was the electrics, see. It musta been instant. I just stood there, stunned. Then Tom come up and he said . . . well, not to repeat what he said. But she's gone. I thought maybe mouth-to-mouth, but it were too late. We managed to find the main fuse box and turned everything off, and I went back upstairs 'cause Tom wasn't feeling too good but she's definitely gone. So I din't know what to do till I thought, well, Mrs Quicke recommended us, and it's her auntie, so she ought to be told. So that's why I'm ringing you.'

'Oh,' said Ellie, feeling faint. Shock. Numbness.

'You all right, missus?'

'Yes,' said Ellie, from a distance. Aunt Drusilla dead? It was unthinkable. Her death would leave a large hole in Ellie's life. Miss Quicke was a miser and a bully. Yes, she was — had been — this and that and probably would tell St Peter to stand up straight and take his hands out of his pockets when she got to heaven, but she'd been part of Ellie's life for ever.

She'd brought up Ellie's husband Frank after his parents died, and though she'd treated Ellie as her personal slave for years, they'd reached an understanding of sorts in recent months. They could almost be described as good friends.

Miss Quicke was perhaps the only person of the older generation left in Ellie's life now, and they'd been able to talk about everything together. Not to mention that both of them were wealthy but didn't want that generally known.

Ellie would miss her terribly. Lord, be with her.

'You still there, missus?'

Ellie made an effort. 'Yes, Jimbo. Have you rung the doctor? You have to get one to certify death, don't you? I suppose you dial nine–nine–nine.'

'You think I should? Thing is, undertaker's needed, not doctor.'

'I understand, but I think you must follow the usual procedures. It would have been over at once, wouldn't it? She wouldn't have suffered?'

'Dead quick. Uh, sorry. Didn't mean . . . well, you know. OK. I'll get nine–nine–nine. You'll be round, then? I mean, not much point my staying here, if the job's not going to come off, right? Got other jobs on, right?'

'Jimbo, you stay right there till the doctor's been. I have a horrid feeling that there might have to be an autopsy and, oh dear, there's so many people who'll have to be told. I'll be round as soon as I can, right?'

She put the phone down. She couldn't think what to do first. Dear Lord, give me strength. Comfort and sustain me.

Midge jumped on to her lap and gently touched her chin with his paw. He was a very loving cat, when he wasn't hunting anything that moved.

She held him tightly and rocked to and fro. Then let him jump down — he hated being cuddled really — and punched in a familiar number.

Roy Bartrick was Aunt Drusilla's illegitimate son by the only man she'd ever loved. She'd been forced by her tyrannical father to give him away at birth so the boy had been adopted into a family living some distance away. Grown-up and about to take early retirement from his job as an architect, Roy had come looking for his real mother some months ago, and chosen to settle into the community.

Six feet of silver-haired, blue-eyed charm, Roy had made more friends than enemies since he arrived, especially since he and his mother went into partnership to develop the site of a dilapidated Victorian house on the Green nearby. He also paid court — now and then — to Ellie, who refused to take him seriously. No, she would not marry him, but there was a loving kindness between them.

For once Roy was available to answer his mobile phone.

Ellie found breathing difficult as she fought to tell him the bad news. 'Roy, this is Ellie. Are you sitting down?'

'What? No, I'm driving down the Avenue . . . wait a mo'. I'll pull into the kerb. What is it, Ellie?'

She tried to speak, but couldn't. She was going to give way to tears. No, she wasn't. 'Roy, it's your mother.'

'What about the old bat, then? Saw her last night. Had a fine old time last week, didn't she? Sacked the cleaner — again. Made the builders repaint the fascia boards. Sacked the plumbers. Went out and bought a new computer. Sacked Diana, who had it coming to her, if you ask me.'

There was no love lost between Diana and Roy. Roy thought her a selfish bully, and Diana thought him a fortune-hunter. Both thought they were in line for a substantial inheritance when Aunt Drusilla died, and only one of them was right.

His voice became uncertain. 'She's also going to sack Stewart, I believe. Says he's not up to the job. She's probably right, though I'm a little sorry for him. It's punishment enough for any man to be married to Diana. Ellie, what's wrong? My mother was full of beans last night. Told me a naughty bit of gossip about the Town Clerk which I must pass on to you sometime. She also told me to get a haircut. Ellie?'

'Roy, she's dead. A fault in the wiring at the house.'

There was a long, long silence. Eventually he said, 'No, no, *no*!'

Ellie began to weep, without sound.

He said, 'I've only just found her. She can't be dead. She's not that old, and there's nothing wrong with her!'

Ellie wept.

He said, quietly, 'I don't think I can bear it.'

'I can't, either.'

'She's so fond of you. But I–I can't think straight. What happened? A fault in the wiring? I've told her over and over!

Those blasted electricians! They were there two days running and then . . . it's over a week since they started tearing out the old wiring. I warned her. I did warn her, didn't I, Ellie? I didn't forget to warn her, did I?'

Ellie didn't know whether he'd warned her or not, but she did know that he'd blame himself for ever if she didn't reassure him. 'No, Roy. You warned her. I did, too. And dear Rose was looking after her so well.'

'What a blessing that woman is. Your finding her to look after my mother made her life so much better. She was enjoying herself so much. I can't . . . I've got to get over there.'

'Don't try to drive, Roy.'

'I'll lock up the car and walk. It's not far. I can't believe it.'

Only after he'd disconnected did she think, Diana will be thrilled . . .

Oh dear. What a nasty thought.

She mopped up, blew her nose and phoned for a minicab. Even if she'd ever learned to drive a car, today was not the day to do it and she had an account with a local firm. Glancing out of the window, she saw it was a nasty blustery day with a cold east wind. Typical of late March. She pulled on a coat, located her handbag and mobile phone and gave the driver her aunt's address.

She had her own mobile phone nowadays and though she hated the nasty little gadget, she did agree that it was useful now and then. As now, in the minicab.

'Diana, is that you?'

'Mother, you've been on the phone for ever. I'm coming round to see you. You've got to help me make Great-Aunt Drusilla see sense.'

'Diana, listen to me. I'm on my way to Aunt Drusilla's now. There's been an accident.'

'Fallen down the stairs again, has she? You never listen to me when I say this, but it really is time that she was put into a home. She's gone completely gaga, you know. Tried to give me the sack . . .' Diana gave a metallic laugh.

'It's worse than that,' said Ellie, steeling herself for Diana's reaction. (Please, Diana, don't be too pleased about this.) 'I'm afraid she's dead.'

'What? Nonsense.' A silence. 'Are you sure?'

'Yes, I'm afraid so. I'm on my way there now.'

Another silence. But this time there was no grief at the end of it. 'Wow! I thought she was indestructible. Sometimes the Gods do listen, then. Well, this is a turn-up for the books. It couldn't be better timed. I'll meet you there.'

Ellie ended the call. At least Diana hadn't crowed with joy, even if she hadn't sounded upset.

Who else ought she to ring? Her own solicitor, perhaps. But he wasn't Aunt Drusilla's solicitor. Ellie didn't know who was. The old lady had kept her life in separate compartments, hardly ever letting her right hand know what her left hand was doing. Ellie winced at the idea of having to sort out the complications of her estate.

It didn't bear thinking about.

Rose. She must ring Rose. She'd become friends with Rose McNally when they were both working at the charity shop in the Avenue. After Ellie's husband died and left her well off, she'd left the charity shop but kept up her friendship with Rose. Ellie valued Rose highly because although she had a habit of twittering on about everything, she had a heart of gold. Recently Rose had moved in with Aunt Drusilla to act as a temporary companion and housekeeper. Rose had also helped Miss Quicke to start on long-overdue renovations to the big Victorian house. Ellie and Roy had fervently hoped Rose would stay on, but were not sure that she'd be able to put up with Miss Quicke's sharp tongue.

Jimbo hadn't mentioned Rose being at the house when he found Miss Quicke so she must have been having a rare day off and would probably be back at her council flat. Rose would be shattered to hear Aunt Drusilla was dead, too. They hadn't been together long but it was an arrangement made in heaven; Miss Quicke had the financial acumen of a City giant, while Rose was a home-loving body who really appreciated the space and original features of the old house and knew exactly how to tempt an elderly lady's appetite.

Perhaps Rose was out shopping, or arranging something for her daughter Joyce's wedding, which was to take place that Saturday, the reception being held at . . . at Aunt Drusilla's. Oh.

What would happen about that? Joyce would screech to heaven if the reception had to be cancelled, so . . . poor Rose. Poor everyone.

The cab turned off the road into the semicircular driveway of Aunt Drusilla's house. The laurels dripped with rain and the dullness of the day brought out the shadows in the pillared portico. The broken steps had recently been repaired and new paint gleamed everywhere, but the house looked unlived-in and unloved, perhaps because of the scaffolding which surrounded it.

Perhaps the house knew its mistress had died. Ellie held back a sigh. The house had belonged to Ellie's husband Frank and on his death it had passed to Ellie. She had never thought of turning the old lady out but together with Rose had finally persuaded Miss Quicke to undertake some urgent repairs. The roof was now watertight, the gutters renewed, plumbing and wiring were next on the list — except that the wiring had killed Miss Quicke before she could get round to replacing it.

Ellie felt the burden of looking after the house settle around her. She didn't want it. Never had liked the house. Oh dear.

A couple of cars and a van were already in the driveway and a lorry was trying to edge its way in but being turned away. She recognized Jimbo's van, and she supposed the others belonged to the doctor and . . . some other visitor.

Jimbo was in the panelled hallway, looking agitated. He started towards her, keeping his voice low. 'Thank God you've come, missus. Look, I've got to go. Can't hang around with jobs waiting. I found her but I don't know nothing, right?'

Someone was coming down the stairs. The front door opened and Jimbo darted out as Roy came in. Roy looked as if he'd aged ten years since she last saw him. Ellie went to him and put her arms round him — or as much of him as she could manage, he being tall and well built, and she on the short side.

Someone coughed. Roy patted Ellie's back and she patted his shoulder.

'Detective Sergeant Willis,' announced the woman at the foot of the stairs. And then, 'Oh. We've met before, I think. Mrs Quicke, isn't it?'

Indeed they had, over a tragic affair of child abuse. Neither woman had thought much of the other then, and it didn't look as if Ms Willis had changed her mind since.

DS Willis was in plain clothes — and very plain they were, too, Ellie thought. DS Willis still hadn't done anything much about her hair, which was thick and untidy and inexpertly coloured mahogany.

Roy gaped. 'Police? What the hell . . . ?'

The woman produced her badge, flicked it open and pocketed it again. 'And who might you be?'

'Roy Bartrick. Miss Quicke's son. But . . .'

'Her son? Really?' The woman had thick eyebrows which she used to good effect. Her 'really?' was a triumph of disbelief.

Ellie stepped between them. 'Roy is her son and my cousin. Miss Quicke is . . . was . . . my husband's aunt . . . We heard that she'd met with an accident . . . but . . .'

DS Willis's eyes switched to and fro in the hall. 'Where's the plumber gone? I told him not to move till I'd spoken to him. There's a policeman on the door, isn't there? How did he get out? And how did you get in?'

Ellie felt as if she'd dropped through the rabbit hole into Wonderland. 'What in heaven's name is going on here? There's no one on the door, and why shouldn't Jimbo leave?'

The front door opened again and a uniformed policeman was thrust back into the hall, protesting loudly that no one was supposed to come in.

It was Diana, loudly informing him that he had no right to keep her out of her own house.

Only an avalanche could stop Diana when she was on the warpath. Power-dressed in an expensive black suit, handbag and briefcase at the ready, she thrust past the policeman and took centre stage. Eyes flashing, dark hair shaped to her head, she made Ellie feel inadequate just to look at her.

'So who is this?' Diana gestured towards DS Willis.

Ellie sank into a hall chair. She began to shiver. The house was cold. Of course, Jimbo had turned off the electricity at the mains, so there could be no heating or lighting on.

The PC said, 'Sorry, ma'am, I had to step out into the road. Two men in a lorry tried to come in, said they had to take the scaffolding down today. There was a bit of an argument and while my back was turned, the plumber got into his van and drove off and this woman forced her way in.'

DS Willis sighed. She said to the PC, 'I'll have a word with you later.' She flicked open her badge again and said to Diana, 'You say this is your house? And who might you be, then?'

'I,' said Diana with magnificent effrontery, 'am my great-aunt's heir, and you are trespassing. Please remove yourself from my house at once!'

The front door was pushed open again. A couple of men walked in as if they owned the place. DS Willis waved a hand and said, 'Upstairs, straight ahead.'

Diana said, 'If you please . . .' and tried to stand in their way, only to be brushed aside as if she were a child.

Ellie put one hand to her head. She found she was holding Roy's hand tightly in her other hand. He seemed to be shivering, too. It was comforting, to hold on to a man in such a time and place.

Roy cleared his throat. 'Sergeant, does this mean what I think it means? We were told that my mother had met with an accident.'

'You could put it that way, but . . .'

Once more the door was thrust open and someone walked the young PC back into the hall. Ellie reflected that the police really ought to send him on a course to show him how to deal with forceful young women.

For this was Joyce McNally, Rose's daughter, who had planned to hold her wedding reception in that very hall in five days' time. Joyce was as hard a nut as any bank cashier could be.

'Well!' said Joyce, almost but not quite putting her arms akimbo. 'What's going to happen about my wedding reception, then? I'm not cancelling it, and that's flat!'

'You'll have no choice in the matter,' said Diana, as icy as could be. 'I'm not having my house mucked up with you lot, and that's flat, too!'

Ellie felt a bubble of mirth begin to rise in her throat. Hysteria, of course. She supposed she ought to try to take command of the situation, but against three such powerful women as DS Willis, her daughter Diana and the bride to be, she didn't think she stood much of a chance.

Roy knew what to do, though. Men of his generation always did. He drew himself up to his full height and spoke over Joyce's head to the detective sergeant.

'Ms Willis, are we to take it that your presence here means there is some doubt about the cause of my mother's death? We were told it was faulty wiring.'

'Ah, it was the missing plumber who said that? I need to question him,' said the DS, responding to Roy's masterful manner. She turned to the uniformed policeman, who was beginning to wilt under this barrage of feminine personalities. 'Find him!' Then back to Roy. 'The doctor who certified death called us in, thinking that there were some suspicious circumstances.'

'You mean,' said Joyce in pleasurable horror, 'that the wiring was tampered with?'

Roy went even paler, and Ellie found he was clutching her hand so hard that it hurt.

Ellie knew she had a regrettable tendency towards flippancy. She sincerely mourned the old woman but couldn't resist saying, 'Murder by accident, you mean?'

* * *

The neighbourhood was naturally enthralled at the sight of so many vehicles piling up outside the old house. Passing cars slowed to have a look. Pedestrians gathered in knots on the other side of the street to discuss what was happening.

A youngish man in a newish Renault was among those who slowed down and gawped. Round the corner he parked, took out his mobile, and reported in.

'It's worked, just like I said it would. Police everywhere. You can stand me a drink tonight.'

He drove off, whistling through his teeth.

CHAPTER TWO

Police reinforcements were brought up, which meant that no matter how cagey the DS had been in speaking of Miss Quicke's death, it was considered suspicious.

Everyone was swept into the big sitting room, which bore so many traces of the life of Miss Quicke that Ellie was afraid she was going to break down. She noticed Roy surreptitiously blowing his nose as he picked up and gently folded the day's newspapers strewn on the floor around the old lady's favourite chair.

Ellie noted that a nearby bowl of early tulips needed water, but lacked the nerve to ask to be allowed to attend to it. A pencilled shopping list lay on the piecrust table and the *Radio Times* had been turned to tonight's programmes. Programmes that Miss Quicke would now never watch.

Ellie picked up some half-finished and rather inexpert knitting — it would be Rose's, since it was impossible to imagine Aunt Drusilla knitting — and sat down in the chair nearest the big bay window. It was still raining outside, but she felt better when she was closer to daylight. That gloomy room had always depressed her, though since dear Rose had moved in and added one or two plants and vases of flowers, it had felt more cheerful. Rose. Ellie brought out her mobile phone, intending to try Rose again.

The WPC who had been wafted in to look after them asked Ellie please not to contact anyone for the moment.

Ellie gave her a look of blind incomprehension and put the phone back in her handbag. Of course, the police must think they might have something to hide, might even try to contact an accomplice. Ellie tried to come to terms with the enormity of this idea and failed, so pushed it out of her mind.

Diana was tittupping up and down the room, making notes. 'All this heavy furniture will have to go to Sotheby's, or perhaps Phillips'. Most of it is too large for modern houses, but it's all antique and should fetch a good price.'

Ellie felt too beaten down to protest, to try to soften Diana's appalling lack of taste, or to correct Diana's assumption that she now owned the house and its contents.

'Mrs Quicke?' The WPC motioned Ellie to her feet. 'The Inspector will see you now.'

Joyce jumped up instead. 'Look, I've got to get back to work, or they'll go mad. I knew nothing about the old lady's death till half an hour ago when I dropped by in my dinner hour to check on the number of plugs in the kitchen — for the caterers on Saturday, you know. It was my mother who—'

'And where is your mother?'

'How should I know? Out running errands for Miss Quicke, I suppose. The old lady certainly got her money's worth out of my mother, didn't she? Go here, cook this, do that from morning to night. And for what? A pittance.'

No, not a pittance, thought Ellie. Aunt Drusilla paid Rose a very fair wage, far more than Rose thought necessary. Rose liked being here. As for working her too hard, Aunt Drusilla knew when she was on to a good thing and had made sure that Rose never did more than she was comfortable with. Rose was a brilliant cook. Aunt Drusilla hadn't had such good meals for ever and a day.

Oh, my dear Aunt Drusilla! You could be difficult, but am I going to miss you!

Ellie said to the WPC, 'Let Joyce go first. I can wait.'

Joyce left. The room was so chilly you could almost see your breath on the air. Roy was staring into space, now and then drawing his hand downwards across his face from brow to chin. Poor Roy. Ellie realized she liked him best when he was not coming the Autocratic over her. Poor dear Roy. He really had come to love his mother and had done his best by her over the short time he'd known her. Why, he'd even moved in to look after her after she'd had that nasty fall back in the early spring. The fact that he'd been proved completely incompetent as a carer didn't mean that he hadn't cared, because he had.

Ellie tried to pray a little; for her aunt, for Roy . . . and for poor deluded Diana, so unhappy, so grasping.

Diana joined Ellie by the window, pulling the heavy floor-to-ceiling velvet curtains backwards and forwards. The lining gave way under her hands, and she exclaimed, 'These are only fit for the dustcart!'

Diana's mobile rang. She went to retrieve it from her bag, but was stopped by the WPC. Diana bridled. 'I have appointments to keep, you know. What about her jewellery? She hasn't much but it is of good quality. I'll have to get it into the bank before they close.'

Ellie winced. 'Diana, you mustn't assume that everything goes to you.'

'Who else would she leave it to? To you? Didn't my father leave you more than enough? Would she leave it to Roy? Don't be stupid. He's just a fortune-hunter and she saw through him in a trice. To my baby Frank? Well, I suppose she might have left him something, family feeling, you know. But he's only a toddler, so who's to look after it but me? After all, blood's thicker than water.'

These sweeping and somewhat inaccurate statements silenced Ellie. Roy raised his head to give Diana a look of blank surprise, opened his mouth, shook his head and shut off whatever he'd been about to say. He didn't feel up to quarrelling with Diana, either.

Ellie closed her eyes and tried to think about something more pleasant. What was it that was eating the geranium leaves in her conservatory? And should she change her hairdresser, go for a more up-to-date, stylish cut? Perhaps even — greatly daring — go up into London to a really expensive salon? It would cost a bomb, but it might be worth it, give her spirits a much needed lift.

As she knew from her experience after Frank had died, it helped to make plans, to be positive, to get out and about. Not to sit at home and mope.

Poor Aunt Drusilla. She'd so much enjoyed her last few weeks . . . what a pity!

Ellie wondered if she'd dozed off. The room was empty except for Roy and the WPC. And even colder than before. Heavy feet were treading around up above her. Now they were descending the stairs. She didn't like to think what they were doing. Aunt Drusilla had always said she wanted to die in her bed. She hadn't been afraid of death. She'd even drawn up a note of the arrangements for her funeral, including a list of hymns to be sung and readings.

Diana had disappeared, presumably to be interviewed by DS Willis. Roy had now picked up the papers, man-like, and was reading every word, shutting out the reality of what was happening.

The WPC touched Ellie on the arm and Ellie got up, slightly stiff, and followed her across the hall into the room originally intended as a dining room. It was certainly large enough to accommodate a dining table to sit a dozen people, but Aunt Drusilla had always used it as an office. There was her computer, the screen now dark. And the filing cabinets containing details of her wide empire; the block of thirties flats down by the river which Diana managed — had managed — for her great-aunt. Also for the older houses which had long ago been converted into flats and which Stewart had been managing for her. Plus, Ellie suspected, a considerable amount of other property, too.

DS Willis was seated at the table, with a younger, tough-looking PC. Tape recorder ready to switch on, and pencil and pad at the ready.

Ellie sat where indicated, and told what she knew of the morning's events.

'This Jimbo. We've been out looking for him. Where is he to be found?'

Ellie gestured to the telephone directory. 'In the Avenue. J.C.J. Plumbing and Central Heating.'

'Why did he leave, when he was specifically asked to wait till I'd questioned him?'

Ellie shrugged. 'I've no idea.' Actually, she had a very good idea. Jimbo had been arrested for being drunk and disorderly on New Year's Eve, and hadn't she heard him grumbling about overdue parking tickets? Jimbo was an excellent plumber but he came from a family which held the police in wary dislike. It wasn't that they were particularly criminal, because they weren't — except perhaps for the odd spot of football hooliganism — but they were on the whole racist in attitude and against petty rules and regulations. They saw no harm in dropping litter on the pavement and often parked on double yellow lines.

The DS led Ellie through the events of the morning. Ellie answered all the questions frankly and to the best of her ability. Then it came. 'Who do you think benefits from Miss Quicke's death?'

'Was it suspicious?'

'Yes. The wiring had definitely been tampered with.'

Tears stung Ellie's eyes. She sniffed. 'I suppose the only good thing about it is that it must have been quick.'

'Yes. Who benefits?'

'Well, I do. At least that's what Miss Quicke told me, though she might well have changed her mind since. She told me I was to get two thirds of her estate and one third goes to Roy, her son.'

'What about her great-niece?'

'Nothing, as far as I know.'

'Diana told me she's going to inherit everything.'

'We'll have to wait till we see the will, won't we?'

'Who is Miss Quicke's solicitor?'

'I've no idea. I suppose you can find the name in her files or on the computer.'

'Yes, they're taking it away in a minute. What about this companion of Miss Quicke's, Mrs Rose McNally. Your daughter seemed to think she was out for what she could get from your aunt.'

'She's quite wrong. Rose McNally's only recently been taken on by my aunt and they got on very well indeed. Rose's daughter Joyce — you've spoken to her, haven't you? — is supposed to be having her wedding reception here on Saturday. I suppose that will have to be cancelled and Rose will lose her job. Rose stands to lose twice over by my aunt's death.'

'Perhaps when we look at the will, we'll find she was in it?'

'Possible, but unlikely.'

'Where does she live?'

'In one of the council tower blocks near the tube station.'

'Her address, please.' Ellie gave it.

The DS looked down at some notes. 'This Roy — your cousin? He was in partnership with Miss Quicke to redevelop a site locally? Your daughter says that he'd bamboozled his mother into putting up most of the money for the redevelopment.'

'Nobody could bamboozle my aunt when it came to finance. She was putting money into the development, yes. But it was a viable proposition and he's a respected architect and no fly-by-night.'

'What will happen to the development now?'

'I haven't the faintest idea. I suppose he may have to sell up at a loss.'

'But you think he's going to inherit a substantial amount under her will?'

'I believe so.'

And then it was the old 'Can you give me an account of your movements yesterday and today?'

She could, and she did. And much good might it do them for she'd been very busy this last couple of days with meetings here and there, going to church, seeing old friends, going to an exhibition at the National Gallery, and going out to supper.

And no, she didn't know anything much about electrics. If a fuse blew, she had to call someone in to deal with it. She was just not mechanically minded.

They let her go at last.

She shut the front door behind her, and walked away without looking at the PC on duty outside. The police had offered her a lift back home, but although it was still raining, she found the fresh cold wind invigorating and preferred to walk. Her brain had gone into fatigue syndrome. She couldn't think, nearly walked under a bus as she crossed the Avenue. Couldn't think whether or not she had anything suitable in the fridge to eat for supper. Stopped at the deli and bought cold meats and some luscious cream cakes. Thought of Rose, who loved the occasional treat of a cream cake. Almost burst into tears.

She had no umbrella with her. She thought of getting out her phone and ringing the minicab firm, but was too beaten down to delve for it. Walked on and on.

Crossed the Green by the church.

The rain was dripping through the branches on the trees.

Down the slope to the gate into the alley. Turn left, the back gardens here sloped up again to the houses. On her right the workmen were getting on nicely with next door's conservatory. It was going to be very much like hers, but intended as an outdoor dining room for Armand and his wife Kate, rather than as a place for growing plants.

Through the gate into her own garden. Plod up the path. Let herself into the conservatory. The phone was ringing again. Let it ring. It would record messages. She needed a cup of tea, perhaps two cups. Or maybe hot chocolate. Carbohydrates for shock. Biscuits. Cream cakes.

Peace and quiet. Midge on her lap. Dear Lord, I don't know what to pray for, but you know what I need most, what everyone needs most. Look after Roy, who really did love his mother. And poor Diana, I really can't think how she got to be so money-grubbing, I suppose it must be my fault. And dear Rose, who must be just about returning from her shopping expedition now, to be faced with police and questions and oh, dear. I must try to think about something else.

The front-door bell rang. It was Roy, looking haggard. Somehow he looked even handsomer than ever. Definitely he was better-looking than her own dear husband Frank had been.

'Sorry,' he said, or rather mumbled. 'I'm afraid I went to pieces a bit just now. They want me to make the formal identification, and I want to do it because I shan't take it in properly till I see for myself. When my adopted family died, first Mum and then Dad and my aunt, it didn't affect me so much. I loved them, of course I did. But it wasn't the same because at the back of my mind I was thinking, They're not my real family and one day I'll find my real mother, and now . . .'

'You're twittering, Roy,' said Ellie, with compassion. 'Yes, of course I'll come with you. I'd like to see her, too.'

He took a deep breath. Let it out. Swallowed hard. Looked at his feet. Mute.

Ellie peered out into the rain. 'Did they send a police car to take you to . . . wherever?'

He nodded, indicating an unmarked car by the kerbside. Ellie collected her coat, handbag and an umbrella. 'What about your own car?'

He stared at her, without words. She shrugged. He'd better not try to drive in his present state, anyway. She would have to organize someone to collect it later. She hoped he wouldn't get a parking ticket for leaving it in the Avenue but if he did, it was just too bad.

She got into the back of the car with him. Rain, rain, go away. Come again another day.

She hadn't been to a mortuary before. Hadn't even known they had one in this part of London. Well, well. You learned something new every day. Would they have to have an autopsy? She supposed so. Shudder.

The place didn't give any hint of what it was from the outside, except for a discreet plaque on the red-brick wall. Inside, it was all tiles and sterile. Roy was like an automaton, one that needed winding up to function. She held his elbow and steered him in the direction taken by the PC.

Pause. Did they both wish to look? It was only necessary for one? Roy gave a great start and said yes, they both needed to see.

The sheet was drawn back. They looked.

Roy stepped back. 'You've got the wrong body. That's not my mother.'

Ellie stepped forward to take a closer look. She frowned. She'd seen that face somewhere before. But where?

'No, this isn't Miss Quicke,' she said. 'She's about the same size but she's a good bit younger.'

The PC said, 'Are you sure?'

Roy exploded. 'Don't be stupid! Would we make a mistake like that? That. Is. Not. My. Mother!'

Ellie put out a hand to touch the ear of the woman on the slab.

'Don't touch.'

'Oh, of course not. Sorry. I was just thinking, that looks like she's had her ears pierced, though the holes have almost closed up. Aunt Drusilla never had her ears pierced. May I see her hands?'

Roy swung her away from the slab. 'Let's get out of here! This is madness. They bring us here . . .'

He was going to say 'under false pretences', she knew it. And she'd giggle if he did. Hysteria. 'Hush, Roy.' She disengaged his arm and stepped back to the slab. A technician — mortuary attendant? — had now joined the PC. 'Would you mind if I saw her hands? Or perhaps the clothes she was wearing?'

'I'm out of here!' shouted Roy and plunged out of the room.

The mortuary attendant drew the sheet back at one side, exposing the woman's right hand. Ellie bent over it, without touching. There was a really bad burn across the woman's palm, which must be where she'd held on to — whatever it was that had given her a lethal shock.

'Mm. What do you think, Constable?'

'I couldn't say, miss.'

Ellie looked at the technician. 'What do you think?' No reply.

Ellie sighed. 'This woman's hand shows signs of rough usage, probably housework. Reddened fingers, some eczema from using chemicals. Aunt Drusilla wouldn't have been seen dead washing up or cleaning a floor. I wonder, do you have her clothes here?'

An exchange of glances between the two men, but no reply. Presumably the clothes had gone for forensic tests. Yuk.

Ellie frowned. 'I am not entirely sure, but I think I've seen this woman at my aunt's. Miss Quicke employed cleaners through an agency. None of them ever lasted for long because she had very high standards and most people failed to live up to them. I have a mental picture of a woman wearing an unsuitable tartan skirt, pleated, very old-fashioned. I think it was a Royal Stewart tartan, with lots of red and green in it?'

The PC and the mortuary attendant exchanged glances. One of them seemed to be smiling, ever so slightly.

Ellie said, 'I can't be one hundred per cent sure, but I think this was a cleaner my aunt employed some time ago. I suggest you contact the agency for which the cleaners work. I'll remember the name in a minute . . . no, it's gone. But there can't be many agencies around here which do that kind of work. I'm sure that if you spend a little time on the phone you'll find the right one, and they'll be able to tell you if they're missing someone.'

'But you can confirm that this is not Miss Drusilla Quicke.'

'No, definitely not.' She hesitated. 'I think I've heard this woman's name mentioned by my aunt, but . . . no, I'm sorry. I'm bad at remembering names. Lucky? No. Booker? Cooker? No, that's not right, either. Sorry.'

'Thank you. Most helpful.'

Ellie let out a long sigh of relief. She needed to sit down. She couldn't quite take in all these reverses of fortune. The body was not that of Miss Quicke. What a relief. Thank the Lord for all his mercies.

She couldn't think which way to the exit, but the young PC steered her out into the open air. Roy was raging up and down on the pavement, hitting the palm of his hand with his fist. It was still raining, but he was beyond noticing things like that.

The PC was on his walkie-talkie, giving the bad news to Ms Willis. 'No, they're both quite sure. The body is not that of Miss Quicke . . .' He turned slightly away from Ellie, but she heard the words 'possibly a cleaner?' quite clearly.

She felt rather shaky. A good cup of tea wouldn't be a bad idea. She could do with some food. Roy had probably missed lunch, too. He was still in a tearing rage, muttering about incompetent police, misleading . . . and so on and so forth.

He'd probably refuse a lift back in the police car, just to spite them. But — she looked around her — they were in the middle of nowhere and she rather thought a lift back would be a good idea.

Roy had got to the inventive swearing stage. So wasteful of energy.

He told the policeman where to put his something car, because he was . . . etcetera. Ellie filtered out the swear words.

She put up her umbrella, dived into her handbag and punched in the number of her minicab firm. 'Mrs Quicke here. I'm stranded at the mortuary, in . . .' She peered into the gloom and read off the name of the road. 'Can you send a cab for me and my cousin? To go home, James.'

The delightful Asian controller the other end of the phone knew her of old. He chuckled and said in his musical voice, 'That's a new one to me. Mrs Quicke? You all right there? My name not James, you know.'

Ellie was embarrassed. 'So sorry. I'm regressing to childhood. My father always used to say "Home, James!" when he got us all safely back on to the train after a day's outing, just as if we were in a coach and he was telling the coach driver to . . . oh, forget it. I'm not quite myself this afternoon. Tell me something. You know my aunt, Miss Quicke? Have you by any chance been called out to take her somewhere today? She seems to have gone missing, you see.'

'Not to me she hasn't called, no. But look, I've been on since noon only. I ask, shall I?'

'Thank you.' She switched off the phone, thinking that it was an outside chance that Aunt Drusilla would have used the minicab firm. She usually called a black taxi when she wanted to go anywhere.

Roy had muttered himself to a standstill. Now he was looking stricken, almost sagging at the knees.

She thought she knew what he was thinking. If the woman in the mortuary was not Aunt Drusilla, then *where was she*?

CHAPTER THREE

They made the journey back to Ellie's place in silence. Ellie was thinking about her answerphone. The phone had been ringing when she got back from Aunt Drusilla's that morning, but she'd ignored it to make herself a cuppa. Perhaps Aunt Drusilla had been trying to ring her? And had left a message?

Then Roy had come and taken her off to the mortuary. So there might very well be a message for her at home.

Alas, when she eased herself and Roy into her house, there was Diana talking away in animated fashion on the phone. And the answerphone light was out.

Diana usually stabbed in casual fashion at the buttons on modern telephones, and had erased recorded messages on Ellie's phone before now. Diana saved money by using Ellie's phone instead of her own. Diana was . . . Ellie stopped that thought.

'Food,' she said to Roy. 'Take your coat off, go and sit down, turn the telly on or something. I'll see what I can rustle up.'

Diana said, 'Kiss, kiss!' into the phone and hung up, all bright-eyed and bubbly. 'Mother, he's coming round to meet you straight away, so do you think you could change into something a little more fashionable?'

'Diana, there's something you need to know . . .'

Diana was not listening, but smearing fresh lipstick on her mouth. 'I know you won't approve, you're so old-fashioned, quite dead in the water, dead as the Dodo, but this is the first day of the rest of my life and I'm determined you shan't pull a sour face, right?'

Roy lifted his hands in despair and went into the sitting room. The rain was beating down on the conservatory roof but it would still be warm in there, because of the central heating Jimbo had installed.

And what was eating her geraniums?

Ellie hadn't a clue what Diana was talking about. 'You've cleared the messages on the answerphone again. Who rang?'

Diana gave her metallic laugh. 'Oh, mother, you're so out of date. It was just Jimbo, that stupid plumber of yours . . .'

'Well, as a matter of fact, we've just come from—'

The doorbell rang and Diana leaped to answer it. In came a dapper little man whom Ellie recognized with dismay. Derek Jolley, her most unfavourite of all estate agents. At Diana's instigation he'd once tried to cheat Ellie out of her house. He'd also acted for some years as managing agent for some — if not all — of Aunt Drusilla's property. Diana and Derek, two people with but one thing in mind — which was doing other people down for a quick buck. This was an alliance made in hell.

'Derek Jolley, you remember me?' The dapper little man held out his hand to be shaken by Ellie. 'From *THE* Estate Agents, in the Avenue. Har, har.'

'And my very special friend,' announced Diana, linking her arm with his. She was taller by three or four inches.

'Ready for anything and anybody, that's me,' pronounced Mr Jolley. 'Pity we had to meet again under such sad circumstances, but still, it's an ill wind that blows no good, as they say.'

Diana simpered. 'Derek and I just got together. Isn't it exciting?'

Ellie gaped. Had the girl forgotten she already had a husband and had borne him a child?

'Come along in, Derek,' said Diana, ushering him into the sitting room. 'I'm sure we can run to a glass of sherry to toast our happiness, though I don't think we'll find any champagne in my mother's wine rack. Oh,' she said, her face hardening. 'This is my sort-of-uncle, Roy Bartick. Illegitimate. You don't need to worry about him.'

Diana always called Roy 'Bartick' instead of his real name, which was Bartrick. This amused Diana, but annoyed everyone who liked Roy — and that included Ellie.

Roy had taken too many blows that day. He wilted. Ellie recovered her voice and her wits. 'Diana, how dare you! In the first place, Roy's name is Bartrick, as you very well know. And in the second place, I don't believe what you've just said! What about Stewart? Anyway, we've just discovered that . . .'

Diana put on her meanest face. 'I've left Stewart. Haven't I, my dearest?' She pressed herself even closer to Derek Jolley. Derek nodded, and patted her hand with his plump paw.

'Does Stewart know that?' asked Ellie.

Roy shook his head as if to clear his ears of something that he simply could not have heard. Ellie gave Roy a push towards the drinks tray, he poured himself a sherry and downed it in one gulp.

Diana preened herself. 'He will by now. I left a note for him with the babysitter.'

Prompt on cue, the doorbell rang and Stewart used his key to enter, wheeling the pushchair containing little Frank before him. He looked harassed, honest and angry all at once.

'Diana, I thought I'd find you here! What the devil do you think you're doing?'

Little Frank started to wail, so Ellie scooped him up out of the pushchair and took him out into the conservatory. Roy followed with a glass of sherry for her, and another for him.

She heard Diana say, 'What a bad loser you are, Stewart!' before Roy closed the door from the living room into the conservatory. Ellie jiggled the toddler up and down. Midge the cat exited by the cat flap. He didn't like Diana any more than Diana liked him.

'Leave them to sort it out between them,' said Roy, speaking for the first time since they got back to Ellie's.

'Words of wisdom. But they still think Aunt Drusilla's dead.'

Roy sank into a chair and sipped sherry. 'It may be reprehensible of me, but I take a certain amount of satisfaction from that thought. Just pray that we're both there to enjoy the moment when she finds out. Here, give me little Frank. He likes me. Shall we walk out and leave them to it? Go for a meal somewhere?'

'I'm too wound up to sit still. Besides, what would we do with little Frank? Suppose I make us an omelette or a sandwich or something. That all right with you?'

He couldn't bring his mind back to mundane things like food. 'Where's my mother gone to, do you think? I'd suggest going back to her house to wait for her there, but the police said they'd sealed off her bedroom . . .'

'Is that where it happened?'

'Apparently, yes. They were putting a man out front so nobody could contaminate the crime scene. She might have returned at any time and been refused admission to her own house.'

Ellie tried to laugh. 'If so, I don't envy the policeman on duty outside.'

Roy almost managed to smile at that. 'But where has she gone? Why hasn't she rung us? Perhaps she's been kidnapped or knocked over in the street.'

'I pity anyone who tried to kidnap her. She'd give them short shrift. I expect she's gone shopping. Or to have an argument with her bank manager — which I'm sure she'd win. To her solicitor's, to sue someone? To inspect the work which Diana ought to have done at the flats? Ten to one she's out with Rose, because I tried ringing Rose and she wasn't at home.'

Roy checked his mobile. 'No messages on it. I'll see if she left any on the phone at my flat.' He pressed keys. 'No, nothing. Has she left any messages on your mobile?'

Ellie tossed him her mobile. 'You can check. I can't work out how to access the messages. If there were any messages on my answerphone, Diana will have wiped them. For a woman who deals with computers all day, she's remarkably clumsy with my answerphone. Try ringing Rose again. The number's in the mobile.'

Yes, where was Rose, anyway? Dear Lord, if anything's happened to her, too . . .

'No reply.'

Frank was getting fractious, so Roy took him to look at the fish in the water tank while Ellie escaped to the kitchen. There were raised voices in the sitting room. 'You said . . .'

'No, I didn't!'

Roy was right, let them get on with it.

Roy followed her out into the kitchen as she threw the ingredients for a Spanish omelette onto the table. Cold potatoes, tomatoes, onions and eggs. Half a pepper, and some leftover ham. Defrost some bread from the freezer. The butter's too hard to use straight away. Leave it out on the boiler and pray Midge doesn't get back to investigate it before it's softened.

Roy had finished his second sherry and was loosening up nicely. He popped little Frank into his high chair at the table and found a spoon for him to play with. Ellie hewed a crust off the loaf, put it under the grill to defrost and gave it to little Frank to keep him quiet. Roy asked for a slice as well. Roy probably hadn't had any breakfast, certainly hadn't had any lunch.

Ellie got out the pans, sliced onions into some oil and set them to soften.

Roy became ponderous. 'My mother told me last night that she was going to sack Diana. Something about invoices not adding up. Stupid girl. Doesn't she know my mother always checks invoices? I wonder if she actually got round to telling the girl she was fired?'

'Yes,' said Ellie. 'Diana rang this morning. She wanted me to get Aunt Drusilla to change her mind. As if I could.'

'Right. Did Diana know that my mother was also about to sack Stewart? She may well have done. In which case, she didn't waste much time finding herself another meal ticket, did she? Do you know anything about this man Jolley? He makes my skin creep.'

'Mm. Nasty piece of work. Not above shading the truth if it suits him.'

'My mother said we'd use a nationally known estate agent to sell the townhouses we're building on the Green. She said something about having used a local man in the past and got rid of him. Would this be the man, do you think?'

'Probably. She has a short loyalty span, though in this case I think she was right to discard him.' Ellie used a wooden spoon to stir the onions. Little Frank had thrown his crust on the floor. He was pretending to count as he worked over Roy's bunch of keys.

Roy's car! She'd forgotten it completely, and he had, too. How was she to get it back to him, or would it matter if it were out there all night?

A chair overturned in the sitting room and someone screamed. Diana, of course. Perhaps Stewart was not taking things as quietly as she'd expected? He did come from a Scottish family and though slow to rouse, he might possibly throw off a tantrum if circumstances were right. Good.

Mushrooms and pepper. Chop them. Mix little Frank a drink in his cup, and find him a biscuit. Leave the biscuit tin out for Roy to dip into.

She said, 'Diana thinks Aunt Drusilla has left her the house but she hasn't, because it was Frank's house and he left it to me. Diana doesn't know that. She probably thinks she can demolish it and redevelop the site rather as you are doing with that terrible old wreck of a place on the Green. Diana also seems to think she's her great-aunt's sole heir. Derek Jolley must see pound signs whenever he looks her way.'

'Two thirds of her estate to you, and one third to me? That's what my mother said. And you're the executor.'

'Yes. Academic, now. And I'm remarkably pleased that it is so.'

'By God. So am I.' He meant it, too.

She broke eggs into a bowl and started whisking them up with some seasoning. 'If she'd died, would you have been able to go on with the development on the Green, or would you have had to sell?'

'Oh no, we could carry on. My mother made me take out a special insurance to cover all eventualities — such as the death of one of us. If she'd died, I'd have been able to pick up the insurance money to finish the development. But no amount of insurance money would compensate for her input. What a clear mind she has. She says, Why did you do this and why are you planning to do that? And do you know what? When I've thought it through, she's always right. I wouldn't mind going into partnership with her any day. She'd actually said that if she was pleased with this development, she might perhaps consider doing another one with me in future.'

'That's brilliant, Roy. I'm so pleased for you.'

It was brilliant in another way, too. It meant Roy would have lost more than he'd have gained if he'd murdered his mother. Therefore, it wouldn't have been in his interest to harm her. Though of course Ellie hadn't thought him guilty for a minute.

Ellie got out her biggest frying pan, tipped the egg mix into it, and topped half of it with all the other things she'd found in the fridge, plus the cooked onions. 'Can you set the table? We'll eat in here, I think.'

Frank screamed, 'Me, too!' He was hungry and it was nearly time for bath and bed. Next door the battle royal raged, with accusations flying around like boomerangs. 'How dare you . . . You drove me to it!'

Ellie carved chunks of bread, rescued the butter from the top of the stove and sought for a bottle of wine in the bottom of her larder. 'Red wine do you?'

'Anything. Ellie, you are a miracle worker.'

She flipped one half of the omelette over the other, while Roy disinterred knives and forks from the drawer and fished out a couple of glasses. Frank yelled 'Me, me, me!' which meant he was serious about wanting some food as well. What could she provide for him? Roy retrieved his keys from the floor, where Frank had thrown them. It was a very domestic scene.

The front door slammed. Was reopened. And slammed again. Frank jumped in his high chair. There was silence next door. 'Momma?' said Frank in a small voice. 'Where Momma gone?'

'Ouch,' said Ellie. 'They must each have thought that the other had taken Frank. Never mind, my little love. You can have supper with Uncle Roy and Granny, and then we'll pop you in the bath and then your nice little bed upstairs.'

'Sleep at Ganny's,' said Frank, quite accustomed to being dumped on his grandmother. Ellie put two thirds of the omelette on a plate for Roy and kept a third for herself, cutting off a large corner for Frank, who loved scrambled eggs.

Roy tied a bib around little Frank's neck and then lifted his glass. 'Here's to your blue eyes, Ellie.'

'And yours.' Frank opened his mouth to yell. 'Wait a minute, Frank. Here's your own special spoon.'

'This is good,' commented Roy, getting on with his food. 'Marry me, Ellie?'

'No, thank you, Roy. How many times is that you've asked me? Three, or four? Move your glass or Frank will have it over.'

'I shall go on asking, you know.'

'Give over, do. You need someone much younger, who'll give you a batch of kids of your own.'

He shook his head. He'd had one failed marriage with a much younger woman. 'I'm not going through that again.' He sighed. 'I wish I knew where my mother was.'

* * *

It was past seven o'clock. It was still raining, Frank had only just settled down to sleep and both Roy and Ellie were tired out, mentally and physically. Messages had been left for both Stewart and Diana on their phones, but neither was picking them up.

Roy was searching the channels on TV, looking for some football. He had the sound turned up just a trifle too loud, which was reason number six why Ellie wouldn't marry him. Reasons numbers one to five tended to wax and wane in importance at any given moment, but included: it was too close to her husband's death, Roy was too like her dear departed but autocratic husband, who had always assumed she would be happy to fall in with all his wishes without complaint or query, Roy was just too charming to be trusted, and she liked her independence.

Oh yes, and he wasn't averse to playing the sex card and she'd had enough of that. For the time being, at any rate.

Ellie was leafing through some paperwork. Part of her inheritance was being put into a trust fund to be used for charitable purposes and there was a lot of paperwork for her to look at every week. The other trustees were Armand's wife, her best friend Kate — the financial whizz kid from next door — and their recently departed vicar from St Thomas' who was now in a larger parish on the other side of London. They joked that Kate was the brains of the organization, Ellie the heart and dear Gilbert — a lean man with a large appetite — was the stomach.

Ellie would have liked peace and quiet to concentrate on the paperwork, but she quite understood that Roy — being a man — needed the distraction of a football match. They'd been ringing Rose and Aunt Drusilla every half hour without result and both were beginning to talk about informing the police.

The only person who had rung them that evening had been Joyce McNally, wanting to know if the police would allow her to hold her wedding reception as planned. She'd rung three times, getting in more of a panic each time. Joyce didn't know where her mother was, either. Ellie felt sorry for her. A little. Joyce was a bit of a bully, but she didn't deserve this.

Ellie's eyes were on the paper in front of her, but her mind was elsewhere. She was trying to work out exactly what must have happened at Aunt Drusilla's that morning. According to the evidence in the sitting room, the two women had been quietly sitting there; Aunt Drusilla had been reading the papers — the *Financial Times*, of course — and Rose had been making out a list of food to buy. That list had been in Rose's handwriting. The cleaner had presumably arrived and been admitted before the two women had sat down in the sitting room? Or had the cleaner let herself in later? Presumably the agency kept the keys because Aunt Drusilla changed cleaners frequently. Note: better check that.

What *was* the name of the cleaning agency?

No, she couldn't bring it to mind.

And the cleaner's name? Copper? Ellie half laughed and shook her head at herself. 'Copper' as in policeman? Cocker? Forget it. It would come back to her presently. Probably when she was in the bath.

Jimbo had arrived at about ten and by that time the two women had gone and the cleaner was dead upstairs. It was a fairly short time span. What could have caused the women to up and go so quickly, without leaving any message behind?

Ellie couldn't think what it might be. Now, if she could have prowled around, perhaps visited the kitchen, she might be able to work out what had happened. But that was not likely to happen with Ms Willis in charge.

* * *

Down at the local, the man met up with his girlfriend. He bought her a pint, and she munched crisps.

'You done good,' she said. 'Comin' back tonight?'

'Might. Or you come round my place? It's quieter.'

She gave him a nudge and giggled.

He caught her round the shoulders and gave her a smacking great kiss.

* * *

Rose McNally had a two-bedroom council flat high up in a tower block about half a mile from the Avenue. Her husband had died some years before and since her daughter Joyce had moved out last year, Rose had lived there alone and lonely. That is, until Miss Quicke had invited her to stay for a few weeks.

Two floors down and in another block on the same site there was an identical flat occupied by the geriatric Mr Tucker — whose lifelong heavy smoking had led to the loss of his left leg. He was looked after by his daughter Mo, who not only claimed all the allowances to which she was entitled, but earned money on the side by cleaning.

Mo Tucker and Rose McNally had never spoken, although they knew one another by sight.

'Mrs' Tucker had never bothered to marry but had had several live-in partners. The present recipient of her favours was a large slug of a man, a beer-bellied soft-porn watcher, out of work for many a year and content to have his meals and pocket money provided for him by Mo.

Mr Tucker sniped at Norm, and Norm ignored Mr Tucker. They were, however, united in their dislike of Mo Tucker's seventeen-year-old son, who'd never had a job and was usually in trouble with the police over thefts from cars and joyriding.

The lad's nickname was Jogger, because he never stood still. Technically, he lived with his girlfriend and their baby, but he often visited his mum for a handout.

For the umpteenth time Mr Tucker said, 'I want my tea. Where's Mo with my tea?'

Norm flicked ash. He too smoked. Even the curtains in the flat were stained with nicotine. 'Get it yourself, old man.'

Jogger said, 'I gotta have some cash . . . where is she?'

Someone knocked on the front door. Jogger slid out of sight. He could smell police even through the door.

Mrs Tucker's death would affect all three of their lives. And Rose McNally's as well.

* * *

Ellie put down her paperwork. 'Is that a taxi?'

She rushed to the window overlooking the road and yes, there was a taxi. Two figures were sitting in the back. 'Roy, they're here!'

Roy was glued to the television set. 'Go for it, man! You can do it! Aaah! You idiot!'

Ellie reached for the remote control and turned the television down. 'They're here. Both of them.'

Suddenly sober, they opened the front door.

Dear Rose twittered down the path to the front door, hung about with various parcels. 'Oh, my dears, what a day! I've never known anything like it.'

Rose was noted for her good heart and poor dress sense but this evening she was transformed, wearing a smart new camel-hair coat and matching beret. Where had she got those from?

The taxi driver was actually descending from his cab to help Aunt Drusilla out — unheard of! She was gesturing with her umbrella, ordering him to come to the other side of the cab, did he think she was a teenager to hop out all by herself? And don't forget those other parcels!

It was still raining.

Ellie kissed Rose warmly. 'Where have you been? We've been so worried about you!'

Roy had grown very tense at Ellie's side. Ellie expected him to rush up the path to help his mother, but he didn't. He stared up at her, looking shocked rather than thrilled to see her again. Or overcome by shyness?

Rose flumped down on the hall chair. 'Didn't you get my message? Is that the time? Sorry we're a bit late, but we've been all over the place and I confess I'm dead beat though dear Miss Quicke is indefatigable.'

Miss Quicke made her majestic way down the path, prodding the unfortunate taxi driver, now burdened with more parcels, down the slope ahead of her.

Roy let out a long-held breath and moved to take the parcels from the taxi driver and pay him. 'We've been worried sick about you. Where have you been?'

'Mind that package, it's got china in it. I can't be doing with Ellie's idea of china. Might as well drink tea out of a thick pottery mug.'

Wordlessly Ellie helped stack parcels at the foot of the stairs, while Roy helped his mother out of her coat. She was wearing her usual dun-coloured but expensive Wetherall clothes.

'A cup of tea would be welcome,' said Aunt Drusilla, making her way into the sitting room. 'Earl Grey, no milk, a slice of lemon. And please turn the television off. It's been a tiring enough day without having to listen to schoolboys doing a war dance over a simple ball game.'

Rose followed Aunt Drusilla. 'If I sit in a comfortable chair, I'll fall asleep. Oh, aren't you watching EastEnders?'

Ellie skittered into the kitchen to set out tea things and put the kettle on. She got out the best china cups and saucers and gave them a rinse, acknowledging Aunt Drusilla's accusation that she usually drank coffee and tea out of a pottery mug.

Taking the tea into the sitting room, she saw that Roy had settled the two women in armchairs, but had still not received a proper explanation for their absence. 'Yes, but what happened?'

Aunt Drusilla looked surprised. 'Didn't you get my message? Rose said you might be worried if you couldn't contact us, so I told her to ring you and leave a message on your answerphone if you were out. You should have got that. Where were you?'

'Out, I suppose,' said Ellie. That must have been about the time she and Roy were on their way to the mortuary. Diana had probably wiped that message in her usual thoughtless fashion.

'Well, no great harm done,' said Miss Quicke, removing her slice of lemon from her tea and holding it in the air, waiting for someone to relieve her of it.

Ellie duly removed the lemon. 'I wouldn't say that, exactly. If we'd only known you were all right! We've been half out of our minds with worry about you.'

'What, even Roy?' Aunt Drusilla was not sure she could believe that.

'Especially Roy,' said Ellie, firmly. 'When we had to go to the mortuary to identify you — only it wasn't you, of course . . .'

'Mortuary, indeed,' said Miss Quicke. 'I am reminded of that witty remark, I don't know who said it, but it was something about the reports of my death being greatly exaggerated.'

Rose clasped both hands together, still very excited. 'We arrived back at the house and I nearly had a fit. Police everywhere. I couldn't believe my eyes. What a fuss! Do you know, they wouldn't even let us go upstairs, not even to the bathroom . . .'

'To start at the beginning,' said Miss Quicke, overriding Rose with ease. 'The cleaner had arrived early — I've had her before and not been at all pleased with her work but apparently she was the only one the agency had free, so I had to put up with her. It's amazing the amount of dust that flies about when builders start work on a house. I told her to start upstairs and I'd just settled down with the papers when Rose said she fancied a cup of coffee. I said I'd have one, too. So Rose went into the kitchen and switched on the kettle but it wouldn't light or heat up.'

'So I went to tell Miss Quicke and she said . . .'

'We'd only bought that kettle last week and it was still under guarantee so of course we had to take it back.'

'. . . though I did wonder if it were the wiring in the house which was responsible . . .'

'Nonsense. The kettle was faulty. The problem was that I'd told Rose to throw away my old kettle when we got the new one, so we couldn't even make ourselves a cup of tea without it.'

'. . . but it had been all right at breakfast,' said Rose. 'Though I'd had to press the switch down three times to make it work . . .'

Aunt Drusilla turned to Ellie. 'That plumber of yours was supposed to have been there at half past nine. I thought he might have fixed the kettle, but it was well after ten and he hadn't turned up. The electrician said he was going to switch off all the power to our side of the house, in order to start rewiring the kitchen. He couldn't say when he'd be finished. Naturally I couldn't have that, because of the wedding on Saturday and the caterers needing power points. I told him he'd have to stop work till after the weekend.'

Rose put in, 'And he wouldn't even look at the kettle, to see if he could mend it for us.'

'It was the last straw. Having the builders thump and clang around the place doing the roof for the previous fortnight had been had enough, and that plumber — I'll never use him again — proposing to use the wrong gauge of pipes, did he think I was born yesterday? — but it was the kettle which finally made me realize that I would have to find somewhere else to live until the electricians and the plumbers had finished.

'Dear Rose suggested I go back home with her but she'd already mentioned what a strain it was to walk up six flights of stairs to her flat when the lift was out of order, which I understand is not unusual. Hotels are out of the question; far too expensive. Then I thought of the flats which Stewart is supposed to be looking after for me, and after some trouble got his mobile — which was switched off, if you please! I asked him to phone me back as a matter of urgency. I get weekly reports on the flats, naturally, and I knew there was one empty not too far away. I planned for Stewart to show it to us and if it were suitable, we would make arrangements to move in straight away.

'I looked at the clock and saw it was after ten and that plumber of yours, Ellie, had still not arrived. I decided he couldn't want the job very much and that I wouldn't wait in for him. So we called a taxi and took the kettle back to the ironmongers in the Avenue, and there was something of an argument.'

'Which Miss Quicke won, naturally . . .'

'While we were there in the Avenue, we took the opportunity to have a hot chocolate at the Sunflowers Café, which

Rose recommended — acceptable if overpriced — and then I thought that we might as well look at some new bathroom fitments while we were out.'

Ellie tried to remember what time Jimbo had phoned her to report the corpse, and couldn't quite pin it down. He said he'd got to the house just after ten? So maybe he'd shaded the truth, knowing he was late? She hadn't looked at her watch, had she? The cab firm would know when she called them, though.

'So we took a cab to that big warehouse place near the A40, and after some trouble Rose found a man to attend to us. Altogether I was pleased with what we saw. We bought two bathroom suites, a complete new kitchen, and selected tiles for both bathrooms and the kitchen all at a very good discount. Rose suggested I might want to replace my old television sets and we looked at the DVDs and I think I probably will have one but not till the men have finished rewiring the place. Oh yes, and Rose fancied a food processor, so we added that to the bill. I think I can say it was time well spent.'

'Only,' said Rose, 'I'd torn my coat pocket on a sticky-out piece of metal, so Miss Quicke said we'd call in at the department store in Ealing on the way back, and she bought me this lovely coat and beret to match, so kind, though of course I could have paid for it out of my wages and I did want to, but she wouldn't let me. That's when I phoned, but you were out, so I left a message. Miss Quicke said all her old bedlinen was rather old, so she bought some new soft honeycomb blankets, too, light as air, some pillows and some fine china and oh, I don't know how many other things for the house. We shall be so grand! Then we had lunch in their restaurant, such a lovely lunch, with waitress service and all, and we had a glass of wine each, so daring . . .'

'And then,' said Miss Quicke, her face darkening, 'Stewart finally rang back and I told him I'd heard he might have a flat to let . . .'

Rose broke in, 'Because it's a secret, isn't it? He's not to know that Miss Quicke really owns all the houses he's looking after, and so we arranged to meet him there . . . oh, and that's when I tried to ring you here the second time, Ellie, but I couldn't get through, you were so busy on the phone . . .'

Ellie nodded. It would have been Joyce on the phone, probably.

'Anyway,' said Miss Quicke, 'I took one sniff inside the front door and smelt damp. Rose looked inside the kitchen cupboards and gave such a scream, I nearly had a heart attack . . .'

Rose nodded. 'Cockroaches.'

'. . . and what Stewart thinks he's playing at, trying to let a flat in such a state, I do not know. So we gave in and took a cab home, only to find a policeman on the door, refusing us entry! To my own house! Apparently the cleaner had managed to electrocute herself and they said someone had tampered with the wiring. Absurd. Why should anyone do that?'

Her voice had trembled. She knew, all right.

Roy took both her hands in his, and held them tightly. 'Mother.' Perhaps it was the first time he'd ever called her that to her face. His voice shook, too. 'Mother, if someone tampered with the wiring in your bedroom, then might it not have been meant for you?'

CHAPTER FOUR

'Nonsense, Roy,' said Aunt Drusilla, refusing to let her voice wobble. 'Of course it was a tragic accident. I never liked the woman and her work was unsatisfactory, but still it was rather a shock to find she'd passed away in my own house, in my own bedroom! I believe she had a partner; not a husband, if you please, but a partner. I try never to listen to the gossip these people pour out, but I think there may have been an elderly relative, too. It's all very upsetting. Now, if you please, Ellie, I'm rather tired and would like to go up to my room. I don't need much for supper — perhaps just a cup of home-made soup and some thinly cut bread and butter. Rose can sleep in the little room at the front for tonight.'

'I'm afraid I've got Frank asleep in that bedroom.'

'Then Roy must take Rose back to her flat and she can come here and help look after me in the morning.'

Ellie knew this meant the end of any peace and quiet for her but said, 'Of course you shall stay here, Aunt Drusilla. I'll go and make the bed up for you at once. What a terrible experience for both of you. Now, dear Rose, are you all right to go home? You could have my bed and I could sleep on the sofa . . . ?'

'No, dear. I'm quite all right. Best be back in my own little flat. There's a corner shop that'll see me right for milk and tea and such, and tomorrow I'll come here and we'll decide what to do.'

Ellie thought Rose was looking pale and shaken but so was Aunt Drusilla, for all her decisiveness. Perhaps it would do Rose good to return to the flat she had left only a short while ago, in order to look after Miss Quicke. Rose's flat was warm and comfortable enough, and if the teenager next door was not playing his stereo too loudly, Rose would probably get a good night's sleep in familiar surroundings.

Roy, too, was making an effort to appear normal. 'I left the car in the Avenue. How about I order a taxi, take Mrs Rose home, buy her what she needs from the corner shop and then collect my own car and get back to my flat?'

'Anything you say,' said Miss Quicke, leaning back in her chair and closing her eyes. 'But please don't try to suffocate me under a duvet tonight. Use the blankets I bought for Rose, and the new pillows.' She drifted off into silence, showing her age at last.

Ellie got busy unpacking the things Miss Quicke had bought, hindered rather than helped by Rose, who was really too tired to do much but yawn and get in the way. When the taxi came, Roy kissed his mother on her cheek, carefully put Rose into the cab and disappeared with her into the night.

Ellie found some toiletries and a clean nightdress for her aunt, and helped her into bed.

'I knew I could count on you, Ellie. I feel quite safe here. Thank you.'

Ellie knew Miss Quicke very well by now. She said, 'You think you know who tried to kill you?'

The reply was terse. 'Certainly not. I would have told the police if I knew anything of the kind.'

'Very well, then. You suspect someone.'

'Suspect? Yes, that's possible. That builder, you know he threatened me? But no, it's extremely unlikely. I don't want to talk about it, too upsetting.'

Ellie frowned. She knew that Aunt Drusilla had had an argument with her builder, but she'd thought nothing of it. Aunt Drusilla enjoyed arguments.

Ellie said, 'We were very worried, you know. Roy was devastated. It was only when he thought he'd lost you that he realized how much you mean to him.'

'And to you, my dear?'

'Yes. I'm extremely thankful that it wasn't you.'

'I suppose it would have been, if it hadn't been for Rose. She was so distressed about the kettle. I've never been particularly concerned about my surroundings as you know, but she's shown me the difference that a little care and attention can make. I don't think I'd ever thought how pretty a vase of daffodils can look till she came to stay. And the plumber — not yours but the one I sacked yesterday — total incompetence — well, he was on at me to get new bathroom suites and kitchen equipment through him and no doubt he'd be getting a hefty discount . . . so I thought, Why not spend a little, make Rose happy, she really likes doing things for me. I can't think why. I know I'm not the easiest of people to live with.'

Ellie realized Miss Quicke was rambling, talking to push away the horror of what might have been her fate that day. The old woman was in her mid-seventies, and a shock like this might have disturbed a much younger person.

Ellie folded up her aunt's clothes and laid them over the chair. 'Rose likes to be of use and she loves beautiful things. She loves your house and she really admires you. It was good of you to buy her a new coat and hat.'

'She thought you might resent my buying clothes for her,' said Aunt Drusilla, with a sharp sideways look at Ellie.

Ellie shook her head. 'Yes, I did for a moment. Then I realized that what I was feeling was guilt, because I ought to have bought new clothes for her myself. I'd been so pleased with myself because I'd given her money for taxis and bought her the odd meal, but you saw what she really needed. I'm very glad you bought her the clothes, and I'm glad you both get on so well.'

'She has perfectly appalling taste in clothes,' said Aunt Drusilla, with a return to her usual acid tone of voice. 'And she may not choose to stay on with me after this. It was only supposed to be a temporary arrangement while I got over that fall down the stairs. Just till after her daughter's wedding on Saturday. Now I don't suppose Joyce will be able to hold her reception at my house and I haven't even got a home to offer Rose. What's more, if I read that cleaner aright, her family will probably sue me for her death. I doubt if I shall sleep a wink tonight.'

Ellie offered a sleeping pill, but the old woman would have none of it. 'I don't hold with such things. Now don't fuss, Ellie. Go to bed early, when you've brought me my cup of soup. You're looking worn out.'

Ellie bent over to kiss the old woman's cheek and for the first time she felt a dampness on the wrinkled skin. Aunt Drusilla crying? No, it was only a stray tear, and best to ignore it.

Aunt Drusilla clung to Ellie's hand. 'I had a narrow escape, didn't I?' A pause. 'Roy really was upset?'

'Believe it. He clung to me as if I were his mother substitute.'

'Marry him, then. I know he's very fond of you.'

Ellie shook her head, smiling. 'I'm very fond of him, too. But that's not enough, and you know it.'

* * *

The huge television set was still on in the Tucker flat, a porn video running. Norm came heavily back into the room, shed his jacket, turfed young Jogger out of the better of the two armchairs and collapsed into it, lighting another cigarette.

'It was her, no mistake. Poor old cow.'

Old Mr Tucker was still in his armchair, with the blanket over his knees. 'I knew it. Soon as they said they'd found someone, I knew it! What we going to do now then, eh? Poor old Mo. She always did her best, did our Mo.'

Jogger was restless. 'Yeah, it's bad. Can't take it in. Thing is, I need some cash.'

Norm knocked over the remains of his can of beer, his temper rising. 'There ain't no cash! There ain't never going to be no more cash, right?'

Jogger was aggrieved. 'She'll have cash on her, in her bag, bound to. Didn't they give it you, down the morgue?'

'Poor Mo, poor kid,' said Grandad. 'Never had much of a life.'

Norm was in shock. 'The police said she was killed by accident, in mistake for that rich old cow she worked for.'

Jogger's bright eyes switched left and right. 'Then we can sue her, can we?'

'Dunno,' said Norm. 'Might. Takes a bit of getting used to, her not being around. Poor old Mo. I'm going to miss her.'

Grandad sniffled, his eyes watering. 'Who's going to get me my tea, that's what I want to know.'

Jogger lost his temper. 'Eff your tea, old man! There ain't going to be no more tea for you. Best get used to it. There's nobody now to fetch and carry for you. The sooner you're put away in an old-people's home, the better.'

The old man quavered, 'I never did you no harm, Jogger.'

'You never did me no good, neither.'

Norm heaved himself out of his chair. 'Mo was going to do us egg 'n' chips. Maybe I can rustle something up. Egg 'n' chips do you, Grandad?'

'I ain't your grandad . . .' He wiped his hand across his face. But the prospect of tea soothed both him and Jogger.

* * *

In the morning all was quiet at Ellie's, except for little Frank burbling away in his room. Ellie sent up a prayer or two as she huddled into some old clothes. There was no point in dressing smartly if you had to feed a toddler his breakfast.

Please Lord, look after Aunt Drusilla and everyone who's been hurt by this, not forgetting that poor woman who was killed. If she had a family, then please keep an eye out for them, too.

She kept a cupboard full of toys for Frank in the little bedroom and by the sound of it, he was renewing his acquaintance with them one by one. Fairly quietly.

Ellie listened at Aunt Drusilla's door before taking Frank to the bathroom, getting him dressed and going down to prepare breakfast. Midge was sitting in the middle of the kitchen table, annoyed that Ellie was late in putting his food down. Frank was in a wonderfully happy mood. Just as well that someone was, thought Ellie. She hadn't heard anything from either Stewart or Diana about collecting the little boy, so Ellie rang Frank's childminder direct and arranged for her to pick him up at Ellie's house.

Ellie didn't much like the look of the day ahead. She had all that paperwork to deal with for her charitable trust, but it wasn't likely she'd be allowed to concentrate on it, with Aunt Drusilla and Frank demanding her attention. And the murder.

No matter how much she tried to reason it away, the conclusion kept returning to her mind. The wiring in Aunt Drusilla's room had been tampered with, and there could be only one intended victim. Aunt Drusilla.

The cleaner had got herself killed by accident, being in the wrong place at the wrong time.

Which meant that, however unpleasant the idea might be, someone had tried to kill Aunt Drusilla and *Aunt Drusilla suspected someone* of having done it. If Ellie had read her aunt aright, then the chief suspect would be . . . Diana. All that talk about the builder being responsible was so much nonsense. Wasn't it? Ellie shuddered, and pushed the thought out of her head.

The police were going to ask who that someone was.

The list couldn't be that large. Friends and family. And possibly the people who worked for her. Sometimes those who worked for her were also family.

Which brought Ellie neatly back to Diana. Ellie realized she must force herself to confront her suspicions.

Diana thought — quite wrongly, but she did think it — that she would inherit everything on Aunt Drusilla's death. That was motive enough, but worse still was that Aunt Drusilla had just sacked her from a very well-paid job.

Ellie had complicated feelings about her only child, who seemed to think the world had been created for her especial benefit. But Ellie could not — would not — believe that Diana would go so far as to kill her great-aunt. Besides, Diana's reaction on hearing of her great-aunt's death had seemed genuine enough. Though it had to be said that she could tell a lie with ease when it suited her.

No, it couldn't be Diana. She wouldn't kill her great-aunt.

Let's look somewhere else, shall we? Let's look at Stewart, Diana's husband. He was also under threat of dismissal and he probably believed he'd gain financially if Diana inherited. But he simply didn't have the temperament, did he? If he got worked up, he might seize the nearest chair and bash someone with it, but tamper with electricity? No, not his style.

Next suspect. Roy Bartrick, Aunt Drusilla's illegitimate son who had only recently been reunited with his mother. Roy was due to inherit a fortune. But no one could fake the reaction he'd had when he thought his mother had died. No, not him.

The cleaner herself was in Aunt Drusilla's bad books. She might momentarily have toyed with the thought of murdering Miss Quicke if she'd been subject to one of the old lady's tirades, but would such thoughts have lasted longer than the next cup of tea? She might perhaps have considered some petty act of revenge, such as smashing one of Aunt Drusilla's favourite cups and saucers, or leaving the fridge door slightly open so that the contents would spoil. Yes, Ellie could quite see that sort of thing happening.

Would she have tampered with the wiring, with intent to kill? Thinking that the next person to touch it would be Miss Quicke? Suppose she had, only something had gone wrong and she'd electrocuted herself, rather like those suicide bombers who blew themselves up halfway to their targets?

Well, it was a possible theory, but the woman worked for an agency and not directly for Miss Quicke, so it seemed a little far-fetched to suggest that being torn off a strip by Miss Quicke would be sufficient reason to want to murder her.

With some reluctance Ellie discarded this theory, which would have been extremely convenient and taken the heat off the family.

How about the plumbers Aunt Drusilla had sacked because they'd tried to use the wrong gauge of pipe? Ridiculous. It was more likely that Aunt Drusilla would wish to sue them for trying to pull a fast one, than that they would want to kill her, the goose that laid the golden eggs.

Ellie smiled to herself. She wished she'd been a fly on the wall when Aunt Drusilla had found out what they'd been doing and confronted them with it. They ought to have known better than to try to pull that sort of nonsense. Ellie could imagine their aggrieved expressions . . . how could they have expected the old — dear — to know about the correct gauge for pipes?

Ellie almost laughed. Knowing human nature, she thought the plumbers were probably feeling angry with Miss Quicke because their scheme hadn't worked. They probably didn't feel at all guilty about having tried it on.

However, if the police didn't find out who'd done it quickly, it might be worth having a word with the plumber.

The electrician who'd walked off the job that morning? No, no, no. He'd been doing a good job until Miss Quicke ordered him to down tools till Monday. Even supposing he'd taken umbrage about the delay and wanted to do her an injury, he wouldn't have had time to go upstairs and tamper with the wiring after she told him to stop work. He couldn't have done that anyway, because he'd have been seen by the cleaner who was working up there. No, no. Strike him off the list.

The builders? Yes, there had been an argument which Ellie had heard about second-hand from dear Rose. Something about letting part of the house to a friend of the builder's? According to Rose, the builder had told Aunt Drusilla she'd soon be dead anyway, so why not let that part of the house?

No, it really was ridiculous to think the builder would have tampered with the wiring. Why should he?

Perhaps to give Aunt Drusilla a fright? No, no.

It sounded as if he'd lost his temper completely with the old lady. What was his name? Ellie had seen it on the scaffolding in front of the house. She ought to be able to recall it. She wondered how long it would be before the police released their hold on the house. That scaffolding was paid for by the week, and it was expensive. Would the builder still charge Aunt Drusilla for its hire, if the police refused to let them take it down? Probably. Hmm. It might be worth a word with them. But as for them wanting to murder Aunt Drusilla? No, it was too far-fetched.

Which left . . . Diana.

No, not even Diana in a temper would kill someone.

A more welcome thought — what about Derek Jolley? Here was a man who'd been managing properties for Aunt Drusilla for years and presumably had learned enough to realize how wealthy she was. A man who was making up to Diana with a view to helping himself to a slice of cake? Y–y–yes. Possibly. Ellie had never liked the man, considering him the sort of estate agent who gave the trade a bad name. Being a man, he'd know how to tamper with the wiring, wouldn't he?

Well, if the police investigation stalled, Ellie would be happy to point them away from Diana and in other directions.

At this point Midge's ears switched towards the hall as the phone and the doorbell rang at once. Ellie suspected that there was some connection between her cat's ears, the front-door bell and the phone, as no matter how long an interval of quiet there was in her life, Midge knew when there was going to be some action and both would ring at the same time — usually when Ellie was in the bathroom, gardening, or feeding Frank.

This time it was Betty, Frank's delightful childminder, at the door. Frank greeted her with enthusiasm and was borne off without a backward look at Ellie. Oh well, thought Ellie.

At least I come second in his affections, after Betty. What a dear little boy he was turning out to be now that he was growing out of the tantrum stage, so different from what his mother had been at that age.

No. Stop that thought. Diana had been a loving child, too. Hadn't she? Of course, she'd had a lot of trouble teething, but no more than was to be expected.

It was Joyce on the phone, almost hysterical. Would she have to cancel the wedding, or the reception, or what? Would someone please tell her this was just a bad dream?

Ellie made soothing noises. She would put her thinking cap on, she said. Had Joyce asked the police when Miss Quicke's house would be released? She had? And? They wouldn't say? Oh dear.

Ellie heard Aunt Drusilla making her slow way down the stairs. The old lady had got herself out into the conservatory and seated herself at the table before Ellie could get off the phone.

'Who,' asked Aunt Drusilla, pointing down the garden, 'is that young man sneaking up the path?'

Ellie looked. The 'young man' concerned was in his early forties, but he certainly did look furtive as he sidled up the path, glancing behind him now and again.

'That's my plumber, Jimbo. Mr Johnson. The one who found the body yesterday.'

'I'll have some porridge for breakfast. With demerara sugar and cream, not salt. I can't abide salt with porridge.'

Ellie unlocked the door to the garden and Jimbo more or less fell in. He looked unkempt and he hadn't shaved that morning.

'Mrs Quicke, you've gotta help me!'

Ellie diagnosed a bad case of panic. 'This is Miss Quicke, Jimbo. Whose house you were in yesterday morning.'

'You aren't dead!' Jimbo stared at the old lady. 'But . . . no, it wasn't you, was it? You mean that you weren't there when . . . Then who was it who . . . ?'

'Sit down, young man, and explain yourself. Ellie, my breakfast, if you please!'

Luckily the kitchen opened onto the conservatory, so Ellie was able to measure out oatmeal, add water and pop it in the microwave — with both fingers crossed that she had pressed the right control buttons, because microwaves were rather intimidating, weren't they? — and put the kettle on while Jimbo seated himself opposite Miss Quicke and began to explain himself.

'I slept in the van, see. Didn't dare go home.'

'Start at the beginning,' said Miss Quicke. 'Take your time. We've got all morning. Start from when you arrived at my house yesterday morning. You were late.'

Jimbo calmed down at this. 'Well, yes. I was. My mate couldn't start his car, see, so I went round there to pick him up, 'cause we were going on to another job once I'd seen what you wanted done.'

Ellie popped her head around the door. 'Porridge suit you, too, Jimbo? Yes? What time did you really get there?'

Jimbo shifted in his seat. ''Bout quarter past ten, I suppose. I din't look. First I thought, no one there. I rang and rang. Then this woman come to the door, let me in, din't say nothing to me. I din't get a good look at her, 'cause it was darkish in that big hall. She just turned and went up the stairs. We could hear the hoover going up top, then we heard it stop. I shouted out, Yoohoo! like I always do, and said we was come to look at the plumbing but she din't say nothing. I thought she was you. I thought she'd gone upstairs to shut off the hoover, and then she'd come down and talk to us, tell us what she wanted done.

'So we hung about, waiting. We peeped in the rooms off the hall, in the big sitting room and the dining room. The kitchen. Still she din't come down. So we called out to her that we were in a bit of a hurry, like. Nothing. In the end I went upstairs and peeped round doors. And that's when I saw her. Lying on the floor. Dead.'

Ellie put two plates of porridge on the table, with spoons, sugar and milk. She hadn't got any cream.

Miss Quicke picked up her spoon. 'No cream, Ellie? Oh, very well, I can make do for once. Toast and tea to follow, please. Go on, young man. I understand why you thought it was me, though anyone with a grain of common sense would have realized . . . However, we haven't all been born with common sense, have we? Especially men. Eat up while it's hot.'

Jimbo picked up his spoon and started to eat. 'Well, I panicked, didn't I? Din't know what to do. So I rang Mrs Quicke here and she said I should get nine–nine–nine, which I did. Though you could see she was deader than anything.'

Ellie put bread in the toaster and placed butter, marmalade, plates and knives on the table. Switched the kettle on. 'So why did you run, Jimbo? You knew very well the police would want to talk to you. Your going off like that is bound to make them suspicious.'

Jimbo shifted on his chair again. 'Well . . . it were the tax disc, see.'

Miss Quicke pointed her nose at him. 'Out of date?'

'A bit. Well, maybe a lot. And maybe a coupla parking fines outstanding. And a bit of a barney with a copper at New Year. And I had this other job on, din't I? Urgent, it was. And it weren't as if I knew anything. I just found her, is all.'

Ellie dumped toast on the table and went back for a big pot of tea. Mug for Jimbo. Quality cup and saucer for Miss Quicke. 'You were only there when she died.'

'You do know how to make life difficult for yourself,' observed Miss Quicke. 'The police will be more suspicious of you for running away than if you'd stayed and been straight with them.'

'No, they wouldn't, missus. You don't know them. Down on me like a ton of bricks, they'd be. Make out it was all my fault, or something. I phoned the wife last night and first thing this morning and she told me they was looking for me real bad. There was a copper sitting in an unmarked all night outside our house. They're fitting me up, I tell you. I din't dare go home, spent the night in the van out by Heathrow Airport. Thought about getting out of the country, but I din't have no passport, no money. My mate Tom's the same. He's all right, been with me for yonks, but he's got a bit of a record, fighting and that, so he said he wasn't sticking around for them to fit him up. Then I thought Mrs Quicke might help me.'

Ellie poured herself a mug of tea and joined them at the table. 'You need a solicitor. I'll ring mine in a minute and he'll take you to the police and see you're treated properly. I suggest you also get all your fines and your tax disc up to date immediately. In the meantime, tell us exactly what you saw when you got upstairs and found the body.'

He downed a mug of tea and ladled butter on to toast. 'I had a bacon butty late last night, in a lay-by. Nothing since.'

Miss Quicke pointed her knife at him. 'Spill the beans!'

Ellie nearly choked on her tea. Had Aunt Drusilla been watching late-night films? Spill the beans, indeed!

'We-ell. It musta been the TV, I reckon . . .'

Miss Quicke was on to that straight away. 'Why would she turn on my television? She was supposed to be giving my bedroom a good turn-out.'

'She'd done the hoovering,' agreed Jimbo. 'You could see that. Nice and clean, the carpet. The hoover was stood by the door, unplugged, cord wrapped up all neat and tidy. We'd heard her hoovering and we'd heard her stop. So that was all right. Then I reckon she'd set about the dusting, turned the telly on for company. 'Cause the telly was on, right, only there were no proper picture. Just them ghost pictures you see when the aerial's not angled right. It's an old TV, right, with an aerial screwed on to the window frame?'

'Nothing wrong with that TV,' said Aunt Drusilla. 'Good for a few years yet. You just have to know how to tweak the aerial, that's all.'

'Yes. Well. That was it, I reckon,' said Jimbo, heavily. 'She was down on her back on the floor with her arms up and her skirts . . . well, you could almost see everything, not that you'd want to, mind. There was a . . .'

'Burn mark across her right palm,' said Ellie, remembering what she'd seen in the mortuary. 'She'd touched something, moved something with her right hand . . .'

'And got a helluva shock and been thrown back by it.'

Silence.

Aunt Drusilla set down a piece of toast, half-eaten. 'You mean, she tried to adjust the aerial because the picture wasn't clear, and that killed her?'

Jimbo nodded, and passed his mug to Ellie for a refill.

Aunt Drusilla protested. 'I often have to adjust the aerial and I've never had a shock from it, never.'

'The wiring had been fiddled with. I could see that with half an eye. Not that I'm no electrical expert, but I do know the basics. There should be a wire leading from the aerial to the telly, right? Well, this time it weren't. It led straight down to an extra plug on the skirting board by the window. I knew enough not to touch *that.* So I yelled to Tom to get out of there fast and we went down those stairs quicker'n we went up, I can tell you. We found the main fuse box in a scullery place off the kitchen and shut the electrics off.

'Then I went back upstairs 'cause I thought there might be a chance she'd just fainted, but she hadn't moved. I wanted to close her eyes, but somehow . . . well, I didn't. I were shaking. I went down to Tom in the hall, and he said . . . we both said it would be better if we hadn't been there. Let someone else find her. Then I thought it weren't decent, leaving her there like that, and someone would have seen the van outside. So I rang Mrs Quicke and told her.'

'You mean,' said Miss Quicke, still trying to come to terms with the horror of it all. 'You mean that the woman died *while you were in the house*?'

Jimbo nodded.

'You mean,' said Miss Quicke, trying to get this straight in her head, 'that if she'd confined herself to cleaning the room as she ought to have done, if she'd kept her hands off my television set, she wouldn't have died?'

Jimbo nodded.

Miss Quicke sat back in her chair. 'If I'd turned the television on to watch the late-night news as I often do, it would be me in the mortuary now?'

'That's about it,' said Jimbo. 'Any more toast, is there?'

CHAPTER FIVE

Bill Weatherspoon was not only Ellie's solicitor, but also a family friend. Ellie had often sat with his wife when she'd been dying of cancer and later spent a lot of time with their two teenage girls. Since Frank's death, Ellie had relied on Bill for advice and sympathy, not only when it came to dealing with the fortune Frank had left her but also for dealing with a daughter who always expected more than she got.

Ellie did realize that asking Bill to look after a plumber with a slightly spotty past was not quite the same as asking him to help her out with her charitable trust, but she couldn't think who else might be able to help.

She phoned him straight away. He listened, as always, with care. 'Ellie, you do get mixed up in the most bizarre cases. I'm not your aunt's solicitor, you know.'

'I know that, but I'm prepared to pay if you'll look after Jimbo for me. Suppose I bring him round to you now? You listen to his story and decide whether you can handle it, or need to pass it on to someone more . . . well, accustomed to dealing with criminal matters.'

Bill said, 'Ellie, are you daring me to take him on? It's true that this firm doesn't do much criminal work. But if all that's needed is for someone to see he isn't leaned on too much by the local police, well, perhaps my junior partner might be able to cope. I'll see what he says.'

'Dear, dear Bill. Thank you. I'll be round in half an hour. Jimbo has worked for me for ever and looked after me well. I'd like to help him out now, but he needs to wash and have a shave first.'

'You mean I have to cancel my appointment in an hour's time, just to please you?'

'Well, it would please me, yes. And Bill . . . I may be asking another favour of you, but I'll think about that while I'm on my way.'

'Heaven forbid!' He rang off, laughing.

Ellie returned to the conservatory, where Miss Quicke and Jimbo were each gazing at a future they didn't much like.

'Jimbo, upstairs. Quick. Shave and wash. Make yourself as respectable as you can. And hurry! I have a horrible feeling that we're going to be descended upon by the police at any minute and it will look much better if you go to them, rather than them hunting you down. Oh, and where did you leave your van? By the church?'

'I left it out by Heathrow Airport, came back in by tube.' He made for the stairs at the double.

'Good. That may buy us some time. Aunt Drusilla, can you cope by yourself this morning? Don't let anyone in. Unless it's Rose, of course.'

Aunt Drusilla struggled to her feet. 'I have some checking up to do. Bring me back a *Financial Times*, will you? Now, if you go round by my house, see if you can persuade the police to let you have a change of clothing for me and my good shoes — the ones with the inserts. I went out in my house shoes yesterday and my knee is feeling it. Oh, and my jewellery case and medication as well. I've written out a list — here it is — of what I need. Your computer is in the study, isn't it? I imagine you're on the Internet?'

'Heavens, I don't know. Oh, yes. I think Frank did get on the Internet, but I haven't dared use it and I haven't a clue what his site — or whatever the name is — was called.'

'Don't worry about that. Leave the dishes. Rose can do those when she comes. Give me a front-door key. If I go out, I'll leave a written message for you. If you want something else to do while you're out, I'd suggest calling on Stewart. He started off creditably enough, but lately he's been as much use to me as a wet sponge. Perhaps you can shake some sense into the lad.'

'Yes, yes,' said Ellie, searching for her handbag, distributing keys, clearing the table. Midge was on the top of the boiler again. She saw his ears twitch towards the front door just before the phone and doorbell rang together.

'Help!' said Ellie, under her breath. She darted into the front room to peer out through the curtains. Who was it? If it were Rose, then she'd let her in. If it were Diana . . . perhaps she wouldn't.

It was Mrs Dawes, the redoubtable flower-arranging lady from church, complete with new black beret over freshly dyed black hair, dangling jade earrings, and an enormous caped mackintosh. As usual she was carrying an outsize bag containing all the tools of her trade. And wearing a determined expression. It was a Thursday morning, so she must be calling in on her way to take her flower-arranging class in the church hall.

She caught sight of Ellie through the window and stepped back, obviously waiting for Ellie to let her in. Instead, Ellie called out, 'Wait a minute!' and dived for the phone.

It was Joyce again. Aunt Drusilla passed Ellie on her way to the study, and shut the door behind her. Joyce was no longer hysterical, but coldly ferocious. She said she was holding Ellie responsible for the failure of her wedding arrangements, and was going to cancel everything and then sue the pants off everyone in sight as they could very well afford it and she was not going to be pushed around like this and her fiancé had told her she should go to a solicitor, and that was exactly what she was going—

'Hold on a minute,' said Ellie. She dropped the phone, unbolted the front door and let Mrs Dawes into the hall.

'Well, I must say . . . !' began Mrs Dawes.

'Hold on a minute,' said Ellie to Mrs Dawes. And then to Joyce, 'My aunt can't possibly be held responsible for a death in her house, or for the police isolating it as a crime scene. She's not able to set foot inside it herself at the moment, let alone allow the premises to be used for a wedding reception. Do go to a solicitor, by all means, if you wish to waste your money. But remember, you've no contract to use my aunt's house for your wedding reception. It was supposed to be lent to you as a favour to your mother. What's more, you have absolutely nothing in writing!'

The phone squawked. Ellie put her hand over the receiver, and turned to Mrs Dawes. 'Sorry about this.'

The study door opened and Miss Quicke said, 'Ellie, will you please finish your conversation? I can't access the Internet with you on the phone.'

Mrs Dawes exploded, 'Well, Miss Quicke, I didn't expect to find you here. What do you have to say for yourself, bringing all our arrangements for the wedding to nothing and a hundred pounds worth of flowers that I've ordered for Saturday going to waste?'

Miss Quicke shrugged and retreated into the study, closing the door behind her. Jimbo came out on to the landing at the top of the stairs, where he hovered with an anguished expression. Ellie rolled her eyes at him, and obediently he slid into the back bedroom out of sight.

Joyce was still quacking on. Ellie tried to interrupt twice, without success. Finally she shouted into the phone, 'Will you shut up and listen, you silly girl! I'm not responsible in any way for the failure of your arrangements, but I'm just stupid enough to try to help you, if I can. Are you at work? No? Well, you'd better go in as usual, hadn't you? I'll give you a ring at lunch time if I've been able to arrange something for you but one more threat from you and I wash my hands of the whole affair. Is that understood? Right. Now, give me a number where you can be reached . . . no, you are *not* to ring me back here. I'm going to be out. Understood? And don't badger your mother. She's got enough on her mind at the moment without . . . Yes, of course I understand that she's your mother and naturally she . . . *Give me your mobile number* and shut up!'

Spluttering indignation mixed with fury from Joyce.

Ellie listened for a moment, then put the phone down. It rang again immediately. Ellie picked it up . . . held it well away from her . . . and put it down again. It rang again. Ellie opened the study door.

'Aunt Drusilla, I'm going to put the phone down again in a minute. See if you can get on the Internet then.'

Ellie picked up the phone again, listened. Laughed in a shocked fashion. Said, 'And the same to you!' And put it down again. There was a clicking sound as Aunt Drusilla accessed the Internet. Then silence.

Mrs Dawes said, 'Well, I don't know, I really don't.' The heat had gone out of her indignation.

'I'll do my best to sort it,' said Ellie, 'so long as everyone realizes that this is something that couldn't have been foreseen. I might have some better news for you at the end of the morning and I might not. Joyce was in too much of a temper to give me her mobile-phone number, but I imagine that you have it since you're doing the flowers for the church and the reception. Would you like to write it down for me?'

'Really, Ellie. You were a little sharp with her.'

'Not half as sharp as I wanted to be. Now, dear Mrs Dawes, I must ask you to excuse me as I have some urgent business to attend to.'

'Yes, of course, if you can find another venue for the reception . . . I have my team of flower ladies all ready to decorate both the church and the house where the reception is to be held and what's more, they want some table arrangements for the party for the new vicar tomorrow night.'

'Exactly.' Ellie bowed Mrs Dawes out and bolted the door behind her. Jimbo ran down the stairs, looking slightly more presentable. 'We'll go out the back way,' said Ellie, and they ran for the back door even as Midge's ears twitched towards the hall and the front door rang again.

'Leave it,' said Ellie. 'My aunt can answer it if she feels like it, and if she doesn't they'll have to go away again. I must ring Rose and tell her to be careful approaching the house. We'll walk to Mr Weatherspoon's office, because it's only at the end of the Avenue.'

Bill was an attractive man in his early sixties, who showed no signs of wishing to retire. Ellie knew that he was fond of her, and she felt slightly guilty about asking him for favours. Today, for instance, this busy solicitor didn't keep them waiting long before ushering them into his office; a reassuringly old-fashioned room with cartoon prints by Spy on the walls. His junior partner was summoned and Ellie prompted Jimbo through his story.

Both solicitors, the younger one and the old, listened with courtesy mixed with scepticism.

When Jimbo had finished, Bill turned to Ellie. 'Are you happy with his story?'

Ellie shrugged. 'It ties in with everything I know. And Jimbo — Mr Johnson — had no motive to tamper with the wiring or harm Miss Quicke in any way. On the contrary, he would be losing out on a big contract.'

The younger partner sighed. 'Very well. Mr Johnson, if you will come with me?' He wafted Jimbo out of the room and Bill asked his receptionist to rustle up some coffee for them, there's a good girl.

Bill was about the same height and build as Roy, both being tall, well-made men. But there the resemblance ended. Bill's dark hair had long since receded backwards over his head and his monkey-like face was thin and deeply lined. Roy was handsome, Bill was not obviously attractive but he was dependable and gave good advice.

'Well, my dear,' he said. 'Who dunnit this time?'

'I wish I knew.'

'You don't think that . . . ? No. Ridiculous!'

'Yes, she has the best motive, but I really can't believe that Diana would do such a thing.'

'Hm.' Bill didn't seem so sure of it.

Neither was Ellie, to be absolutely truthful.

The coffee came and they chatted about the setting up of the trust. Then Ellie looked at her watch and exclaimed that she must go, she had lots to do.

'You wanted to ask me another favour?'

Ellie got to her feet, embarrassed. 'No, I couldn't. It would be presuming far too much and really, why should you?'

'What is it?' He was resigned, amused.

'Well, if you must know, really it is out of the question and I wouldn't dream of asking . . .'

'Ellie!'

'Oh, very well. Dear Rose McNally's daughter is getting married on Saturday. She was going to have the reception at Aunt Drusilla's house but of course that's out of bounds. Now you do have that nice big house by the river, and both your girls are away at university. Dare we ask if we might use your hall and sitting room for the day? Say until four in the afternoon? I could have the rooms professionally cleaned before and after. Flowers brought in. Caterers would need to use the kitchen, of course, but . . . no, it's impossible!'

Bill laughed. 'All right, Ellie. I'll do it, if you agree to come to the golf club dinner dance with me. Is it a deal?'

'Done,' said Ellie, who had already refused two invitations to go to the dance, one of them being from Roy. Well, she'd have to deal with that when she saw him. 'Oh dear, but I've nothing to wear.'

* * *

What next? She sighed, looking over Aunt Drusilla's list. Would the police let her in to the house? If not, clothes could be bought elsewhere, but shoes for an elderly lady with difficult feet were another matter. Ellie knew all about that, having been with Miss Quicke on many a shopping expedition for shoes *and* escorted her to the podiatrist before now.

The best thing to do would be to phone the police and get their authority to let her into Aunt Drusilla's house. But what would be the right number to phone? You couldn't dial 999 for this, wasting police time. Ellie bought a *Financial Times* and asked the girl behind the counter at the newsagents if they knew the number of the local police station. The girl didn't, and looked at Ellie as if she'd come from outer space.

She could use her mobile to contact directory enquiries. Well, she could if she hadn't left it at home. How had that come about? Well, never mind. She could dial directory enquiries from a public telephone box — except that it was occupied by a young girl having a chat with a friend, who refused to acknowledge Ellie's presence even when she tapped on the window.

Ellie gave up. She hailed a taxi and directed him to the quiet side street where Stewart and Diana lived. She could use their phone to ring the police. She could also ring dear Rose as well, with the good news about the wedding reception.

Diana and Stewart had married, believing her to be the most wonderful girl in the world. She deserved — they both thought — the best of everything. Diana's father had given them a generous wedding present, enabling them to buy a modest house up North where Stewart worked. Instead, Diana had persuaded Stewart to buy a large executive-style house far beyond his middle-management means. Even though Diana was also working, they had begun to slip into debt.

After baby Frank arrived Diana had gone back to work in a series of jobs which she'd complained were never quite right for her. At the same time, she'd become increasingly impatient with Stewart, who was slow to provide the glamorous lifestyle she considered her due.

Ellie was fond of her honest, stalwart son-in-law, but as Aunt Drusilla had noted, he was not the sort to set the Thames — or any other river — on fire. In the spring Diana had come down to London with little Frank, leaving Stewart to sell up and follow her — if he could.

Diana had thought she had taken a step up the ladder when she had persuaded her great-aunt to let her manage a block of flats, a position which she greatly relished. Diana had energy and ideas and the job might have worked out well enough if it hadn't been for her tendency to cut corners. Diana had assumed she could fool her great-aunt; Ellie knew better.

When Stewart did manage to sell the house and follow his wife down to London, Ellie had persuaded Miss Quicke to give him a job similar to Diana's; this time looking after some of the old lady's housing-to-let empire. No one knew how much money and property Miss Quicke had, and she liked to keep it that way. Accordingly she had stipulated that Stewart was not to know who his employer was, and all arrangements had been made through a holding company.

As Miss Quicke had said, Stewart had appeared to do well — at first.

To cover the gap between Diana's moving down to London and Stewart's selling their house up North, Ellie had been paying the rent of one of Aunt Drusilla's flats on behalf of her daughter and her husband.

The money was now in from the sale of their house up North, Stewart and Diana were both in work and Ellie had assumed that they would soon take out a mortgage on a small house or flat somewhere nearby and settle down.

All that, of course, was before the bombshell that Diana had dropped the previous evening.

Ellie got out of the cab and looked up at the first-floor windows of the house in which Stewart and Diana had their flat. The house was large, solidly built in Edwardian days with black and white wood facings imitating the style of Tudor mansions. There was only a tiny front garden and no garage, but that was only to be expected in this area.

The front porch was spacious, with three bell pushes on the side. Ellie rang the middle one. No reply. Weren't they up yet?

She rang again. It was quiet in this street. Just the occasional passer-by walking a dog. The pavements were dotted with small council-planted trees. An aeroplane droned overhead, taking off from Heathrow Airport. Ellie hoped Jimbo's van hadn't been clamped for illegal parking. With his luck it might even have been towed away by now.

A tinny voice; 'Who is it?'

'Ellie Quicke.'

The door popped open and Ellie entered, crossed a tiled hallway and went up the wide, uncarpeted wooden stairs. A door at the top was open and she went through a tiny hallway into Stewart and Diana's sitting room.

Her mouth formed a soundless 'Oh!'

The place had been wrecked. Chairs were on their sides, books strewn about higgledy-piggledy among videos, ornaments, cushions, china, and Frank's toys. In the middle lay an empty whisky bottle.

Stewart was sunk into a leather armchair — the place had come ready-furnished — and holding his head in his hands. There was no sign of Diana.

Ellie patted him on one big shoulder. He smelt sour. Hadn't shaved. What was it about these big-framed men, that they fell to pieces so quickly?

'Dear me,' she said. 'Got drunk last night, did you?'

Stewart nodded, groaned, clutched his head.

She went into the kitchen. Untidy. Evidence of a junk-food meal — everything dried up. Yesterday's? More junk-food packaging in the waste bin. Fridge pretty empty, except for a heel of a loaf of bread, a few eggs, a scrap or two of bacon. In the cupboard there were a few staples such as tea and coffee, sugar and flour, but there was hardly any food except baby food in tins. Yuk. She put the kettle on to make some instant coffee for both of them before noticing the door of the washing machine was ajar, the interior stuffed with clothes ready to wash, dark and light clothes all jumbled up together. Luckily Stewart hadn't started the machine up, or everything would come out blue or pink, including underclothes. Ellie pulled the dirty clothes out on to the floor and quickly sorted them it into two piles.

When the kettle had boiled, she made instant coffee and took it into the sitting room. Stewart was staggering around, eyes squinched up, trying to right the furniture. She pushed him back into his chair, put the coffee mug in his hands, and seated herself on an upright chair.

'Drink that. Then tell me all about it.'

In her experience it was an opening that never failed to produce the goods. Stewart told. After the first few sentences, Ellie could have written the script for him.

'I've failed her. Let her down. No wonder she's left me. I don't blame her.'

Stewart blamed himself for everything. Ellie fitted the pieces of what he said into her knowledge of Diana and felt compassion for the lad. He'd done his best. Ellie knew how Diana could work on you, make you think everything was your fault.

'We were so happy at first. We were both working. I loved my job. It did worry me a bit that we'd bought such an expensive big house but, well — as Diana said — it was nothing less than she deserved and it showed people where we were going.'

Ellie held back a sigh. Diana had always had an inflated idea of what life owed her.

'Then little Frank came along and though Diana was angry about having a baby so soon, she said that nowadays no one expected a career woman to stay at home and look after babies. She left the firm she'd been working for, because they wouldn't give her the promotion she had every right to expect. Although I did say that I thought . . . but of course she was right, and I never should have tried to hold her back from reaching her full potential. Only it wasn't so easy for her to get a really good job again after little Frank was born . . . not her fault, of course. Up North they discriminate against career women, don't they . . . ?'

Poor Stewart, thought Ellie. You *know* what she's like really, but you can't admit it.

'. . . and she got so restless at home all day, that I offered — perhaps I didn't really mean it, although I thought I did — to go part-time to look after little Frank while she got the sort of job she could really get her teeth into, but that didn't go down too well with my boss and to tell the truth, I'm not much of a hand at housework and cooking, though I do try.'

Ellie sighed, patted his hand.

'That's when I got passed over for promotion. But it didn't matter, because Diana got this really good job, only somehow it wasn't quite right for her and I'd lost the knack of . . . well . . . making it come right for her . . .'

Ellie shook her head. He meant he hadn't been able to get it up in bed. Oh dear. But in the face of Diana's critical nature, not at all surprising.

Stewart blushed, clearly wishing he hadn't referred to sex. 'Then she got her big chance down here and I was really happy for her, of course I was. To tell the truth, I was rather pleased that we had to give up that big house. It was killing us financially to keep it going and pretend all the time that we were doing just fine, keeping up with the Joneses, you know. I tried for a transfer down here but got turned down. Don't blame them. Fresh out of ideas. I did look for something else up North but somehow, when Diana took little Frank away with her, I lost heart. You know?'

Ellie nodded and continued to pat his hand.

He heaved a great sigh. 'Then I got a really good offer for the house. Well, I thought it was a good offer. It was way above average, but Diana said . . . and of course she was right. I ought to have held out for more. But you came to my rescue. Dear Mother-in-law, you really saved the day for me, didn't you, finding me this job down here? I really enjoyed myself at first, caring for these grand old houses, talking to people, finding out what they wanted, organizing the end-of-tenancy cleaning, getting the contractors to do the repairs and the decorating.'

'What went wrong, my dear?' Though she thought she knew already.

'I'm afraid I'm just not sharp enough to know when I'm being taken for a ride. Diana pointed out that I shouldn't have taken the contractors' word for it, but used people she knew who'd do the job for less and were more reliable. Only, it never seemed to work out that way. I used to get on well with the cleaners I had at first, and the builders, too. But Diana would interfere . . . no, I don't mean interfere. She meant it for the best, of course.

'Only, I didn't think the people she recommended were as good. The work seemed slapdash to me, and when I said so they downed tools. Diana said it just shows how little I know about it, trying to teach them how to do their business. I mustn't criticize her. She does know a lot more about it than I do. Only . . .'

'Yes.' Ellie squeezed his hand. 'Stewart, you didn't by any chance find another woman to talk to about this, did you?'

He looked shocked. 'How did you know? I mean, it wasn't anything, really it wasn't. It was just that we were both left in a corner at a party — a really exciting do, just the thing that Diana enjoys so much — but I was a bit tired, I suppose, and I couldn't sparkle as she does and this girl was the same, dumped by her boyfriend, who'd gone chasing some blonde or other. We just talked, honest! You could have heard every word, but Diana made out that I . . . that she . . .'

'She was a nice-looking woman, sympathetic, and Diana got the wrong idea?'

'Honest, Mother-in-law. It never crossed my mind. I mean, I wouldn't.'

'You'd no idea that Diana was making up to Derek Jolley?'

Stewart hesitated and then said, unwillingly, 'I suspected there might be someone else, a bit on the side, that sort of thing. But I didn't think she'd leave me and Frank. I still can't believe it. But I'm beginning to see that she's right. If I can't give her what she needs out of life, then I have to let her go.'

Ellie sighed. What a mess. She could see how Diana had worked on poor Stewart, destroying his confidence in himself as the hunter-gatherer, and as a man. Once she'd got him down and there was no more fight in him, she'd kicked him out.

Ellie thought that Derek Jolley and Diana probably deserved one another. Stewart certainly hadn't deserved what happened to him.

Ellie Quicke, who had always believed in the sanctity of marriage, and that if a couple fell out, you must try, try, try again . . . made the instant decision that Stewart was better off without Diana and that her immediate task was not to work for a reconciliation, but to rebuild her son-in-law's confidence.

Stewart groaned. 'She said I could make arrangements to see little Frank when it was convenient for her, because she's moving in with her boyfriend. She's coming back to fetch her things tonight.'

'What about Frank's things?'

He lifted his shoulders and let them drop. 'She didn't say. I got your message, saying he was with you. I suppose he's with the childminder today? Poor little beggar. I'm going to miss him terribly. Last night, when it came to his bath time, I nearly . . . that's when I got the bottle out and . . .' He gestured to the mess around them.

Ellie wanted to shake him, but realized it wouldn't do any good. He was too far down to be shaken into action. He needed building up, not knocking down.

'Well, first things first. How do you feel about your job here?'

'I've failed there, too, haven't I? You should have seen Miss Quicke's face when I showed her that terrible flat yesterday. I'd been meaning to do something about it all week, but somehow it seemed too much trouble. She's bound to tell the agents that I'm hopeless and I can't blame her. Then I'll be out of a job again.'

'If you can put the past behind you and make a fresh start, I'll have a word with her for you, if you like. First things first. Go and have a shower. Clean clothes. Get down to your old cleaning agency and charm them into taking you back on. Get the flat that you showed Miss Quicke fumigated, redecorated, whatever needs doing to it. Can you do that?'

'What's the point?'

'Because if you don't, Stewart, I'm going to box your ears!' She hadn't meant to say that. She was appalled at herself.

To her enormous relief, Stewart's face went through outrage to laughter. She, too, began to laugh. 'Oh, I'm so sorry, Stewart. I didn't mean that.'

'Yes, you did. And I deserved it.' He looked around at the mess. 'Do you know something? I've never liked this flat. I'd imagined we'd get something modern, light and airy. I've got one or two on my books at the moment with stripped floors, minimal furniture, all pale colours. In this area I can charge more for them, too. Nothing vacant, unfortunately. The lease on this flat is up soon, isn't it? Do you think I could really make a fresh start . . . ? No, I'm kidding myself, aren't I, Mother-in-law?'

'No, you're not. Stewart, you are a really nice man who needs to start believing in himself again. And would you please start calling me Ellie instead of Mother-in-law.'

She bustled him off to the bathroom — dirty towels on the floor, laundry basket overflowing — and tried to think what she needed to do first. She dived for the phone book. Ah, there was the number of the local police station. Now if she could only get through to DS Willis, then . . . but no; DS Willis was interviewing someone at the moment. Jimbo, probably.

Ellie asked to speak to someone else and got a heavy breather, who laboriously took down her details and what she wanted to know. He might be slow, but he did seem to understand that an elderly lady would end up crippled if she wasn't able to get hold of her special shoes. Perhaps he had a mother with bad feet. Heavy breather said DS Willis would get the message when she was free, but he couldn't say when that would be. Ellie wanted to scream, but refrained. She gave them Stewart's telephone number, and rang off.

Next she rang Rose to give her the good news about a new venue for the wedding reception. Dear Rose was thrilled and said she would pass the good news on straight away to her daughter, to the caterers, the cleaning firm which Miss

Quicke always used, and to Mrs Dawes. Rose said Ellie had only just caught her, as she was about to leave for Ellie's house to look after Miss Quicke. So far so good.

Ellie looked around her, and set about righting the sitting room. The sun came out and brightened everything up. The rooms in this flat were of a good size, the furniture solid if not inspiring, but there was dust everywhere, stains on the paintwork, and the carpet . . . ! Best not to think what's been spilt on the carpet.

Ellie had worn old clothes that day because breakfast with little Frank was a splattering experience. She found an ancient apron in the kitchen, set the washing machine going on the whites-only programme and started to make a large, satisfying breakfast for Stewart with odd bits and pieces from the fridge and store cupboard.

He emerged from the bathroom looking neat and tidy but plucking at the collar of his shirt. 'I couldn't find a clean shirt. Will this one do? I was going to do some washing last night, but . . .' He grimaced. 'I lost it, didn't I?'

Ellie's priorities in married life were first food, and next clean clothes. 'You look perfectly all right,' she said, and set a crowded plateful in front of him, pouring tea into the largest mug she could find. She thought she'd better deal with all the washing before she left the flat.

He started to eat while she picked up toys and newspapers and threw out a pot plant that had died. Didn't Diana ever do any housework? On the evidence, possibly not. She removed a bag full of rubbish from the kitchen bin and put in a new one.

'You know it wasn't Aunt Drusilla who died yesterday?'

He frowned. Shook his head to clear it. Frowned some more. 'Sorry. I don't follow you. Aunt Drusilla, dead? No! You're pulling my leg.'

'Didn't you hear that someone was electrocuted yesterday at Aunt Drusilla's?'

CHAPTER SIX

Stewart stared at Ellie as if she'd gone out of her mind. 'Aunt Drusilla dead? No, really? But . . . Who . . . ? I don't understand. No, Diana would have said something if . . . You really mean it?'

'It wasn't Aunt Drusilla. It was a cleaner from an agency.'

'Oh? For a moment there, I thought that if it had been her great-aunt, Diana would have been over the moon. Wouldn't she have been thrilled? The plans she's made for when the old girl pops off . . .' He pulled a face. 'I always said to her, Don't count your chickens. Besides, I rather like the old girl. So, an accident, was it? That's terrible. But that wiring . . .' he shook his head. 'Anyone could see. Poor Diana. Foiled again. I bet she's fit to be tied, missing out on her inheritance by chance. A good thing, really, though I say it as shouldn't. I was brought up to think we should make our own way in life and that inherited wealth is somehow wrong.'

Ellie slapped some more toast in front of him and he seized on it hungrily. When had he last eaten, she wondered.

Well, it was definitely not Stewart who'd tampered with the wiring. Though the police would probably want to question him about it at some point. And how was Jimbo getting on at the police station?

'Do you know,' said Stewart, 'I'd rather not be here when Diana comes for her things. I haven't got much here. All our own furniture is in store still, up north. Suppose . . .'

Ellie dumped another mug of tea in front of him. 'First things first, Stewart. I know I'm going to sound as bossy as my daughter, but may I ask what has happened to the money from the sale of your house up north?'

'It's in the bank here, of course. Diana couldn't make up her mind what we should do with it.'

'Joint account, bank in the Avenue?' He nodded. 'Well, I suggest you go straight to the bank, open a new account in your own name only, and transfer half of whatever is in the joint account to yourself.'

He blinked. Put his mug of tea down slowly. Did some quiet thinking. As Ellie watched, the lines of his face tightened. Suddenly he looked older and, yes, more capable.

'She'll take everything if I don't?' It was only half a question.

Stewart lumbered to his feet, looked blindly around the flat and checked his pockets for car keys and wallet. Ellie helpfully found a jacket for him, and saw that his tie was straight before pushing him towards the door. On the threshold he paused, turned round and gave her a hug, lifting her off her feet. Then vanished.

'Gracious me,' said Ellie. The phone rang. It was the heavy breather from the police station with a message for Ellie.

DS Willis couldn't come to the phone but had sent a message saying that she was sending a WPC down to Miss Quicke's straight away to escort Ellie into the house to collect what her aunt needed. Also, would Mrs Quicke please tell the builder — who'd been phoning every half hour to get permission to start removing his scaffolding — that this was all right provided he didn't try to enter the house itself.

Ellie cast a distracted look around the flat. All her housewifely instincts reacted against leaving it in such a mess, with the washing machine still working away. But if DS Willis said straight away, she didn't mean in an hour's time. Ellie phoned for a minicab, and helped herself to the spare door keys from the kitchen cupboard. She would pick up Aunt Drusilla's things and come straight back here to take the washing out of the machine and tidy up a bit.

As she'd expected, there was still incident tape across the driveway at Aunt Drusilla's. The builder's lorry was outside in the street, and the builder himself was arguing with a policeman on the pavement. There was no sign of the WPC who was supposed to oversee Ellie's entry into the house, but a number of local people were hanging around, gaping and gossiping. Perhaps they hoped the builder would lose his temper and hit the policeman; he certainly looked capable of it.

'Look,' said the builder, snatching at calmness and missing. 'I've got to get that scaffolding down. It's due on another site today and if I don't get it up there, I'll lose the contract. You've got to see it my way.'

The policeman gave him a wooden look and shook his head. Ellie's minicab driver was curious to know what was happening. Someone dead, then?

Mr Strawson, the builder, raised his fists in the air and stamped around in fury. He was a big, bulky man with something of a paunch. His clothes were rag-tag, his lorry filthy, his workmen looked no better, but he had the reputation of doing a good job. He caught sight of Ellie and moved in on her.

'Look, can you tell this man that I've got to get on and—'

Ellie said, 'I know.' She approached the policeman. 'Good morning. I don't think I know you, do I? I'm Mrs Quicke, Miss Quicke's daughter-in-law, and I quite understand that you have your orders to let no one into the house. Now, I've been on the phone to the police station this morning and DS Willis has sent me a message that it's quite all right for Mr Strawson to remove his scaffolding, provided he doesn't try to go inside. Oh, and a WPC is coming to help me get some things for my aunt from the house.'

The policeman was no more susceptible to charm than he had been to Mr Strawson's bluster. 'Sorry, miss. Don't know nothing about that.'

Mr Strawson's blood pressure was going through the roof. Ellie cursed herself yet again for forgetting her mobile. 'I assure you I was speaking to the station not fifteen minutes ago. Couldn't you get on your mobile phone and check with DS Willis?'

The policeman unfolded his arms and with an air of extreme reluctance he spoke into his mobile. The bystanders were joined by a man walking his dog. Mr Strawson folded his arms over his ample frontage and glared. The policeman reported their requests as if they had been demands made with menaces. He nodded once or twice. Said to Mr Strawson and Ellie, 'Hold on. There's someone on their way.'

The minicab driver was enjoying this. He asked Ellie, 'Want me to wait?'

'Thank you, but no.' With evident reluctance he drove away.

Mr Strawson joined one of his workmen in the cab of his lorry and unscrewed the top of a thermos to pour out a cup of coffee. Ellie immediately craved a cup of coffee herself. She saw the policeman avert his eyes and thought he could probably do with one, too. The wind was brisk, if not chill. There was a large camellia in full flower in the garden of the house across the road. A splendid sight. And beyond it a japonica spread its red blossom against a wall. Now why hadn't Aunt Drusilla put some flowering shrubs into her garden? They would have made all the difference. But there, she'd been brought up on laurel and privet, hadn't she?

A lumpy, youngish woman detached herself from the onlookers and approached Ellie. She had pale eyes, pale-brown hair drawn back into an unbecoming ponytail and looked as if she could do with a good wash and brush up.

'Hi! Remember me? I used to work for Miss Quicke, was thinking of making it permanent. Bad luck about the accident. Thing is, I could do with the job now. Any chance of a word with Miss Quicke?'

Ellie recognized the girl as one of the procession of cleaners who had passed through Miss Quicke's hands. 'I'm afraid she's not able to get back into her own house yet. I'm sure when she does, she'll need help and will contact the agency.'

The woman nodded, but Ellie could see she was not satisfied.

'Where's she gone, then?'

'Oh, moving around,' said Ellie, which was an honest answer but didn't satisfy the woman, who looked as if she'd like to press the matter. An unmarked car drove up with a WPC in it, and the cleaner walked away with a rolling gait.

Mr Strawson leaped down from his cab, cup of coffee in hand. 'Now we're getting somewhere.' He launched into his plea with gusto.

The WPC hadn't thought to equip herself with a windproof winter coat, and was shivering. 'That's all right,' she said. 'Take down the scaffolding if you wish, but you're not to set foot in the house. Understood?'

Mr Strawson threw a triumphant look at the policeman on duty, chucked the dregs of his coffee into the bushes and yelled at his workmen to 'Get in there, then!'

The policeman shrugged, wound up the incident tape and let the lorry in.

'And what precisely is it you want?' demanded the WPC of Ellie.

Ellie showed her Aunt Drusilla's list. 'Clothing we could perhaps buy for her, but she needs her medication and the orthopaedic inserts in her shoes can't be replaced overnight. She usually wears them all the time but yesterday she went out in such a hurry that she forgot and it's almost crippled her.'

DS Willis nodded. Perhaps she was convinced as much by the force of the chill wind as by Ellie's argument. 'That's all right, if you're quick. I've got to get back.'

The WPC shadowed Ellie into the house. It seemed eerily quiet, now. And somehow, Ellie thought, sad. Abandoned.

She pushed aside such fanciful notions and led the way up the stairs to the main bedroom. Ellie couldn't help looking towards the window where she'd been told that the cleaner had died, but there was nothing now to see. The television set and aerial had been removed. There was a dusty powder everywhere. Ellie shuddered. For fingerprints?

She thought that the young woman outside had had the right idea. There was going to be a lot of cleaning needed before Miss Quicke could move back in.

Ellie showed the list to the WPC, who stood over her while she collected her medication, sorted out clothing, and retrieved Aunt Drusilla's best brown shoes — complete with orthopaedic inserts and shoe trees — from the bottom of the enormous mahogany wardrobe. Aunt Drusilla's jewellery box was also at the bottom of the wardrobe. It had a heavy lock on it, and the lock seemed undisturbed. All the time there were crashings and clonkings going on outside the window as the builders dismantled the scaffolding.

Ellie thought the WPC looked almost human so said, 'My aunt only has what she wore yesterday, so you won't mind if I take a couple of changes of clothes, and her night-wear, will you? And her toiletries? All I need now is a suitcase to put everything in. I think she kept her luggage in the box-room at the end of the corridor.'

'My instructions are only to let you into this room and then see you out.'

'Oh. Well I suppose I could find some plastic bags to put everything in. I expect there's some downstairs in the kitchen. Everyone keeps once-used plastic bags, don't they?'

The WPC hesitated, but agreed that it was all right to collect some plastic bags from the kitchen. She even volunteered the opinion that plastic bags bred like mice. So down they went to the kitchen, which seemed very dark and cheerless today. Perhaps it was going to rain again?

Together the WPC and Ellie found two large plastic bags and stowed everything inside them.

'Thank you,' said Ellie. 'I don't know what I'd have done without you.'

'Yoo-hoo!' Mr Strawson was tapping on the kitchen window. 'Mrs Quicke. Can I have a word before you go?'

The WPC said she had orders not to leave Ellie alone on the premises, so Ellie said that was fine by her. She'd go out the back way to talk to the builder. The WPC said the back door was locked, and she'd have to see Ellie out by the front, so this is what she did. Ellie then carted all her bits and pieces round the side of the house into the yard by the garage.

Mr Strawson was there, rubbing his hands, shifting from foot to foot. His lorry had drawn up nearby and his men were piling the scaffolding onto it.

'Want to show you something,' he said, and ushered her into the cavernous depths of the old garage, which contained no cars, but an assortment of junk furniture. Miss Quicke never threw anything away, because 'it might come in useful'. A set of wooden stairs in poor repair led up to rooms which had once been lived in by a full-time gardener-cum-chauffeur.

'It's like this, see,' he said to Ellie. 'The old dear's stuck way back in the old days when she had servants living in and everything was delivered to the door. It's good she's doing something about the house now, tiles, gutters, drainpipes. But she wants to think bigger. This house must cost a mint to keep going, and she tells me she doesn't know where the money's coming from to pay the bills, so why not make it work for her? She could live easy, if she'd just let me handle it.'

Before Ellie had a chance to disabuse the man of his notion that Miss Quicke was a pauper, he beckoned her up the stairs. 'See these rooms above the garage, there's running water up here already, and a loo. This cubbyhole here's the kitchen, and then there's this big room overlooking the garden at the back, and a bedroom up front. It would make a proper little flat with its own entrance, wouldn't it?'

Ellie looked and saw that, under the grime and cobwebs, Mr Strawson was right, and the rooms above the garage would indeed make a nice little flat. So this was the cause of the row which Rose had reported Mr Strawson having with Aunt Drusilla?

'The stairs aren't too safe, are they?'

'New stairs, of course. Outside. You'd have to put some money into it, strip back to the plaster, new ceilings maybe, new plumbing, new kitchen and shower room. Then below you could make that big garage space into another flat to rent out — or sell.'

'Yes, I do see,' said Ellie. He didn't of course know that the house belonged not to Miss Quicke but to Ellie, and she wasn't sure whether to tell him or not. Perhaps it would take the heat out of the situation if he knew he'd have to deal with a younger woman?

But there, her aunt wouldn't like the idea of people living in her garage at all. Miss Quicke liked the idea of being detached from the neighbourhood and she didn't need the money which she might get from tenants, whatever she might have told Mr Strawson. Ellie shook her head. She was not about to force change upon her aunt.

'I heard something about your plans from Mrs McNally, but I'm afraid it's a non-starter,' she told Mr Strawson. 'My aunt would never agree and I would never force her to do so.'

'You can at least see the possibilities?' said Mr Strawson. 'Good. Now perhaps we're getting somewhere. Apart from the garage, there's the back part of the house where the servants used to live, which could be turned into a separate living unit. The present back door leads out into the yard and that would become their front door, so Miss Quicke needn't even see people coming and going. That part of the house has got a nice sitting room downstairs and two bedrooms upstairs. It's got its own staircase and bathroom already, and all you'd need to do would be to put in another kitchen in one of the sculleries. Then you'd block up the doorway to the main part of the house, making it a completely separate unit. Understood?'

'You have vision, Mr Strawson,' said Ellie. 'But I'm afraid that neither my aunt nor I—'

'Look, tell her she wouldn't have to lift a finger, nor raise any money for the job. She could sit back and let the money roll in from selling off the parts she doesn't need, and which she admits herself she never goes into.'

Ellie sighed. 'Yes, but my aunt doesn't think like that.'

'Are you telling me!' He was grim. 'I've argued with her till I thought my blood pressure would go through the roof and I'm on beta blockers already. That great-niece of hers, Diana, the one that's going to inherit the house, she understood what I was on about, told me she was after getting the old lady into a home. I thought it was all set. I'd have to give her a cut, of course. But . . .'

'Ah,' said Ellie. 'Now this gets interesting. Can you explain how you intended to finance all this?'

He spread his hands wide. 'Well, naturally, if I have to finance it, there's got to be something in it to make it worth my while. Architects and planning permission, they don't come cheap. But I'd raise the money, do all the work, see to the selling of the properties. Of course, I'd need to make a profit, but I'd be willing to make a nice little present to anyone who could see that the deal went through.'

'I'm curious. You'd try to sell the two flats outright?'

'And the little house we'd make out of the back part. Of course. Give the old lady a nice little sum of money to put in the bank, cover the council tax for years to come. Right?'

'How much of a cut were you going to give Diana?'

'Plenty, I can tell you. She promised me she could talk the old dear round, only she couldn't, could she? Mind you, I think she tackled it at the wrong time. Last week, it was. The old dear had just had a barney with the plumbers . . .' He laughed, remembering. 'Can she tear a strip off when she gets going! Sent them off with a flea in their ear. That's when her great-niece came along and wanted to know what the row was about. Bad timing. Seems to me that Diana of yours didn't read the old girl right, started straight in talking about the conversions and, well, I thought the old girl would have a fit. She said she wouldn't hear of it, and I wasn't to bring it up again. Diana lost her temper, too, and they were shouting at one another fit to bring the neighbours round. So I made myself scarce.

'After, Diana came round to see me, said she was sure it would all go through, that she had some scheme or other in mind.'

'What scheme?' asked Ellie, appalled by the thought that Diana might have been contemplating an electrical 'fault'.

Mr Strawson shrugged. 'I dunno. She just said she'd thought of something would do the trick. She said she'd get back to me, and I could start on the conversions after the next job I'm down to do, easy. Now everything's gone pear-shaped and I don't know what to do. Time's getting on, and I've got my men to pay whether there's work out there or not.'

'And you've already got someone waiting to buy the flat?'

'What if I have? There's nothing wrong with that, is there? The thing is, after everything that's happened, the old dear won't want to come back here to live, will she? Not after finding a dead body in her bedroom. She'll be going into a home, just as the great-niece says. But I've been trying and trying to raise Diana on the phone to get it sorted and I can't get her. So, seeing you here today, I thought you could have a word with her.'

'She's a little preoccupied at the moment. She's just started seeing an estate agent, you see.'

It took a moment for that to sink in. Mr Strawson's mouth fell open. He stared at Ellie. Then stared all around him. He was doing his sums. If Diana were to inherit the house but was seeing an estate agent, then said estate agent would be in charge of letting or selling the new units and Mr Strawson could whistle for his large profit. Ellie saw him work that out. Then saw him come to the conclusion that at least he could try for the building work that needed to be done.

He said, 'Well, if she'd only told me! But there's still all the work to be done, to do the units up, and I've got a buyer already lined up for the top flat, no problem, no need to advertise it.'

Ellie felt sorry for him. A little. But it was time to disabuse his mind of various misconceptions, and at the same time, take the heat off Miss Quicke. 'Mr Strawson, I think this may be the first time you've worked for my aunt? Yes? Then I'd advise you to ask around about her among your colleagues. My aunt has plenty of money to pay for your bill, and for any number of conversions such as you describe. She has no intention of going into a home, and I am sure she will wish to return here as soon as she can. Oh yes, and despite what my daughter Diana may have been saying, my aunt doesn't actually own this house. I do. And I wouldn't dream of distressing her by making the alterations you describe — however sensible they may appear to you or me.'

He turned purple in the face. He looked like a bull ready to charge. Ellie held her ground with an effort, because he really could be quite intimidating. For a moment she wondered if he himself might have thought of tampering with the wiring in order to scare Miss Quicke into leaving. But no. That was too far-fetched. He wouldn't murder.

She said gently, 'I'm sorry to disappoint you. Perhaps some day we'll be able to do business together. Now I must go as my aunt will be waiting for her things.'

Also, she remembered, after that she had the washing machine at Stewart's to empty, and another load to put in. She told herself she didn't have to go back to the flat. Stewart could do the washing when he got home this evening. Or ignore it.

Ellie sighed again. The trouble with being brought up to help other people is that it's hard to know when to stop.

'Might I borrow your phone to call a cab?' she asked.

She thought he was going to refuse, but after a moment's struggle with himself, he held it out to her. Within his limits, he was a nice man.

* * *

Peace and quiet. Ellie stood in the middle of Stewart and Diana's sitting room and considered what she should do next. The first load of washing was in the tumble-dryer, and the second now going through the machine. She had plenty of paperwork to do back home but it was bedlam there, with Aunt Drusilla issuing one order per second, and Rose fluttering around. Rose had even volunteered to cook the supper for them. She wondered how Jimbo had got on at the police station, and spared a moment of prayer for the poor woman who'd died, wondering who she'd been and how her family were coping.

She supposed that if both Stewart and Diana vacated this flat it might be a good-enough bolt hole for Aunt Drusilla until her own house was habitable once more. But not in its present state of disarray.

Ellie could call in contract cleaners, of course, to put the place right. Or, as she had nothing better to do, why not do it herself?

Then it occurred to her to wonder if the cleaners Stewart had originally used also covered domestic work. If so, might they not be the same ones Aunt Drusilla used to clean her own house? It might well be worth checking that out.

Diana, she thought.

No, it wasn't Diana. Please let me stop thinking that it was her, though she had by far the best motive. If it was Diana, then she had killed the cleaner by accident.

Ellie felt responsible. What could she do about it? Well, she supposed she could go to see the family, at least to say how sorry they all were . . . not that Aunt Drusilla seemed to be very sorry, but she ought to be, especially if it were Diana who . . . Cut that thought.

Now, could she remember the name of the contract cleaners Aunt Drusilla always used? Some time ago she'd asked Ellie to oversee the cleaning of a flat in the block by the river, so Ellie must have heard it at some point. It was some months ago, before Diana took over the management of the flats. All Clean? No. Spring Clean? No. Something with the word 'clean' in it? Perhaps if she were to look it up in the Yellow Pages, the name would jump out at her. Now where would the Yellow Pages be in all this mess?

She was on her knees working at a stain on the carpet when the police came.

CHAPTER SEVEN

Ellie was startled to hear a voice somewhere above her head, demanding entry to the flat. It took her a moment to realize someone was speaking on the Entryphone. Before she could struggle to her feet, heavy steps came up the stairs, and two large young men entered the flat. She couldn't have closed the door properly when she came in.

'Hello there!' said the first one in. Sandy hair, a twitchy nose. Plain-clothes police? 'You the cleaner? Police, dearie. We're looking for your boss, Stewart. Seen him today?'

Ellie didn't like being called 'dearie'. And surely he should have shown her his badge and announced his name? She sat back on her heels, suddenly conscious of her bedraggled state. The front of her apron was sodden, she was wearing her oldest clothes and her hair was all over the place.

Behind the sandy-haired one came another man, with pale-brown skin, flashing a badge at her. 'DC Baptiste.' He looked slightly more intelligent. She didn't recognize either of them, and they certainly didn't know her. Fancy mistaking her for a cleaner! Although to be fair, she supposed she was giving the wrong impression, dressed in old clothes and scrubbing at the carpet . . .

Sandy Hair ignored her, pushing open doors. DC Baptiste talked into his mobile. 'Not here. Just a cleaner . . . yeah, all right.'

DC Baptiste squatted down to her level and spoke loudly, as if to someone slightly deaf. 'Where's your boss, eh?'

'I'm not . . .'

'Not here, any rate,' said Sandy Hair. 'Bed's been slept in, though.' And to Ellie: 'Mind if we look around a bit, dearie?'

'I most certainly do!' said Ellie, getting rather painfully to her feet. Her left leg seemed to have gone to sleep while she'd been kneeling. She bent over to rub it.

'Thing is, dearie, your boss is in a spot of bother, know what I mean? So you just sit quiet and we won't be five minutes, right?' To his mate: 'Bank statements, that sort of thing, right?'

Ellie drew herself up to her full height, which didn't even bring her up to the policeman's shoulder. 'What's Stewart supposed to have done?'

'He's been a bad boy, has Stewart. Now never you mind about him, dearie. You just make us a cuppa and we'll be through in no time.'

Ellie was getting angry. 'No, we won't, young man. And if you dare to call me "dearie" once more, I–I won't be answerable for the consequences. Now either show me your warrant to search this flat, or get out.'

'Does it bite, then?' Sandy Hair thought she was screamingly funny.

'Indeed it does,' said Ellie, with a grim smile. She reached for Stewart's phone. 'And if you're not out of here by the time I count ten, I'm ringing my solicitor . . .' If she could find the number. Yes, it was in her diary in her handbag, wasn't it?

DC Baptiste looked doubtfully at his partner, but Sandy Hair seated himself on the corner of the table and swung his leg. He looked amused.

'You remind me of my son's hamster, dearie. Ever heard of obstructing the police in the course of their duty?'

Ellie found the number, and punched it in. 'Will you put me through to Mr Weatherspoon, please? It's Ellie Quicke here.'

'Quicke?' echoed DC Baptiste, looking alert. 'You some relation of the old girl's?'

'Niece,' said Ellie. On hearing Bill's voice, she said, 'Bill, dear. There are two policemen in Stewart and Diana's flat, who want to search the place. They don't seem to have a warrant, they won't tell me what Stewart's supposed to have done . . . and one of them thinks it's amusing to call me "dearie"! Would you like a word with them?'

She passed over the phone to Sandy Hair, and watched with considerable pleasure as he first lost his grin, then slipped off the table and stood upright. He nodded once or twice. Said, 'Yes, yes, of course,' and handed the phone back to her.

'Ellie, is that you? Shall I come and rescue you?' asked Bill. 'Problem: I do have a client with me at the moment.'

'Thank you, dear Bill. I think I can manage now. Speak to you later.'

She snapped the phone back on the hook and faced two increasingly embarrassed policemen. 'Well? Are you prepared now to tell me what this is all about?'

DC Baptiste tried to make up for his partner's bad manners. 'Look, we just need to ask this Stewart a few questions, so if you know where to find him . . .'

'I haven't a clue.'

Sandy Hair had recovered his nerve. He was also flushing red with anger at the way Ellie had made a fool of him. 'I reckon you do know where he is, and that you're obstructing the police in the course of their enquiries. I reckon you should come down to the station with us, right now, to answer some questions.'

Ellie was amazed. 'You must be joking?'

'Never more serious. So if you'll get your coat on . . .'

'Certainly not,' said Ellie, moving towards the kitchen. 'I've got one lot of washing to take out of the dryer and another to go through. Also the table needs polishing.'

'You refuse?'

Ellie thought it over. The flat was a lot cleaner now. It might even be feasible to bring Aunt Drusilla over to have a look at it later that day. As for these two Keystone Kops, they had no warrant and they were just doing this to annoy her.

On the other hand, she realized she had misled them. Unintentionally, of course. And she had nothing to hide.

'Very well. I have an appointment with someone just off the Avenue in half an hour and after that I need to go home to change, see that everything's all right. I'll report to DS Willis at about . . . oh, half past two?'

'Are you refusing to come with us?' asked Sandy Hair, who couldn't believe his ears.

'Of course not,' said Ellie. 'If you can tell me that it is of the utmost urgency that I speed down to the police station to answer vitally important questions this very minute, then of course I'll ring to cancel my appointment, check up on my elderly aunt and come with you. I don't think it's that important, do you?'

'Give you a lift?' said DC Baptiste, who had never called her dearie.

'Take her straight in,' said Sandy, whose blood pressure seemed to be mounting by the minute.

'Thank you, no. I'll call a cab,' said Ellie. 'And while I'm waiting for the washing machine to finish its cycle, I'll just polish the table.'

Sandy swung out of the door, banging it behind him. DC Baptiste politely pulled the table further into the room so that she could get right round it. She flicked him a small smile and he flicked her one back.

'He outranks me,' said DC Baptiste. 'We'll call for you at home at two fifteen, if that's all right with you?'

'Do you two play "bad cop, good cop" all the time?'

* * *

He was on his break when his mobile rang.

'Hi,' he said. 'How d'you get on?'

'I hung about, waiting for her, but she din't come. That snotty cow came, though, and got the police to let her in. And the builders to take down the scaffolding. The police is still there.'

'What she come for?'

'Dunno. She was in there ages, then called a cab and went off, taking a whole pile of stuff from the house. Thieving under the nose of the police, I call it.'

'Did you have a word, find out where the old biddy's gone, then?'

'Had a word. No dice. The snotty cow wouldn't say. The builders don't know, neither. Din't you say you knew where she lived?'

'Sure. Done some work there, not long back. You think the old woman's gone there?'

'Might have. Worth checking.'

'Will do. See you.'

'See yer.'

* * *

The cab dropped Ellie in the Avenue, almost opposite Bill's offices. She resisted the temptation to call in on him and have a little weep on his shoulder. She really must learn to stand on her own two feet.

But not, she remembered, relying on her own strength. No.

Dear Lord Jesus, help me. I'm so desperately afraid that Diana—

No, kill that thought. But could you just keep an eye on me, on all of us, at the moment? Help me to discover the truth, even if it leads back to . . . Kill that thought, too.

Just . . . help, please!

The offices of Trulyclean Services, Offices, Flat Clearance and Domestic, were situated above the hairdresser's that Ellie had used for twenty-five years. She hesitated about going into the hairdresser's first to make an appointment, but a glance at her watch informed her that she would be late for her appointment with Maria at the cleaning services if she did.

Ellie hated being late.

She trod the stairs to the top office, where a nice-looking woman in her mid-thirties was working at a computer. Ellie diagnosed an Indian father and a white mother.

'Ms Patel? I rang earlier . . .'

The woman swivelled round, her practised eye giving Ellie the once-over.

'Looking for a job? I've not much on at the moment, but if you like to fill out a form . . .'

Ellie felt herself go red. For the second time that day she'd been mistaken for a cleaner. 'Sorry to disappoint you. I'm Ellie Quicke, Miss Quicke's niece.'

'Ah, one of our best clients.' The woman gave Ellie a practised smile, and the words were spoken in a discreet, uninflected tone. Ellie could read the subtext, though. Her aunt was known as a difficult customer.

Clearly Maria Patel was no fool. Though not precisely a beauty, she was good-looking in a calm, statuesque way. Her hair was well cut — probably not done by the hairdresser below — and carefully streaked with blonde. Her figure was good though the bust was perhaps a trifle on the large side.

Ellie, unasked, took a chair and treated Maria to a friendly, open, smile. 'Yes, I know my aunt can be very particular, but she is getting on and that house . . .'

Maria's impersonal smile widened. 'Some of my cleaners refuse to go there anymore.'

'I can well believe it. My aunt's standards are those of a previous age.' Ellie crossed her fingers. 'She was extremely shocked at the unfortunate death of your cleaner.' Ellie thought that if Aunt Drusilla hadn't appeared to be terribly shocked on the surface, she probably had been underneath.

'We all were. Never had such a thing happen before.' Maria shook her head, expressing her own shock and dismay in the formal words required by the situation. It seemed her sorrow was about on a par with Miss Quicke's. 'So, what can I do for you?'

'I wondered if you could give me the woman's address. I'd like to express my condolences on behalf of my aunt. Also, there's something else . . .'

Maria's eyes registered calculation. She decided to play the gracious hostess. 'Would you like a cuppa and a biscuit? I was just thinking it was time for a cuppa and my sandwich.'

'Thanks, yes.' Ellie took stock of the office while Maria busied herself with making two mugs of coffee. The place smelt clean. The carpet was immaculate, and all the office furniture was speckless, polished wood. There were framed flower prints on the walls, and the computer system was bang up to date. A stack of invoices lay ready for mailing. A locked cupboard on the back wall probably contained keys to the various properties for which the agency was responsible on a daily or weekly basis.

Maria herself was well turned out in a black trouser suit over an emerald-green T-shirt. She wore glinting silver bands on all her fingers except the fourth finger of her left hand. So, not married but possibly divorced? A hatstand supported an elegantly rolled umbrella and an expensive raincoat. A copy of the *Telegraph* was on the desk.

Ellie came to the conclusion that Maria was a good businesswoman and that the business was prospering in her capable hands. Judging by the evidence of the newspaper and the lively look in Maria's eyes, it would be best to treat her as an intelligent equal, woman to woman.

'Thanks, no sugar, but a biscuit would be welcome.'

Maria unwrapped a sandwich. 'You don't mind if I . . .'

'No, of course not. My aunt had to move out of her house, of course. She's moved in with me, temporarily. Did the police tell you?'

'They rang me for Mo's address, which I gave them. I haven't seen them, and they didn't tell me anything else. What's happening at the house, then? Did the police close it up?'

'For the time being, yes. My aunt has decided to stay away till all the work's finished, which seems sensible, but at the moment the workmen can't get back in, so goodness knows how long it's going to be before she returns. I wondered if I — or my aunt — ought to visit the cleaner's family — did you say her name was Mo? What can you tell me about her? I seem to remember seeing her at my aunt's some time ago but I hadn't seen her recently, and I'm not sure I even remembered her name correctly.'

'Mo Tucker. She called herself "Mrs" but I don't think she ever married. What else can I tell you? She used to do domestic work for me regularly, years ago. I use women for regular contract cleaning in houses, and men for cleaning flats at the end of their tenancies, for the heavy work, cleaning specialist floors, spring cleaning and the like. About a year ago Mo stopped working for me on a regular basis, saying she'd got herself a job with more convenient hours, somewhere down the other end of the Avenue, cleaning offices out of business hours? Something like that. She didn't get the job through us, so I don't know exactly what it was.'

'Would it be fair to say she wasn't one of your best cleaners?'

Maria grimaced. 'Now she's dead, poor thing . . . well yes, I suppose it's fair to say that. I pay them a sliding scale and she was on the lowest. About a month ago — yes, it was at the beginning of this month she came back to me, said she wanted some extra work — some family difficulty? — and could I help her out. I used her on, oh, about half a dozen occasions, all domestic, nothing too heavy. She was getting on, had put on weight. There were a couple of complaints and if she hadn't been on our books for so many years I might well have said there wasn't anything else for her.

'Then earlier this week I was at my wits' end to get another cleaner for Miss Quicke, who's been through all my good ones, so I asked Mo if she'd mind, because she'd worked for the old lady for a while, some time back, so she knew what she was like. I asked her to take extra care, not to bang the furniture about, which was what clients were always complaining she used to do.'

She lifted her hands, open-palmed, in a gesture of despair. 'And then . . .'

'It was a dreadful thing,' said Ellie. 'But at least she couldn't have known anything about it, it was so quick.'

Maria shrugged. 'We're insured for accidents. I've alerted the insurers. Let them sort it out.'

'Forgive me, but you don't seem very distressed . . .'

'Tell the truth — and it won't go any further, will it? — I rather agreed with Miss Quicke when she rang to complain about Mo having been sent to her. I had to do some fast talking to persuade your aunt to let her work that day. I wish now that I hadn't. Mo really wasn't a very pleasant . . . no, I shouldn't say that. She had her crosses to bear in life, and it's no wonder she was a bit, well, sharp at times. Forget I said that about her.'

'So there'll be some insurance money going to the relatives?'

'No husband, far as I know. Ancient grandad, wastrel son. That's about it. I suppose they'll get something. I'll let you have the address before you go.'

Ellie clicked her tongue, and both women shook their heads at the pity of it all. Ellie placed her empty mug on the table. 'There's just one other thing. My son-in-law Stewart. You know that he was managing some older houses and flats?'

Maria nodded again. She also straightened her shoulders and sat more upright. 'We were sorry to lose his business. It was all part of Miss Quicke's little empire, wasn't it?'

'What do you know about Miss Quicke's empire?'

'We've known the old dear for years. My father started this business thirty years ago and got to know her when she was just setting up, buying up old houses and flats, renovating them and selling them on. He always said she was one to keep an eye on and even when she demanded better rates than she could get elsewhere, he said it was worth keeping in with her. And it was . . . until recently. Then she handed the riverside block of flats over to her great-niece to deal with, and we found ourselves edged out. To tell the truth, I was happy enough to let that contact go.'

Ellie took a deep breath. 'She's my daughter, but I don't hold with all her business methods.'

'Oh?' Maria chewed the last of her sandwich, looking sideways at Ellie.

'Did she ask for a better discount, perhaps?'

'She wanted a backhander, on top of the special rate we always gave Miss Quicke. I refused and she went elsewhere.'

Ellie looked down at her fingernails. She was ashamed of Diana. Not, of course, that Diana would ever be ashamed of what she'd done. 'And Stewart?'

'He was fine at first. Miss Quicke informed us that he was going to look after the older houses and flats for us, and that we were to report back if at any time we were unhappy with the situation. Everything went along as it always had done for months. We were pleased and so was Miss Quicke. Then one day he came in and said he was changing contractors. To give him his due, he didn't seem happy about it. I know who he went to and frankly, though I say it as shouldn't, I didn't think he'd be satisfied with their services for long.'

Ellie narrowed her eyes. 'I believe he very much regretted dispensing with your services. He might perhaps be thinking of approaching you again.'

Maria doodled on a pad, keeping her eyes down. 'He rang me this morning and asked if he might drop in — to discuss things — later on this afternoon.'

'You won't be too hard on him? He's feeling rather disillusioned at the moment.'

Maria doodled some more. Ellie revised her first estimate of the woman's age. She was probably in her early-to-mid-thirties, no older. The thought popped into Ellie's head that Maria and Stewart might make a match of it. They'd look good together, both tall and well built. Both with a naturally calm temperament. With his genial nature and good sense in dealing with people and her business acumen, they'd go far.

What was she thinking of? It was an outrageous idea! Ridiculous! It would mean a divorce and Ellie reminded herself that she didn't believe in divorce. And anyway, what would happen to baby Frank if Stewart divorced Diana? But the thought of a possible divorce returned, muted, as a background to the rest of the conversation. Cold common sense fighting with the ideals she'd been brought up on.

Maria continued to doodle. 'I also had a call from Miss Quicke this morning to say that her great-niece was no longer in her employ, and that she would be advising me who would take over the management of the flats in due course. She didn't mention Stewart. Am I to understand that Stewart is still to be employed by Miss Quicke? It would be helpful to know before I see him.'

'Yes, I think so. Stewart and my daughter have separated for the time being.'

Maria didn't look up and she didn't smile, exactly. But her shoulders — which had been rather tense — relaxed.

Yes, thought Ellie, Maria is definitely interested in Stewart as a man. I really don't know how I feel about that. Poor baby Frank. Oh dear, poor Diana. Does Diana know that Stewart has caught this woman's eye? But then, he is a fine-looking man and why shouldn't he look elsewhere if Diana dumps him?

Ellie suddenly realized what the time was. The police would be on the lookout for her very soon. 'I must go. Thank you for giving me so much of your time.'

'Not at all. I hope I was able to help.' She looked up an address, and scribbled it down on a piece of paper. 'Mo Tucker's address. Perhaps we'll meet again.'

They shook hands briefly, with surface smiles.

Ellie went down the stairs with a great deal to think about as she sped home.

* * *

The police car waited outside while Ellie went in to change her clothes, collect her mobile — most important — and make some phone calls about the wedding reception. She made and ate a sandwich and drank a cup of coffee on the run. Rose was in the kitchen, busily putting together the ingredients to make some little chocolate cakes, while listening to the radio. Rose wondered if Ellie could manage to drop by the shops for this and that in the food line. Midge was waiting under the table for titbits from Rose's cooking. Aunt Drusilla was so intent on the computer screen that she barely acknowledged Ellie's flying visit.

There was no sign of Jimbo, and no messages on the answerphone.

Sandy Hair was sitting in the driving seat of the police car, with DC Baptiste beside him.

'May I sit in the front?' Ellie asked DC Baptiste, when she was ready to depart.

'No!' said Sandy Hair.

Ellie meekly got in the back of the car and tried not to feel seasick when he rounded corners on two wheels. Arriving in one piece at the station, Ellie straightened her jacket and said, 'Really, young man, I would recommend you take some driving lessons soon, or you'll lose your licence.'

Sandy made a sound like steam escaping from a kettle. Ellie smiled, allowing herself to be ushered into the police station, and guided down a corridor to an interview room.

She was left there for some time. She wondered if this was to show her who was boss in this situation but as it happened, she'd got plenty to think about. In addition, because she'd thought it might be a good idea to take her mind off her grinding anxiety about Diana, she'd had the forethought to bring some paperwork with her and was soon engrossed in that. Concentration was definitely required.

All these legal terms . . . it was all very well setting up a charitable trust to administer some of the funds her husband had left her, but it was all so complicated. She rather thought that she now understood the first four pages, but . . . she shook her head and sighed. Bill would have to explain the rest to her.

'Hah!' It was DS Willis, looking almost as angry as the "dearie" policeman.

'Oh, hello again,' said Ellie, casually. 'Are you ready to ask me your questions now, or shall I go on with this for a while?'

DS Willis sat opposite Ellie and DC Baptiste came in to sit with her. Ellie carefully checked over her papers, put them in order, placed them inside her bag and smiled at DS Willis. 'Now suppose you tell me what this is all about?'

DS Willis switched on a tape and recorded that she and a colleague were present, at 1430 hours . . .

'Goodness,' said Ellie. 'Is that really the time? I feel quite hollow. Might I have a cup of tea? A little milk, no sugar. And a biscuit, if you have one.'

DS Willis took no notice. 'Mrs Quicke, you have been accused of obstructing the police in the course of their duty.'

Ellie sighed. 'I suppose I can always get my solicitor down here to defend me, but really, why waste time for both of us? You know perfectly well — because I give you credit for listening to both the men you sent to Stewart's flat — that one of your constables made a complete fool of himself and then tried to take it out on me. I think your dragging me down here for no real reason could be called harassment. I'll have to ask my solicitor about that, won't I?'

The muscles along DS Willis's jawline shifted as she ground her teeth. 'They were acting on information received when they went to ask your son-in-law Stewart a few questions.'

'Really? What information? What's he supposed to have done?'

'You were deliberately obstructive.'

'They asked me if I knew where he was and I said I didn't. Which was the truth. They wanted me to turn a blind eye while they searched for bank statements, and I refused to let them because they hadn't a warrant. Is that being obstructive? I don't think so.'

DS Willis appeared to be on the point of losing her temper. Ellie watched her with some interest. She considered telling the woman that if the policemen had asked her nicely if she had any suggestions as to where Stewart might be found, she might have told them. Or perhaps she wouldn't.

'Well, if that's all . . . ?' said Ellie, drawing her bag towards her.

'No, it certainly isn't.' DS Willis was going to make the most of her opportunity to grill Ellie. 'Let's start from the beginning.'

CHAPTER EIGHT

DS Willis leaned forward slightly. 'For the record, what is your name and what relation are you to Miss Drusilla Quicke?'

'I am Mrs Ellie Quicke. I was married to her nephew Frank, who died last year.'

'You stand to inherit the most under her will?'

'So she says. I'll believe it when I see the will.'

'She informed you that was the case?'

'Yes, but she may well change her mind and leave it all to her son, Roy. And even leave some to her great-niece, my daughter Diana, if it so pleases her.'

'Surely it bothers you that she may change her will?'

'No. My husband left me very well provided for.'

'No one ever has enough.'

'So they say. Personally, I've found a big inheritance brings its own problems. That's why we're setting up a charitable trust to get rid of some of the money.' Ellie showed DS Willis some of the paperwork from her bag. 'You see?'

'You could be getting rid of some of the money because you know you have a lot more to come.'

'Believe me, dealing with Aunt Drusilla's estate would be no picnic. I know she owns a lot of property in the immediate vicinity, most of it flats to let. There may well be more that

I don't know about. Looking after property to let is not my idea of fun.'

'There's that big house, too. That should fetch a bomb if the site were redeveloped.'

'It's the Quicke family house. It belonged not to Miss Quicke, but to my husband Frank — who left it to me. Miss Quicke now has it on a repairing lease. What about that cup of tea?'

DS Willis snarled at her colleague, who left the room. A fact which was then recorded on the tape. With the tape switched off, Ellie said, 'Has that fool of a constable ever tried to call you "dearie"?'

DS Willis fought to hold back a smile. She won. Just. Ellie went through her handbag looking for a handkerchief. The air was perhaps a trifle on the dry side in this interview room. A pity she hadn't thought to put in some sucky sweets. But there, you can't think of everything.

A cup of tea arrived, and the tape was switched back on again.

DS Willis said, 'We have established that you have the best motive for killing your aunt, so . . .'

'No motive at all,' said Ellie. 'In fact, I'm rather fond of her and I think she is of me, too.'

'—so I'd like you to tell me when you were last at her house.'

'Apart from this morning when your WPC let me in, and saw me out again?'

Ellie tried to think why it should matter when she was last at Aunt Drusilla's house. Then she got it.

'Ah. For fingerprints purposes? The day before it happened, I suppose. I've been there almost every day . . . no, make that every day . . . for the last week or so because of the renovations and the wedding on Saturday. Although I can't think when I last went up into her bedroom.'

'Try.'

Ellie sat back and thought about it. 'I'm really not at all sure. I was up there quite a bit when she had that bad fall some time ago, because she had a spell in bed. Then Rose moved in to look after her temporarily, and I don't think I had any reason to go up there after that. Maybe to fetch something for her . . . ?' Her voice trailed off. She shook her head. 'Maybe Rose might remember or Aunt Drusilla, but I honestly don't think I went up there after Rose moved in.

'I was in and out downstairs, of course. There were a lot of workmen around. My Aunt found them intrusive but refused to consider moving out of the house till they'd finished. I acted as mediator between my aunt and the workmen on occasion. I was pretty successful at keeping the peace until my aunt found the plumbers were proposing to use the wrong gauge of pipe, and sacked them on the spot. She was, of course, quite right to do so. That's when I suggested my own plumber, Jimbo Johnson. But you know all about that.

'The builders seemed efficient enough. She didn't have any quarrel with them, apart from turning down their proposal to redevelop the garage and the back of the house into self-contained units. I believe she did have an argument with them about that but I wasn't there and only heard about it after it was over.

'It was the electricians who caused me the most grief. They were slow. I had to keep popping in to see that they were providing enough power for the caterers who were doing the wedding on Saturday. The caterers need to bring in a great deal of electrical equipment and there simply aren't enough power points in the kitchen. That's why I was pressing the electricians — who were rewiring the unoccupied back part of the house first — to finish before the weekend, which they promised to do.'

'Let's get back to the wiring. The old wiring. It had been condemned?'

'No. No one had come along and slapped a notice on, saying, "You must not touch." Nothing like that. I agree that the wiring in what used to be the servants' quarters was quite appalling, but then, nobody had lived there for years. That was where the electricians started, putting in a new ring main for that part of the house, which included the old servants' sitting room and bedrooms, the larders and the scullery. You can check with them about that.

'The wiring in the rest of the house was in need of replacement but it was still serviceable. I know, because when we were married about thirty years ago, my dear husband put in a new ring main for the part of the house which Aunt Drusilla used. That is, the kitchen, downstairs living rooms, bedrooms and bathrooms above. It cost a pretty penny and we had to scrimp and save to pay for it. Before you point out that Aunt Drusilla is as rich as Croesus, in those days we thought she was as poor as a church mouse and couldn't afford to do it herself.'

'So the wiring you put in has developed faults.'

'Not as far as I know, but it was certainly in need of attention and that's what was happening. The electricians have been working there on and off for, oh, ten days or so. On the day of the accident I'm told they were due to start on the kitchen, but to do that they had to turn off the power there and to the rest of the house. Do I make myself clear?

'Miss Quicke had promised Mrs McNally's daughter that she could hold her wedding reception there this Saturday. The electricians couldn't guarantee the rewiring would be done in time, so Miss Quicke told them to leave it till after the weekend. You can ask my aunt about this, surely? I can only tell you what she told me.'

'Go on.'

'Well, at that point my aunt realized she would have to look for somewhere else to stay until the workmen had finished. Exit Miss Quicke. End of story.'

'You seem to know a lot about electricity. How handy are you with a screwdriver yourself?'

'Hopeless. Ask my husband. Oh. You can't, of course.'

'Do you mean to tell me—' with an air of menace — 'that you have never in your life changed a plug?'

'Of course I have,' said Ellie cheerfully. 'I had to put a plug on an electric toaster before I was married — do you remember that in those days they used to supply electrical equipment without plugs? I hadn't a clue how to do it, so I undid the plug on my radio to see how the wires went, and copied them. I was so pleased when the toaster worked, but Frank — we'd just got engaged at the time — he thought I'd be bound to have got it wrong, took it all apart and did it up again. Of course, he did everything like that about the house himself after we got married.'

DS Willis looked stunned, but recovered. 'You could have got someone else to interfere with the wiring in your aunt's bedroom.'

'That's a good point,' said Ellie, drawing her chair nearer to the table. 'I was wondering if you'd thought about a contract killer — is that what they call them? Contract killers? Forget about the wiring being old. Jimbo says that the cleaner was using the hoover all right in the bedroom, that she coiled up the flex, indicating she'd finished the job. Then she turned the television on, which of course she shouldn't have done on her employer's time. The point is that the wiring does seem to have been working perfectly normally up till then, don't you agree?'

'It is possible, yes.'

'Well, what I think is that someone who knew what they were doing tampered with that television set. It couldn't have been done by accident, could it? Perhaps it was done by one of the electricians who was in and out all week? Or one of the plumbers? Was it very hard to do, this rewiring job?'

'I'm asking the questions, if you please.'

Ellie shrugged. 'I just wanted to help. But if that's all . . . it's getting quite late, isn't it, and I have so much still to do today.' She looked at her watch, and stood up. 'I really must go. Shopping to do, phone calls to make. And tell that young man that if he calls me "dearie" again, I'll have him for libel . . . or is it slander?'

'Slander,' said Ms Willis, absent-mindedly.

Ellie began to button up her jacket when there came an interruption. Sandy Hair poked his head round the door and signalled to Ms Willis, who turned off the recorder and left the room.

Ellie picked up her bag and looked around to see if she'd left anything else in the room, which she hadn't. Before she got to the door it opened again, and in marched Ms Willis carrying a file and wearing her most forbidding expression. Ellie sighed. Really, if the woman would only pluck her eyebrows, she'd be far easier on the eye and would probably have an easier ride in life.

'Don't go,' said Ms Willis, sitting down and switching on the tape again.

Ellie hovered. 'Is it really important? Because I do have a lot on.'

'It's important. We've just got the result of the autopsy in. Your cleaner, Mrs Tucker, had a heart condition. We have also had the voltage that was going through the television aerial checked. It was not sufficient to kill anyone.'

Ellie gaped. 'You mean that Mrs Tucker wouldn't have died if her heart had been all right? That a mild shock from the aerial triggered off a heart attack?'

'Yes.'

'You mean someone tried to frighten Aunt Drusilla, but not to kill her?'

'That's what it looks like, yes.'

Ellie thought about that. If the voltage had not been sufficient to kill, then it opened up all sorts of possibilities. A lot of people — not just Diana — might have liked the idea of giving Aunt Drusilla a nasty shock, while not wanting to kill her.

Ms Willis said, 'So let's go through your story yet again, shall we? You were irritated with your aunt for various reasons and decided to give her a fright, not intending to kill her.'

'Dear me,' said Ellie, 'you do have a one-track mind, don't you?' She didn't sit down again, but looked for her mobile phone in her handbag. She was more than a little surprised by how well she was standing up to this intimidating woman. What would her dear Frank have said, if he could have seen her now? Six months ago she would probably have sat down with a meek expression and obeyed Ms Willis. Now, oh no! She'd had it up to here with the woman.

'I can see you've got to start all over again but I've told you all I know. For the record, I did not try to give my aunt an electric shock — and in any case, her heart's as strong as an ox — and I don't see any point in going over and over the same ground. So I'll call a cab and be on my way. I'm not risking life and limb in a police car with Sandy Hair again.'

'Wait a minute. You can't go yet.'

'Can't I? I don't see why not. Oh, I almost forgot. What did you want to speak to Stewart for?'

'To eliminate him from our enquiries.'

Ellie started to punch in the number for the minicab firm that she always used. 'What enquiries? He's a law-abiding soul, never even got a speeding ticket as far as I know, so that means you wanted to talk to him about the accident. Well, he hasn't anything to do with it, I can tell you that. He didn't even know someone had died till I told him. He's actually rather fond of Miss Quicke, you know.'

'That's just your opinion. Sit down again, please, Mrs Quicke.'

Ellie spoke into the phone. 'Yes, Mrs Quicke here. Can you send a cab to the police station for me, as soon as possible? I'll need to do some shopping in the Avenue, then drop it back at my house and then go on to my solicitor's . . . it's a big house down by the river. Five minutes? Thank you.'

Norm helped old Mr Tucker back into his chair and tucked him in. The room looked dingier than ever, partly because Mo hadn't been there to tidy up, and partly because for some reason the television was not on.

Norm sat on the edge of his chair, instead of sinking into its depths as he usually did. 'You oughta tell your granddaughter. She's a right to know, even if . . .'

Mr Tucker screwed up his face. 'Tell that bitch nothing.'

'She's Mo's niece.'

'Blood isn't thicker than water where she's concerned. You know Mo never got on with her. It's number one all the way with that one. She'd be round soon enough if there were any money in it but there ain't, so we won't see nothing of her.'

'You're her grandad. She might want to take care of you.'

Mr Tucker sucked in his cheeks, noisily. His upper plate didn't fit too well. 'You want to be rid of me, then?'

Norm shook his head.

Mr Tucker cackled. 'Know which side your bread's buttered, eh? Too old to go on the pull nowadays, are we? Not so easy to find yourself another bread ticket?'

'Mo was all right. I'll miss her.'

Mr Tucker nodded. Mo had been all right. She'd done her bit by them. She'd had a sharp tongue but her heart had been in the right place. Family first and last, that was Mo.

Norm said, 'I been thinking. I could go down the Social tomorrow. Tell them what's happened. There'll be money for the funeral. She'd got a bit saved, in the Building Society. She din't make a will, did she? So it's yours. Not your granddaughter's, nor Jogger's.'

Mr Tucker nodded vigorously. 'And the flat's in my name. Not Jogger's.'

'Jogger lives with his girlfriend, don't he? The flat's in her name, what with her having the baby and all.'

My Tucker nodded. 'They'll stop Mo's allowances. Bound to.'

'Suppose I were registered as your carer, 'stead of her?'

Mr Tucker relaxed. 'Thought you'd get round to that. A fine carer you'd make. Be better off in a home.'

Norm grinned. 'No, you wouldn't. You always said you wouldn't. If I stay . . .'

'And where else would you go?'

'. . . I can be your carer. With some help from the Social. Right?'

There was a long silence.

It was about the best arrangement they could come to, and both knew it.

'Chip butties for tea?' said old Mr Tucker.

Norm nodded. 'And tomorrow, I'll see about some compensation from the old bitch, right?'

'Turn the telly back on. I like to see those big girls shaking themselves all over the place.'

* * *

Her house was much as it had been before when Ellie got back, except that nearly all the chocolate cakes Rose had been making had vanished. And there was a fresh pile of dishes in the sink. Rose fell on Ellie's food purchases with cries of joy, and set about making supper. Aunt Drusilla was snoring lightly, in the conservatory. There was no little Frank today; no doubt the childminder was looking after him till six.

Ellie had a quick cuppa, checked the messages on the answerphone, and was on her way out again.

Bill's house stood in a quiet cul-de-sac with its back garden looking out over the Thames. At low tide, mud flats were about all you could see, but at high tide the river presented a constant source of entertainment, with boats rocketing up and down, oarsmen sculling, gulls wheeling. At all times the willows on the towpaths provided a touch of rural beauty.

Bill was waiting for her and so was Joyce McNally, together with her scoutmaster fiancé and the flower-arranging lady, Mrs Dawes. The caterers drew up shortly after. Joyce was torn between pleasure at having her wedding reception in such a beautiful setting, irritation at having to alter existing arrangements, and annoyance at having to be grateful to Ellie and Bill for making everything possible.

'You mean, we can use the garden and it goes down to the river? But will the tide be out? I mean, mud flats are not exactly . . . though of course I do realize that . . . I suppose we'll have to run off some notices to let everyone know about the change of venue, and none of this would have been necessary if only . . . though of course, I don't mean to sound ungrateful and this really is quite the most . . . Mrs Quicke, you are indeed a marvel . . .'

Bill was quietly enjoying the spectacle of Joyce's changing facial expressions. He took Ellie's elbow and guided her into his den at the back of the house. This was the small, untidy room in which he spent most of his time now that his two girls were away at university. There was a superb view from this window. Early narcissi were spangling the grass, and a splendid magnolia was bursting into flower all over. Because his house was so old, the garden was surrounded with red-brick walls, which provided protection for the plants within.

'It's very beautiful here,' said Ellie, a touch wistfully. 'You are a very kind man to let us take over your house like this.'

'Be sure I shall exact every penny of my fee. The Golf Club Dinner on Saturday night will only be the start of what I shall require by way of repayment.'

'Good,' said Ellie. 'I shall look forward to it. Full evening dress? I shall have to buy something, you know. And maybe have my hair restyled. What do you think?'

'You always look just right to me,' said Bill and seemed to mean it.

'You should have seen me this morning,' said Ellie, and proceeded to tell Bill all about it. She liked talking things over with Bill. She knew he liked her a lot, but he'd never tried to pressurize her into a more intimate relationship, as Roy did. Also, they'd known one another for ever. You never needed to explain anything to old friends.

Bill smoothed out a smile when she reported how she had stalked out of the police station. 'So Mrs Tucker's death really was an accident? But you didn't find out what the police wanted Stewart for?'

'If I were a fanciful woman . . .'

'Which you are not . . .'

'. . . I'd wonder who might have wanted to harm poor Stewart, and the answer would be . . .'

'Diana. A little tacky, getting involved with a new man while still married to another, don't you think? I wonder. She arrived at my office this morning shortly after you left, demanding to know if we were Miss Quicke's solicitors.

Stormed into my office, frightened a client out of her chair, had to be taken outside and informed of the facts of life.'

Ellie was intrigued. 'You mean, even this morning she thought it was Aunt Drusilla who had died? But . . . oh, I suppose if she spent the night with Derek Jolley — which she may well have done because she certainly didn't spend it at the flat with Stewart — she might easily not have heard. The police wouldn't have known where she was. I didn't know where she was. Nor did Stewart. So you told her that Aunt Drusilla was still alive?'

Bill grinned. 'Her reaction was extreme. She nearly fainted. I had to get my girl to sit her down and push her head between her knees. Then feed her some sugared tea. You'd have thought I'd just told her the sky had fallen in.'

'Which it had for her, I suppose.' Ellie sighed. 'Oh dear. I do love her, of course I do, she's my only child. But there's no denying that all she thinks about is number one.'

'She demanded the use of my phone. I said she might. She punched in a number and then changed her mind, crashed the phone down and exited in a hurry.'

'Exit left, pursued by a bear,' Ellie quoted from some half-remembered play of Shakespeare's. 'Though I've always wondered why it had to be a bear. She may have realized that she'd burned her boats a little too quickly, that Derek Jolley might not be so keen to have her if she didn't bring Aunt Drusilla's millions with her. Her first thought might be to make it up with Stewart? No, her first thought would have been to go down to the bank to close the joint account and transfer all the money into her name. I do hope Stewart got there first. He was going to transfer half to himself.'

'Hah!' Bill applauded.

'Suppose he did get there first. She'd be so angry she'd look round for a scapegoat. Do you think it possible that it was she who denounced Stewart to the police? Telling them that Stewart wanted Aunt Drusilla dead so that he and Diana could inherit? And that's why the police went round to question him? Is that far-fetched?'

'I fear not,' said Bill, gloomily. 'What are you going to do about that daughter of yours, Ellie? You can't go on protecting her from the consequences of her actions for ever.'

'Dear Bill.' Ellie rested her head against his shoulder and he put his arm about her. In companionship. In fondness. And then drew away again. 'You really think Diana denounced him to the police?'

'Haven't a clue. She's devious enough. Single-minded enough.'

'Yes, but . . . she's my daughter, Bill. A poor, unhappy creature who lashes out at anyone who gets in her way. As I should know. I used to think it was all my fault that she was like she is. I used to be really afraid of her. Now, I don't know whether I can help or not. I can't think — no, I really can't — that she'd go so far as to murder. No, really! She wouldn't.'

'You'd agree she'd be capable of wanting to give Miss Quicke a bad fright? Push her off balance? Force her to see great-niece in a new light? Diana the strong, the one who knows how to solve everyone's problems? Perhaps Diana just wanted Miss Quicke to become more dependent on her.'

Ellie sighed deeply, but didn't reply. She remembered Mr Strawson and Diana's plot to convert Aunt Drusilla's out-buildings into self-contained units for sale. Suppose Aunt Drusilla *had* received a bad shock and it had made her disinclined to return to her house? Diana would have thought she'd inherit. She'd been wrong in that assumption, but suppose . . .

Ellie didn't want to think Bill was right, but she had to agree there was a lot of sense in what he said. Only, if it wasn't Diana, then — as Ellie had suggested to the police — probably someone else was involved. An accomplice who knew how to tamper with the wiring.

There was a lot of squawking from Bill's kitchen, which finally got through Ellie's musings on the subject of unsatisfactory daughters. 'I'd better go and sort that out, I suppose,' said Ellie. 'I'll be glad when this wedding is over.'

Bill gave her a hug. 'You've changed, Ellie Quicke. When Frank died, you couldn't have stood up to anyone, let alone that appalling female in the kitchen — what's her name, Joyce? I've met her mother, a delightful woman if a little fluffy for my taste, but I hope I never see the daughter again after tomorrow. I'm filled with admiration for you, Ellie. You seem to be able to cope with everything and everybody. Come to think of it, I'd back you even against Diana.'

Ellie kissed his chin, which was all she could reach, even standing on tiptoe. 'Thanks for that vote of confidence, Bill. Now let's see what all the fuss is about this time.'

* * *

The man whistled through his teeth as he got through on his mobile.

'Have you heard? They say the old bat had a bad heart, and it was that which killed her.'

'What!'

'Yeah, I got it from one of the builders taking down the scaffolding. That Norm was round, asking about the old 'un, and he told the scaffolders. Yeah, he was surprised, too.'

'Have the builders left, then?'

'Should be clear of the place this afternoon.'

'And then what?'

'Anybody's guess. No sign of her highness, though. Nor the lady in waiting.'

'I need to see her. You thought she might be at the stroppy cow's place? How do we find out?'

'I done some work there a while back. Maybe I'll go round that way on the way back.'

CHAPTER NINE

The days were getting longer, but it was still dusk just after six and the lights were on in Ellie's house when she returned home. She had sorted out Joyce's last-minute whims, the caterers' demands for serving tables, and Mrs Dawes' need for access in the morning to prepare the flower arrangements. Ellie wondered at her recently developed talent for telling other people what to do.

As she left her cab, she noticed a rusty old car parked in the road opposite. Not one of the neighbours.

Letting herself into the house, she found the central heating had been turned up higher than normal. Rose opened the kitchen door and beckoned Ellie within, with one finger on her lips. The study door was ajar and through the gap Ellie saw that one of her armchairs had been eased into the study. Miss Quicke was sitting in it, with her eyes closed. Rose closed the kitchen door with exaggerated caution.

'Having a little doze. Such a trying afternoon we've had. I'll tell you all about it later. I've started supper. You did mean us to have a lamb stew, didn't you?'

'Bless you, Rose. You're a marvel. Listen, the police told me something that should make my aunt feel better. Mrs Tucker, the cleaner, had a bad heart. The shock from the aerial wouldn't have been strong enough to kill her. It was her heart that did it. I've got her address and I thought I'd call on the woman's father tomorrow.'

Rose brightened. 'That is good news. I'll tell Miss Quicke when she wakes up, but in the meantime, Diana is in the sitting room.'

Ellie blinked. 'Whaaaat?' Soundlessly.

Ellie metaphorically girded her loins. She was not at all sure that she was prepared to tackle Diana at this, or at any other time. Despite Bill's faith in her. She clasped her hands tightly in front of her, and realized that she was in fact praying for help.

Dear Lord, what a mess. Please help me say the right thing. Or at least, help me not to say the wrong thing. And please, don't let Diana have been responsible for that poor woman's death . . .

She went across the hall into the sitting room. Diana was sitting in a huddle on the settee. One of the side lamps was on, but the curtains were still open. By the look of her, Diana had been crying. She looked up when Ellie came in, but didn't speak.

'Diana.' Ellie didn't know what to say to her difficult daughter, so she drew the curtains and switched on another side light. 'Would you like a sherry, or coffee or something? Who's looking after little Frank tonight?'

'I asked the childminder to keep him over, tonight. I couldn't take him to Derek's and I can't go back to the flat.'

Ellie sat down beside her daughter and spoke the magic words. 'Tell me all about it.'

Diana stared straight ahead of her, plucking at a button on her smart black jacket. 'The police think I did it. Killed that woman. But I didn't.'

'No, no.' Ellie did her best to believe it.

'The inspector was on at me for hours and hours. Going over it again and again. Did I expect to gain by my great-aunt's death? Yes, of course I did. Had she given me the sack? Yes, of course she had . . . the stupid . . . ! Great-Aunt can't see beyond the end of her nose, she's totally out of date, it was only good business practice to . . .'

'Cheat her?'

'It wasn't cheating.' But it had been cheating and Diana knew it. 'Anyway, I didn't do it.' She was sullen, obstinate. Not at all remorseful. Then self-pity turned to anger. 'If she'd only given me my fair share of the money, acknowledged me as her heir, none of this would have happened.'

'You mean, Mrs Tucker wouldn't have died?'

'I mean . . . I don't mean that, of course. What I mean is that . . . oh, it's all such a horrible mess! Why couldn't she be a normal, loving great-aunt, someone who looked after her relatives and helped them when they needed it?'

'You didn't *need* her money, Diana. You were earning a very nice salary, you had a loving, faithful husband and a lovely child. You had money in the bank to put down on a house, you had a car and a wardrobe full of good clothes.'

'It wasn't enough,' said Diana, in a hard, tight voice. 'I want much, much more than that. I want to be up there with the best. I want a house in Mayfair and an attractive, powerful man at my side. I want . . .'

'The stars and the moon. Well, you could have got it, if you'd worked for it.'

Diana turned on her mother. 'Look who's talking! You could have helped me, given me my half of this house, given me a loan to start up in my own business.'

'No, I couldn't, Diana. And please don't go round repeating that you own half this house, because you know very well that you don't. I own half outright, and the other half is mine for my lifetime and only after my death comes to you. If I had given you all the money you asked for, you'd only have wanted more. Then more. It would never have been enough.'

'It would! It would! All I ever wanted was—'

'Fairy gold, Diana. Do you remember the story? The fairies gave the hero what he asked for, but because he hadn't earned it, it turned to dust in his hands.'

'I hate you! You've never loved me! Why did I think you'd be able to help me? You never think of anyone but yourself!'

Ellie winced, absorbing the hurt but not giving in.

Diana blew her nose, wiped her eyes and threw the tissue in the direction of the waste-paper basket. It missed.

'Drink?' said Ellie, who felt the need for a sherry. A large one.

Diana turned her shoulder on her mother but didn't get up to leave, which Ellie thought was a good sign. Ellie got herself a sherry but paused in the act of pouring one out for Diana.

'Diana, have you eaten anything today?'

Diana shrugged. 'I couldn't possibly eat. You've no idea what a terrible day it's been. Last night was quite something. Dinner out, down by the river. Making plans, such marvellous plans Derek has. His flat's superb, in a brand-new block in Old Isle-worth, also overlooking the river. We drank champagne and it was just wonderful. Then this morning he said I must check with Aunt Drusilla's solicitor, and I didn't know who that might be so I went to see your famous Bill and he said . . .' She gulped.

'He told you Aunt Drusilla was very much alive.'

'Yes. I damn near fainted. I realized I ought to ring Derek and tell him, stop him from putting the money down on . . . well, if I'd had the money, we could have really made a killing, but now . . . I don't know what he'll do.'

'You know very well what he'll do,' said Ellie, with compassion. 'He'll dump you.'

'No, he won't. He loves me!' She went and got some sherry for herself and gulped it down. 'You've got to see it from his point of view. Without Aunt Drusilla's money, he can't . . . won't . . . and then I'm still married to Stewart . . . unfortunately . . .'

Ellie sighed. 'So you went to see Derek and he dumped you . . .'

'No, I haven't spoken to him since . . . he's been leaving messages on my mobile all day, but I haven't got back to him yet. Well, I thought that at least I still had the money from the sale of the house up north although it's not nearly enough, but when I got to the bank . . . I could kill Stewart!'

'You don't really mean that, Diana.'

'Oh, you know what I mean. I was so furious with him that I . . . well, I was passing the police station and I went in to ask where my great-aunt was because she wasn't back at the house, and they gave me a really hard time.'

'So you told them to look at Stewart . . . which, if I may say so, Diana, was both unkind and unfair.'

'I wasn't thinking straight. He shouldn't have taken the money out of our account.'

'Why not? Half of it is his and you dumped him last night, remember?'

'Yes, well. That was . . . then. Things are different now.'

'Having second thoughts about dumping Stewart?'

Silence.

Diana finished off her sherry. 'I can get him back any time.' Defiantly. 'Not that I want him, of course. He's just so deadly dull, and boring. I can't think why I married him.'

Ellie wasn't so sure that Stewart would take her back. 'So have you taken your things out of your flat yet? Have you told Derek that the money is not available anymore?'

Diana looked away. The answer was no to both.

So Diana had yet to break the bad news to her new boyfriend, who would ditch her if Ellie knew anything about him. She had nowhere to go, no job and no loving husband to pick up the pieces. And was under suspicion of murder.

Ellie tried to put her arm around her daughter, who pulled away. Ellie contemplated her daughter's averted face with compassion mixed, it must be said, with irritation. 'What do you want out of life now, Diana? I know what you thought you wanted in the past, but what do you want now?'

Diana shrugged. 'Something'll work out.'

'You can't stay here.'

'I can move back into my old room upstairs.'

'Aunt Drusilla has moved in there. Either Rose or little Frank has the little bedroom. I think you'd better go back to the flat and have a talk with Stewart. But remember, the lease of that flat is up soon.'

'You can get it extended for me, I'm sure.'

'No, I don't think I can. It's time you stood on your own feet, Diana. And I'm not going to ask you to stay for supper, because I think it might be a little awkward for you to sit down at table with Aunt Drusilla. Off you go.'

Diana got to her feet, closed her eyes, fists clenched at her sides, opened her mouth and screamed. And screamed. And screamed.

Ellie watched her, feeling detached. She was sorry for the girl in a way, but chiefly she wondered how much she herself had been responsible for Diana's selfishness. With sorrow.

'What's all this?' Aunt Drusilla, leaning on her stick, eyes snapping. Rose peered over her shoulder.

Diana cut herself off in mid-scream and dissolved into tears.

'Oh, Great-Aunt, everything's such a mess and I've been such a fool.'

'That's true,' said Miss Quicke, making for the most comfortable chair in the room. 'I'll have a sherry, too, Ellie.'

Diana's remorseful tears froze on her cheeks and she switched into the high-handed mode which came more easily to her. 'You don't understand. I've always done my best by you. I've saved you thousands of pounds by using different contractors . . .'

'Who paid you thousands of pounds to make the switch . . .'

'. . entirely for your own good . . .'

'For whose good?'

Diana hesitated for half a beat. Then, 'For both our goods. You benefit and so do I. I deserve to benefit because of all the hard work I put into . . .'

'Giving me an inferior service. Don't you think I know the difference? Did you think I wouldn't bother to check up on what you'd done? I gave you the job to—'

'To save yourself money,' said Diana, smiting the palm of her left hand with her fist.

'No,' said Miss Quicke, with a small sigh. 'I gave you the job because I wanted to see for myself what you were made of. Also, a little, to please your mother. I gave you the opportunity to prove yourself as a businesswoman, and I warned you right from the start that you would have to follow my guidelines.'

'Yes, but I—'

'I warned you. Your mother warned you. You chose to disregard our warnings, and continued to deliver a second-class service while drawing a first-class salary. You can't say I haven't been fair. You've had three written warnings from me. You shall be paid till the end of the month, plus whatever is due to you by way of holiday pay, and that is the end of it.'

'You don't understand!' Diana seized a chair and drew it up close to her great-aunt. 'The kind of work I was doing for you, well, it was boring. All the time I was thinking, making contacts, laying the groundwork to move into something that would really bring in the money. At long last, I've found it. There's this big property on the other side of the shops, been derelict for ages and then was done up by a man who put in new windows, extended into the roof, put up garages. He's got to sell because he's over-extended. I can get in on the ground floor, make a large profit.'

Aunt Drusilla cackled. 'I know the property. The man hasn't planning permission for all the alterations and extensions he's had done, and yes, of course he wants to get out quickly, before he's made to put it all back as it was.'

Diana went white. 'Are you sure?'

'Of course I'm sure. By the way, whose money were you proposing to use to "get in on the ground floor"?'

'Well, I thought you'd be pleased to . . . then of course yesterday we heard that . . .'

'The reports of my death have been much exaggerated.' The old woman laughed, a dry coughing sound. 'Would I be right in thinking that you've fallen victim to Derek Jolley? That he persuaded you to put up your own money, the money from the sale of your house up north?'

'Derek and I are . . . we have an understanding, yes.'

'I heard. More fool you. That Stewart's a nice lad, you won't find many like him growing on trees. Or he was a nice lad till you corrupted him.'

'Corrupted?' That stung. 'How dare you!'

'Easily, when it's the truth. I'm not sure whether he can be saved or not, but I know I'm not prepared to give you any more leeway. You are out, young lady.'

'You can't do that. I'm your great-niece. I have every right to—'

'To expect something under my will? For your information, I did make a new will recently. I left two thirds of my estate to your mother, which she will probably waste on charitable causes but that's her problem, and one third to my son Roy. Oh, and a small legacy to Rose. I set you down for ten thousand pounds, if you can stay out of jail till it's time for you to collect your inheritance.'

'Out of jail?' Diana gasped. 'What on earth do you mean?'

'That's where you're heading, in my opinion.'

'Why, you . . . !' Diana raised her arm to hit her great-aunt. Both Rose and Ellie cried out. Diana realized at the last minute what she was doing, and recoiled.

Aunt Drusilla tipped the last drop of sherry into her mouth and said, 'Now, if the police ask me tomorrow who might have wanted to kill me, what shall I say?'

'If I'd tried to kill you — old woman! — you'd be dead by now.'

Ellie drew in her breath. All of them heard the hate in Diana's voice, and all three believed her.

Someone rang the doorbell. Rose went to answer it while Ellie lowered herself gently into a chair. Diana seemed frozen, standing over her great-aunt.

'Hello there!' It was Derek Jolley, rubbing his hands, half uneasy and half jocular. Ellie thought, He must be fifty if he's a day. Too ripe a complexion and going bald already. What does Diana see in him? Money, I suppose.

'Darling.' He tried to kiss Diana's cheek. 'Miss Quicke. So glad to hear that you're still with us and not . . . well, laid low. How delightful, quite the family gathering.' To Diana, 'I thought I might find you here. Something's wrong with your mobile, I haven't been able to get through to you all day.'

Diana said. 'Derek, I have some bad news. I haven't been able to persuade my great-aunt to invest in our little venture, and half my capital has been removed from my bank account.'

His nose seemed to become more pointed. 'My poor dear! It's been a bad day, has it? Never mind, a bottle of the old Jolley champagne should buck you up a treat.'

Ellie put her hand over her eyes. Derek was going to stick by Diana. Why? There must be something in it for him. If not money, then what? Or did he still hope to get money through her from somewhere?'

Aunt Drusilla said, 'Mr Jolley, may I ask whether my great-niece has been foolish enough to sign something in the property line?'

'If she has, dear lady? She has done nothing improper, I can assure you. A sound proposition, just waiting for the right person to . . .'

'To pick up the tab. Well, that is her affair. Again and again I have warned her and now I wash my hands of her. Not another penny does she see of my money. Now, Rose, I rather think I'd like to sit quietly in the conservatory till supper.'

Rose steered Aunt Drusilla out into the conservatory and shut the communicating doors behind them. Ellie looked from one hard-set face to the other. The distressing thought came to her that Derek and Diana were wearing identical expressions, wary and speculative. A trifle mean. Did they deserve one another? Ellie hoped not. She would have one more try.

'Diana, little Frank will be missing you. Why don't you pick him up from the childminder's, take him home, have a good talk with Stewart?'

Derek Jolley didn't speak, but Ellie imagined she heard him say that he wasn't interested in the brat.

The doorbell rang again. Ellie went to answer it. A stranger stood there. A heavily built man in well-worn casual clothes that looked as if they could do with a good clean.

'Miss Quicke? Can I have a word?'

'I'm Mrs Quicke. I'm sorry, but I don't think I know you, do I?'

'I'm Norm. Mo Tucker's partner. Mind if I come in a minute?' He wasn't threatening, but somehow he managed to get himself into the hall and close the front door behind him.

'Mrs Tucker?' Fresh from the scene next door, Ellie took a couple of seconds to connect. The cleaner who'd died. 'Oh, yes. A terrible thing. She had a heart condition, apparently. You must be shattered.'

Rose poked her head out of the kitchen. 'Miss Quicke wants to know who it is.' Rose looked as if she'd seen the big man somewhere before but couldn't quite place him.

Norm half glanced towards Rose, but concentrated on Ellie. 'I want a private word with Miss Quicke.'

'With my aunt? Rose, is my aunt up to it at the moment?'

He turned on Ellie and being such a big man so close to her, she quailed.

'Ain't you Miss Quicke? You said you was Miss Quicke.'

'No, I'm *Mrs* Quicke. *Miss* Quicke is my aunt. But she's been through a very difficult couple of days and I'm not sure—'

'Not half as difficult as my days have been missus. I've got Mo's old grandad on me back an' her son too, an' all.'

'Oh dear.' Ellie eyed the still-closed sitting-room door and then led the way out through the kitchen to the conservatory, where Miss Quicke was leaning back in a chair, leaning back, with her eyes closed. 'Aunt Drusilla, this is Norm, Mo's husband. I mean, partner.'

Miss Quicke's eyes opened halfway. 'My condolences,' she said, using the formal phrases that came naturally to one of her generation, 'Very shocked. It must be a very difficult time for you.'

'It could be easier.' Unasked, he sat on a chair, planting big hands on knees and leaning forward. 'It's her old father, see. Lost his leg. Mo was his carer. Then there's her boy, Jogger we call him. Got a girlfriend an' all, an' a baby. Mo did the lot, looked after all of us.'

'I'm sure she did.' Miss Quicke's eyelids began to sink again.

'Well. Hah!' Norm rubbed his thumb across his finger-tips. 'We wondered what you wanted to do about it.'

'Do?' The aged voice faded. 'I can do nothing. I am turned out of my own home, having to take refuge in my niece's home, which is comfortable enough in some ways, I suppose, but not what I have been accustomed to. I have no idea when I shall be allowed back.'

Norm shifted on his chair. 'She was killed in your house, by your telly.'

'Which she had no right to turn on. She was supposed to be cleaning, not sitting down to watch the television.'

'Well, there's no harm watching the telly, listening while she worked, was there? There's no getting away from it, is there? Your telly killed her.'

'I believe it was her heart condition which killed her. I am told that the aerial delivered a slight shock, not enough to kill a normal, healthy person. Her theft of my electricity — for it was theft of my electricity to watch my television without permission — her theft gave her a shock and her bad heart did the rest.'

The old eyes closed completely.

Norm reddened. 'Look, lady. That's not good enough. Mo died on your premises, doing work which you'd asked her to do. I think we deserve a little understanding, don't you? A little . . . compensation.'

Silence. Then a thread-like voice. 'See my solicitor, if you wish. I don't think you'll find him very helpful, though. You haven't a leg to stand on.'

'I bet you don't want a court case, though, with all the publicity. If the papers get hold of this, it'll be "Millionairess' Telly Kills Cleaner. Refuses Compensation!"'

Miss Quicke yawned. 'I dislike being blackmailed even more than I dislike publicity. Publish and be damned, as the Duke of Wellington is supposed to have said. I rather agree with him. Now, if you please, I am exceedingly tired.'

Ellie touched Norm's elbow and, rather to her surprise, he left the conservatory with her without any more argument. 'I'm so sorry,' she said, in the hallway. 'I called at the agency this afternoon, asking for your address. I intended to come to see you tomorrow. What you must be feeling! I think I only saw your . . . Mrs Tucker . . . once or twice. It must have been a terrible shock.'

Norm's face was still red. 'We're due something for losing Mo, aren't we? You tell that old . . . that old woman that I'm down the Social tomorrow first thing, and they'll give me the name of a good solicitor. She's taken Mo from us and she has to pay for it. Right?'

'I wouldn't count on it. May I make a suggestion? The cleaning company for whom Mo worked have insurances. Maybe they can help you in some way? Why don't you go to see Maria, discuss it with her? There may even be some wages due.'

He didn't seem to take that in. 'It's that rich bitch back there that should pay, and I'm going to see to it that she does!'

Ellie showed him out. Watched him climb back into his rust bucket of a car and drive away with a farting of blue exhaust fumes. Ellie listened at the sitting-room door. Quiet voices. Derek and Diana were still there.

'I need peace and quiet,' said Ellie to herself. 'I need to get out of here for a while. And think!' It was getting dark. The builders had departed and both her neighbours' cars were parked up front. On impulse she called to Rose that she would be back in half an hour, and went next door.

CHAPTER TEN

Ellie heard raised voices inside as she rang her neighbour's front-door bell. Armand and his wife Kate were having an argument.

As the door opened, Ellie said, 'Is it a bad time to call?'

'Come in.' Tall Kate drew Ellie in and banged the front door to behind her. 'We were only arguing about what tiles to put on the floor of the extension. Perhaps you can make my dear husband see sense.'

Ellie began to giggle. 'Sorry. I was looking for somewhere to have hysterics, quietly.'

Kate's handsome face lost its frown. 'You can't have hysterics quietly. I hear you've been having all sorts of trouble. Have a seat, a glass of wine and tell us all.'

Foxy-faced Armand was a teacher at the high school, and possibly an inch shorter than his wife. He'd been red with anger when he answered the door, but his naturally kind heart won out. 'Ellie, you know you're always welcome here.'

'Red wine do you?' asked Kate, handing Ellie a large glass full, and pressing her down into one of their angular but comfortable chairs.

'I daren't,' said Ellie. 'I've been trying to drown my sorrows already.'

Armand drew up a chair beside her. 'Tell us all the gory details. Who killed who, why and wherefore.'

'And was that your holy terror of an aunt in your conservatory? We couldn't help seeing she'd moved in when we went out into the extension to see what the builders have done today.'

'We will not,' declared Armand, 'discuss the tiles.'

'For the moment,' said his wife with a darkling look. Kate was something of a financial whizz kid in the City and earned three times as much as Armand. They had been through a rough patch when they were first married, but had won through to a more or less permanent truce, disturbed by the occasional flare-up.

'Well, my dears,' said Ellie. 'I would welcome your reactions. Was it only yesterday morning that I heard from Jimbo that he'd found a body? It seems like a lifetime ago . . .'

Kate and Armand heard her out without comment. Ellie concluded, in a voice which tried not to wobble, '. . . and I suppose I'm so shattered because I've never been accused of trying to kill someone before.' Or more than half believed that her own daughter had done it.

She realized she was holding an empty glass. Had she really drunk all that wine? She'd better not try to stand up too quickly or she'd fall over.

Armand stabbed the air with a forefinger. 'Whoever arranged the "accident" wasn't too bright. Why not pick on a method which would definitely take out the target, instead of an innocent bystander?'

Kate shook her head. 'You think it was Diana, don't you?'

Ellie struggled to put her thoughts in order. At all costs she must defend Diana. 'No, I don't think I do . . . now. I did suspect it might be her, of course. She was the first person that sprang to mind because she had the strongest motive and she's in contact with dozens of builders and decorators and plumbers and electricians. Yes, it did cross my mind that she could have asked someone to alter the wiring for her, meaning she'd never need to go near the house to kill her great-aunt.

'Only, this evening she nearly hit Aunt Drusilla and said that if she'd tried to kill her, she would have succeeded. It was the voice of truth.'

Kate brushed back a wing of dark hair. 'From what you say, the police are interviewing everyone who might possibly gain from Miss Quicke's death. It sounds as if they're floundering around, trying to get a lead. What about Roy?'

'I don't know where he is. Possibly being interviewed by the inspector who saw Diana. I had DS Willis and so, I think, did Jimbo. You think Roy's been in with the police all day? He's in the clear. Granted, he'd know how to fiddle with the wiring, but his reaction on hearing that she'd died . . . no, it wasn't him.'

Armand was still brooding on the means used to kill. He could be very obsessive at times. 'I still say it's a strange method to use. Suppose Mrs Rose had turned the television on, while seeing Miss Quicke to bed. Then it would have been her that got killed.'

'Apparently not,' said Ellie, trying not to show how much the idea of Rose being killed upset her. 'There was only sufficient current going through the wire to shock someone, not to kill them. It was Mrs Tucker's heart condition which did for her.'

'Did the person who set the trap know that? Did they intend to kill, or did they intend to give someone a shock?'

'Dear Armand, you always think so clearly,' said Ellie. Her head was swimming. She had definitely had too much to drink. She tried to heave herself out of the chair and failed. 'Oh dear, I think I've had a little too much to drink.'

Kate made for the kitchen. 'I'll get you something to eat.'

Armand was continuing to think about the 'accident'. 'It would have been less risky to loosen the bolts of a wall radiator, and make sure it fell into the bath while Miss Quicke was in it. That would kill. Or make sure the voltage going through the wire to the television aerial was sufficiently strong. Or fiddle with a kettle . . .'

Ellie rubbed her forehead. 'There was trouble with a new kettle. Rose said that it wouldn't work and so they took it back to the shop yesterday morning — which was why they were out of the house when Mrs Tucker died.'

'Have the police looked at the kettle? Are they considering the other options?'

'What other options?' Ellie couldn't think straight any more.

'Have they checked the rest of the wiring in the house? Have they asked the electricians what they think about the wiring? Has Miss Quicke sacked any of them lately? Or any of the other workpeople who've been swarming all over that house recently? It seems to me that if the aim was to shock and not to kill, then you should be looking at some workman she'd sacked, rather than a member of her family. What point would there be in some member of her family giving her an electric shock?'

Ellie thought muzzily that there might have been a reason, but couldn't for the moment remember what it was.

Kate put a plate of thickly buttered bread and some cheese in front of Ellie, and told her to eat up. Ellie took a small bite and chewed. She ought to be hungry but somehow it was difficult to get interested in the food. Kate was not a great cook. She and Armand lived mostly on take-aways and frozen meals. Ellie's own house and the supper Rose was preparing seemed a long way away.

'If I'm right,' said Armand, 'it lets you and your family off the hook.'

Ellie nodded. Wished she hadn't. The room was gently tipping onto its side.

Kate put her arm under Ellie's, heaved her to her feet and guided her out of the sitting room and into the kitchen. 'Let's get some coffee or tea into you.'

Ellie drank a couple of mugs full of tea, which didn't seem to help much. She couldn't eat a thing. She visited the bathroom, but didn't feel much better afterwards.

Armand had gone off to tackle some of the marking he had to do, but Kate sat opposite Ellie, ready to help in whatever way she could.

'Your colour's not very good,' said Kate.

'I don't usually drink more than half a glass of anything. Stupid me.'

'I suppose everyone's entitled, once in a while. So tell me, what about this dinner dance on Saturday? Have you something to wear?'

Ellie started to shake her head. Remembered it made the room tip sideways. Mumbled, 'No.'

'Tell you what,' said Kate, stretching long legs at the side of the table. 'I'm taking the morning off tomorrow. I need a new suit, something in grey, not the usual black. How's about us going shopping together?'

Ellie blinked. Some vestige of reason thrust through her woozy mindset. 'I'd thought that the charity shop in the Avenue might . . .'

'No way. Harvey Nicholls? No, I've got it. Bond Street. I know just the place. You need some elegant clothes, understated, well cut. No black or midnight blue, understand?'

Ellie blinked again. 'Retail therapy? As in taking my mind off things?'

'Retail therapy, as in presenting the real Ellie Quicke to the world. Over the last six months you've changed a lot. You've stopped being a downtrodden housewife who thinks men always know best, and become a personage in your own right. I know you think it's wasteful to spend money on yourself, but one or two good outfits will last ages. You know what colours suit you, but you haven't quite got the hang of what necklines flatter you and it's never too late to learn that a lined skirt hangs better than a skirt over a slip. That top you're wearing doesn't do anything for you. The neck's all wrong. And the skirt sags.'

'You sound like Diana. She's always on at me to smarten up, but says it's no use my buying new clothes till I've lost a couple of stone in weight.'

'Your figure's good. Don't let her tease you into dieting. Older women need to have a little softness on their bones or they start to look haggard. I don't suppose you'll believe me, but you're a pretty woman and could be a smasher. You're feeling better. Sorry we pushed so much alcohol down you. Nine o'clock tomorrow, we're off up Town. Right?'

Ellie reached for her handkerchief. Couldn't find it. Kate pushed a box of tissues in her direction.

'I did think of having my hair cut somewhere in Town.'

'I'll make an appointment for you at my hairdresser's in the afternoon.'

'Dear Kate, I . . .'

Kate made a shushing movement. Ellie wobbled to her feet. The floor stayed put. Perhaps she could make it back home without disgracing herself. But eating lamb stew might not be a good idea.

'I really cannot think why people get drunk in order to forget. It seems to me a most unpleasant experience.'

Kate laughed, and said she'd see Ellie back to her own front door. As they went down the path to Ellie's house, Roy's car drew up and he got out, slamming the door behind him. 'What a day I've had . . . !'

'Oh dear,' said Kate, under her breath. 'His Master's Voice . . .'

Ellie tried not to giggle, but couldn't help it. 'I forgot to bring my key out with me so I'll have to ring the bell and get Rose to open up. I'm all right now, Kate. Really. I can cope.'

Roy strode down the path, emitting sparks of frustration, expecting Ellie to open the door for him. Kate dodged round him. He probably didn't even see her.

'Do you realize, I've wasted a whole day at the police station with that something inspector? They think that I . . . ! Ridiculous!'

'Come in, dear Roy,' said Ellie, pressing the bell. She didn't add, And tell me all about it. That was, of course, what he was expecting to hear. But she didn't think she was up to giving the right responses of 'Ooh,' and 'Aah,' and 'Oh, you poor dear'. It was all right saying that women could think of three things at once, but what Armand had said — which had seemed extremely profound and of maximum importance at the time — seemed to be slipping in and out of her head.

Rose opened the door, looking worried. 'Oh Ellie, dear. Thank goodness you've come back. I just don't know what to do. Miss Quicke is having a little nap, quite tired out, and the supper's almost ready but Diana and that rather nasty little estate agent are still in the living room and the supper won't stretch to five, never mind that Miss Quicke won't want to sit down at table with Diana . . . and the dining table's in that room, too.'

'Dear Rose,' said Ellie, enveloping her in a big hug. 'You are the best thing that's happened to us for mears. I mean years. I love you dearly. Roy dear, can you hang up your own coat? You can have my supper. I don't want many. Any. I'll get rid of Diana and Mr Jolley, don't you fuss. Yes, that's the right word. Fuss. Did you know it was probably an electrician that Aunt Drusilla sacked who tried to give her a fright?' She frowned. 'Is that right? I've had too much alcohol, you see, but I'll be all right when I've had a little lie down.'

She looked at the staircase. The treads seemed somewhat steeper than usual, and the banister further away. One step. There. Managed it. Another step. And another. Someone seemed to be calling her name. Well, let them call. Bed beckoned. Reckoned. That wasn't right.

Could she bend down to take off her shoes? No, better not. She lowered herself on to her bed with care, managed to lift her legs up . . . and away she went . . . whoops, off and away . . .

* * *

The man whistled between his teeth as he punched in his favourite combination of numbers.

'Hi. Look, I got delayed. Spot of overtime. Nearly done here, though. Leave in a half, probbly. Everything all right your end?'

'I went round to see the lady in waiting, but she'd already gone. Her neighbour said she's back looking after her highness again. Did you find out if they'd gone to the stroppy cow's?'

'I can check on the way home, like I said.'

'You do that. I want to get moving on this. And she'd better listen this time.'

* * *

Ellie woke to darkness. Where was she? Why was she so thirsty?

And why was she lying on her bed, fully dressed?

Ah. She remembered. Put the light on. Four o'clock. The worst time of the night, when nasty things came crawling out of the back of your mind and pounced on you and wouldn't let go. When you knew that if you woke up at that time, you wouldn't sleep again properly. When hope vanished to be defeated by despair. Oh, Diana . . .

It was raining again. The builders still hadn't mended her gutter or been to look at the toilet and with three people in the house, this was getting serious. What's more, she could hear the overspill from the gutter thumping down on to the window ledge . . . thump, thump, thump . . .

Got out of bed, moving with care. Undressed. Couldn't have a bath or a shower because it would wake Aunt Drusilla. Gentle snores were coming from both the other bedrooms, so dear Rose must be sleeping here as well. Went to the bathroom and strip-washed. Felt even more thirsty.

Cup of tea required.

Ellie eased herself down the stairs in her dressing gown and fluffy slippers, closed the kitchen door firmly behind her and put the kettle on. Midge plopped in through the cat flap and got in the way while Ellie made herself some tea. So she fed him.

The kitchen was tidy enough, though Rose had left the plates on the draining board to dry, instead of putting them away. Ellie told herself that that didn't matter and she was not going to let herself get irritated by it.

Ellie hooked her ankles round a kitchen chair and slumped down, hoping the tea would make her brain kick in with something positive.

Because at the moment all she could think of was that Diana was going to be the chief suspect in the case of the murdered cleaner. No, not murder. Manslaughter. Probably. Hopefully.

Diana's attempt to implicate Stewart would soon be seen for what it was — an act of spite, without foundation. Diana had told far too many people that she expected to inherit a considerable fortune from her great-aunt. Diana had been sacked for bribery and corruption and it had been done officially, in writing. The police would be able to build a good case against her for motive. As for means and opportunity, wasn't Diana in contact with those who could have rigged the wiring, every day of the week?

Then there was the interesting matter of her moving in on a man whose ethics Ellie had always considered slightly suspect, while she was still married to Stewart. Also, Diana's manner . . . Ellie shuddered. Suppose Diana were to lose control and start screaming at the police, as she had done at Aunt Drusilla the previous night?

Ellie told herself that Diana hadn't done it. No. Ellie was absolutely sure that she hadn't. The way Diana had threatened Aunt Drusilla had convinced Ellie, but would it convince the police? Wouldn't they probe and investigate and question till Diana lost her temper and admitted that she had threatened to kill Aunt Drusilla?

Ellie shuddered. She poured herself a second cup of tea. The boiler was ticking over, pushing out heat in friendly fashion. Ellie usually had it closed down at night, but someone — probably Aunt Drusilla — had managed to reset it to provide heat throughout the night. For once Ellie didn't think about the heating bill, but was grateful for the warmth.

So, let's look at what's likely to happen. Diana will be taken in by the police for questioning again. It would depend on how much evidence they had amassed against her, whether or not they would keep her in. Diana would no doubt yell for a solicitor as soon as she realized the danger.

Would Bill help Diana? Hmmm. Possibly not.

If Ellie were to ask him to help, would he do so? Possibly not. But he might ask his junior partner to look after Diana, if Ellie agreed to pay his fees.

Yes, that would be the best thing to do. She must speak to Bill tomorrow first thing in the morning. Friday was going to be a busy day, shopping with Kate, having her hair done.

No, she couldn't possibly go out shopping while so much was happening. Aunt Drusilla and Rose needed looking after and that wretched gutter had still not mended. Then there was the party tonight at the church to welcome the new vicar, who would be installed on Sunday.

Before that, on Saturday there was Joyce's wedding and the Golf Club dinner.

Ellie groaned. How could she think of such things when so much was going wrong in her family? Take Stewart, for instance. How was he coping? And little Frank? Would Diana give him a second thought, having committed herself to Derek Jolley? How could she put the little boy out of her mind so easily?

Oh, surely Diana would remember him. She was devoted to him. Of course she was. It was ridiculous to think that she would throw little Frank out with the bathwater, with Stewart. Quite ridiculous.

Nevertheless at half past four in the morning, Ellie did think it and tried to formulate some plan of action to rescue her grandchild, and Stewart, and . . . have them to live with her? In this house? Which was already occupied by Aunt Drusilla and Rose?

Well, Rose could go back to her flat in the daytime, and surely the police would soon release their hold on Aunt Drusilla's place and everything would go back to normal.

Well, no. It couldn't go back to normal with that poor woman lying dead in the morgue and her family bereft. Aunt Drusilla had been a little hard on that man, what was his name? Norm? Short for Norman? But there, Aunt Drusilla had been within her rights, hadn't she? And Maria at the agency would probably be able to help them file an insurance claim of some sort.

So.

Who had killed the woman? (Apart from Diana, that is.)

Ellie tried hard to remember what Armand had said to her. Both Armand and Kate thought very clearly. And they had said . . .

No, it had gone.

Midge jumped on to her lap and nuzzled her chin. He purred so loudly that Ellie felt herself smile. She hadn't meant to smile, but Midge had made her. She stroked him and he half closed his eyes and trod money on her dressing gown. Ouch. His claws had gone through the material.

She gathered him up over her shoulder, switched off the lights and went back up to bed. Midge snuggled close to her back, and then decided to give himself a good wash all over. He shook the bed each time he changed position. Ellie lay there, trying to think about nothing at all . . . and drifted into a prayer or two.

Dear Lord, help us all. Help Diana. I wish I understood her. How did she get this way? Was it our fault? Her father and I, perhaps we did spoil her, but . . . she was his little princess, nothing too good for her . . . she only had to put on that wheedling tone and he would buy her anything she wanted. When I tried to object, they'd both turn on me and call me a spoilsport.

Ellie turned over in bed and sighed. Midge protested, but she ignored him. Diana had always been a difficult child, demanding to be first in everything.

Like . . . like her father. Ouch. Ellie hadn't liked to admit it before, but it was true. Frank had been equally demanding and she, as his loving wife, had thought it her duty to please him. But Frank had loved her, in his own way. He had looked after her, had thought for her, had left her well provided for. Whereas Diana . . .

Diana loved no one but herself, thought of no one but herself.

Ellie turned over yet again, much to Midge's annoyance.

She checked the time on her digital clock. Nearly five. She wouldn't sleep again now. Her eyes half closed and she dozed. Tomorrow — no, it was today already — was going to be difficult.

* * *

Friday morning. It was eight o'clock! She'd overslept, after having been awake so long in the early hours of the night. She groaned and turned over, willing herself to go back to sleep, but the scent of frying bacon brought her sitting upright. For a moment she couldn't think who could be in her kitchen frying bacon. Then she remembered that Aunt Drusilla and Rose were staying in her house, that Diana was in deep trouble, Stewart likewise.

She remembered the death of the cleaner and that little Frank had been handed from mother to father to childminder.

And she was supposed to forget everything and go out for the day, shopping? What on earth for? For clothes, to make her look like something she was not.

What on earth would her own dear Frank have said about it? He would have snorted and said that she shouldn't throw good money after bad, trying to look like something she was not. He liked her as she was, he'd always said that. Not trying to show off. Not trying to be a dolly bird, yes, that had been his very expression.

Well, she was no dolly bird, never had been. But it wasn't a sin to make the best of oneself, and one new dress and a haircut wasn't going to break the bank.

Ellie cringed a bit when she remembered that Kate was going to take her up to Bond Street. Then she grinned. Well, why not? Ellie was sure that Diana spent more on her clothes and hair than Ellie had ever done.

Ellie showered, put on her one really good suit — the coffee stain was hardly visible — and went down the stairs to find Rose and Aunt Drusilla finishing their breakfast in the conservatory. It had stopped raining at last, and the sun was trying to break through. Maybe it would be a nice day.

'Sorry I'm late.' She kissed them both. 'I had a bad night.'

'I slept like a log,' said Rose, faded blue eyes sparkling with enjoyment. 'I do enjoy a night in a really soft bed.'

'I didn't sleep a wink,' declared Aunt Drusilla, which was a lie, of course. But there were prune-coloured shadows under her eyes. 'Worrying about that stupid little girl.'

Rose giggled. She could be very girlish at times. 'You should have seen us, trying to get Derek Jolley to leave, with or without Diana . . .'

'A disgusting sight,' said Miss Quicke. 'Sex rampant. Wrapped round one another.'

'We got Roy to tell them to go eventually, because they wouldn't take the hint and you'd disappeared. Poor Roy was in a state anyway, because of having been questioned by the police all afternoon, and he did rather lose his temper with them and shout but it worked, thank goodness, and the lamb stew was as tender as could be . . .'

Ellie put some bacon and mushrooms on to fry, and made some more tea for herself. 'I'm worried about Diana.'

'So am I,' said Miss Quicke. 'Little though she deserves it. The way she's been carrying on, the police will think she had a good motive and would know how to interfere with the wiring. Personally, I don't believe she did it, but I can see why the police would think so.'

'I agree,' said Ellie, bleakly. 'I'll ring her after breakfast and give her the name of Bill's junior partner, so that she has someone to represent her if the police haul her in.' She took her meal to the table and sat down with them. She was hungry.

Rose clattered used plates and cutlery together and piled it on a tray. 'I'll just pop these in the sink for now, and tidy up the bedrooms. I have to be at the hairdresser's in the Avenue at eleven, and then check on everything for the wedding tomorrow.' She drifted off. The buttons on her cardigan had been done up wrongly, her skirt dipped at the back, and she was a thoroughly contented woman.

There was silence when she'd gone. Aunt Drusilla appeared to be dozing in the sun that streamed into the conservatory.

Finally Ellie said, 'I'm going shopping today with Kate.'

'Running away from your problems?'

'Yes. It's too close to home. Too painful.'

Aunt Drusilla said, 'To return to the matter of the accident. It occurred to me — no doubt I am being fanciful — that the wiring had been interfered with in order, not to kill me, but simply to give me a shock. To make me realize that I couldn't continue to live in the house. So who would benefit? You, of course — but I dismissed that idea immediately. Roy? No, it's not his style. So that's why I gave DS Willis the name of Mr Strawson when she came round to see me yesterday afternoon, after you'd gone to visit Mr Weatherspoon. She wanted to know who might have had a motive for meddling with the wiring, so I told her that my builder, Mr Strawson, had threatened me.'

'Did he actually threaten you? He told me all about his plans yesterday, when I went round to collect your things. I understand why you didn't mention his proposal to me, but . . .'

'You might have seen what an opportunity it was to make some more money, and I didn't fancy anyone else living there, so close to me. If I had told you, you might have done a deal with the builder behind my back.'

'I wouldn't, you know. I told him so, too.'

Miss Quicke softened. 'No, I don't really think you would but that's what I told myself. He didn't help his case by bringing Diana into it. That merely put my back up further. He is, of course, quite right. It's a disgrace to leave all that accommodation standing empty. Why don't you do up the garage yourself, and move in?'

Ellie hid a smile. 'You've been on at me for ever to move in with you, but you know perfectly well that I like my own house and garden.'

'Well, it was worth a try. Mr Strawson did threaten me, you know. And Diana. They made remarks about my frailty, about my needing to go into a home to be looked after. Mr Strawson knew about the fall I'd had down the stairs. In front of Diana he said he could see me having another accident soon and having to leave the house anyway. Mr Strawson deserves to be questioned by the police, if he thinks I can be intimidated into selling.'

'Poor man,' said Ellie, with a twist of her lips. 'How little he knows you.'

Miss Quicke twitched a smile and smoothed it out again. 'Exactly, I have no intention of going into a home. But I have been thinking about the garage and how much money it could bring in if converted into two flats. You have my permission to do that and find me some quiet, respectable tenants.'

'Thank you,' said Ellie, hiding a smile. 'I'll do that.' She thought that Rose could do with moving from her council flat into a pleasant place of her own. Would a ground-floor flat in the garage suit her? 'So you tossed Mr Strawson to the police to take their minds off Diana. Will it work, and won't they haul Diana into it, anyway?'

'That is why I wish to speak to your friend Kate, whom you've always said was a paragon of financial virtue. Perhaps she can help me provide the police with another suspect.'

CHAPTER ELEVEN

Ellie said, 'Another suspect? Another red herring? Won't the police catch on?'

A twitch of a smile. 'I did not find Ms Willis sympathetic.'

'No. She's honest, dogmatic, persistent. I think she's probably a good policewoman, though not intuitive.'

'You are intuitive, Ellie.'

'I know when you are trying to bamboozle me, if that's what you mean. Who is this other person? Anyone I know?'

Aunt Drusilla shifted in her chair, 'I rather think that one of the stockbrokers I use has been cheating me, though it's going to be difficult to prove — hence my need for the services of your friend.'

'I don't suppose I'd understand what he's been doing, but . . .'

'Put simply, the stock market has taken a hammering recently, and I was not particularly surprised to find that I was losing money. Naturally, I check the performance of my stocks daily. Then I noticed that he was moving my money around far more than seemed appropriate. You look puzzled. Every time stocks and shares are bought or sold, my stockbroker charges me a fee. Unnecessary movement is called "churning", and can provide a nice little income if it remains undetected. I want your friend Kate to detect it, and then I'll pass the information to the police for action.'

'But even if you're right, would it provide him with an incentive to harm you?'

'Probably not,' admitted Miss Quicke. 'But it might help to muddy the waters.'

Ellie went to switch on the kettle. So Miss Quicke really did believe Diana was guilty. Ellie felt hollow inside. It was one thing for her to suspect Diana, but quite another to have her suspicions echoed by the astute Miss Quicke. She made herself some instant coffee and took it back to the conservatory.

Miss Quicke sighed. 'I tell myself that I must be wrong, that Diana would never mean to murder me. However, I fear she would not in the least worry about giving me an electrical shock, if it meant she could throw me off balance enough to get her own way. I understand Diana. I was like her myself, once. She takes after her father . . .' She shook her head.

Ellie was horrified. 'Frank was an honest man. He'd never have . . .'

'Oh yes, he would, my dear. As I did when I was younger and thought I could get away with it. When I first started out buying up flats and doing them up for resale, I tried to gloss over any problems but was soon found out and had to learn the hard way that honesty is the best policy. This tendency to cheat must be in the genes. My father cheated his customers and was proud to "do the fools down" as he put it. Frank's father was a weakling, always took the easy way out. I could never get him to see that cutting corners was the quickest way to lose his reputation.

'I struggled to bring Frank up correctly but he broke out, time and again . . . until I despaired of him. Then he met you and tried to change. He'd quickly realized what a diamond you are, and that he'd have to be completely straight if he wanted to keep you.'

'Frank was always straight!'

'No, he wasn't, but your honesty kept him that way. He always had to fight a tendency to shade the truth in business.

It was something of a pleasant surprise to him to find that he could be straight and still make money. He was always afraid of losing you, though. He used to tell me that he had to keep a firm hand on you lest you stray.'

'Me? Stray? I loved him.'

'He was afraid that if you went out into the world more, got a better job, you'd see him for what he was and stop loving him. Perhaps you would, because you've changed a lot since he died and you've had to take charge of your own life.'

'I loved him,' repeated Ellie, wounded. 'How could he think I'd ever change towards him?' Every word Aunt Drusilla said had dropped into her mind and stuck there. Had Frank really been like that? And she had never noticed?

Miss Quicke shook her head. 'You closed your eyes to his occasional lapses, as you closed your eyes to Diana's. She's just like her father. She married an honest man, but I'm afraid Stewart is not as strong as you, and hasn't been able to keep her straight.'

'Your theory breaks down when it comes to Roy. He's straight.'

'He's been well brought up,' said Aunt Drusilla with a grim smile. 'My theory holds good for the rest of the family.'

There was a bad taste in Ellie's mouth. She'd always respected the older woman's brains, thinking them a good deal sharper than her own. If Aunt Drusilla really thought Diana was responsible and was prepared to go to considerable lengths to divert the police from her great-niece, Ellie supposed — with a feeling of dread — that the older woman must be right.

Aunt Drusilla had acted with her usual efficiency when she'd understood the danger she was in. She'd ensured there would be no repeat performance by telling Diana that she wouldn't gain anything by her great-aunt's death, and she was planning to confuse the police investigation to such an extent that no jury would be able to try her great-niece without reasonable doubt.

'Well, girl? Are you with me in this?'

Ellie thought about honesty and family feeling, her love for her only child, and Frank's attitude to her.

Time for an arrow prayer. Dear Lord, what would you like me to do? I don't know what to think, or feel. Am I really sure that Diana is guilty? It looks as if it must be her, but . . . I can't help remembering her joyful response when I broke the news of the accident to her. It didn't sound as if she'd known anything about it. It had sounded as if she were really surprised. Could she act that well? And surely Diana had been speaking the truth last night when she'd said that if she'd tried to kill Miss Quicke, she would have succeeded.

I really don't know.

Ellie's instinct was to play for time.

'I'll ask Kate to speak to you about your stockbroker. And yes, I will back you up with the police over the builder's threats. In fact, I have already mentioned it to them. As for the rest, I must do some phoning before I go out, give Diana my solicitor's number, check on Stewart and little Frank. And on poor Roy. I'm afraid I was a little rude to everyone last night, going to bed so early, but I was not quite well. We have such a busy weekend ahead, what with the party for the new vicar tonight, the wedding and then the Golf Club dinner.'

'I gather Roy has asked you to go with him to that.'

Ellie started guiltily. Yes, he had asked her and she had turned him down, only to agree to go with Bill. Oh dear, trouble ahead.

'Bring me in the *Financial Times* when you return.'

* * *

Ellie had never been shopping in Bond Street in her life before. Kate was obviously used to it, striding into the most discreet and expensive of establishments without even glancing in the window, and commanding the attention of the sales girls without effort. Ellie followed on her heels rather, she thought, like a lady in waiting trailing after a princess.

Kate bought herself a new suit in dove grey — very handsome — in record time. Ellie quested up and down, trying to work out what might suit her from the rows of beautiful but slimline clothes displayed, and refusing to flinch when she checked the price tickets.

'That's settled, and now I'll take you to the kind of shop you'll love,' promised Kate.

Ellie couldn't believe that there might be a shop which would cater for her unfashionable figure, but there was. In fact, there was more than one. But the first one Kate took her to provided such a revelation that Ellie thought she would never, for the rest of her life, try to buy clothes in Marks & Spencer's or the charity shop.

Of course, it did help that she had a Gold Card to pay for her purchases. Underwear — 'You have a very pretty figure,' said the saleswoman, 'and beautiful shoulders.'

Skirts that swirled and clung in the right places. Ellie exclaimed in delight, 'I could even run for a bus in this.'

'And turn heads,' added Kate. 'If you've got a pretty bum, then flaunt it.'

Colours: 'With that beautiful, natural complexion, I'd suggest clear colours, not too heavy,' said the sales woman. Ellie gasped, seeing her skin tones enhanced by sweet-pea colours, by apricots and her favourite blues.

Evening wear: 'Oh, I couldn't possibly,' said Ellie, giving a twirl in front of the glass. And then, 'I don't think I can bear to take it off.'

Kate laughed. 'You'll knock their eyes out. How many men did you say were after you at the moment?'

'Oh, Kate! Don't. It's not funny, indeed it's not.'

'It's no more than you deserve,' said Kate. To the saleswoman: 'She'll not be wearing very high heels, so that length will be perfect. We'll take the evening wrap as well — that's a present from me.'

'Oh,' cried Ellie, reaching for her handkerchief. 'But you mustn't.'

'Yes, I must,' said Kate, giving her a hug. 'Now, an early lunch before I deliver you into the hands of my hairdresser. Don't worry, he won't do anything dreadful to you.'

Burdened with packages, they found a quiet corner for lunch and Ellie, whose imagination had been filled with daydreams of herself in designer gear, walking down a catwalk on eight-inch heels, pulled herself back to reality. She told Kate what Aunt Drusilla wanted.

'Churning,' said Kate. 'Difficult to prove, and the market is not kind to investors at the moment. However, she's a shrewd old bird and if she wants me to look into it for her, then consider it done.'

'I wasn't quite myself last night,' Ellie confessed. 'But I seem to remember Armand being very clear that it wasn't murder, but an effort to give Aunt Drusilla a fright. She seems to think it was that, herself. Only, it's so dreadful, thinking that someone's died as a result.'

'Miss Quicke thinks it was Diana?'

'Yes, but I'm not so sure.'

'From what I know of your daughter, forgive me, Ellie, but . . . it doesn't sound impossible.'

'I know that,' said Ellie, unhappily driven to agree. 'But she doesn't act as if she were guilty. Last night she threatened Aunt Drusilla and said that if she'd wanted to kill her, then she would have succeeded. I believed her. Only that makes everything worse and not better, doesn't it? I'm so muddled, I don't know what to think.'

'What's your gut reaction?'

Ellie answered without hesitation. 'She didn't do it.'

'Then there's everything still to play for, isn't there? Where are you going to start looking?'

'Me? No, no. This is far too big a job for me. It would mean looking at all the people Aunt Drusilla might have upset over a period of, well, years. Give or take a name or two, that might well add up to fifty names. I can't do that.'

'Then concentrate on motives. She's given you a couple to go on, and you must know of more. Anyway, you may tell

Miss Quicke that I'll be at the welcoming party for the new vicar this evening, if she'd like to talk to me. I'm not invited to the wedding tomorrow, so I could go in to work and see what information I can dig up on this famous stockbroker. All right?'

Ellie couldn't help but laugh. 'Kate, I've never known you go to church before.'

'It's not church, is it? It's only a party in the church hall. Oh, as to church, I used to go now and then. Christmas and Easter, you know. I haven't been for some years and I don't know how Armand would react if I said I wanted to go now. I suppose I might go back some day. I'm curious as to what keeps you so serene in the middle of chaos. And,' with a wolfish grin, 'I wouldn't miss seeing you slay the opposition tonight for anything.'

'Kate, there is no opposition and I don't want to slay anyone.'

'What about Roy? Isn't he sniffing at your heels, and doesn't he tend to take you for granted, just as your husband used to do? Won't it be a salutary experience for him to see you being admired by other people as well?'

'Well, yes, but . . .'

'What about the church treasurer, can't remember his name, but didn't he make a nuisance of himself, always asking you to go out with him just after your husband died?'

'Well, yes. Archie did . . . but honestly, Kate, I never liked him enough to go out with him, and anyway it was too soon and he's got a girlfriend now — not that anyone at church seems to like her, but . . .'

'There's your solicitor friend, as well, isn't there? You always said how nice he was, though possibly,' Kate considered this, 'a little too old for you? In his sixties? Wouldn't you find a younger man more, well, rewarding?'

Ellie was scandalized. 'Kate, you stop this right now! The very idea! I'm no flirt and I'm not looking for another husband. I do very well as I am, thank you.' She remembered what Aunt Drusilla had said about Frank. She'd been burying that in her mind but she knew she was going to have to deal with it some time. Oh dear, had he really been a bit of a tyrant? Like Diana? Oh dear, oh dear.

Kate merely laughed, and said they must be on their way to the hairdressers. Ellie felt considerable trepidation about going to a new hairdresser — and one in such an expensive street as well. What on earth was she going to look like? She would refuse to be permed, or coloured, or made to look outlandish. But, would he listen to her? How much should she tip?

She was so accustomed to going to her usual hairdresser in the Avenue, that this was going to be an ordeal.

They were a few minutes early for their appointment, so Ellie took the opportunity to phone Diana on her mobile, grimacing as she tried to remember how to access Diana's mobile-phone number. It was in the address book, or whatever they called it, but had she pressed the right button? The phone only rang twice before Diana answered.

'Mother? Where are you? I've been ringing and ringing at home, and you weren't there. Great-Aunt Drusilla was, though, and she was in such a temper. I've never known her so horrible.'

'I'm up in Town, shopping. Where are you, Diana?'

'I'm at the new project, of course. Forget what Great-Aunt was saying yesterday; it's an absolute snip, just needs redecorating in imaginative fashion, new kitchen units and bathrooms. I want you to come round and see it before the light goes.'

'Sorry, dear. I'm busy today. Diana, you don't expect me to fund this new project of yours, do you? You know very well that I can't do that.'

'I don't see why not. It's just my scene, this. Far better than working for fuddy-duddy old Great-Aunt. The market's changing and she's stuck in the last century. We must go for the young professional look now, something minimal, clear bright colours, inventive fitments. I know this is where I belong and . . .'

Ellie broke in. 'Diana, did you get the message I left on your answerphone? My solicitor's telephone number?'

'What would I need that for? Anyway, I wouldn't use your solicitor for anything. You have no idea how rude they were to me. Why don't you take a cab? I'll give you the address, it's on the main road down to the A40 from West Ealing. You can't miss it . . .'

'Diana! Please, listen to me. I have another appointment this afternoon that I am not prepared to miss, and I am not going to put money into your latest wild venture, however much you want it. Now, have you seen Stewart, and is little Frank all right?'

Diana turned sulky. 'No, I haven't seen him. I went round there and he was out and the place had been tidied up and the washing all done and hung up to air. I expect he got one of his girlfriends round to do it . . .'

'I did it, Diana.'

'. . . so I just packed some clothes and got out. I've arranged with the childminder to take him round to Stewart's for the weekend, and then we'll have to see what happens, right?'

'But won't he miss you, Diana? It's not right to dump him on just anybody . . .'

'He loves his childminder, and if you won't take him I don't see what other option I have.'

Ellie gave a defeated little sigh. Poor little Frank! Though what Diana said was correct, and Frank did love his child-minder and she was good to him. Possibly he was better off with her than anywhere else. At least he knew exactly where he was and what he could and could not do with her. Ellie had hoped that even at the last minute, Diana would relent towards Stewart, but there never had been any holding Diana when she got an idea into her head, and Ellie had a horrid feeling that Stewart would lead a happier, quieter life without her. 'Well, look after yourself, my dear. And don't forget to keep that telephone number with you all the time.'

Ellie ended the call with a sigh for her difficult daughter.

Kate smiled and shook her head. 'You think the police are going to pick Diana up and question her again? You've done what you can to safeguard her interests and now, Ellie Quicke, you are going to meet the sharpest pair of scissors in London.'

* * *

'Is that you? Listen. I dropped the note in, like we planned. She was there, came to the door herself but when I give it her, she just looked at me as if I was nothing and said she wasn't interested.'

The man whistled through his teeth. 'That's a bummer!'

'I know I said she wouldn't give me the drippings of her nose, but she could at least have read it, not just tossed it aside. I'd like to wring her neck.'

'Calm down. She'll come round to it. Bound to. At least we know now where she is for sure and certain. It's easier to get at her there than at the old house.'

'What you think we should do, then? Give her another shock? The house'll be empty. Her toady was there, reminded her to have a rest because they're going out this evening.'

'All of them?'

'Dunno. Suppose so. You can get in there, can't you? What will you do, then?'

'The kitchen's best, probbly. I'll think of something.'

* * *

Ellie tilted her bedroom mirror and stepped back to admire the overall effect. The woman in the mirror looked back at her first with doubt and then appreciation. And finally, with a giggle.

'Ellie Quicke, what would your husband have said, if he could have seen you now?'

To which there was only one answer. He would have disapproved. He'd have said, 'That top is a bit revealing, isn't it? I thought you didn't like people staring at your hips? What in heaven's name possessed you to choose such a peculiar colour to wear?'

Or he might have said, 'Come here, woman, and give us a cuddle.'

She sighed. She knew which he'd have said. He wouldn't have liked her short-cut but gleaming cap of silvery hair either, because the expert had encouraged the ends to curl, just a little. No perm, no colouring. Just a hint of . . . well, of mischief? And the golden-brown colour of her new outfit brought out the blue in her eyes, in a way she didn't understand, but could recognize.

Poor Frank, she thought. She sighed. She did miss him, still. Then she brightened as she considered what effect her makeover might have on Roy and Bill. And possibly even on Archie, although she really did not want men chasing after her. No, she didn't. But it was nice to be appreciated, wasn't it?

Ellie Quicke clicked her fingers at her image, and said, 'Danger, experts at work!' And then, 'Do I really want to be considered dangerous?'

No, of course not. Or did she?

She giggled again. Wasn't this fun?

She picked up the creamy leather jacket which Kate had persuaded her to buy at the last minute, took one last look at herself in the mirror, and went downstairs to escort her aunt and dear Rose over to the church hall.

* * *

Ellie had been surprised when her aunt announced her intention of attending the welcome party in the church hall. Miss Quicke didn't go to church, hadn't been for ever. Possibly not since a clever young fortune-hunter had got her pregnant and then abandoned her. Miss Quicke probably considered herself a great sinner because of that long-ago pregnancy. Or did she?

Ellie was never sure what her aunt believed in, if anything.

Rose, of course, was a member of the church, as was Ellie. Rose had had her hair permed again in preparation for the wedding on the morrow, and she was wearing the best of her two-piece suits, the one with the heather fleck and the blouse underneath of just not quite the right colour.

Dear Rose was full of admiration for Ellie's new clothes and haircut. 'Ellie, my dear! How splendid you look!' Dear Rose had the most loving, generous heart it would be possible to find.

Miss Quicke, on the other hand, took one look at Ellie. 'I've always said a fool and her money were soon parted.'

'Be happy for me,' said Ellie, almost beseechingly.

'You look lovely,' said Rose. 'But you won't be able to do the washing-up in that, will you?'

Ellie swallowed her disappointment. It wouldn't have hurt Aunt Drusilla to pay her a compliment for once, would it? Then she saw that her aunt looked tired. 'Rose and I have to go, but wouldn't you rather stay in and have a rest?'

'Certainly not. Your dear husband left some money for the church-hall rebuilding fund and I promised I'd contribute something too, in memory of him. You told me the plans will be on show tonight, and naturally I want to see what I'm going to get for my money. Besides, that girl Kate said she'd be there, didn't she? I want to talk to her. Hand me my stick and open the door. We don't want to be late.'

Ellie turned off all the lights in the house except for those in the conservatory, which she left on to guide them down the back-garden path. She glanced around her, somehow feeling uneasy. Had she double-locked the front door? Yes. And turned off the lights in the sitting room? Yes. So . . . what had she forgotten?

She shrugged. She couldn't think of anything. Well, it wasn't far to the church hall and she could always pop back later if she thought of something she'd overlooked.

CHAPTER TWELVE

Ellie shivered. How dark the trees looked against the night sky! But it was getting lighter in the evenings all the time, wasn't it? She really must get the electrician back to put some lights in the garden so that she could see her way down the path. Something quite low and tasteful. Perhaps set flush with the ground?

She locked the conservatory door and put the key in her handbag while Rose carefully watched Miss Quicke negotiate the steps down on to the path. Ellie glanced back and up at next door's half-finished conservatory, wondering whether Kate and Armand had decided their argument about the floor tiles . . . and then wondering if the builders had forgotten about the repair to her guttering. She must remind them tomorrow. No, tomorrow was Saturday. They might not be working tomorrow. Bother. But it might not rain so heavily again.

One after the other they negotiated the path down the garden and passed through the gate into the alley. She looked back up at the house. She still felt uneasy. What was it she had left undone that she ought to have done?

She still couldn't think of anything: She followed Rose and Aunt Drusilla as they took the path up through the

Green around the church. It was quite dark now, of course, but the paths around the church had been tarmacked and here and there were a few Victorian-style lamps to lighten the gloom. The daffodils under the trees were just about going over now, and had lost their colour in this light. Now the rain had stopped, it was a pleasant place to walk. Looking up at the moon through the branches of the trees, Ellie wondered in idle fashion if they would have a wet or dry summer. If she could find an oak and an ash tree close together — and she knew there were some in the park nearby — then she'd make a special trip to see which leaves were coming out first.

'Ash before oak,
We're in for a soak.
Oak before ash,
We're in for a splash.'

'What's that? What did you say?' Aunt Drusilla had paused, waiting for Ellie to catch them up. Ellie noted with a thrill of sadness that the older lady was now walking with her head dropping forward. Perhaps she had arteriosclerosis? Would it be a good idea to suggest that she saw the doctor? The problem was that Aunt Drusilla did not 'hold' with doctors.

They passed the church, sombre and silent at this time of the evening, and entered the already crowded church hall. Instant Babel. Everyone was there who had any connection with the church; organist, stewards, curate, choir. Members of the church and those who only came occasionally. Mothers' Union and Toddlers group. The flower-arrangers under their redoubtable figurehead, Mrs Dawes. The playgroup, the line dancers, the house group, those who ran the coffee mornings and those who polished the brass candlesticks. Members of the Parish Council and the church treasurer, Archie Benjamin, with his gold-glinting smile and the bottle blonde hanging on his arm.

'My very dear Ellie,' said Archie, trying to disentangle himself from his dolly bird in order to clasp Ellie's hand in both of his. 'I hardly recognized you. What have you been doing to yourself?'

Dolly bird resisted his attempt to shed her. 'Had a perm dear, did we?'

'Nothing like that,' said Ellie, trying in turn to disengage herself from Archie. 'Do you know my aunt, Miss Quicke? Aunt Drusilla, this is Archie Benjamin, the church treasurer who's responsible for masterminding the rebuilding of the church hall.'

'Not before time,' pronounced Miss Quicke, surveying the tired-looking interior. 'Mr Benjamin, I would like to see the plans.'

'Of course, dear lady. I understand that you may be willing to contribute to our little fund.' He wafted Miss Quicke away, his dolly bird still clinging to his arm.

'Ellie, is that you?' Roy, edging his way towards her with plate and glass in hand. He whistled in admiration. 'Pawned the family jewels, have you? I must say, you do look splendid.'

'Thank you, Roy. And you, too. Sorry I was so unsociable last night . . .'

'Not feeling too good, I understood. Never mind, let me get you something to eat and drink. Have you met the new chap yet? I thought he'd be like the old one, Gilbert, who was like a stick figure, looked like something out of a Lowry picture, didn't he? But this one's Humpty Dumpty. Got a sense of humour, though, give him that . . .'

Kate, looking amused. Tall enough to see over the heads of most people. 'Ellie, where's your aunt?'

Mrs Dawes, the crowd breaking apart as she thrust, her bosom leading the way, through the crowd. 'We got the flowers done only just in time . . . they had the rehearsal in church just as we were tidying up . . .'

Their curate — Timid Timothy — was working the room, sweating slightly, aware that this congregation had given him the thumbs down, but ever hopeful of receiving a pat on the back.

Joyce, looking a trifle wild-eyed and dishevelled, holding on to her fiancé's arm as if he'd disappear if she let go. 'Mrs Quicke, the most dreadful thing's happened . . .'

The Reverend Gilbert Adams, their old vicar, put his arm around Ellie's shoulders and drew her through the crowd. She'd been expecting to see him as he was returning by special arrangement to take the wedding tomorrow. The new vicar would be installed by the bishop on Sunday.

'Ellie, you look perfectly splendid. What have you been doing to yourself, eh? Come and meet my old friend, Thomas. We always used to call him Tum-Tum at college, you know, after our king of glorious memory, Edward the Seventh — not that you'd remember him . . .'

Ellie said, 'Gilbert, do be careful, you know how nick-names stick . . .'

Gilbert laughed, spectacles at the end of his nose as usual, 'Thomas, meet Mrs Ellie Quicke, who looks as if butter wouldn't melt, but who's the best person to go to if you're ever in hot water . . .'

'Which I'm sure will be more often than she wishes to see me.' Tum-Tum — no, she must remember to call him Thomas — shook her hand warmly. He was surrounded by a semicircle of the usual groupies who had once been devoted to Gilbert, had never quite taken to their curate Timid Timothy, and were now preparing to transfer their allegiance to Tum-Tum. Thomas.

Ellie liked the look of Thomas. He was indeed a roly-poly creature, but he had dark quirky eyebrows rather like Gilbert's, and eyes that told her he'd seen most things in his time but still had hope for humanity.

'Come along,' said Gilbert, steering Ellie away as one of the stewards brought up an important lady to introduce to Tum-Tum. Thomas. 'I managed to tear my dear wife away from her clients and she's been looking for you to have a chat. It seems a long time since we had a quiet day together.'

'Quiet is what we don't have, at home,' said Liz, kissing Ellie on both cheeks. 'We have to get away from the parish in order to get any peace. You're looking lovely, Ellie. A new man in your life?'

'Certainly not!' said Ellie, going pink. 'Why does everyone think . . . ?'

Joyce thrust her way between them. 'Mrs. Quicke, I'm in dead trouble . . .'

Gilbert put a soothing arm around Joyce's shoulders. 'My dear, it will all get sorted in the morning. Just you see.' And to Ellie. 'You know our dear John at the charity shop, who was going to give Joyce away? Well, his wife's been poorly again and now he's not sure he can make it, so . . .'

'Will I do?' asked Roy, handing Ellie a plate of assorted bites to eat. 'I seem to remember that I offered to act for the bride in case of need, some time ago.'

'Oh. Would you? So kind,' said Joyce, giving the opposite impression. Gilbert, Liz and Ellie struggled not to laugh. Joyce was the most graceless of girls, almost as bad as Diana.

Diana. Ellie looked at her watch. Was Diana all right? Ellie wished she'd rung her before she came out.

Joyce's fiancé, the scoutmaster, shook Roy by the hand. 'Would you really do the honours? We'd be so grateful. Joyce here was so distressed.'

Joyce didn't look distressed. She looked angry. Ellie held back a sigh and bit into a mushroom vol-au-vent.

'Got your soup and fish?' asked Gilbert. 'Morning suit, the full works? Got to do Joyce justice, haven't we?'

'Can do,' said Roy. 'But what are you two doing here, when you should be out with your friends celebrating your last night of freedom?'

The scoutmaster opened his mouth to reply, but Joyce quelled him with a look. 'Oh, we don't want any of that silly nonsense, people being made to get drunk and tied to lamp posts without their trousers on, and strippergrams . . .'

The scoutmaster looked as if he might quite have enjoyed having a strippergram at a bachelor party, but it was not to be. Joyce had said so.

Ellie tried not to giggle and moved closer to Liz. 'Have you heard we've had another little problem here?'

'Mm,' said Liz, round a mouthful of cheese and pineapple. 'Someone said the police had made an arrest. I was never so shocked.'

Oh, Diana, thought Ellie. 'No,' she said. 'I hadn't heard that.'

'Stabbed four times, they said in the papers. All over a parking space which each of them claimed as theirs. Makes you think about putting a chain on the door. Have you got one, Ellie?'

'Chain on the door? Er, no.' Relief. It was nothing to do with *their* murder. Or accident. Whichever.

'Must ring you, Ellie. The most exciting thing has happened, and we thought you might like to come, too. That is, if you're free . . .'

Someone rapped on the table, calling for silence.

'Speeches!' said Gilbert, in disgust.

Someone rapped even more loudly, even longer. The hubbub was beginning to die away. People jostled for position, trying to see who'd called for silence. The new vicar was completely hidden, being on the short side. At least Gilbert had been easily visible, standing six foot four in his socks.

Someone clutched Ellie's arm and whispered, 'Ellie, can you come and help?'

It was Rose, wearing an apron over her blouse, buttons already awry. 'There's mountains of washing-up and someone's dropped out so there's only me to do it.'

Ellie nodded. She slid her plate, still half full of food, into Roy's willing hand and threaded her way through the throng to the kitchen at the back. Someone had been round collecting dirty plates and had dumped them on the end table where the food had been laid out. There were also about a dozen plates with a few slices of quiche or a couple of biscuits on them.

'Pray silence for . . .'

A burst of laughter behind them. Gilbert was getting into his stride. Everyone said he could make a cat laugh and he probably could, if he'd tried. Not that he would bother. Full of common sense, was Gilbert.

The kitchen looked as if it had been hit by a landslide, with toppling piles of plates, cutlery and glasses everywhere. Ellie found herself an apron and some rubber gloves, and started on the washing-up. She wondered why the social committee hadn't gone in for paper plates and cups this time. She cleared soggy pieces of pastry out of the plughole and looked for a new bottle of washing-up liquid, as the old one was finished.

Rose fluttered in with a tray full of oddments and set it down with a clatter. The sound of speeches drifted into the kitchen when Rose opened the door and shut off when she let it fall to behind her.

'. . . for goodness knows when we'll be finished here. I thought that at least Jean would have come to help us as she's supposed to be organizing everything today, but no . . .' Rose dumped the contents of her tray on the draining board and disappeared with her tray, still talking. Jean was not one of Ellie's favourite people, being of a jealous, quarrelsome disposition. It didn't really surprise Ellie that Jean's arrangements had come adrift. She'd probably quarrelled with whoever it was who'd agreed to do the washing-up.

Ellie cleared the draining board by the simple process of transferring everything to the floor and started again.

'. . . and for all that she's putting a brave face on it, I can see she's dead worried, and so should I be in her shoes, wouldn't you, Ellie?'

'Aunt Drusilla?'

'Who else should I mean? It's taken it out of her, I can see. It's a real effort for her to hold her head upright, so soon after that fall that she had, it's done her no good at all.'

Ellie nodded, which was all that Rose needed to continue. Rose seized a tea towel and started to dry the cups Ellie had washed. Jean — a tiny dynamo of a woman with faded hair — crashed into the kitchen with another tray of dirty things, gave them a black look and disappeared.

'. . . I'm really glad to have this chance to talk to you about her, Ellie, because I don't want to put myself forward where I'm not wanted, and I can see you're up to your eyes with other things. I thought that if I could catch you on your own, we could have a little chat and I could ask you if you thought it would be all right, because I wouldn't dream of doing it if you didn't like it, as I'm sure you know, us having been friends for so long . . .'

'What is it you want to do, Rose?'

'Miss Quicke's asked me to move in with her permanently. She really does need someone to be there all the time, just to see that she eats regularly and takes her pills. Oh, she told me not to tell you about the pills, but I really think you ought to know, don't you, Ellie? It's only for her blood pressure.'

'Blood pressure? I picked up some bottles of pills by her bedside yesterday, but I didn't think to look what they were for. I didn't even know she had high blood pressure.'

'She didn't want you to know. She says you've got enough on your plate and indeed I had to agree with her. It seems as if it were meant, don't you think, that I should move in with her? Only, I won't if you think I'm interfering, pushing my nose in where it's not wanted. I'd better get on with the clearing up, hadn't I? That new vicar, what's his name, he's a real card, isn't he . . . ?' Still talking, she disappeared back into the hall.

When she returned, still talking, Ellie cut across her words. 'I think, Rose, that you're the best thing that could possibly have happened to my aunt. She's very fond of you already, and I know she's worried that you won't want to live with her any more, after that terrible accident . . .'

'She says I saved her life. What do you think of that?'

Ellie tipped out the bowl of dirty water and refilled with fresh. 'In what way?'

'Well, when she was by herself, she always went up to bed early because she was bored and she couldn't get comfortable in her chair so it was better to lie in bed. She'd switch on the telly in her bedroom and maybe not even bother to turn it off but leave it on all night, to keep her company. Only, I found her a couple of special cushions for her chair, which makes it so much more comfortable for her, and in the evenings we've been watching the ten o'clock news together and waiting for the weather forecast so that we could plan what to do next day, and of course she knows I'm within call if she wants anything in the night though she never does, or hardly ever. So she hasn't been turning her television on upstairs at all for . . . oh, a long time now. She says I saved her life because I've made it so much more interesting that she didn't need to turn the telly on at night, so she hasn't and that's why she didn't get the shock. Wasn't that a lovely thing to say?'

Like the White Rabbit she seized another tray and disappeared again. Jean reappeared, carrying a pile of dirty serving plates, which she dumped on the table without a word and retreated.

Rose reappeared, saying, 'That's almost the lot, except for those who've left their cups and plates under their chairs and we won't find them till they've cleared the hall, and everyone thinks that Tum-Tum is the best thing . . .'

Oh dear, thought Ellie. That nickname's going to stick. She hugged Rose. 'I do love you, Rose. Aunt Drusilla is absolutely right. You've made a great difference to her life and I'd be absolutely thrilled if you did move in with her permanently. But are you sure you want to give up your independence for her?'

'Oh, we've thought it all out,' said Rose, drying up as rapidly as she talked. 'I'm to have my own rooms furnished as I want them, with whatever pieces I want to bring over from my little flat, although really, dear, I'm not sure I want to bring any of my old stuff except perhaps one or two things of my mother's. And my plants, of course. Then I'm to have as much time off as I want, with a minimum of two days a week, she says, plus every afternoon when she's having a nap. And Miss Quicke wants to buy me an annuity, and .

. .oh, but this is where I need to ask you about it, Ellie, for she wants to give me — actually give me! — one of her little flats, to be rented out to give me an income till I have need for it. I'm to keep it for ever! Only, I'm afraid she can't really mean that. I mean . . . it's too much, isn't it?' She seized plates and cups and began slotting them back into the cupboards.

'It's only what you deserve,' said Ellie and meant it. 'You must also hold out for a cleaner to come in several times a week, and a gardener. And a proper wage.'

Rose squeezed her eyes shut. 'It's too good to be true. I keep telling myself I'll wake up one day. A flat — not a council flat — but a retirement flat just for me! In the meantime I get to live in that lovely house — well, it will be lovely when it's finished, with a proper tiled bathroom that I can choose the tiles for myself, and my own television in my own rooms! The peace and quiet of it! No noisy radios and stereos from next door. No shouting and screaming and filth on the stairs. No lifts out of order and needles left on the staircase! Just for helping to make someone's life a bit easier! I think I've always needed to have someone to look after, and I've been so lonely since Joyce left, not that she ought to have stayed with me, of course . . .'

'Dear Rose, it couldn't happen to a nicer person and I personally am very grateful to you. Roy will be, too. He loves his mother dearly, but handy about the house he is not.'

Rose seemed to shrink into herself. 'Yes, but Diana . . .'

'If we can put up with her moaning, then so can you.'

Rose sighed. 'It's so sad, though. Miss Quicke feels it, I know. Her only great-niece.'

'Cheer up, we'll get Roy another wife and maybe he'll produce some little ones to run around and upset your peace and quiet.'

Rose giggled. 'Oh, do you really think he would? Wouldn't that be lovely?'

Jean bashed her way back into the kitchen. She avoided having to speak to Ellie if she could, but tonight it wasn't possible to do so. 'They're nearly all gone. Can I leave you to finish clearing up?'

Rose was alarmed. 'Is dear Miss Quicke waiting for me? I'd better go to her.'

Jean said, 'Is that the old woman who's promised to give some money for rebuilding the church hall? She's talking to some strange girl, over by the door. Ellie, can I rely on you to see the place is clean and tidy before you go?'

Ellie nodded, slipping the last stack of plates into the hot water. She suspected no one had as yet bothered to tidy up and sweep the floor clean next door, and that she would have to do it before she left.

Jean disappeared and someone else bumped their way into the kitchen.

Stewart, manoeuvring a sleeping Frank in his pushchair before him.

'Ellie, thank God I've found you!'

Ellie pulled down a rubber glove to check on the time. 'Stewart, what on earth are you doing, bringing little Frank out at this time of night?'

'I tried phoning you at home, no reply, and you've got your mobile switched off as usual. Little Frank was fractious so I popped him in his pushchair, thinking I'd walk over with him — he always goes to sleep quickly if I walk him at night, and it worked a treat. You weren't at home though the lights were on in the sitting room, but your neighbour was passing — that big woman, does the flower arranging — she saw me at the door and said you were probably still here.

'The thing is that Diana left a message on my mobile to say that the childminder was bringing him back to me for the weekend and of course I'm thrilled to have him with me, but I really have to work tomorrow and I can't ask the childminder because she doesn't do it over the weekends and I'm really stuck.'

'So you thought I could have him with me?' Swiftly she reviewed what was going to happen tomorrow, singing in the choir at the wedding, the wedding reception, and then the Golf Club dinner dance. If she dropped out of the choir, there'd be trouble. If she didn't go to the wedding reception,

Bill would be justifiably upset. The same with the dinner dance. Besides, she'd bought all those new clothes and had her hair done—

No, that was being selfish.

'Let me think. I've various things arranged, but . . .' She balanced the last plate on the draining board, tipped out the water and drew off the rubber gloves with a sigh of relief.

Stewart picked up a drying-up cloth and got down to work. There was something to be said for a man having a virago for a wife, if it taught him to take his share of the household chores. Catch her husband Frank in the kitchen!

He said, 'You were quite right, what you said yesterday morning at the flat. I don't know what came over me, letting things slip like that. So I went down to the cleaning agency and made it up with them, and I got rid of the people that Diana uses.'

Ah-ha, thought Ellie. Making a clean sweep of everything that reminds him of his wife?

'I've got the cleaners to meet me first thing tomorrow at that appalling flat that I showed Miss Quicke the other day, and they said they'd work through, time and a half on Saturdays, but it will be worth it.'

'Good boy,' said Ellie, stacking dried plates. 'Did you get your own money transferred out of the joint bank account?'

'I did.' He grimaced. 'As I left the bank, I noticed Diana arriving. I didn't hang around.'

Ellie considered telling him that he couldn't always run away, but forbore. The poor lad was doing pretty well, considering. She said, 'I could look after little Frank till eleven o'clock, but I have to sing at a wedding at half past and then go on to the wedding reception.'

'Couldn't you take him with you? Or perhaps Mrs Rose . . .?'

'She has enough to do, looking after my aunt.' She hesitated. 'I suppose I could drop out of singing at the wedding, but it would be pushing my luck to take him on to the wedding reception.'

He gave her a hug. 'You're wonderful. I'll just help you clear up here, shall I, and then see him safely to your place.'

'No, I've got Rose and Aunt Drusilla staying. You'll have to take him back with you tonight.'

He looked devastated. 'This is a miserable affair, isn't it?' he said. 'Trying to find somewhere to put one small boy, who's quite blameless? I'm sorry, Mother-in-law. Ellie. I ought not to have asked you to help. Frank's my responsibility now, and I'll work something out. I'll take him with me to work. Why not? The cleaners will be delighted to have someone else to make a fuss of.'

'You're a good boy, Stewart. I know little Frank's safe in your hands. Would it help if I had him till I'm due at church? As to the future, I'm sure Aunt Drusilla and Rose will be able to go back to their place soon, and then I'll be more free to help out.'

He was a handsome enough lad, she had to admit. Squared shoulders, head held high. Honest, dependable, and a good father. Diana would regret dumping him one day. Perhaps.

She'd finished up in the kitchen. Frank was still fast asleep, clean and sweet-smelling in his pyjamas under his cosy outdoor suit. She opened the door into the hall. Dismay. There was no one there, but the chairs had been left higgledy-piggledy, and the floor was littered with crumbs and sugar. None of the tables had been put away, either. Stewart was preparing to leave.

Suddenly she remembered something he'd said. 'Stewart, did you say that there were lights on in the sitting room when you called at my house? I turned them off when I left. The only lights I left on were the ones in the conservatory, so that we could see our way down the garden path.'

Stewart thought about it. 'I went to the front door, rather than try to drag the pushchair up your garden path. Yes, there was a light on in the sitting room, and in the hall. That's why I spent a few minutes ringing your doorbell, thinking you must be in. Then that flower-lady woman came past, and saw me. You think someone has broken in?' He squared those broad shoulders of his. 'I'm coming back with you, see you in safely, right?'

She looked around at the mess in the room. There would be all hell to pay in the morning if the place was left like this, but her anxiety was mounting. Aunt Drusilla and Rose had left some time ago and would have gone back into the house without seeing anything wrong in lights having been switched on where they ought not to have been. She grabbed her jacket and handbag, switched off the lights. If she had time in the morning, she'd come in and tidy up. Jean ought never to have left Ellie alone to clear up in here and in the kitchen. Under normal circumstances, Rose would have stayed to help her. But Rose had her mind set on looking after Aunt Drusilla and it would never have crossed her mind that Jean would dump it all on Ellie.

They rushed across the Green, into the alley, and through the gate into Ellie's back garden. Ellie seized one end of the pushchair and Stewart the other, and they carried Frank up the garden path between them.

All seemed quiet. As normal. The conservatory lights were on, as they should be. The house showed no other lights at all.

CHAPTER THIRTEEN

Ellie touched Stewart's arm, indicating that they stand still for a moment and listen. Armand had the radio on next door. A classical concert of some kind? The music was hardly loud enough to identify.

Ellie unlocked the door into the conservatory and they carried the pushchair up into the house. All was quiet, very still. No Midge. No Aunt Drusilla or Rose.

Ellie preceded Stewart into the kitchen. The light wasn't on there, nor in the hall, nor in the sitting room. The place seemed to be just as she had left it. No burglars. No intruders. Television and VCR still where she'd left them.

Stewart hovered. 'I could have sworn there were lights on in the hall and the sitting room. If there hadn't been, I'd not have spent so long ringing the doorbell.'

'Yes,' said Ellie, throat constricting. The sitting room felt all right, and so did the hall. But the kitchen. What was it about the kitchen that felt wrong?

There was a sharp ring at the front-door bell and Rose entered, flushed and rosy, using her key. Aunt Drusilla came after her, leaning on her stick.

'Did you give us up for lost, then?' asked Rose, all bright and cheerful. 'Your kind neighbour Kate asked us in for a chat as you hadn't finished up yet.' Then, on seeing Ellie's face, 'What's wrong?'

'I don't know exactly,' said Ellie. 'Stewart called round when we were out and said there were lights on in the sitting room and hall. Only, I didn't leave any lights on there when we went out.'

Aunt Drusilla seated herself on the hall chair. She looked tired. 'I expect it was Diana. She has her own key. I'm going up to bed now. I like that Kate of yours — she said she'd pop into work tomorrow and check one or two things out for me. Bring me a cup of tea up, will you, Rose?'

Ellie barred the way. 'Wait a minute. I don't think Diana was here. She always disturbs the furniture in the sitting room when she comes in, and the furniture looks fine to me. If you don't mind, I'll just check around upstairs.'

She looked in all three of the bedrooms, and the bathroom. Nothing seemed to have been disturbed. Midge was asleep on her bed. Fine.

She told herself that there was absolutely nothing wrong. Stewart had been in a bit of a state. He'd been mistaken about seeing lights on downstairs.

Only, Stewart wasn't the sort to make mistakes like that. So, someone had been in the house this evening and it hadn't been Diana.

'False alarm,' she said, in a bright voice as she went downstairs. 'Off you go to bed, you two.'

Aunt Drusilla glared at Ellie. 'You'd pack us off to bed like children, would you? Is anything missing?'

Ellie shook her head. 'Something's worrying me about the kitchen.'

'Not the kettle again,' said Rose, trying to make a joke of it.

Stewart peered into the kitchen. 'Looks all right to me.'

Ellie went past him and stood by the table, looking at every unit, every piece of equipment. Thinking that wires could be tampered with more than once, thinking that maybe she ought to ring the police.

In the cold weather Midge either slept on a folded tea towel on top of the boiler, or on Ellie's bed. His tea towel was now on the floor. Why? Had he started off the evening there and been disturbed?

The tea caddy and sugar bowl were now on the far side of the microwave. Why? They were usually kept next to the kettle, for obvious reasons. 'Rose, did you move the tea caddy and sugar bowl for some reason?'

'No,' said Rose, looking worried.

'There!' said Stewart, pointing to something which had drifted into a corner by the back door. 'Don't touch it!'

'It looks like a screwed-up cellophane wrapping from something. A packet of cigarettes, perhaps?' It hadn't been there when she went out. No one Ellie knew smoked any longer. So someone else had definitely been in the kitchen. She felt quite light-headed. 'So what's been tampered with? Electric kettle or microwave?'

Stewart exclaimed, 'Ellie, don't touch anything. Step back here. At once!'

Ellie stepped.

'What is it? Let me see.' cried Rose.

'It's the kettle. I can see it from here,' said Stewart. 'The wiring into the plug has been frayed. Anyone who switched that on would get a nasty shock.'

'That kettle's not new,' said Ellie, keeping her voice steady. 'But the wiring wasn't frayed when I left here this evening.'

'What we need is an electrician's screwdriver,' said Stewart. 'You know the sort? It's rubberized, protects you from electric shocks.'

Ellie shook her head. She'd never seen one.

'Very well. We'll find something else to use for insulation. You've got a rubber bath mat, haven't you?' asked Stewart. 'I don't want to touch that plug till I'm standing on something made of rubber. And your rubber washing-up gloves will help, too.'

Rose fetched the bath mat. Stewart donned the rubber gloves, stood on the mat, leaned across and switched the kettle off at the mains. He unplugged it and carried it out into the conservatory. Ellie sank onto a chair. 'But who . . . and how?'

'It's Diana, of course. But why?' added Aunt Drusilla. 'She can't expect to frighten me again now. It doesn't make sense. Well, I vote it's too late to ring the police tonight. They'll keep us up till all hours, if we do. I'm going to bed, with or without my late-night cup of tea.'

Ellie passed her hands distractedly back through her hair. 'I can't believe it's Diana, but . . . it's too late, I can't think straight. Aunt Drusilla, I believe I may have an old kettle somewhere that I can put on the gas to make you a cuppa. Stewart, you can't walk back through the streets at this time of night. Could you bear to sleep on the settee down here, and we'll leave little Frank in his pushchair? It won't hurt him this once.'

* * *

When Ellie finally got into bed, she couldn't sleep. Diana and Stewart. The mess she'd left at the church hall. How could she look after little Frank with all that she had going on? She wasn't at all sure of the soprano part in the anthem for the wedding, and Bill would expect her to be at his side at the reception tomorrow.

Who had got into the house? How had they got into the house? And above all, why?

Rousting out the old kettle and giving it a clean in order to make her aunt a cup of tea, Ellie had come across an envelope addressed in biro to Miss Quicke. It had been torn across and thrown away. It had missed the bin and fallen to the floor. Ellie checked inside the envelope. Naturally. There was nothing inside.

Why would someone be writing — by hand — to Aunt Drusilla at Ellie's? How many people knew she was now living there? Ellie might have expected bills to be forwarded here, perhaps. But this? The handwriting was minute, painstaking.

It was an oddity, and Ellie was suspicious of oddities.

Dear Lord, see us through this. Please?

* * *

It was the morning of the wedding, and chaos ruled in Ellie's house.

Rose had to return to her flat to collect her wedding outfit, before going on to Joyce's to get her ready for the wedding. So Rose wasn't around to help with Aunt Drusilla.

Frank woke early and screamed to be let out of his pushchair. Ellie rushed down to rescue him. Stewart was still asleep on the sitting-room settee. She thought it best to let him sleep, while getting Frank an early breakfast. She then brought down some of the toys she always kept handy for her grandson and let him play in the conservatory, while keeping an eye out for him. Which didn't leave her any time to shower or dress before Aunt Drusilla called out that she would take her breakfast in bed, and where was the *Financial Times*?

Stewart, bleary-eyed but more or less in command of his senses, used the bathroom — reporting that the loo wouldn't flush properly — wolfed down some breakfast and volunteered to go out and fetch a *Financial Times* before setting off to work.

Before Ellie had finished all three breakfasts, she was called to the door to face DS Willis plus the 'Dearie' constable. DS Willis was as usual in a belligerent mood.

'For heavens' sake, not now!' Ellie exclaimed, running her fingers back through her hair and noticing that she was still wearing her old dressing gown and slippers. Now, if she'd only been wearing one of her brand-new outfits, she'd have been able to cope better. 'What is it this time?'

'We've had a report of another attempt on Miss Quicke's life. Your kettle, I believe?'

'What?' Ellie clutched her head. 'But I haven't rung in to report it yet. There's so much to do this morning that I forgot. We only discovered late last night that . . . who told you?'

Frank, who'd been happily engaged piling toys into his pushchair and shoving it around the conservatory, now set up a tremendous howling. No doubt he'd got a wheel stuck under a chair and hadn't the wit to pull backwards to extricate himself.

Ms Willis clamped her lips in a 'torture wouldn't get it out of me' gesture. She stepped into the hall, followed by 'Dearie', though Ellie had not really intended to let them in. 'Information received. So why didn't you inform us?'

'I give up,' said Ellie. 'We didn't tell you, but someone else did? Only, you're not going to tell us who it was, when it was probably the person who tampered with the kettle? Has the world gone totally mad?'

Ms Willis frowned at the row which Frank was making. Aunt Drusilla limped out into the landing above and called down, 'Ellie, can't you hear that Frank's in trouble? And where's my *Financial Times*?'

'It's Detective Sergeant Willis again, Aunt Drusilla. About the kettle.'

'I suppose Stewart rang them. Well, you can tell her I'm not available for interview. I am about to have my shower, if you will put out some clean towels for me. Also some better soap. I don't like the one you have out at the moment. It's too harsh for my skin.'

Frank had reached the dry-throated screaming point. Ellie darted into the conservatory, rescued his pushchair and pulled him on to her lap to calm him down. Ms Willis followed her. 'Dearie' hovered. At the same moment Stewart thrust his head round the door to the garden. 'Here's the paper. See you about half eleven.' The paper flopped on to the conservatory floor and he vanished. Of course, he'd need to get back to the flat and shave before he went about his business.

'Who was that?' 'Dearie' joined them in the conservatory. Too late.

'That was Stewart,' said Ellie. 'Helping out.'

'What,' demanded Ms Willis, 'is going on here? Don't you realize how serious this all is? I came here expecting to find you all distraught, while you seem to have decided that these attempts on Ms Quicke's life are totally unimportant. If you've been wasting police time . . .'

'Do sit down,' said Ellie, 'I'll just run up with the paper to Aunt Drusilla, and then I'll do my best to put you in the picture.'

When she returned, she did so, finishing, '. . . and of course you may think we're not taking this seriously, but we are. Indeed we are. Aunt Drusilla is very worried, though she appears to be taking the matter lightly. She's been turning over in her mind every contact of hers who might wish her harm, and she has come up with two. She has asked a financial expert, a friend of mine, to investigate one of these possibilities and the other she has already mentioned to you, I believe.'

'The builder, yes. Someone is interviewing him at this moment.'

'What I think, is that it's a question of access. Who's got access both to Miss Quicke's house, and here. The list looks quite manageable at first; members of the family . . .'

'Including her great-niece, Diana, who had an excellent motive . . .'

'But has none now, since her great-aunt has informed her that she will not gain a fortune in the event of her death . . .'

'Diana might have engineered this latest development after she heard that she'd been cut out of the will, in an attempt to persuade us she wasn't responsible for the first effort.'

'It is possible but not likely, don't you think?'

Frank wriggled out of her arms and flumped to the floor, where he made for his pushchair again.

Ellie said, 'I think we ought to look at who else might have keys . . . and there are a good many possibilities there, aren't there?'

'Not for your house, surely.'

Ellie sighed. 'I've been thinking about that. I've had quite a lot of work done here since my husband died. I've given keys to my builders — who are currently working next door now — to Jimbo, the central-heating engineer. I'm not sure but I think I gave one to my electrician, as well. I'm not a complete fool and I've always asked for my keys back at the end of a job, but last week I gave a key back to the builders because I've got a piece of guttering that needs fixing and the loo isn't flushing properly and they promised to fit me in as soon as possible. Now I'd stake my life on my builder and his two mates, but he does get contract workers in now and then, and one of them could easily have pinched a key. As for Aunt Drusilla's house, who knows how many keys there are floating around?'

'Each and every one of which might have been copied at some time?'

Ellie winced. 'Yes. It presumes that someone we've employed is a criminal intent on a future burglary. But yes, it could be.'

Ms Willis didn't like this line of thought, either. 'Which takes the heat off your family.'

Ellie sighed. 'I don't think any of them did it.'

'Not even your daughter?'

'No,' said Ellie, firmly. 'I don't see it.'

Ms Willis got up and started to prowl around, looking at everything. 'Dearie' leaned against the doors leading to the sitting room and cleared his throat. Ms Willis ignored him. Little Frank frowned at her because she was standing just where he wanted to drive his pushchair.

'Well, let me have a look at this famous kettle of yours. You've been unlucky with kettles, haven't you?'

Ellie showed her where the kettle with its frayed cord sat on the conservatory table. 'I suppose we can be grateful that the kettle at my aunt's was faulty, as it got her and Mrs McNally out of the house before the cleaner received her fatal shock.'

Ms Willis put on protective gloves and lifted the kettle into a large bag.

'I don't know whose prints are on the handle. Probably not Stewart's, since he used my rubber gloves to handle it when he made it safe. He very kindly disposed of it for us last night. In fact, it was he who pointed out the problem.'

'Having first caused it himself?'

'No,' said Ellie, trying to be patient. 'Stewart wouldn't, didn't and anyway doesn't have a key to this house.'

'He was here first thing this morning?'

'He slept here because . . . oh, never mind that. It's a long and complicated story. He and Diana have split up, so he brought little Frank over for me to look after for a couple of hours while he gets some work done.'

'Stewart is the person best able to tamper with electrics around here?'

'Yes.'

There was a grinding crash from the sitting room, followed by a horrible two-second silence before Frank filled his lungs with air and bellowed. He had a very loud voice. Ellie leaped back into the sitting room to find Frank had run his pushchair into the coffee table and managed to tip it over, and with it two pot plants in ceramic containers. He'd also tipped himself over and banged his head against a corner of the table.

Ellie snatched him up and inspected the damage. He was going to have a bump there. 'There, there!' she said. 'Granny's here. Let me kiss it better.' She took him into the kitchen and bathed his head. He was scarlet with fury and hurt. Ellie found a drink and a biscuit for him, which he rejected. A scoop of ice cream went down better and soon his sobs subsided as he sat on her knee and kneaded a biscuit into crumbs while she fed him the soothing mixture.

Ellie glanced at the clock. Time was hurrying on, and she had to be at the church, showered, properly dressed and in her right mind for the service in half an hour. Still there was no sign of Stewart.

'I'll just have a word with Miss Quicke, then,' said Ms Willis.

'Please do. If you can get her to come down. I haven't got her the clean towels for her shower yet and she won't appear till she's properly groomed and ready to meet her public.'

'Forgive me,' said Ms Willis, in a tone at variance with the words, 'but you don't appear to be taking this matter very seriously.'

'Oh, I do. I assure you,' said Ellie, putting the damp cloth to Frank's temple again. 'And if it weren't for all these domestic chores, I'd probably be able to put my thinking cap on and help you.'

Ms Willis snorted. 'We don't need your kind of help, thank you.'

Ellie lifted an eyebrow, but didn't argue. Little Frank was clinging to her like a limpet. His breathing was slowing. He slid further down her lap, still holding on to her. Was he actually going to have a little nap? The poor little love.

Also, Praise be, because she needed to get herself ready and to church.

Ms Willis said, in her inimitable menacing way, 'Why do I get the impression that you're hiding something? That you know exactly who's been tampering with the electrics, and don't want to tell me? Have you forgotten that a woman died?'

Ellie sighed. 'No, I haven't forgotten, but you're quite right. I do have a lot on my mind at the moment and her death was just an accident, wasn't it?'

Ms Willis pointed. 'That kettle wasn't an accident, was it?'

Ellie had to admit that it wasn't.

Ms Willis finally left with 'Dearie', without having seen Miss Quicke, but with a promise to return later that day. To which Miss Quicke replied that she would be hither and yon, and she was not prepared to wait in for anybody.

Surprisingly, Ms Willis kept her temper. Only, as she left with the kettle, she gave Ellie a sympathetic look. 'You have your work cut out at the moment, don't you?'

Ellie nodded, saw the policewoman out, deposited Frank in his pushchair and fastened him in. His head lolled to one side. He looked like a fat cherub, with biscuit crumbs all over his face. He needed changing, too, but if she tried that he'd wake up . . .

It could wait.

Ellie dived back into the sitting room, righted the coffee table, scooped most of the earth back into the flowerpots, took a brush and pan to the rest, mopped up some spilt water, regretted that the water had stained the coffee table, but couldn't stop to polish it again. She stepped backwards onto the waste-paper basket which immediately upended itself on the floor.

She could have wept with frustration. Until she saw that among the debris was a piece of paper, torn into pieces and thrown away. She pieced the bits together like a jigsaw.

It was a letter, handwritten in the same biro as the discarded envelope that had been addressed to Miss Quicke. There was an address, some flat in the same tower block in which Rose lived. No phone number.

'Dear Miss Quicke,

I am sorry you have no cleaner. I can work for you again, full-time, or move in as discussed. ASAP.

Tracy Samantha Sugden.'

'Tracy,' murmured Ellie to herself. 'Now where have I heard that name before? Is she one of the cleaners my aunt used to have? Sounds like it. I suppose I may well have seen her at some time. A bit pushy, isn't she? Aunt Drusilla obviously isn't interested, or she wouldn't have torn the letter up.'

Into her mind came the image of the lumpy girl who had accosted her outside Miss Quicke's. Was that Tracy? Ellie supposed it might have been. She nearly threw the pieces back into the waste-paper basket but had second thoughts. She took them through into the study and put them in a clean envelope in the bureau.

A glance at the clock showed her it was time to get ready for church.

CHAPTER FOURTEEN

There was the usual fever of excitement and expectation in and around the church as people arrived for the wedding. Women air-kissed one another, tilting their heads so their hats didn't collide. Cars drew up, failed to find a parking space and disgorged passengers so that the drivers could explore the side roads for a vacancy. Parishioners crowded into the back pews to see Joyce married to the scoutmaster. Those who hadn't been invited to the reception wore ordinary clothes.

In spite of the March wind, there were lots of summery outfits and hats on view. The ushers wore morning coats, as did the bridegroom. The Reverend Gilbert Adams, back for this one occasion only, stood in the porch, cassock fluttering in the breeze, greeting old friends. Ushers dodged past him, guiding guests to their pews — more or less evenly divided since both parties to the wedding were local born.

Ellie glanced despairingly up and down the road but Stewart's car was nowhere in sight. Aunt Drusilla had managed to ease herself down the stairs and was now installed in the conservatory with her newspaper and a third cup of coffee. She couldn't be expected to look after little Frank.

Ellie had tried to raise Diana on her mobile but had no luck. It was switched off. Diana was probably still in bed with Derek Jolley.

'I really must go,' Ellie said to her aunt. 'Tell Stewart I've had to take Frank with me to church. I'll try to find someone to look after him during the service. If not, I'll have to drop out of singing in the choir.'

Aunt Drusilla nodded. 'That charming girl Kate said she might pop in later if she's got any information for me.'

'Don't let anyone into the house while I'm gone. Workmen, I mean.'

Aunt Drusilla didn't reply to that.

Ellie looked over the garden to the church grounds. Dear Rose was descending from a car and straightening her hat — or rather, pushing it further awry. The mother of the bride looked both happy and fraught.

Ellie put her wedding hat into a large plastic bag, hung it from Frank's pushchair and manoeuvred it down the garden path to the alley. For some reason she was loath to leave the house. Anxiety fluttered along her nerve ends. Surely nothing could happen to Aunt Drusilla if she didn't let anyone into the house?

She eased the pushchair up into the Green and took the path to the vestry door. If Stewart didn't arrive by the time she reached the church, she was going to have to make her apologies to the choir . . . and what about the mess the church hall had been left in last night? She'd thought she might be able to get up there early this morning to put it to rights, but of course that hadn't happened. She felt both guilty and defiant.

No Stewart. She drew a deep breath and went in by the vestry door, tugging the pushchair behind her. Frank was waking up, grunting and squirming. Pray heaven he didn't fill his pants again now. When Ellie had been a young mother, everyone automatically trained the children to the potty. Nowadays it seemed you waited for the child to train itself. Which might be fine for some people, but not for a granny with a bad back.

Jean saw her first. 'Well!' she exploded. 'Look who's here! I thought you of all people could be trusted to clear up last night! You said you would and . . .'

Ellie opened her eyes wide. 'I did clear up. Every single cup and saucer and plate was washed and dried and put away and the kitchen left spotless. It took me hours, but I said I would do it and I did. I didn't know who was supposed to clear up in the hall. I suppose they had to leave early and meant to come back this morning to do it?'

Sympathetic looks were sent in Ellie's direction and Jean subsided, grumbling. They all knew Ellie would have done her share. They all knew that Jean ought to have found someone else to clear the hall, and she knew that, too.

Mrs Dawes' majestic head emerged through the neck of her gown. 'Ellie, you're late. And why have you got the child with you?'

'A breakdown in communication between the parents,' said Ellie. 'Is there anyone I can leave him with, do you think?'

'There's a couple of young mothers who've come to see the wedding and are looking after their children at the back of the church. Try them.'

Ellie flew around the outside of the church and found a cluster of young mums with pushchairs making their way into the pews at the back. They did agree to look after young Frank, who had woken up and was eyeing a brightly coloured toy which another boy was holding. Then she fled back to the vestry and rushed into her gown, thanked Mrs Dawes for having found her the right sheets of music and the first hymn in the hymn book, and tried to still her breathing.

Timothy the curate popped his head round the vestry door. 'Ready, everyone? I don't think Joyce will be late, do you?'

Everyone smiled or tittered. Joyce was never late.

They filed into the choir pews and looked down the aisle while the organist played for time. The church was reasonably full. Mrs Dawes scanned her flower arrangements, checking to see that none of the flowers had drooped when she'd turned her back on them. White and blue. Of course. There were two magnificent arrangements by the rood screen, and little baskets of flowers on the end of every other pew, all the way down the church.

Rose sat in the front pew with a dour-looking cousin and his wife who'd come up to Town for the occasion and didn't look as if they were enjoying it. Rose's hat was still askew. Ellie wanted to jump out of her pew and rush across to give Rose a hug and straighten her hat for her.

The scoutmaster and his best man waited opposite, looking as if they'd got the wrong size shirt collar on, but otherwise neatly turned out. The vicar appeared at the end door, now fully robed.

There was a stir at the big doors. A chill wind lifted skirts and hats. And settled. The organist brought her hands down and everyone stood as the bride entered on Roy's arm. She was wearing white with a long veil. A very long veil. No wonder they'd had to have a practice for the wedding, or she'd have lost the veil halfway down the aisle. Two bridesmaids in blue, chosen for their homely looks and lumpy figures, by the look of them. They certainly made Joyce look like a film star by contrast.

Joyce looked up at her husband-to-be with a misty smile. At least for the duration of the service it was possible to believe that she would be a loving wife instead of another shrew.

For a second or two, Ellie felt tears gather as she remembered Diana's wedding to Stewart, not so many years ago. Her dear husband Frank had been so proud, displaying his handsome daughter on his arm as he walked down the aisle. Diana had worn a slender robe of ivory satin with a short veil, and all her flowers had been white . . . on bridesmaids. Stewart had turned his head to watch her come up the aisle, just as the scoutmaster now turned his head to watch Joyce.

And that was ending in tears.

Ellie prayed that Joyce and the scoutmaster would have a better life. She prayed that Joyce would be understanding and forbearing when required, and that he would be able to stand up to her, assert his rights as an equal partner in the marriage.

Rose had her handkerchief out.

Ellie remembered herself standing in that place, wearing a hat chosen for her by Diana. The same hat she had brought with her this afternoon to wear to the reception. Diana had said, 'Now, don't disgrace me, mother . . .' and Frank had said, 'Don't fuss, Ellie. Who's going to look at you?'

That thought hurt. Frank had sometimes been a little unkind. Without meaning it, of course. It just showed what a good marriage hers had been, her making allowances for things he didn't really mean, and his taking good care of her.

Well, it was one sort of marriage. Not the sort she understood they usually had nowadays, with both parties claiming pole position and only too ready to seek divorce if they didn't get it.

Ellie listened to the old, old words of the marriage service and slipped into prayer for those about to be married and those thinking of divorce. For all her friends. For her family. Especially for poor, unhappy Diana . . . who was probably at that very moment having it off with Derek Jolley . . .

No, perhaps not on a Saturday. Estate agents were always very busy on a Saturday. Perhaps he'd asked Diana to help him out, show customers around houses for sale?

Ellie thought she heard Frank give a yell of frustration during the anthem. Her first impulse was to go to him but she couldn't, hemmed in as she was by the substantial figure of Mrs Dawes on one side, and an equally large alto on the other.

She began to fret about Stewart's absence. Where was he? It wasn't like him to forget his son. How much longer before they could all be released from the service?

* * *

After the service there was the usual interminable wait while the photographer posed the newly married couple in the doorway of the church. No one could leave till they had finished that.

Ellie stripped off her gown in the vestry, and rescued her handbag. Pretty nearly all the choir had been invited to go on to the reception, but Ellie's mind was on little Frank, wailing at the back of the church. How could she have left him for so long? She ought never to have sung in the choir. Her first duty must always be to look after her family.

She almost ran down one of the aisles inside the church to the back — the photographer was still holding everyone up in the porch and no one could get out. Frank had by this time got to the stage of red-faced yelling. Ellie rescued him, unstrapped him from his pushchair, and tried to soothe him. She apologized to the two young marrieds who'd been trying to keep him quiet and thanked them for looking after him. All the time she was wondering what had happened to Stewart.

Instead of waiting for the main door to clear, Ellie carried Frank back to the vestry, tugging the pushchair after her. Then out through the vestry door into the sunlight. The wind was keen, but the daffodils were quite a sight.

Round the corner of the church she could hear whoops of laughter as confetti was thrown over the newly married couple by the guests, to be captured on film and video by photographs both amateur and professional.

Ellie put Frank down, encouraging him to toddle along beside her. He couldn't walk far yet, but the effort usually wore him out satisfactorily, and she really couldn't carry him that far, no, she really couldn't.

His attention was caught by the daffodils. He strutted among them, somewhat unsteadily, making whooshing sounds. Ellie hoped he wasn't going to move into destructive mode.

Where on earth was Stewart?

She encouraged Frank to walk along by the pushchair, holding on to it. Making remarks about 'din-dins' soon.

Frank loved his food. He grabbed a daffodil and tore it off its stalk, retaining just the head in his hand. Stood and stared at it. Picked at it. Tasted it.

Were daffodils poisonous? Ellie hoped not. No, she remembered now. It was the bulb that was poisonous, not the flower.

She tried to urge Frank on, but he wouldn't budge. Daffodils were something new to him. So brightly coloured. He breathed heavily, exploring the feeling of this new toy.

Ellie almost danced with impatience, but controlled herself. There was no use trying to hurry a toddler. And toddlers couldn't understand the notices that were all over the Green, 'Please do not pick the flowers'.

Eventually Frank consented to move on a few paces and there, thank goodness, came Stewart striding up through the trees, looking anxiously around for them.

'Ellie, you've got him safe? Such a terrible thing happened . . . no, no. Nothing that desperate, don't look so alarmed.' He picked up little Frank and gave him a hug. Frank dropped the remains of his daffodil and crowed with pleasure.

Stewart seized the pushchair in one hand and set off back to Ellie's house, throwing words over his shoulder at Ellie. 'I was on time, well, early in fact, and just on my way back here to relieve you when Diana rang me.'

'*She* rang *you?*'

'I couldn't believe it was her at first. The thing was, she said she was being taken to the police station for questioning, she didn't know how long she was going to be, and would I fetch her!'

Ellie gasped. Her worst fears had been realized. 'You mean, they've arrested her?'

'I shot down there, of course, but I couldn't get them to admit it or deny it. They said she was helping them with their enquiries. This was about half past eleven.'

Ellie tried to get her mind working again. 'Why did she ring you? I gave her the number of my solicitor.'

'Did you? She said she didn't know who else to ring.' His voice was grim. 'I suppose I ought to be flattered.'

'But . . .' Too many questions, too few answers.

He opened the gate into Ellie's garden. 'I couldn't get through to you — you'd got your mobile switched off. I tried ringing Derek Jolley, thinking he ought to take responsibility for her now, but his secretary said he was out all day today. I tried ringing Great-Aunt Drusilla, but she's permanently on the phone. I couldn't remember the name of your solicitor. I knew it was Bill something . . . but what? So I prayed you'd be able to look after little Frank for a bit longer. I waited around for a bit, at the police station, trying all three of you again. Then I thought it best to come back here, see what you think we ought to do.'

Ellie let them into the conservatory. No Rose, of course. She was probably still at the church, part of the wedding-group photos. The phone in the hall was off the hook — why? — and there was no sign of Aunt Drusilla.

Frank started to yell again as soon as they got inside. Stewart put him down, remarking that he needed changing again.

Ellie ran her fingers back through her hair. What to do first?

Bill. Phone Bill's office. She got through at the first try. His secretary said that Bill had left for the day, and no, his junior partner wasn't there, either. It was Saturday afternoon, didn't she realize?

So it was.

What to do?

She was due at the wedding reception in a minute. Rose would flutter and get in a state if Ellie were not there to calm things down. Joyce would be livid if there was the slightest crumple in the rose leaf of her most important day.

But Diana . . . !

Ellie tried Derek Jolley. No, he was still out and they didn't think he'd be back for hours.

Yellow pages. Solicitors.

Who was Aunt Drusilla's solicitor? Did any name jump out at her? No, no, no . . . possibly. She rather thought she'd seen this name on some correspondence which Aunt Drusilla had left lying around in a moment of uncharacteristic indiscretion.

Brr . . . Brr . . . No reply. They'd gone home for the day, too.

Stewart was changing little Frank. Stewart looked haggard with anxiety. Did he still love Diana, perhaps? Was her phone call to him a sign that she perhaps still had some feeling for him? Was that a wise thing to hope for?

She tried another solicitor. No reply.

A third. Someone was there, in a hurry, about to leave for the weekend. But he was still on the other end of the phone, and possibly their last chance. She took a deep breath in, and out. Must be calm. Be reasonable. Explained.

No, he wasn't interested. Put the phone down.

Ellie went into the kitchen and ran the cold-water tap. Dashed cold water over her face, washed her hands. Got out a tin of pasta rings in tomato sauce and some cheese and handed them over to Stewart, to heat up for Frank.

Went back to the phone.

There was only one thing for it. She rang Bill at home. He would be there, of course . . . or would he have made himself scarce because of the wedding reception? She prayed he would be there, but with her luck he'd have gone out.

He was a long time answering the phone and perhaps had already been at the sherry before he spoke.

'Bill, thank goodness. Listen, we need some advice, urgently. Diana has been . . .'

He listened as courteously as ever.

'Has she been charged?' Apparently not. 'Arrested? Just "helping with their enquiries?" Hmm. I can't get hold of my partner, he's away this weekend.'

'Yes, I know. What do we do, Bill?'

'May I ask, Ellie, why you think Diana needs a solicitor?'

Ah. That was the question, indeed.

'Well, I don't think she did it, of course not. The very idea! But there's no denying that she did think Aunt Drusilla was going to leave her a lot of money, and of course she's in touch with electricians all the time in her job. The keys to Aunt Drusilla's house must have passed through many hands because she's had all those workmen in. Almost anybody could have got hold of one.'

'Surely the same thing applies to you? And to Stewart? You've both been called in to "help with enquiries" before now, haven't you? I seem to remember that it was only on Thursday that you yourself needed me to put in a good word for you with the police. So why are you panicking?'

'I'm not panicking. Of course I'm not panicking. It's just that she rang Stewart to let him know that she was being taken to the police station, she didn't know how long she was going to be, and she asked him to fetch her. It was a cry for help, you see, because she and Stewart are not on good terms. In fact, they've just separated and she's moved in with someone else.'

Ellie improvised. 'I'm sure this separation has given her a bad shock . . .' That sounded all right, anyway. 'She must be feeling rather fragile at the moment. So you see, even if we think it might be just routine, Diana has taken it very seriously. It might, well, upset her balance.'

A long silence.

'Bill, are you still there?'

'Yes.' A sigh. 'Jimbo's case was different, because he'd got a spotty past. A totally innocent person — the police might think — doesn't need a solicitor.'

'No, but a foolish one might. I do think Diana is in a fragile emotional state and she has been very foolish. She's uttered threats against Aunt Drusilla.'

'She's done what?'

Silence on Ellie's part. Stewart appeared in the doorway, carrying Frank. Stewart was continuing to look anxious.

'Yes,' said Ellie, quietly. 'She did. The police could make out a case that she intended to give Aunt Drusilla a shock, though not of course to kill her.'

'So that's what you're afraid of? If you send me down there, the police will realize that you think she's guilty. If she did it, she's facing a manslaughter charge, Ellie.'

'Oh, she didn't do it. Of course she didn't. But she's so volatile at the moment, she might do or say something to rouse their suspicions.'

'You do think she's guilty, don't you?'

Ellie didn't reply.

Stewart said, 'Can I have a word with him?'

Ellie took Frank off Stewart and returned to the kitchen, where she popped him into his high chair and dished up his food. He plunged both hands enthusiastically into the tomatoey mess . . .

Oh, her best blue suit!

She would have to change before she went on to the wedding reception. If she ever managed to get there. She persuaded Frank to eat with a spoon plus his fingers — he seemed to have decided that fingers were best, after some months of using a spoon alone. She gave him a drink. He threw it on the floor. She picked it up, washed it out, gave him some more. Mopped up the mess. He hit her on the back of her head with his spoon. With more tomato on it. Whatever had persuaded her to give him something with tomato in it? She peeled a banana for him. He liked bananas.

He threw that on the floor, too. He lunged sideways, yelling, 'No!'

Why was 'No!' the first word they ever mastered? Was it because it was always being said to them? Don't do this, don't do that. No!

Stewart came back to the kitchen and sat. Heavily. 'Well, he'll go down there. It's against his better judgement, but he'll go. I said she was in such a state that she might lose her temper and say the first thing that came into her head. Even admit something that's not true.'

'You think she's guilty, as well.'

'No, I don't.' His eyelids flickered. He wasn't a good liar. He doubted Diana as much as Ellie did. She held her hand out over the table and he closed his own hand around hers. For a count of ten, Frank ceased to pound on his chair and yell. He was watching a sunbeam tremble on the wall opposite. Ellie used those moments to pray for Diana and Stewart. Stewart had closed his eyes. Perhaps he was praying, too. Then he took his hand away and passed it over his face.

'I said I'd meet him down there. She asked for me, so I'd better go. Can you cope with Frank this afternoon?'

She wanted to say that she couldn't, but of course she could. She wanted to go upstairs, strip, have a shower and fall on her bed for a nap so as to be fresh for the dance tonight.

Instead she must clean herself up as best she might — Frank, too — and get them both to the wedding reception. Return home, organize supper for Aunt Drusilla and then get ready for the dance.

'Of course I can,' she said. 'Will you let me know what's happening? I promised to go to the Golf Club Dance this evening with Bill.'

'I've got tickets for that, too. Somewhere. Diana bought herself a new dress for it, and we arranged for a babysitter, but . . .' He shrugged. 'Could you remember to keep your mobile switched on? Then I can ring you as soon as we know what's happening.'

He went off, with little Frank waving him goodbye. 'Dadda?' yelled Frank. And then, to Ellie, 'Mumma? Mumma come soon?'

'Yes, darling. Of course she will. Now we've got to clean up the kitchen and have a nice walk in the sunshine, go to see the seagulls on the river. Won't that be nice?' She lifted him out of the high chair and set him on the floor.

'Want Mumma,' said Frank, hitting her on her leg. Oh dear. And if she put him back in his pushchair while she washed and changed, he'd yell blue murder.

'A little sleepy-byes?' she suggested.

'No!' He charged at the coffee table in his railway-engine mode. 'Choo-choo-choo! Bang! Crash!' Over went the table again, plant pots and all. He then looked at her with a wicked, 'that'll larn you' grin.

Ellie was torn between bursting into tears and giving him a good smack. She had heard that grannies in this situation normally put a video on to soothe the child. Well, she hadn't got a video, but perhaps it was time she acquired one. She picked little Frank up and carried him up the stairs. He yelled all the way. She dumped him on the stool in the bathroom and proceeded to get him comparatively clean and tidy, in spite of his yells and squirms. Then she laid him on his bed in the small room, closing the door on his bellows of fury, hoping Kate and Armand were out and wouldn't be disturbed by the noise.

She had a hurried shower, washed her hair, put on one of the outfits she'd bought yesterday, decided not to wear a hat, and called for a cab.

Frank was mercifully silent.

Oh. It wasn't good news when toddlers were that quiet. What was he up to? More mischief?

No. Relief. He was flat on his back on his bed, arms flung above his head, long eyelashes fanning out on red cheeks, the whole of that energetic little body relaxed in sleep. The little cherub! He was quite edible when he was asleep and she loved him dearly.

She tiptoed down the stairs and telephoned Kate next door. Armand answered the phone.

'Hi, Ellie. Yes, Miss Quicke's here, been here for hours. We're just about to have a spot of lunch. Want to join us?'

'No, no. I just wanted to make sure my aunt was with you safe and sound. I'm taking Frank off to the wedding reception, back in a couple of hours, I suppose. Tell my aunt . . . no, not to bother. I'll see her this evening.'

The cab arrived and she loaded Frank's pushchair into it. Then she carefully carried the sleeping little boy down and held him in her arms all the way to Bill's house.

CHAPTER FIFTEEN

It was the perfect setting for a wedding reception. The sun was out, the tide was up and gulls swooped everywhere. The garden sparkled with spring flowers, the women floated around in their light-coloured clothes — except for the few who insisted on wearing black even for a wedding. The men mingled, the waiters and waitresses served and poured wine. Joyce and her new husband were the centre of attention, which was where Joyce liked to be. Dear Rose had discarded her hat; a good idea. She looked much better without it. Dear Rose had had perhaps a little too much to drink, but was so pleased to see Ellie.

'Because you know, my dear, I had to speak to one of the waitresses rather sharply a moment ago and it was most unpleasant, and I couldn't help thinking that you'd have done it so much better than me. You never upset people when you tell them off, but I'm always too much one way or the other.'

Ellie smiled and smiled, and apologized to the bride and groom for being late — a little family upset. Her apologies were graciously accepted, though with the distinct subtext that Joyce would have managed much better and been on time, too.

Frank woke up when they arrived and declined to be bundled back into his pushchair, so Ellie led him around — or rather he led her around. She encouraged him to throw some oddments of leftover canapes to the gulls. He threw scraps a yard and screamed with joy when the gulls came close to retrieve them. Joyce frowned. She really did not want children taking the limelight off her on her wedding day.

Tough! Thought Ellie. I didn't want to bring him, either.

Oh, Diana! She checked that her mobile was switched on, which it was.

Roy was doing his duty by Rose, shepherding her around, making sure the drink and food flowed in the right places. He looked good in a morning suit. Ellie felt proud of him and when he looked her way, she blew him a kiss, to which he replied with another. Ellie noticed he'd also got his eye on a mega-thin blonde in an executive-style suit which proclaimed her a career woman. She wore heavy rings on the third finger of her right hand, but none on her left. Divorced?

Mrs Dawes loomed at Ellie's shoulder. 'That's a cousin of Joyce's that he's making eyes at. Drives one of those cars which you can't get into without difficulty, low down on the road, you know? Something in marketing. What do you make of that, eh?'

Mrs Dawes wanted to see if Ellie would react on seeing Roy pay attention to another woman, and indeed she did feel a pang — but only a small one — of jealousy. She smiled. 'I'm really pleased for him.'

'Oh,' said Mrs Dawes, disconcerted. 'Have you seen the flower decorations in the drawing room? Someone had the nerve to tell me that I should have put some colour into them. What do they know about it, eh? Tell me what you think.'

Ellie managed to persuade Frank to follow her into the drawing room, where there might be some nice little sweeties for him to eat, and duly admired the all-white flower arrangements. 'No, Mrs Dawes, they're perfect as they are. Virginal.'

'Hnh! Not that *she* is!' said Mrs Dawes. A remark which Ellie pretended not to hear.

Frank had found a tray of canapes on a side table but just as he was about to cram some smoked salmon into his mouth, a waitress swooped on him and struck it out of his hand. 'Not for you!'

Ellie wasn't sure whether to agree or be angry at her interference.

Frank bellowed his irritation at being deprived of his titbit, so Ellie said to the girl, 'Can you find something he can eat?'

'Egg do you?'

With reluctance and great put-upon sighs, the girl sorted out a couple of tiny sandwiches and put them on a plate for Frank, who promptly collapsed himself on to the floor and got stuck in.

'Thank you,' said Ellie, wondering where she'd seen the girl before. Because she had seen her before, she was sure of it.

The girl stalked off. She had stout legs and rolled in her walk, which rang a bell somewhere with Ellie. The girl — no, she was not a girl, she was probably in her late twenties, maybe early thirties — was a bit of a lump, really. Her black skirt was too cheap, too short, the black tights laddered. The white top was not as clean as it might be and certainly hadn't seen an iron recently.

The other waitresses were all looking very smart and well groomed, with shining hair pinned back or kept short, immaculate white blouses and unwrinkled black skirts. This one girl stood out from the rest. Perhaps she wasn't one of their regulars.

Well, it didn't matter, did it? What did matter was that Stewart hadn't rung yet. She checked her mobile phone but it was still on, and still unresponsive.

There weren't many people inside the house. Most were standing around in the garden, thrilled to be out in the sunshine, ignoring the chilly breeze. The Reverend Gilbert Adams was there, of course, having taken the wedding ceremony. He was talking animatedly to a group of old friends from the church. Tum-Tum was also there . . . she really must not call him Tum-Tum, even to herself. Thomas. The new vicar was called Thomas, and the church was also called St Thomas', so she ought to be able to remember it.

Rose was listening to that sour cousin of hers complain about something. Roy had drawn the blonde down to the river's edge to admire the seagulls. Or to admire her?

Frank hauled himself to his feet and made for the three-tiered wedding cake in the bay window. What he'd do to that if he got his hands on it, Ellie dreaded to think. She picked him up and sought for a tray of sandwiches to keep his mouth filled. He objected. He wanted to get down, have a bash at the cake. If he got his hands on the white cloth under the wedding cake, he could easily pull it all off and bring the cake smashing to the carpet. It didn't bear thinking about.

A waiter rushed in, calling for 'Tracy' to take out some more champagne. The lumpish girl obliged, very very slowly.

Tracy, thought Ellie. I know that name. I have seen the girl somewhere before. Yes, she'd seen her outside Aunt Drusilla's house the day after the accident, and possibly working at Aunt Drusilla's before that, too? Someone called Tracy wrote to my aunt. Aunt Drusilla tore the letter up and I rescued it from the waste-paper basket.

Well, what of it?

The caterers probably called on a wide variety of people to service their contracts. This Tracy was a cleaner who'd once worked for Aunt Drusilla and now picked up the odd afternoon's wages working for the caterer. And why not?

She carried Frank out into the garden again. He protested, but was charmed by the Reverend Gilbert Adams coming over and tickling him. 'Well, little man? How you've grown.'

Banal words, but Gilbert exuded pleasure at the sight of Frank and Frank responded, reaching out to clutch at the pen in Gilbert's top pocket.

'No, you don't, you little terror,' said Gilbert. 'And how is your grandmother today? Looking very well, if I may say so. What happened to you last night? Liz and I wanted to talk to you about . . .'

'Oh, there you are, vicar.' This was Jean from the choir, giving Ellie a look of dislike, preparing to take Gilbert away. Gilbert tried to adhere to Ellie, who'd always been a favourite of his.

'Jean, lovely to see all my old friends again. The choir was in good voice, too.'

'I want you to meet . . .' Gilbert was dragged away, calling back that he'd ring Ellie.

Tum-Tum materialized at Ellie's side. Frank took one look at him, and decided he didn't like him, so twisted right round in Ellie's arms and pretended he was invisible. Tum-Tum seemed amused rather than annoyed at this.

'You're Mrs Quicke, aren't you? I've a terrible memory for names, but Gilbert made me promise to look you up. May I drop in to see you sometime?'

'Time to cut the cake!'

There was a general move indoors, led by the bride and groom. Ellie's arms ached with holding Frank, but he resisted being put back into his pushchair. Ellie managed to find a chair to sit on, so that she could hold Frank on her lap. But where was her handbag with the all-important phone in it? She must have dropped it somewhere, trying to look after Frank and see that he didn't get into mischief. She looked to see if she'd left it by the table which had held the canapes, but they'd all been cleared away now. She peered down through people's legs, to see if it had come to rest on the floor somewhere.

Speeches were going on over her head. People were laughing. Glasses were being refilled. She hadn't got a glass. A waiter thrust one into her hand. Frank grabbed it, and she spilt some champagne over her fingers, trying to prise it out of his grasp. More laughter. The first toast. She sipped.

Quite a good champagne. Not too sweet, but not acid. An apple-like taste.

It went to her head. Heavens, when had she last eaten anything?

Another speech. She wondered if she could ease herself out of the chair and edge around the room to the door, see if she could find her handbag there. She was hemmed in. Ten to one the phone would ring in a minute and everyone would look around to see if it were theirs and she'd be so embarrassed.

Another gale of laughter. Louder this time. Someone had made a good joke, then. Was it the bridegroom? She hadn't thought he'd have it in him. Another toast.

Frank tried to grab the glass again. She allowed him one tiny sip. He pulled a face and pushed the glass away. He really needed a good run around, but she was surrounded by people who, judging by their looks in her direction, thought it a poor show to bring such a young child to a wedding reception. She rather agreed with them.

There. Someone's mobile had gone off. Was it hers? What was happening to Diana?

It wasn't hers. A woman removed her mobile from her bag, spoke low down into it, and wriggled her way out of the throng into the hall to continue the conversation. If only Ellie could do the same.

More laughter. Another toast.

Good, no reading out of telegrams or cards or whatever it was they had nowadays. It always took up so much time, and none of the guests would know the people who'd sent them. Or care. The bride and groom disappeared, led away by one of the waiters to another room to change. Still Ellie couldn't move from her chair for people around her. A noted bore from church suddenly realized he was standing right in front of her, and began to give her his opinion of the service, which hymns ought to have been chosen, and which not.

She abstracted her mind while nodding and smiling, she hoped, in the right places. Frank became ever heavier in her arms. It was possible he would go off to sleep if she kept very still.

People were looking at their watches, wondering how soon they could get away, trains to catch, staying overnight, where did I leave the car?

The bride and groom returned to the far end of the room. Ellie couldn't see them from where she sat, but she could tell they were there by everyone's reactions. The room emptied as if the plug had been pulled out, as everyone but Ellie and the waiters and waitresses followed the bride and groom out into the drive at the front of the house. Ellie could hear shouts of 'Throw the bouquet this way!' 'Here, Joyce!'

Frank was drowsy in her arms.

She looked up and saw the lumpy Tracy holding a handbag which she recognized. The bag was open. Tracy had been looking inside. Perhaps had taken money out?

Tracy saw Ellie watching her. 'This yours? I found it under the chair.'

'Thank you,' said Ellie. 'It must have slipped off my shoulder when I was dealing with my grandson.'

Tracy shrugged and turned away, leaving the bag with the flap still undone, on a side table. Ellie watched her go.

One of the waiters approached her. 'Is there a problem, madam?'

'I hope not. I lost my bag. Your waitress picked it up. I just hope nothing's missing.'

'I'm sure not, madam. Let me bring it over for you, and you can check it. Though if it's been lying around for some time, anyone might have picked it up.'

'I realize that.'

He brought the bag over. Frank came fully awake again and wriggled. She let him down onto the floor. Where was his pushchair? There were some toys, attached to that which might keep him occupied for a few minutes. With one eye on the toddler, Ellie checked over the contents of her bag, which looked all right at a quick glance. She flicked open her purse and paused. There should have been some twenty pound notes in there and a fiver. There were no notes there at all.

She held the purse up so that the waiter could see. 'I rather think I'm missing some money.'

He didn't want to know, she could see that. She could also see that making a fuss at a wedding reception — at Joyce's wedding reception — was going to make her unpopular.

'You must be mistaken, madam.'

So that was how it was to be played? She was sure the notes had been there this morning. Now they weren't. Was it worth making a fuss? Possibly not.

She delved into the bottom of her bag for her mobile phone. Why hadn't anyone rung her?

She tipped the bag towards the light. She couldn't find the mobile.

Because — it wasn't there.

The waiter was hovering, looking impatient. They would be wanting to clear up, get away. Rose would be coming back in soon, probably having a little weep. It would upset Rose a lot to have a theft discovered at Joyce's wedding.

Ellie said, 'I'm sorry to make a fuss, but my mobile phone is missing as well. Perhaps you'd better let me speak to whoever's in charge?'

'I'm in charge, madam.' He didn't look old enough, and he didn't look as if he relished the position, either. 'I'm sure you're mistaken. All our staff are vetted. Anyone could have picked up a bag which had been carelessly mislaid. Anyone. Not just my staff.'

'I agree. But you see, I have to think it might be your girl Tracy, because I saw her handling my bag. Will you speak to her, please? I don't mind so much about the money, but I must have my phone back immediately.'

He didn't take his eyes off her, but went to the doorway and called for Tracy. She came, slowly, insolently, hand on hip. Her fair hair had been tied back in a scanty ponytail but wisps were escaping in untidy fashion. Her shoes were scuffed.

'Yes?'

'Madam is missing some money and her mobile phone. She thinks you might have picked them up when you found her bag. Perhaps it was open and the contents tipped out?'

'No.' Tracy's eyes were bright and bold, fixed on Ellie. Her body language said, 'You can't pin this on me.'

Ellie thought, She's ditched the stuff somewhere. Or passed it on to an accomplice. Now where would she have put it, if she had so little time to dispose of it? She let her eyes roam around the part of the room in which the girl had been standing when Ellie saw her with the bag in her hand.

The waiter didn't want any trouble. Also, time was passing and he wanted to get off. 'Perhaps, madam, you left the mobile at home this afternoon, and just thought you had it with you.'

'No,' said Ellie. 'I'm expecting an important phone call. I checked several times this afternoon — after I arrived here — to see that the phone was switched on.' She narrowed her eyes. Tracy had been standing halfway between the door and the corner of the room where there was a big stand of flowers. She'd been standing right in front of a glass-fronted bookcase, but there wouldn't have been time for her to open the doors of the bookcase and stash something inside, would there?

'Accusing me without any evidence,' said Tracy, enjoying herself. 'I'll have the Law on you.'

Ellie grabbed little Frank, who was just about to dive under the table where the cake had been. She spoke to the waiter. 'You see that stand of flowers in the corner by the door? It's supposed to be all white flowers, but I think I can see a bit of blue. My mobile phone has a blue cover. Would you like to look for me?'

The waiter looked and produced Ellie's mobile phone. Plus a small bundle of notes. He looked at Tracy and then he looked at Ellie.

Ellie said, 'You can check the first few numbers on the memory bank in the mobile to see if it's mine. They are for my daughter Diana, son-in-law Stewart, and cousin Roy.'

'Yes, it's yours,' said the waiter. He shot a look at Tracy, who rolled her shoulders at him.

'I expect you carelessly left the bag open and someone picked it up and the things fell out, then they popped them into the flowers for safety. Madam.'

The waiter looked at Ellie. Would she go along with this explanation, false as it sounded, or was she going to make a fuss? 'Do you want me to call the police?'

Ellie shook her head. She'd got her phone back, and there wasn't really enough evidence to take to the police. Tracy did a slow turn and removed herself from the room, her apology for a ponytail bouncing behind her.

The waiter said, 'Our apologies, madam, that you've been so inconvenienced.' He handed over the phone. It had been turned off, so even if someone had tried to contact Ellie, they wouldn't have got through. Frank had crawled under a chair and was going to bump his head when he sat upright. Ellie dived for him and pulled him out, protesting.

Ellie said, 'Tell me, have you ever employed that girl before?'

'Well, no. We were one short today so got her through an agency.'

'Which agency, may I ask?'

'Ladies in Waiting. We often use them, because their people are Silver Service trained.'

'That girl isn't.'

'No. We'd booked her for a function this evening too, but I'll make sure she's not required. Will that be all, madam?'

Ellie bounced Frank on her knee and turned on her phone. There was one message waiting for her.

Stewart; 'Ellie, turn on your phone, for heavens' sake. Diana threw a wobbly and they had to call in the doctor to calm her down. We should all be able to leave shortly.'

Ellie was still gazing at the phone when Rose came in, having a little weep.

'What a lovely wedding, wasn't it? I don't suppose they remembered to thank you for everything that you've done to make it happen, but dear Ellie, I do thank you from the bottom of my heart and I'm sure dear Joyce will when she has recovered from the stresses of the day. Oh dear, my poor feet. I shouldn't have worn these shoes really, they do pinch, but Joyce said I mustn't wear my usual old clodhoppers. Wasn't the garden the most marvellous place to have the reception? And the waitresses and waiters — superb, except for that one, but we won't mention her on this lovely day, will we?'

Frank ran to her and hugged her leg. She loved Frank, and Frank loved her. With a touch of envy, Ellie watched Rose pick up Frank and give him a cuddle, to which he responded with lots of giggles.

Dear Rose. She was just like one of the family.

Rose put little Frank down, smoothing back his hair. 'I suppose I must go and deal with my cousin and his wife, poor things, no chick nor child of their own so they don't realize that children can love their parents without showing it. I wish I could come back to you tonight, Ellie — how is dear Miss Quicke managing? — but I shall have to take them out to supper and after that I'll be so tired I'll just go home to my own little bed, which doesn't seem like my own any more, isn't that odd, but I suppose it's because I've got so used to a bit of peace and quiet and the boy next door — well, I suppose we were all young once . . .'

She drifted away to where her cousin and his wife waited for her, grim-faced.

Then Bill was there, also looking grim-faced. No Stewart and no Diana.

Ellie and Bill took Frank out into the garden to look at the gulls, while the catering staff moved into the drawing room to clear out the traces of the party.

Ellie asked, 'What happened?'

'I don't know what happened before I arrived, but when I did she accepted me as her solicitor without turning a hair. I used the excuse you gave me, that Diana was so upset about the separation from Stewart that she was not perhaps as calm as she looked. Diana picked up the hint and within five minutes she was in floods of tears, following it up with a full-scale temper tantrum.

'I suggested we take a break. The police were nonplussed. They'd picked up somehow that Diana and her aunt were daggers drawn and they wanted to question her about it. Eventually Diana settled in to a good long weep, unable to lift her head and certainly unable to answer their questions. The police suggested she might like to see the doctor, take a sedative. She refused the sedative, said she'd be perfectly all right once she'd had a good rest. So they said they'd send for her again tomorrow. She put on a lovely act, I must say. All noble innocence, wrongly accused.'

'You think her guilty, then?'

'It's not my place to think such things. I don't particularly wish to represent her, but if they call her in again tomorrow and I can't get my partner back in time — which I don't think I can — yes, I'll represent her.'

'Thank you, Bill. It's more than I asked of you.'

'I must say, she gives a lovely performance. It would be a hard-hearted jury who would convict.'

So Bill did believe her guilty.

Ellie sighed. She wished she could be as sure, one way or the other. 'So where is she now?'

'She went with Stewart to get some things she needed from the flat. Stewart has more backbone than I thought. He behaved well. He didn't reproach her, or bother her with questions. Just asked her what she wanted to do. He gave me a message for you, asking why your phone had been turned off, said he'd pick up little Frank as soon as he could. End of story. I'll run you back home, shall I? Can you face the dance tonight?'

Ellie stiffened her back. She could take this. Of course she could. Bill deserved a lollipop for all his trouble. 'Certainly I can. I owe you so much. I have a new dress to wear and I'm going to knock everyone's eyes out.'

'That's my girl.' He gave her an absent-minded hug and a kiss on her cheek.

* * *

Stewart arrived at Ellie's just after Bill had dropped her there. Aunt Drusilla was ensconced in the conservatory with her paperwork and called for Ellie and Stewart to join her.

Ellie explained what had happened and asked Stewart, 'Where is Diana?'

'She wanted me to take her to the flat and then get lost. I asked her what she wanted to do about Frank. She said she was sure you'd look after him for a bit. I said I wanted to keep him with me and she just laughed as if I'd made a joke. Then I asked if she intended to keep the flat for herself, in which case I'd move out. She said the flat was a dump and she wouldn't be spending any more time in it, that I was welcome to it.'

'Is she still very distressed? Bill told me she cried a lot at the police station.'

'No. She was perfectly all right. She can turn it off like a tap, you know.'

Ellie did know. Diana's two-year-old tantrums had lasted until she went to school, causing terrible battles with Ellie, who had tried in vain to teach her daughter that this was not a good way to carry on.

Ellie said, 'I thought she'd grown out of throwing tantrums.'

Stewart grimaced. 'Until she can't get her own way about something. It was a nasty shock when she first threw a wobbly at me on the day she learned she was pregnant. I was thrilled that we were to start a family so soon and we could have managed, easily, if we'd moved to a smaller house. She didn't see it that way. So we compromised; she had the child but we kept on with the big house — much against my better judgement.'

Aunt Drusilla said, 'Do you still love her?'

Stewart shook his head. 'No, but I married her and I'll stick with her, as long as she'll let me.'

Stewart picked little Frank up, gave him a hug, and took him out into the garden.

'You can't help admiring a man who's letting himself in for a life of misery,' said Aunt Drusilla.

Ellie watched Stewart as he ran around the garden with his son, playing hide and seek. Frank loved it. He shrieked and ran, and shrieked again.

Ellie took the opportunity to go upstairs, have a shower and change into her new dress, hoping the neighbours wouldn't complain about the noise Frank was making. He was such a dear little boy and was probably suffering from the tensions between his father and mother.

Ellie managed to get some food on the table — with her largest apron covering her dress. She only needed to feed little Frank and Aunt Drusilla, luckily, as she'd eat at the dinner dance and Stewart had said he wasn't hungry.

'By the way, Ellie, thank you for the introduction to your friend Kate,' said Aunt Drusilla. 'She's given me a lot of useful information about that scoundrel who has been mishandling my affairs. I'll pass it all on to the police on Monday.'

'Giving them something else to think about? Isn't it a bit late for that?' asked Stewart, nursing little Frank on his knee. Neither Ellie nor Aunt Drusilla said anything to that. A heavy silence settled upon them.

Ellie switched on the electric light. The fine spring day was drawing to a close and though the nights were getting lighter, it would be some time before they could eat without artificial light. Stewart looked tired, she thought.

'Did you say you'd got a babysitter coming tonight?' she asked.

Stewart looked at his watch. 'I'd better get going. At first I thought I'd cancel her, but then I thought I might as well go out somewhere tonight, give myself something else to think about.'

He went off, carrying Frank under one arm — much to the little boy's delight — and the pushchair under the other.

'She doesn't realize what she's throwing away,' observed Aunt Drusilla. 'Loyalty like that, when love has gone. It's rare.'

* * *

The man whistled through his teeth as he got through to his favourite number. 'Hi. How'd it go?'

'Don't ask! That cow! I only lifted a few quid from her purse to see me over the weekend, but she caught me at it. I thought for sure she'd

call the police, but she didn't. Probably didn't want to upset dear Rose. Lost me a job this evening, though. I was counting on that. I could spit!'

'Nothing happened about the kettle I fixed, then?'

'Nothing.' Silence. 'There's one thing, though. Dear Rose is going to be back at her flat tonight. If we could just choke her off, mebbe I could get back in with the old woman. What do you think?'

'A pleasure. But how?'

'Been thinking about that. We could bust in — I could get the boys to help — and give her a good fright. Give her a shock or two, to make the point. Tell her to get out or else.'

He started to laugh. 'I got a better idea. How about I feed a cable in from your flat, rig up a gantry with wires going all over the place so whatever she touches will give her a nasty shock? I'll do the front-door knob as well. A coupla hours in a hot-wired flat should do the trick!'

'I like it!'

CHAPTER SIXTEEN

The annual Golf Club Dinner and Dance was one of those functions attended by everyone who was anyone. Ellie thought, Happy days, remembering how she used to go with her husband. Frank didn't play golf — perhaps it would have been better for his health if he had — but he knew many of the members and it had always been a pleasant occasion. Ellie had usually worn a dress from the charity shop, something plain and dark.

She couldn't help feeling a flush of excitement as Bill took her arm and led her into the dark but cosy bar where they were all to meet before going in to dinner. She'd missed this sort of socializing in the months since her husband had died when she'd hardly felt like going out of the house. The Reverend Gilbert Adams and his wife had chivvied her to do this and that, and what with problems in the family and at church, she supposed the time had passed quickly enough.

This was the first time she'd been able to dress up — this time not in a charity-shop dress — and go out with a man.

Not that Bill was thinking of it as a date, of course. It wasn't that. It was being friendly and helping him out on a social occasion. She checked on her appearance in a nearby mirror as Bill fought his way to the bar to get them a drink.

She thought she looked all right. The new hairdo was definitely a success, framing her face but not drawing too much attention to itself. Her dress was of a deep dull rose colour with a draped bodice that showed rather too much cleavage for her taste, though Kate had assured her that it was modesty itself compared to what other people would be wearing.

Most of the other women — and she knew most of them — were wearing black, which made the dark room even darker. She was afraid she stood out amongst them, flaunting that pink. One or two of the women came over to her, saying how delighted they were to see her out and about again. Ellie thought they meant it. Probably.

Bill came back with drinks. He looked down at her and said, 'You could always knock their eyes out, Ellie. I'll be lucky to get one dance with you tonight.'

Ellie blushed and shook her head at him. And then saw Roy. He was with the stick-thin woman — Joyce's cousin — but he was staring at her with an expression that combined shock and indignation.

He bore down on her, leaving his partner isolated. 'Ellie, you said you wouldn't come to—'

'I was blackmailed into it,' said Ellie, trying to forestall a scene. 'Bill here took advantage of me. Who's the lovely girl you've got in tow?'

'Oh. Her? Someone I met at the wedding reception.' The 'girl' in question wasn't going to be left out, and had followed close behind him. 'Helen, this is my sort-of-cousin Ellie Quicke, and this is Bill Weatherspoon, our local solicitor.'

'Delighted,' said Helen, assessing the cost of Ellie's dress and Bill's air of solid respectability. 'I'm in marketing. Do you work, or are you retired? Didn't I see you at the wedding reception today?'

'It was Bill's house and garden they used,' said Ellie, determined to be affable, while noting that Helen's outfit — black with sequins — was showing far more cleavage than was wise.

What if Helen shrugged, and the straps fell off her shoulders? She hadn't enough flesh on her bones to flaunt a cleavage like that. In fact, there really wasn't much cleavage to shout about.

Ellie permitted herself a tiny smile, a smug smile. In a moment of self-knowledge she realized that she was not — as she had thought — completely dead to the impression she aroused in the opposite sex. The admiration she was seeing in Bill's and Roy's faces was getting through to her. Perhaps Aunt Drusilla's revelations about Frank had had something to do with it? Perhaps this moment was just a natural step forward out of grief? Perhaps she would sink back into feelings of worthlessness again tomorrow.

For the moment, she was a woman enjoying the attention of two good-looking men. Wow! Mark that one up, Ellie Quicke!

The smile vanished as she thought she saw a familiar face across the room. No, surely she must be mistaken. Diana couldn't have come here, after having been wrung out by the police this afternoon?

'My dear lady.' An unctuous voice, a moist hand pressing hers. Archie, the church treasurer, wearing a cummerbund too tight under his evening dress, and his blonde bimbo with her talons firmly on his arm. 'Splendid to see you. How we've missed your lovely smile at these little functions.'

His bimbo was also wearing black, and she was comparing it with Helen's black-with-sequins and Ellie's dark pink. Bimbo looked sour. Bimbo obviously hadn't paid very much for her dress, and her lipstick definitely did not match her nail varnish.

There was a general movement through to the big lounge, now set up with round tables squeezed into every available corner. There were floating balloons above the tables, pretty favours for women and men, flowers and shining silver and glass. Waiter service, of course.

Ellie scanned the crowds as Bill led her to their table. She must have been mistaken in thinking Diana was here. How could she possibly be?

Their table seated other old friends and acquaintances, men and women she'd once known very well but had withdrawn from in the months of Frank's illness and her early widowhood. It was pleasant to meet up with them again. After a moment or two she could remember most of their names and almost all the names of their children and what they were doing. The noise level in the room was high. Wine was poured. The first course was served.

Some of the waiters and waitresses were the same as those who had served at the wedding reception. Tracy was not among them. A group of latecomers were crowding in.

Stewart among them.

Ellie clutched her wine glass and asked for a drink of water, please. Yes, it was definitely Stewart. He'd told her he'd got tickets, of course, but she hadn't thought he'd want to come.

He was with . . . a waiter moved away and she saw that he was with Maria from the cleaning company. Of course.

Bill asked if she were feeling all right, so she nodded and smiled and asked him if the waiters had left his house and garden spick and span.

Maria was wearing a cool sheath in dove grey. With her superb carriage she looked statuesque, serene. Not beautiful, exactly. But handsome. And in some indefinable way, she gave the impression of having integrity. She was nearly as tall as Stewart and together they made a handsome pair.

Ellie closed her eyes for a moment, and prayed. What ought I to do about this, Lord? If anything? It's all going pear-shaped. I thought Stewart would stick with Diana, no matter what. He said he would. But Diana has made it quite clear that she wants nothing more to do with him and, dear Lord, what a mess!

Bill nudged her arm. 'Who's that stunning woman with your son-in-law? I'm sure I've seen her before somewhere. Or is that a tactless question and ought we not to have noticed him being here without Diana?'

'To be quite truthful, Bill, I'm not sure what to think. She's Maria something, and runs the Trulyclean Services in the Avenue. They're one of the few contractors that my aunt approves of, and that's how they met. Stewart's been using another firm, but wants to return to Trulyclean. I think he's right. They have an excellent reputation.'

'I notice you've talked your way all around my question,' said Bill.

'Yes, I did, didn't I? Well, the answer is that I don't know. Diana left Stewart and as far as I know she moved in with someone else. She only went back to the flat she shared with Stewart to collect some clothes. He's feeling very disillusioned about his marriage but he did say he'd stand by Diana. He's had the tickets for this evening for some time, had already arranged a babysitter, said he might as well take advantage of having a babysitter to go out for the evening. He didn't mention Maria. That was at five o'clock this afternoon. What's happened since . . .' She shrugged.

'Diana's here with Derek Jolley, I see.'

'What?' Ellie nearly upset her glass of wine. 'How could she! I mean, I thought I caught a glimpse of her but I told myself I must be mistaken.'

'Larger than life. In the far corner.'

Ellie craned her neck but couldn't see Diana for all the people in the way. The woman on Bill's other side demanded his attention. Was she a parent-governor at the local school? Husband a magistrate? Ellie was drawn into a discussion about a project for a tram down the Avenue which was being mooted by the council.

She ate. She drank. She smiled, and listened and put in the occasional word to keep the conversations around her going. She sat on her anxieties.

After supper everyone drifted back to the bar while the centre of the room was cleared for dancing, and at long last Ellie caught sight of her daughter. With Derek Jolley, as Bill had said.

What could she do about it? Nothing.

Ellie thought Diana's behaviour tasteless. If she had done something like this as a girl, she'd have been cold-shouldered by everyone she knew. Friends would have remonstrated. Parents would have thundered.

As it was, nobody did anything. Stewart and Maria kept to one side of the room, smiling, talking softly to one another or to others around them. Never calling attention to themselves. Moving among friends and acquaintances with their heads held high but without making a fuss.

Diana was noisy, possibly half seas over? Derek's face was red, his hands all over her. She was wearing a black sheath with a glittering choker around her neck. She'd removed her wedding ring. She was shameless.

Or so thought Ellie, checking to see if any of the people on her table were raising their eyebrows at Diana's behaviour.

She felt ashamed for all four of them, though less so for Stewart and Maria, who had the quiet, slightly dazed air of those to whom a revelation of future happiness has been given. When they turned their heads to one another, their eyes searched each other's faces. But their manners were good and when they spoke to others, they did so with good humour. They danced with other members of the party they were with, older people, possibly Maria's relatives? A tall, well-built man with a dark complexion and a heavy moustache. A woman of Ellie's age, quietly but expensively dressed.

Bill said, 'I've placed her now. Her father's a councillor, her mother does a lot of voluntary work at the hospital. Maria doesn't usually come to these affairs. I don't think I've seen her for years, which is why I didn't recognize her at once. There was some gossip about her . . . a long-lasting live-in affair with a man who couldn't make up his mind whether he was coming or going? I imagine that's over now.'

'Marrying someone on the rebound is not a good idea,' said Ellie, while observing that Stewart was dancing with Maria's mother.

Diana had got hold of a bottle of champagne and was spraying it over Derek and everyone else in the vicinity. She laughed too much, threw her arms carelessly around Derek's neck. Hugged him. Refrained from noticing her husband taking Maria on to the dance floor.

'Shall we?' Bill touched Ellie's elbow.

She left her drink untouched and followed his lead. She sighed, relaxed, and confessed that it was a long time since she'd danced a foxtrot. Mentally she said sorry to Frank, who'd been a poor dancer. She'd forgotten that Bill was so good at it.

'Enjoying yourself in spite of everything?' he asked.

'To my surprise, yes.'

'You are not responsible for the rest of your family.'

'Am I not?'

'I know your tender conscience would have you face the firing squad for them, but not tonight, eh?'

'The firing squad doesn't appear to have brought any bullets with them,' said Ellie, noticing that though people drew back from the vicinity of Diana and Derek, the couple were not being ostracized. Stewart and Maria were dancing decorously together, absorbed in one another.

Bill said, 'How would it be if I took my fee for looking after Diana not in money, but in some more hours of your company?'

Ellie giggled. 'Are you trying to flirt with me? Shame on you!'

'You should say, "Fie on you!"'

'I would if I had a fan and knew how to use it. I would rap you on the knuckles and say, "Oh, Sir!"'

He laughed. 'You *are* flirting with me, Ellie.'

'Am I? Is that how it's done? I'm a bit out of practice, I'm afraid.'

Frank had never liked her to talk like that. She liked doing it, though. It made Bill smile and look happier than he'd done for ages. She liked that, too. And then the strangest thought popped into her mind, that Mrs Weatherspoon was not the most ridiculous name in the world and that if she ever had to leave her cosy little house, his house on the river was rather beautiful and could be made to feel like home with a congenial man at her side.

She'd never thought anything like that before. She hadn't thought it in connection with Roy, or with Archie.

She felt bewildered. What was happening to her? Was it just the new dress and hairdo, the lights and the music? The feeling that Bill really enjoyed her company, really liked *her* as opposed to wanting something from her?

There came another treacherous thought; had Frank ever really *liked* her as opposed to loving and wanting her?

Roy appeared at Bill's shoulder. 'My dance, I think.'

Ellie floated away with Roy, only to discover that he wasn't quite as good a dancer as Bill. But she managed to enjoy that dance, too. Perhaps she was just coming out of the depression she'd experienced after Frank's death.

Then she danced with Archie, with the bimbo standing at the side, waiting for him to return to her. And then, surprisingly, with Stewart.

'I expect you think I've taken leave of my senses,' he said, leading her into a sedate waltz. 'But there was a message from Maria on the answerphone when I got back. Her father's on the committee here and had asked her to come, but her partner had let her down. She knew — I think I'd told her, or you had, or somehow the news had got around — that Diana had given up on me. She wondered if I could help her out, if she provided a babysitter.'

Ellie gave a little sigh. So that was how it was done? With style and grace. You saw the man you wanted, you gave him an excuse to come after you and . . . snap. You caught the little fish. Maria was a clever woman.

Stewart was looking worried. 'You've been so kind to me, Ellie. If you think this is wrong . . . ?'

'I understand how it is, Stewart. Diana is under tremendous pressure at the moment and so are you. I'm very fond of you.'

The music finished, and they walked to the side. He looked across the room, and his face lightened. Ellie followed his glance, and saw Maria glance up from her conversation with the older woman and meet his eyes. Just for a second.

Ellie felt a little tired. That tiny glance across a crowded room had said it all. This was no wild romance, but an instant understanding that the pair of them would find it easy to move through life together. There would be no great highs, but no great lows, either.

There was a wild shriek from the bar end. Ellie saw Diana race around the room, closely followed by Derek Jolley. Both were drunk.

Stewart turned his face away. 'I know I promised I'd stand by Diana, but she doesn't want me anymore. She isn't the girl I married.'

'That's a typical modern excuse, saying that he or she isn't what I expected when I married. I can't advise you, but I can whisper one word: be discreet. You won't want to lose your son. Maria will wait for you, if that is what you want.'

Bill appeared at her side. 'They're going to have a change of band — some heavy metal, I shouldn't wonder. We've all had a long day. Would you like me to take you home now?'

'Dear Bill, your timing is impeccable.'

As he guided her back to the cloakroom, they came face to face with a flushed Diana, being crowded against a wall by a red-faced Derek Jolley. Ellie said, 'Goodnight, Diana.'

Incredibly, Diana turned her back on Ellie.

Bill put his arm around Ellie's shoulders and gave her a little push towards the cloakroom. When she'd retrieved her coat, he put her in his car and turned on the heater. The night was clear of cloud, and cold.

He said, 'Will she listen if you try to warn her?'

'You saw.'

'That's tonight. That's the wine speaking and excitement, and consciousness of danger. In the morning it may be a different story.'

'She's living with that man.'

'A highly respectable businessman with a tidy fortune stashed away.'

'A nasty little man. He reminds me of a satyr, half goat and half man.'

'In the morning . . .' he paused to change gear, thinking. 'People drop me hints, you know. Friends. People I meet socially, at work. Someone told me Diana's being watched.'

'By the police?'

He drew up at her gate. 'I can only do so much, Ellie. If she wants to commit suicide, I can't prevent her from doing so. Tell her to keep her mouth shut from now on. No hysterics. No tears. Just "no comment". I've given her my business card and put my home number on it.'

'You think she's guilty.'

Silence. 'I think she's capable of losing her temper and acting rashly. If I were the police, I'd be obtaining records of mobile-phone calls, looking at diaries and worksheets. If they do find she's had much to do with a jobbing electrician, say . . .'

'Of course she has, all the time. It's her work.'

'Yes. But there was a rumour going around some time ago . . . it's probably nothing. A client who was signing a lease for one of the riverside flats told me . . . well, it's easy to be wrong about such things. Call me if you need me.'

* * *

Ellie did not sleep well and woke to the scent of newly ground coffee. She prised open her eyelids to look at the clock. Nearly nine o'clock. *What?* It couldn't be that late, surely. Why, she was usually out of bed every morning by seven. And who was brewing coffee?

Rose was staying over at her own flat. Aunt Drusilla wouldn't descend from her bedroom till she'd had her breakfast in bed. So who could it be?

Ellie hurried through her toilet and almost ran down the stairs. The scent of coffee grew stronger. Someone had been making toast, too.

There wasn't anyone in the kitchen, but Diana was sitting cross-legged on the settee in the living room. Diana didn't even look heavy-eyed, particularly. She was wearing a low-necked black T-shirt over tailored black trousers. Her hair was brushed and shiny, she had made up her eyes, and she was still wearing the sparkling choker from last night.

On the coffee table in front of her was a cafetière of coffee, mugs, toast and butter. And orange juice. Ellie helped herself to orange juice, and Diana poured her out a mug of coffee.

Ellie thought of asking, To what do I owe the pleasure? But waited for Diana to declare herself.

Diana glanced at her watch. 'Let's get down to business. I don't think they'll track me down here yet.'

Ellie took a deep breath. '"They" being the police? Have you got Bill's number with you?'

'Yes, but it won't do any good. I didn't do it, and what's more I didn't ask or even hint that anyone I know should fix that wiring. It would never have occurred to me. But I realize I did have a motive and I could also have had means and opportunity if I'd used an accomplice. They'll say I did it, because of Ahmed. They've tracked him down, you see. He left a message on my answerphone last night to say they'd been around his place asking for him, so he's gone missing. Easy enough for him. He's got relatives in every major city in Britain. A change of name, he'll get by.'

Ellie put her hand to her throat. 'Who's Ahmed?'

'Oh, just someone I was shagging before Stewart joined me down here in London. I never thought the police would check up on my phone bills. It's not something that occurs to you when you're having good sex, is it?'

Ellie let the implications of this roll around her brain. Diana had been having an affair with someone else before she took up with Derek Jolley. How long had it been going on? Where had they met and done it?

'Did Stewart know?'

Diana shrugged. 'I got bored with Stewart a long time ago. Ahmed's not the only one I've been with, here or up north, but they'll jump on him because he's an electrician. Oh, don't look so shocked. You Oldies haven't a clue about what a modern woman needs. I don't suppose you've ever had an orgasm in your life.'

Ellie swallowed all manner of retorts to this. Was Diana trying to wind her up, or did she truly believe that her mother's generation knew nothing about sex? Ellie gave a passing thought to the good times she'd had with Frank in bed before he became so ill, and pushed them out of her mind. This was not the time to argue about who had and who hadn't had orgasms and with which partner. She said, 'You met him through work?'

Diana smiled. 'I jumped straight into bed with him. Or not bed, come to think of it. We usually did it on the floor wherever he happened to be working. His wife's still back in Pakistan or wherever it is that he comes from, and I was bored out of my skull with Stewart's milk-and-water love-making. I'd tried one or two others but they didn't hit my button, as they say. Ahmed showed me what I was missing: excitement, passion . . . fulfilment of myself as a person. I'll always be grateful to him.'

'What of your husband?'

Diana shrugged. 'Oh, he'll divorce me, no doubt. The sooner the better, as far as I'm concerned.'

'And Derek Jolley?'

Diana's finger explored the curve of her lips. She smiled. 'Derek and I understand one another. He's another one who understands what a real woman wants. He's said he'll wait for me, and perhaps he will. I don't think they can get me for anything but conspiracy and if they fail to find Ahmed, they won't even be able to do that. I shouldn't be held up too long. At least, that's what I'm telling myself.'

'But Diana . . .'

'Don't bleat, mother. Accept it. Your little daughter is all grown up now and knows what she wants out of life. You asked me what I wanted out of life, didn't you? Well, now I know. I want a man who can match me in every way, in business and in bed. And that's Derek.'

'He's old enough to be your father.'

'I need someone older, someone who knows what's what.'

'He makes my skin creep.'

'Mine, too. But for a different reason.' Here Diana smiled again.

There was a thump from overhead. Aunt Drusilla was signalling that she required her breakfast in bed. Ellie looked at the clock, and realized that at this very moment she ought to be getting ready to go to church for the installation of their new vicar . . . the bishop was coming . . . and piles of dignitaries and practically everyone in the parish, and she ought to be there right now, struggling into her choir gown and sorting out the music for the service.

Bother the service. This was more important.

But Aunt Drusilla? She half rose from her seat. 'How long do you think we have?'

Diana made a dismissive movement with her hands. 'Oh, go along. Attend to the old moneybags first, by all means. We all know I come last in your life.'

'What? Diana, that's not true!'

'Oh yes, it is. You've always put your *principles*,' and here she pulled a disgusted face, 'and your husband before me. I'm used to it. Go and see to the old dear and if the police don't pick me up before you get back, we'll continue our conversation then.'

'Diana, I do love you and worry about you endlessly.'

'Then you'd do just one thing for me.'

Ellie was not to be caught so easily. 'What is it you want?'

'I'll tell you when you come back.'

CHAPTER SEVENTEEN

Ellie called up to Aunt Drusilla that she wouldn't be a minute, prepared a light breakfast and took it up on a tray. Aunt Drusilla was not in her bedroom at the back of the house but standing in the little bedroom looking out on to the road, looking out on to the road where Diana's car was in full view.

'Hasn't the silly girl even got the sense to hide her car? Are we to expect the police?'

'She thinks so, at any rate. She thinks they're about to arrest her because she knew an electrician rather too well. She wants to ask me to do something for her, but I don't know what.'

'To take care of her business affairs, I imagine. Maybe to look after little Frank.'

'She says she didn't do it. That it hadn't even occurred to her. I think I believe her, but I can see why the police would think she did it.'

'Hm. She must have brought that ground coffee in with her, because I know you haven't any. Tell her to make me some proper coffee if she's got time.'

Aunt Drusilla returned to the back bedroom and indicated that Ellie place the breakfast tray on her knees. 'Ellie, don't tell her this, but I'm prepared to go halves with you to fund her defence.'

So Aunt Drusilla did definitely think Diana was guilty. And Ellie didn't? She didn't know what to think.

Diana was standing by the window looking at her car when Ellie got back. 'I could have left the car somewhere else, but then you'd have to search all over the place for it. The keys are on the table there. I've left a whole lot of my stuff at Derek's, but he said he'd see they were collected up and brought here. I've packed a suitcase of things I'll need to begin with and I suppose you'll see to it that I get the little extras I'll be allowed. I believe you can wear your own clothes when you're on remand and I don't suppose for a minute that I'll get bail.'

'Suppose I ring Bill now . . .'

'No. I need to ask you something first.'

'To look after your business interests?'

'Derek will do that.'

Ellie blinked. 'Some people might say that he wasn't the ideal person to trust in a business relationship.'

'I trust him. He knows what I'd do to him if he played me false.' She smiled, and bit down on her lower lip, still smiling. 'I told you, we're two of a kind. I want you to promise me something else.'

'Not without knowing what it is.'

'Don't you trust me?'

'No, I don't think I do.'

'Which only goes to show how little you love me.'

'I love you, but perhaps you've taught me not to trust you.'

Diana shot her mother a keen glance. She frowned. 'Well, it's quite simple. I don't want that cow Maria taking little Frank. It's going to be hard enough for him as it is, with his mother accused of murder.'

Ellie leaned back in her chair. 'So you knew about Maria?'

'From the first moment she laid eyes on Stewart at that party, I could see she wanted him and intended to have him. He couldn't see it. Probably still doesn't. It takes one to know one.'

Ellie wondered if Diana's objection to Maria was because she was mixed race, or whether she was just being a dog in the manger. 'She seems a nice girl and you've said yourself that you want Stewart to divorce you.'

'But you don't approve of divorce, Mother dear, do you? So you'll work your socks off to keep Stewart and little Frank away from her. Right?'

'You don't want him, but you don't want him to be happy with another woman?'

'You think that sounds harsh? It's nothing to do with colour, either. Do you really think little Frank will thrive if Stewart and Maria start producing their own family?'

'Do you think that he would be happy as the stepson of Derek Jolley? What makes you think Derek wants Frank? I got the impression that he didn't.'

'Oh, Derek and I are not talking about marriage. We're just enjoying ourselves.'

'Where does that leave your son? At least Stewart loves him dearly.'

'Stewart is not to have little Frank. And that's flat.'

Ellie didn't like this conversation at all. 'If you refuse to let Stewart have his own son, then there's nothing to stop him having more children by Maria.'

'No, but I'm betting he'll feel responsible for Frank when I'm in jail and that if you refuse to have anything to do with Maria, he'll go along with that. I want to make you Frank's guardian and to have him live with you.'

'In spite of my old-fashioned ways and beliefs? What would Stewart have to say to that? Quite rightly, he'd get the courts to let him have Frank.'

'Not if you fight it.'

Ellie realized this was crunch time. She didn't like refusing Diana, but it had to be done. 'I wouldn't fight it. He's a good father and Frank adores him.'

Diana clenched her fists. 'So you won't do this one little thing for me? The only thing I've ever asked you to do? Not even to save your grandson from misery?'

‘Don’t twist things so, Diana. When we began this conversation I wasn’t sure what I felt about you and Stewart divorcing. I know what the Bible says, which is that marriage is for life. I still believe that marriage is for life but I can see that you don’t. Stewart told me he wanted to stand by you . . .’

‘Pfui! As if I’d want him. The sooner I’m rid of him the better.’

‘You were happy enough to marry him.’

‘I didn’t know what I was doing. I was too young.’

‘Nonsense. You saw a decent man who promised to love and honour you in sickness and in health . . .’

Diana covered her ears. ‘Oh, stuff that! Will you take little Frank in, and bring him up for me? You can even take him to church if you must, and teach him all that stupid nonsense about God.’

‘I won’t take Frank away from his father, and you should be ashamed of yourself for suggesting it.’

‘Not even when it’s for the best for him?’

‘You didn’t approve of the way I brought you up. So why inflict that on your son? No, Diana. I will not. I will do my best to help Stewart to bring him up, but I will not try to separate him from his father.’

‘You’ve never loved me!’

‘Oh yes, I’ve loved you,’ said Ellie. ‘And agonized over you. As did your father. And as Stewart is doing now. Even your great-aunt loves you in her own way. But you never give anything back, do you? You don’t love anyone but yourself. You don’t love Derek Jolley, although he might think you do. You didn’t love this Ahmed, who’s had to run for his life because of you. You know what, Diana? I’m tired of this one-way love. I shan’t stop loving you and worrying about you and praying for you . . .’

‘Oh, pullease! You’ll have me in tears next.’

‘If they were real tears, I’d be happy to see them. But tears of rage don’t do anything to me. Now I think you’d better be going. I can see a police car drawn up outside.’

‘They’ll hang me out to dry!’

'Nonsense, they don't hang people any more. I'll ring Bill and ask him to follow you down to the police station.'

'You're so hard. You're not like a mother at all.'

'I've been well taught.'

The front-door bell rang. Diana showed the first sign of panic. 'Mother, I didn't do it, I swear I didn't.'

'I believe you,' said Ellie. Perhaps for the first time, she really did believe her.

'Kiss little Frank goodbye for me.'

'Yes.'

Ellie stood up, and so did Diana. They looked at one another for a long moment. In that moment Ellie learned to appreciate Diana's strength. She wondered what Diana saw as she looked at her mother. Someone on whom she could rely, perhaps? Ellie held out her arms, hoping that Diana would give her a hug. Diana kept her own arms at her side. Ellie kissed her daughter's cheek. 'Would you like me to come with you?'

'No. I'll do this by myself.' Diana picked up her handbag and a suitcase and went to the front door. There was a mumbled conversation and Diana walked up the path to the police car between DS Willis and the Dearie constable. Ellie watched as Diana was steered into the back of the car, the others got in, and the car drove off.

Ellie reached for the phone and rang Bill.

* * *

The church service must be in full swing by now, and her name would be mud with the choir members. Tough.

Ellie made some proper coffee from the bag that Diana had brought with her, and took it up to Aunt Drusilla.

Aunt Drusilla sipped. 'I ought to have told the police yesterday about that crooked financial adviser. It might have helped.'

'No. They traced her phone calls. She's been having an affair with an electrician, so the police can make out he was her accomplice. He's scarpered. She knows how bad it looks. I've rung Bill and he'll go straight down there.'

Aunt Drusilla sipped her coffee, and refrained from comment.

Where was dear Rose? Recovering from the excesses of the previous night, when she'd had to look after that sour-faced cousin and his wife? No doubt she'd bob up again soon.

Ellie went downstairs and phoned Stewart. He was at home. Ellie could hear little Frank talking to himself in the background as he played with his toys.

'Stewart, dear. Nice to see you enjoying yourself last night.'

'Yes, it was good, wasn't it. We're going to take little Frank to Kew Gardens this morning, feed the ducks, that sort of thing.'

'"We" meaning Maria?'

'Yes.' No excuses, no comment.

Ellie thought, What did I expect? She said, 'Diana was here this morning, very concerned about little Frank. I said you were an excellent father.'

'I hope so.'

'The police caught up with her and took her down to the station. I phoned Bill and he'll look after her as best he can. The thing is, the police knew she had a motive, and now they can tie her up to an electrician, whom she met in the course of her work.'

'Ah.'

Ellie was surprised. 'You knew about him?'

'I knew there was some workman or other. She didn't make a great secret of the fact that she'd found someone who could give her satisfaction. Apparently I can't. There was more than one man, you know. And now, Derek Jolley. I'm sorry, Ellie. I know you believe that marriage is for life but Diana has smashed all that. If she wants to be free, then so be it, but I'll keep Frank.'

Ellie felt she could understand his position exactly. She didn't agree with it in her head, but she did agree with it in her heart. He'd said he'd stand by Diana, but that was before Diana's latest perfidy . . . and before he'd had more contact with Maria. He wasn't going to wait for Diana at the police station this time.

She said, 'I can't blame you, Stewart. She's my daughter and I love her, but I can't blame you. I don't know what the future holds. She says she didn't do it, that it would never have occurred to her to do it, and I think I believe her.'

'I don't. She's capable of it, you know.'

Ellie sighed. 'Well . . . she asked me to kiss little Frank for her. I'm happy to help out with looking after him, but you know that.'

'Yes, I do. Thanks, Ellie. Must go. Maria's just arrived.'

He put the phone down.

Ellie phoned Rose to see how she was. The line was dead. Perhaps she'd misdialled. She tried again. Still no ringing tone. She'd try again later.

Lunch was a strained affair. Aunt Drusilla came downstairs, but immersed herself in the Sunday papers. There was no conversation.

It wasn't raining exactly, but there was a fine cold drizzle which made it a miserable job to do any gardening. Ellie pottered about her conservatory — what was it that was eating her geraniums? She felt rather tired after the dance the night before, and had a little nap.

Roy came round at tea time. Very subdued. He sat with his mother for a while, though neither seemed inclined to talk. He asked Ellie if she'd enjoyed the dance. She said she had and that it was good to catch up with old friends every now and again.

She asked him if he'd enjoyed himself and he said he had. He said that Helen was a delightful woman whose company he'd enjoyed, and it was a pity she lived so far away, up in the West Midlands somewhere, and yes, she'd already gone back up there.

They didn't speak about Stewart or about Diana.

In fact, they were rather formal with one another.

Ellie phoned Bill's house. No reply.

They were all suspended in time, waiting.

At four o'clock Bill telephoned. Diana had been charged with the manslaughter of Mo Tucker. Bail had been refused.

Worse still, Bill told Ellie that manslaughter carried a wide sentencing range, and could be more than life.

* * *

The news that Diana had been charged released them from the house. Aunt Drusilla said she'd like to take a walk to look at progress on the housing development she'd gone into with Roy. It was just across the Green and if Roy took her arm, she'd quite fancy it.

The sun came out, rather inefficiently trying to dry the ground. Aunt Drusilla set off with Roy. Ellie put on her long winter coat and wandered over to the church. That morning the place had been thronged, but now it was deserted. Everyone had long since gone home; the bishop, the dignitaries, the worthies of the parish. The church would probably be all locked up.

Ellie wondered if it would help if she went in and prayed quietly, all by herself. She tried the vestry door, but it was locked. As it should be.

'I've got a key, if you want a quiet time in the church.'

Tum-Tum was sitting in a sheltered nook, on a wooden seat near the main entrance. He was eating a banana and looked relaxed. He radiated serenity.

Ellie said, 'Oh. I didn't see you. I'm sorry I missed the service. Family problems. Was it good?' She thought, That was a silly thing to say.

'Terrifying,' said Tum-Tum, patting the seat beside him. 'Have a banana? They're only small.' He produced a couple more from his pocket. 'Give you strength. Someone said the pundits on the Antiques Road Show always eat a banana to recoup their strength at the end of the day.'

Ellie accepted the banana, then stared at it as if she didn't know what to do with it.

'First you peel it,' said Tum-Tum. 'And then you eat it.'

'I'm sorry. I'm a bit distracted today. Oh, you won't remember, but my name's—'

'Ellie Quicke, widow of this parish. Yes, Gilbert told me to look out for you.'

'I must apologize again for missing the service . . .'

'Yes,' he said, cheerfully. 'I gather your name's mud around here. There's nothing like a parish get-together to spread gossip.'

'Oh dear. They'll be telling you that I have too much money and ought to have handed it all over to the church, that I encourage men to hang around me, that I take in stray dogs and paedophiles and that I left the church hall in a mess the other night.'

'That's about it, except I didn't pick up the bit about the stray dogs. Gilbert told me you had a daughter from hell, an unusual capacity to see the bigger picture, and that I was to go to you if I were in trouble at any time.' He smiled at her, clasping his hands over his capacious stomach. 'So tell me all about it.'

'What? I mean . . . you won't want to hear . . .'

'Have I got anything better to do?' He started twiddling his thumbs, which made her smile.

'Very well, then. My daughter's just been arrested for manslaughter. They'll allege that she tried to murder her great-aunt for a possible inheritance — or got someone else to do it. Only, she killed a cleaner instead. That's what they'll say.'

'And did she do it?' He was as inquisitive as a robin.

'She's capable of doing almost anything when she's in a temper, and she did believe that my aunt would leave her a substantial fortune. As to whether she did it or not, she says she didn't, that it had never occurred to her.'

'And you believe her?'

Ellie winced. 'I was so afraid Diana had done it that I haven't been able to think straight since it happened. The same with everyone else in the family. But now, yes, I do believe her. First because she said she didn't, and second because she wouldn't get someone else to do something she wasn't prepared to do herself. If she'd picked up a heavy object and hit someone in the middle of an argument . . . yes, I can see her doing that. But this was a devious sort of crime so . . . no, I don't think she did it.'

'I love detective stories. Read 'em all the time. So who are the other suspects?'

'I've been over and over in my mind, thinking about the other people who stood to gain by my aunt's death and I can't believe any of them would do it. Oh, there are lots of people whom she'd irritated. She has high standards and she sacked workmen, builders, cleaners . . . you name it, she's fired them. But is that enough motive to want to kill someone . . . and in such a complicated way? I can see why the police think they've got the right person. I don't know what to do about it.'

'You could do nothing . . .'

'Not an option,' said Ellie, suddenly disliking him.

'There's always one option open to us. So as I said at the beginning, would you like to borrow the key to the church?'

'Thank you, Tum-Tum . . . I mean . . . oh dear, I didn't mean to say that.'

He laughed. 'Now I know I can cope. Starting a new job is always a frightening experience, however much you realize it's what God wants. I've been out of parish work for some years, you see. Been teaching at a theological college. Tried and failed to write a book, went a bit haywire, Bishop said I needed a different sort of challenge. So here I am in a new parish, dumped down in the middle of a lot of strangers, with only my bananas and my detective novels to keep me company, and you greet me by my pet name. Thank you, Ellie. Here's the key. Drop it through the letter box at the vicarage when you're through. I've got to come back later for Evensong. I'll pray for you, of course.'

'Surely you don't want people here to use your nick-name, do you?'

'Why not? It keeps me humbly aware that I can't do this in my own strength, but must always rely on Him.'

Ellie gaped. He was telling her she'd been relying on her own strength, instead of God's. Quite true. Though he'd probably be called by his nickname behind his back, she didn't think, somehow, that anyone was going to take advantage of him. He might have twinkling bright eyes and a rotund figure, but he also had an impressive dignity of his own.

She took the key. 'Thank you.'

He nodded and set off down the path to the vicarage, only to turn and shout back at her, 'Think outside the box, right?'

* * *

Whatever did he mean by that?

The church was still warm from the morning's service, the flowers still splendid — most of them had been left where they were after the wedding yesterday. Was it only yesterday that she'd stood in the choir pew and watched Joyce walking down the aisle? So much had happened since.

She didn't sit in a choir pew, but took a seat near the back of the church by a pillar. She'd sat in that pew, or thereabouts, all the years she'd been coming to the church, before Gilbert had pushed her into the choir as a diversion after she'd been widowed. Dear Gilbert . . . but he'd been right about his friend. Tum-Tum would do them proud.

She wanted to pray, but her thoughts simply would not obey her. 'Dear Lord, I can't think straight' didn't seem an acceptable sort of prayer. Nor, 'Here's a pretty mess', which might be an accurate quote from one of W. S. Gilbert's better comic operas, but didn't have quite the gravity the situation deserved.

'Think outside the box.'

Whatever did he mean by that? Something very clever, no doubt. She wasn't clever. She'd never understood the first thing about stocks and shares or philosophy or algebra, come to think of it.

'You know people.' Well, yes. She did think she knew a bit about people. Usually. Only, they would go and do unexpected things, like . . .

She couldn't think of a good example for the moment.

Like Rose leaving the phone off the hook, which she never did, normally.

Or Diana taking up with Derek Jolley.

Ellie wondered whether she had ever known her difficult daughter. In fact, could you ever really know anyone, ever? Not really, not deep down.

She sighed. Here she was sitting in church, trying to pray and not getting anywhere. She supposed Jesus must be used to that. People coming in, looking for answers and then all they could think of was whether they'd turned the gas down under the roast.

She could hear that it had started to rain again outside. She hadn't an umbrella, so she'd just sit there till the rain stopped. If it did. And think about nothing at all, if she could manage that.

Diana . . . no.

Think outside the box. She'd heard someone else talk about that, perhaps on the radio? It meant . . . widening the scope? Thinking laterally? Extending your lines of thought beyond the immediate vicinity? Something like that.

She hadn't a clue how to do it.

She leaned her shoulder against the pillar and let herself relax. It was quiet in here. At home Aunt Drusilla and Roy would be expecting her to provide them with supper. But not just yet.

Thinking laterally. Thinking about all the people involved . . .

She sat upright. 'I should be praying . . .'

Then relaxed. What was the use? If Jesus were here, he knew all about it and would forgive her wandering mind.

Which kept homing in on one particular face and figure for some unknown reason. It had popped up everywhere this week. Stupid name, Tracy.

All right, turn everything around. Stand it on its head.

Begin at the beginning. Mo Tucker had turned on Aunt Drusilla's television set, and got a shock which — because she'd a bad heart — had killed her. An accidental death. You couldn't get away from the fact that it was an accident.

It was the starting point. A known and accepted fact.

All right, try standing that on its head.

It wasn't an accident. It had been meant. If Aunt Drusilla had turned the television on as usual, she would have had a bad shock but she would have survived. Except of course that Aunt Drusilla hadn't been using that television set since Rose moved in.

And where did Tracy fit into this? Nowhere. Forget Tracy.

All right. Who would know that Aunt Drusilla wasn't using that television set? No one. How could they?

So it really was meant for her and to think otherwise was ridiculous. Consider the scenario as our would-be murderer knows it. Aunt Drusilla goes up to bed. Rose goes up with her to see that Aunt Drusilla had everything she needed for the night. Whoever had fixed the electrics would imagine that Aunt Drusilla would then turn on the television and . . .

No, she wouldn't. Of course she wouldn't. She'd tell Rose to turn it on. Rose would then reach out to adjust the aerial and . . . bingo, get a nasty shock.

Why would anyone want to give Rose a bad shock?

(And why hadn't Rose answered her phone?)

Tracy?

No, don't be stupid. What's Tracy got to do with anything?

Except that she wrote to Aunt Drusilla offering to work for her. Silly girl.

No, it was all too thin. It didn't make sense.

Think outside the box. Ellie drew a box in her mind, and in it she put little doll figures labelled Aunt Drusilla, Roy, Diana and Stewart, the builders and so on. They all fitted neatly into the box. They had a reason for being there and they had a motive but not a good enough motive.

So what players were left outside the box? Well, Ahmed, obviously. And Tracy. Who else? Maria? No. The Tucker family, including Norm? No, no, no.

It suddenly seemed clear to Ellie that it hadn't mattered who'd got the shock from the aerial. The person who arranged it couldn't have known who'd get it, unless they were as familiar with what was going on in the house as Aunt Drusilla and Rose.

So if it didn't matter *who* had got the shock, then perhaps she could work out *why*. The possible recipients were Mo Tucker, Aunt Drusilla and Rose. The electricians couldn't be ruled out, either, though they hadn't yet started on that part of the house.

So what it came down to was that someone wanted to unsettle Aunt Drusilla, perhaps get her out of that house? And they'd succeeded, of course. But why?

Random thoughts about buried treasure wavered in and out of Ellie's mind, till she laughed them away. Ridiculous.

The light was going. Soon people would be arriving for Evensong, she must return the key to the vicarage and get back and see to the supper. She found she'd eaten the banana while she was doing her thinking. She put the skin in her pocket to take home with her.

Tracy.

No. Why should Tracy want to shock anyone? Unless the real target was not Mo Tucker, nor Aunt Drusilla, but Rose. If someone had known that Rose was doing everything for Aunt Drusilla . . . but how could they? And why should they care?

Why had Rose not answered the phone?

Ellie eased herself to her feet, and looked up at the cross on the altar. She'd come in with a lot of questions and was leaving with more. That was her fault, she knew. Not His.

'Sorry, Lord,' she said. 'A bit preoccupied today. Hope you understand.'

He seemed to smile.

'Well, thanks, anyway. And . . . see you again soon.'

CHAPTER EIGHTEEN

'Aunt Drusilla, did you ever have a cleaner called Tracy something?' 'Dreadful girl. Banged the furniture about. Couldn't stand her. Pass the salt, dear. Can I taste garlic in this?'

'No, I know you don't like garlic. Did Tracy come to you through the agency?'

'I wouldn't recommend her, if that's what you're getting at. Besides, you do all your own cleaning, don't you? When you've time.' Which was a dig at Ellie for not having cleaned the kitchen floor that day.

Roy ladled some more spaghetti bolognaise on to his plate. 'Lines your stomach, this. I've had some of the frozen stuff from the supermarket. Doesn't taste like this. What do you put in it?'

'Oh, this and that. Start with an onion, fry the meat, add tomatoes and seasoning. It's quite simple.'

'I'm not eating mine with a fork,' said Aunt Drusilla. 'Get me a spoon, there's a good girl.'

Ellie complied. 'How long did this Tracy work for you?'

'Oh, I don't know. A couple of months, I suppose. I kept on at the agency to send me someone else but they said they didn't have anyone available. Then Rose came to me, thankfully, and that solved the problem.'

Rose's phone was still out of order.

Ellie passed Roy some more grated Parmesan cheese to sprinkle on his food. 'Did you sack Tracy when Rose came?'

'Sack her, dear? No, we still needed someone for the heavy work with the builders in the house and everything. She stayed on for a bit, just to help Rose out. Rose said she'd try to train her but it was hopeless, of course. Dear Rose has such a soft heart. I keep telling her sob stories don't do anything for me, but she felt she ought to try. Where is Rose, anyway? I thought she said she'd come back tonight.'

Roy pushed his empty plate away. 'That was good. If her phone's still out of order, I'll pop over and see what's happened to her after supper if you like.'

'I meant to give her a mobile phone,' said Aunt Drusilla, fretting gently. 'But she said she couldn't cope with one at her age.'

'What sob story?' asked Ellie. 'Tracy, I mean.'

'Something about her boy being excluded from school. Stays at home all day and plays loud music. Vandalizes cars. Terrorizes the neighbourhood along with a couple of other lads. I didn't really listen.'

'Did Rose know the family, then? I know she's always saying that some neighbours played their music too loudly.'

'It was all the fault of the school, Tracy said. She wanted to move into the house with her son, be my official carer, or some such nonsense. Naturally I told her I wasn't interested.'

Ellie gaped. Could this sordid little story really be at the root of the mystery? 'So when she pressed you to let her be your carer, you finally got rid of her and got someone else instead?'

'She was a nasty piece of work. She tripped Rose up, coming down the stairs. Dear Rose said it was an accident, but I was just coming into the hall and I saw it all. I told Tracy to go that minute and of course she cried. Why do these women think tears will solve everything? Her tears might have fooled Rose, but they didn't fool me. I got on to the agency straight away. I was going to tell them that the woman had tried to make Rose fall down the stairs but Rose begged me not to. So I didn't. And then they sent me the Tucker woman instead.'

Roy turned his head from Aunt Drusilla to Ellie and back again. 'You think this Tracy might have had something to do with the accident? That it was nothing to do with Diana?'

'I really cannot be responsible for the way such women's minds work,' said Aunt Drusilla magnificently. 'So what are we having for a sweet, Ellie?'

* * *

After supper Ellie rang Rose again. Then she rang the engineers, who reported that there was a fault on the line and they'd look into it.

Roy was pacing up and down, driving Aunt Drusilla crazy. Aunt Drusilla liked to have a quiet time after supper to digest her food and the business section of the Sunday paper.

Ellie washed up and tidied the kitchen. Roy didn't offer to help, but came in to perch on the kitchen table and generally get in the way.

'You think this Tracy person had something to do with the wiring? But how could she have got at the kettle here in your kitchen? She can't have.'

'I don't know. But it seems to me that the two events are connected, not least because the person who did it didn't seem to care who got the shock. Aunt Drusilla, Rose or Mo Tucker at the big house. Any of us, in my kitchen. I can't work it out.'

'You're worried about Rose, I can see that. Suppose I take you round there, set our minds at rest. Bring her back here with us if you like.'

'That's a good idea. But first I need to speak to Maria.'

'Who's Maria?'

'The girl who was with Stewart last night. She runs the agency which supplied Aunt Drusilla with domestic help.

None of this makes sense unless there's some kind of connection between Tracy and Mo Tucker.'

'She's a looker, that Maria,' said Roy, meditatively.

'Not your style,' said Ellie, with a sharp look.

'As if you cared.'

'I don't want to see you making a bad mistake.'

'What about that Helen then? She was a looker too.'

Ellie laughed. 'You're winding me up. She's not your style, either.'

'So what's my style, Ellie Quicke . . . if it's not you?'

'I don't know, Roy. I really don't. Now if you could take me round to Stewart's place, I think Maria may be there.'

* * *

Maria was there. Maria was cooking supper, with an apron on. Stewart was bathing little Frank and a great deal of laughter was coming from all three. Roy followed Ellie into the flat, which seemed to have undergone a sea change since Ellie was last there. Then it had had a cold and comfortless air, with junk-food containers lying around.

A bunch of daffodils was on the table in a blue jug. A bottle of wine had been uncorked and left to breathe, and both the cutlery and the glassware shone. The furniture had been slightly rearranged, but to good effect. The curtains were drawn against the night, and a delicious scent of roast chicken drifted from the kitchen, while the radio played something lively in the background.

Roy muttered, 'How unlike the home life of our own dear Diana.'

Stewart appeared in the doorway to the bathroom. He was in his shirtsleeves, with his hair tousled. There was colour in his cheeks and he looked relaxed and very much at ease. He was carrying little Frank wrapped up in a big towel. Frank was crowing along to some song he alone knew.

Maria smiled a welcome to Ellie and Roy. Her smile became even warmer, though, when she looked at Stewart.

She tucked the towel more firmly around little Frank, and retreated into the kitchen.

'Have you been trying to contact me? We've been out all day,' said Stewart, vigorously rubbing Frank dry.

Roy said, 'They've charged Diana with manslaughter.'

'I'm sorry for it,' said Stewart, not pausing in his job. 'But she's made it clear she doesn't want anything more to do with me.'

'We know that,' said Ellie. 'We won't keep you a minute. I just wanted a quick word with Maria.'

Stewart immediately looked belligerent. 'Maria has nothing to do with all that.'

'No, indeed,' soothed Ellie. 'Just a quick word about one of her cleaners, that's all.'

Ellie side-stepped Roy — who was standing in the way as usual — and went into the kitchen, where Maria was busying herself at the stove. Maria had overheard.

'What do you want to know?'

'Was there a connection between the girl Tracy, and Mo Tucker?'

Maria frowned, stirring away. 'They didn't like one another, I know that. Someone said . . . I can't be sure about this, but I think I heard someone say they were related. Aunt and niece? Half-sisters?'

'They both live in the high-rise flats on the other side of the Avenue?'

'Yes, but not in the same block, if I remember rightly. Most of our cleaners come from there, or from the hostels.'

'As does Rose.'

'Rose?' Maria didn't know the name.

'Forget it. It doesn't matter.'

Maria put down her spoon and turned to face Ellie. 'I hope you don't mind my being here with Stewart?'

'You're old enough to know your own business.'

Maria pulled a face. 'That's pretty cold.'

'Yes, I'm sorry. I can see you're good for Stewart. Perhaps I just wish that . . . Diana is my only child, and I know that she's not been happy with Stewart for some time, but . . . no. I wish you well.'

'Thank you. I will take good care of him, and of the child.'

* * *

'On to Rose's?' asked Roy as they returned to the car.

'Mmm. I notice you've been looking at your watch. Are you due somewhere else?'

'Well, I half promised to see some people I met at the golf club for a drink, but . . .'

The habit of a lifetime kicked in, and Ellie immediately put her own plans on the back burner. Oh well. Tomorrow would do. 'Drop me off back home, then. I want to ask Armand something. I expect Rose will be back on the phone by now.'

Roy duly dropped Ellie off at her house. She went indoors to make sure that Aunt Drusilla was all right — she was — and to check if Rose's phone was back on — it wasn't. But then, you'd hardly expect telephone engineers to work hard on a Sunday.

Rose would be all right. Of course she would.

In the meantime Armand — who taught at the high school — would be able to tell her something about vandalism and boys being excluded from school. He and Kate were stretched out on recliners sharing a bottle of wine and watching something mindless on the television. They were glad to see her, they said, because they'd finally settled — well, Kate had settled — on the new tiles for the conservatory and wanted her opinion of them.

Which meant that Armand hated the sight of them, but was giving in more or less gracefully.

Ellie looked at the samples, which were in a black and white geometric design and said, 'Very interesting.'

Kate threw up her arms in despair and Armand crowed. 'You see? I told you they were duds.'

Ellie laughed. 'What was Armand's choice?'

Armand dug out some warm terracotta tiles with a faintly orange random pattern on them. Ellie said, 'These would be perfect for an outdoor dining room, wouldn't they? Warm enough in winter, and remind you of the Mediterranean in the summer?'

'All right, you win,' said Kate, and gave Armand a hug to prove that she still loved him even though he'd won that particular fight.

Foxy-faced Armand tried to hide his pleasure. 'So what can we do for you, Ellie, now that you've saved our marriage yet again?'

'Tell me about aggressive parents of young teenage boys who've been excluded from school, and vandalism.'

'You want a doctoral thesis, or generalized gossip?'

Ellie picked her words with care. 'One of my aunt's cleaners, someone she's sacked recently, wanted to be her live-in carer. She tried on a sob story that her boy had been excluded from school.'

'What's she like? Describe her appearance.'

'Lumpy. Thirtyish. Overweight. Clothes, hair and skin ill cared for. Manner, aggressive. Of limited intelligence and education, I would say. As a cleaner Aunt Drusilla said she banged about, scarred the furniture. I think she tried to steal money and my mobile from my handbag when she was waitressing at the wedding reception, but I couldn't prove it so I didn't make a fuss.'

'Overweight and belligerent, of limited intelligence . . . you're describing the type of parent who's the bane of all teachers. Most parents are delightful, but there's just one or two who encourage their children to flout the rules. They drop litter in the streets, shout insults at anyone who gets in their way. They think it's clever to avoid paying fares on buses, and to elbow their way to the front of queues at check-outs. They take any attempt to discipline their children as a personal attack on themselves and have even been known to break into the lessons to attack teachers . . . sometimes even physically.'

Kate stroked Armand's cheek. 'But not yours, my darling.'

'Grrr. I should think not. But others . . .' He leaned forward to tap Ellie's knee. 'There was a fine teacher I knew, twenty years' experience, she was verbally abused and shoved about in front of her own class by a woman such as you describe. That teacher is sitting at home now in tears, had a complete breakdown, will never be able to face a class again. Another excellent teacher resigned because a fifteen-year-old stabbed her in the arm with a knife. Why? Because she'd pushed through a door ahead of him. And what happened to the aggressors? A slap on the wrist, that's all.'

Kate was less emotional, more detached. 'They think it's partly the diet, the additives in the junk food they eat, which makes them aggressive. Both parents and children. It's true that the type of woman you describe probably eats nothing but junk food.'

Armand glared at her. 'Now you'll tell me that that fifteen-year-old was not responsible for his actions.'

'The courts say that the children who act like that are not yet capable of telling right from wrong. I think they're wrong, but that's what the Law says. Ellie, is this something to do with the murder? We saw Diana going off with the police this morning.'

'Yes, she's been arrested and charged. She says it would never have occurred to her to fiddle with the wiring at Aunt Drusilla's, and I believe her. The more I think about it, the odder the whole thing appears. It seems such an inefficient way of killing someone. How could you be absolutely sure you'd get the right person? I've been trying to think myself into the mind of whoever did it, and it seemed to me that they didn't care whether they killed Aunt Drusilla, or Rose. Or anyone else — like Mo Tucker — who might accidentally handle the aerial.

'I've been over and over in my mind all the people who had a financial motive for killing or even giving Aunt Drusilla a shock, and I'm not convinced that any of them did it. As for killing Rose, who'd want to do that? Except that Aunt

Drusilla told me today that her cleaner Tracy tried to trip Rose up as she came down the stairs. But that's so trivial, isn't it? It felt like, well, like spite. Sort of, "I know I'm getting the sack, so I'm going to get my own back on you, Rose, because you're staying and I'm being pushed out."

'Then I remembered that Tracy wanted to move in with her son as Aunt Drusilla's carer, and had even gone to the lengths of writing her a letter to that effect. Her son had recently been excluded from school but that was all the school's fault, she said. And I think — though I'd like to check this out — that there was bad blood between Tracy and Mo Tucker. They may even have been related in some way.'

Kate frowned. 'You think this woman always lays the blame on others? You think she resented Miss Quicke sacking her, and resented Rose and Mo Tucker for replacing her, so rigged the aerial to give any one of them a bad shock? She didn't intend to kill, only to give one of them a shock? I must say, I like it.'

'It explains the random nature of the incident,' said Armand.

Ellie said, 'Then my kettle was sabotaged when Rose and Aunt Drusilla were staying with me. Any one of us could have switched it on and got a bad shock, perhaps even been killed. Again, it didn't seem to matter who got the shock. Doesn't that fit the bill, too?'

'Random spite,' said Armand. 'I see why you asked about vandalism. Yes, I think it's all part of the same mindset. "I want to lash out at the school for trying to correct my son, I want to lash out at society because my life's a mess, and to hurt anyone who gets in my way." She probably smokes and drinks to excess and spends all her spare money on lottery tickets.'

Ellie said, 'I have to hang on to the idea that she didn't intend to kill, only to give people a shock. Mo Tucker didn't die because of the shock, but because she had a bad heart.'

'Does this woman have the know-how to fiddle with wiring?' asked Kate.

'I don't know. I don't even know where she lives exactly. I have the number of her flat, but I don't know which block she lives in. What I do have is the address for Mo's father and her live-in boyfriend, Norm. I thought perhaps they might be able to fill me in with some details about Mo and Tracy. And tomorrow when I see Rose — her phone's out of order — I'll get her to tell me what she knows about Tracy.'

Armand looked grave. 'Rose's phone is out of order, Rose is a target for spite — and Rose has gone back to her flat in that sink estate?'

Kate said, 'Ouch. It's giving me the heebie-jeebies even to think about it.'

Ellie glanced at her watch. 'It's late and it's dark. I admit I'm worried about her. Roy was going to take me over there but he had something else on. I really don't fancy going by myself but have I got enough to justify going to the police?'

'I'll take you,' said Armand. 'I know how to deal with those yobs over there. Heaven knows I've enough of them in my class at the moment.'

'We'll both go, Armand,' said Kate. 'I don't want you getting into any fights behind my back. We'll take our mobile phones and ring the police if there's any trouble.'

* * *

It was a cold, wet night. The windscreen wipers on Armand's car creaked as they swung to and fro. His heater was inefficient. Ellie wished she'd thought to bring gloves and a scarf with her. March could be such a chilly month.

The three tower blocks had been built on what had once been an industrial estate near the river and were reached by a slip road off the bus route. There were wide car-parking spaces around each of the tower blocks, with a high percentage of wrecked and burned-out cars. The ground-floor apartments were mostly boarded up. Graffiti ruled OK.

'Rose lives in the second block on the right,' said Ellie, peering out of her window. 'You can park anywhere, but I suggest you stay in the car and keep the engine running to keep the heater going. I shouldn't be long, provided the lift's working. Rose lives on the sixth floor.'

'I'll come with you,' said Kate. 'You don't want to go up there on your own.'

The rain slackened off as they reached the doorway. Four hulking teenagers were sharing cigarettes in the foyer, and stared at them as they walked in and tried the lift button. The foyer smelled of urine and cigarettes. Ellie felt four pairs of eyes on her and wished she'd left her handbag behind. Kate wasn't carrying one, wise girl.

The lift came — to their relief — and they piled in and took it up to the sixth floor. The lift also smelled bad. Ellie tried to breathe shallowly.

'Along here.' Ellie led the way. One of the lights along the walkway had been smashed, so it was difficult to see which door belonged to Rose's flat. As usual the thump-thump and high-pitched monotonous sound of rap music permeated the corridor. They found Rose's door at last. The doorbell didn't work. At least, they assumed it didn't because they could hardly hear anything above the music from the next-door flat.

Kate mimed to Ellie that she'd gone deaf. Ellie nodded. Dear Rose had not been exaggerating when she complained of the noise.

Kate lifted the letter flap and looked inside. Kate put her mouth to Ellie's ear.

'No lights on. She must be out. Perhaps she's gone back to your house while we've been on our way here.'

It seemed reasonable. Ellie nodded and they turned to go back the way they'd come. Three of the four lads they'd seen downstairs now blocked their path. They didn't speak and when the two women threaded their way between them, they didn't react. But all three turned their heads and watched as Ellie and Kate got back into the lift and closed the doors.

'Nasty!' Kate laughed, partly in relief. 'I'm actually trembling.'

'Me, too. How Rose can put up with it I don't know!'

'I expect she's known them from birth and they wouldn't bother her.'

'I know the music bothers her, though. The sooner she's out of there, the better.'

The night air, though damp, came as a blessing on their faces. Armand was sitting in the car, hunched up, scowling. Two more lads had joined the fourth member of the original gang. They had their hoods up over their heads, and their hands in the pockets of their joggers. One played around with a skateboard. All were on the large side.

As they opened the car door, Armand said — or rather snarled, 'See that big one? I know him well. Excluded from school three times, so far. He carries, they say, though I haven't actually caught him at it. No Rose?'

'Not in. We assume she's gone back to Ellie's, while we were on our way here.'

Ellie sank into the car, thankful to hear Armand lock the doors after her.

'Ellie, suppose you ring your aunt and see if she's arrived yet.' said Armand.

Ellie got out her mobile phone and rang her own number. Eventually Aunt Drusilla condescended to come to the phone. 'Yes?'

'Aunt, it's me. Ellie. We've come over to fetch Rose, but she's not in. Is she with you?'

'No, she isn't, and I wish she were. I can't get Channel Five on your television set. Rose got it for me the other night. I thought you said she was coming back to us tonight?'

'She was. Look, if she turns up, would you ring my mobile? I'm a little worried about her.' Ellie rang off. 'She's not there. So where is she?'

'Visiting a neighbour, presumably. Who's she friendly with around here?'

'This is not exactly Happy Families territory. She's never mentioned anyone's name, that I remember, especially since Joyce moved out a while back. The only person I can think of is Norm, Mo Tucker's boyfriend. When he came round to see Aunt Drusilla, it crossed my mind that they recognized one another. I suppose we could try him.'

'He lives in the next block, right?' Ellie looked around as one does when a driver reverses, and saw that the group of lads had grown to seven or eight. Perhaps the ones who'd followed her up to Rose's flat had come down to join their friends below.

As Armand drove sedately along, looking for the right tower block, the group followed them. The one on the skateboard almost caught up with them at one point.

Ellie felt her uneasiness grow. Some of the lads seemed to be on their mobiles, possibly phoning their girlfriends? Possibly asking for reinforcements?

'They're a bit threatening, aren't they?' she said. 'Do you think we ought to hang around here? Perhaps we should get out of the estate and call the police.'

'I'm not afraid of them,' said Armand robustly. 'They wouldn't dare interfere with me.'

'Hmm.' Kate wasn't so sure. 'I agree with Ellie, but we can't call the police just to see if Rose has gone visiting a friend.'

'Rose said the police don't like coming into the estate after dark.'

Armand huffed and puffed. 'You'll be making out this is a No Go area for them next.'

Ellie wasn't at all sure that it wasn't. They parked near the second tower block. Security lights were on in the foyer and all up the stairs. It wasn't raining and it wasn't far to the entrance. But . . . she hesitated. She glanced around but the lads seemed to have drawn back into the shadows. All but one.

There was a knock on the window at Armand's side. He opened it because he knew the lad.

'It's Jogger, isn't it?'

''Sright. Ain't seen you round here before. Who you looking for? Mebbe I can help?'

Armand saw no reason to refuse the information. 'Mrs Quicke is trying to trace a friend of hers, Mrs McNally. She thought perhaps Mr Tucker might know where she is. Mr Tucker lives in this block, doesn't he?'

'Sure. He's me grandad. Take her up there, shall I? Your quickest way out with the car is, take a right turn, go back the way you come.'

'We'll wait,' said Kate.

CHAPTER NINETEEN

'Thank you,' said Ellie, getting out of the car and following Jogger to the front door of the flats. 'What's your real name? Not Jogger, I assume.'

'They call me Jogger, 'cause I don't like standing still. Up the stairs do you? The lift's out again.'

'How far up?' asked Ellie, when they reached the third floor.

'Almost to the top.' Jogger didn't seem to feel it, but Ellie did. She refused to be beaten, though. Stop for a breather. Hold on to the banisters. Don't try to hold a conversation with Jogger, who was skittering up the steps ahead of her.

Finally they made it and stepped out on to a windy walkway. Doors led on to the flats at intervals. It was just like the block in which Rose lived, probably built at the same time by the same builders.

Jogger did a rapid knock on a door and used a key to let them into a bright, fuggy flat. An elderly man sat in an armchair with a rug over his knees. Big fat Norm sat nearby. The television was on full blast. Both men were comfortably drinking beer out of cans and smoking. Neither wore shoes and the state of their socks and clothing made Ellie pinch in her lips. The room was centrally heated, and the fumes from constant smoking made it hard to breathe easily.

'Hey up,' said Norm, turning his head fractionally to see who had come in. 'It's Jogger . . . with . . . hang about, I know you, don't I?'

'Mrs Quicke. We met when you came to see my aunt, remember? I was so sorry about Mrs Tucker. How are you coping now?'

The old man tried to twist round in his chair, but failed. 'What does she want?'

'Well, I was trying to find Rose McNally — you know her, don't you? Her phone's out of order and she's not in. I wondered if you might know where she might have gone and . . . excuse me, but how do you manage to get out, being so high up, and the lift out of order?'

'It's hard, it's very hard,' whined the old man. 'Me having but one leg an' all. Norm said we should try the Housing again, get us a ground-floor flat . . .'

'I'll go on Monday,' said Norm, looking uneasy.

Jogger, who hadn't stopped jogging on the spot, said, 'Norm's not that good at reading and writing, see? He gets as far as saying what he wants and they says, "Fill in this form here," and then he forgets what's he's come for.'

'You shut your lip,' said the old man. 'Norm's been looking after me all right, gets me my meals, don't he? Helps me in and out of bed? I'd like to see you helping out.'

Jogger grinned. 'Nothing gets you nothing in this world.'

Ellie was distressed for them. 'Can't you explain about the reading and writing, Norm? I'm sure they'd understand. I mean, it's quite a common thing, not being able to cope with forms. I had ever so much difficulty after my husband died, trying to understand the forms. If the worst comes to the worst then surely Rose — or even I — could help you fill out the forms to get you a ground-floor flat.'

'Could you get me another wheelchair?' asked the old man, with a leer. 'Jogger here broke the one the hospital give me and I can't go nowhere without it.'

Ellie seated herself, unasked, trying to deal with this problem. 'Haven't they given you an artificial leg?'

'It don't fit proper, and I can't keep going back for them to have another go at it. Mo was going to write to the doctor about it, but . . .' He pinched out his cigarette butt and took another from the pack at his elbow.

'Mo was a bit of all right,' said Norm, doing the same.

'I'm sure she was. By the way, did she ever talk to you about someone called Tracy?'

There was an instant change in the atmosphere. Neither man had moved, but it was there. Then she got it. Jogger had stopped jogging.

'What is it? You know her?'

'She's my granddaughter,' said the old man. 'Jogger's her brother. They live over the other block. We don't see much of her, but Jogger comes by now and then.'

Ellie was puzzled. 'You mean, she's Mo's daughter?'

'Nah. She's my other daughter's, that died a couple years back. She's Mo's niece, got it? Got a kid of her own, going on fourteen, fifteen now. What about her?'

Ellie became wary. 'I've met her, I think. She used to clean for my aunt at one time. Then I think I saw her at a wedding reception, waitressing?'

Jogger was listening, hard. Still not jogging. So all this was important to him? Norm was staring at the television set as if enthralled. His cigarette was burning down between his fingers. What was going on here?

'That'd be her,' said the old man. 'But you didn't come round to see her, did you? We don't know where this Rose might be, so you'd best be on your way.'

Ellie got to her feet, feeling uncomfortable. She got the impression that these people knew something that she didn't. She also understood that they were not going to tell her what it was. Jogger was on his mobile phone, talking into it, turning away with a hunched shoulder to hear the reply.

'Well, thank you for seeing me,' said Ellie, and then was conscious that this form of social dialogue was not exactly appropriate here.

Jogger snapped his phone shut. 'One of me mates says Rose has just got back, gone up to her flat. Take you over there, shall I?'

Norm and the old man turned to look at Jogger, who ducked his head and started jogging on the spot. Ellie looked at the older men, wondering if they'd give her a clue as to what was going on . . . because something definitely was going on here. Neither man said anything, so she murmured, 'Goodnight', and followed Jogger out of the flat.

He led her rapidly along the walkway. She hesitated, called after him, 'I thought the stairs were at the other end?'

'This way's quicker.' He sped along the walkway at a great pace and held the door open on to another staircase. He had taken out his phone again, and was talking rapidly into it, but too quietly for her to hear what he was saying.

She looked out of a window and saw what she had expected to see; a car-parking area surrounded by a landscaped lawn with pathways leading off in different directions. Except that Armand's car was nowhere to be seen.

'I ought to tell my friends . . .'

'They'll be on the other side of these flats. We'll catch up with them after you've seen Rose.'

Well, that was what she had come for, to see Rose. They left the flats by a different door from the one they had entered by. She tried to orientate herself, and failed. She'd never had a good sense of direction. She followed Jogger out into the night. He moved smoothly along the path, always a little too far ahead of her so that she couldn't question him.

Now why did she think he didn't want to be questioned? He'd been very helpful, hadn't he?

Ah, now she recognized the name of the building in which Rose lived. She looked around — why was she so uneasy? — wondering where all his friends had gone to. There was no sign of them.

Jogger opened the front door and made for the stairs. 'The lift's out. We'll have to take the stairs.'

'It was working earlier.'

'It's out now.'

She toiled up the stairs after him. She had to stop on the third landing to catch her breath. Jogger waited for her, impatiently.

Then up the last few stairs and on to the walkway. The rap music was still blaring. The light outside Rose's flat was still out. Two of Jogger's mates were standing outside the door of the flat from which the music was coming. They nodded to Jogger as he came up.

Jogger opened the door into the noisy flat and motioned that Ellie should go inside.

'This isn't Rose's flat.'

'No, but Tracy knows where she is.'

This was Tracy's flat? Oh. So Tracy lived next door to Rose? They were the ones who'd made Rose's life such hell? And when Tracy was cleaning for Aunt Drusilla, she would have known all about Rose being asked to move in as carer. Tracy had tried to trip Rose up as she came down the stairs. Tracy was on the books of at least two cleaning companies. Tracy had tried to steal from Ellie at the wedding reception.

Ellie did not feel she wanted to meet Tracy again, but Jogger had pushed her inside the flat and closed the door behind him.

* * *

Norm squirmed in his chair as the door closed behind Jogger and Ellie. 'Not a bad sort.'

Mr Tucker stared hard at the television set, not noticing that his cigarette was about to burn his fingers.

Norm said, 'Perhaps we had ought to have stopped her going over there? I mean . . . Trace can be a bit, well . . . sharp.'

Mr Tucker yelped and killed his cigarette. 'You know what she's like. We can't do nothing.'

'Yeah, I know. But if they've done something to Rose McNally, well . . . see what I mean?'

'It was an accident,' said the old man, fiercely. 'Mo's death was an accident. We got to put it behind us.'

'Yeah, but that woman there . . . she seemed all right, din't she? We shoulda warned her, is what I'm saying.'

'And had our flat trashed, too? Change the channel. I'm sick of this one.'

* * *

Tracy was also sitting in an armchair, watching the telly. Or perhaps not watching it, but letting her eyes rest on it. The sound was turned down. Or perhaps it was merely being drowned out by the noise from a bedroom next door? The air was as thick with cigarette smoke as it had been in Norm's place, and there were several beer cans in evidence, some empty and some not yet opened.

Tracy swept back one arm and thumped on the wall behind her. 'Pack it in, Trev!' The noise next door didn't change.

Jogger said, 'He's on the walkway. Shall I tell him you want him to turn it down?'

Tracy didn't reply directly but grumbled, 'It's doing my effing head in.'

On the two-seater settee sprawled a youngish man with spiky hair who Ellie — after a moment's thought — recognized with a feeling of dread.

She managed to smile at him, as if she hadn't just put two and two together to make five. 'Hello, I know you, don't I? You do some work now and then for my builders? I think I've seen you working round at my aunt's, too? Good evening, Tracy. I'm looking for my friend Rose. Jogger said she's just returned to her flat.'

'Yeah, that's what I told him to say,' said Tracy, inhaling smoke and letting it drift out of her nostrils. 'She's gone.'

'Really? That's surprising. Well, I'll just check for myself, if you don't mind. My aunt's been asking for her and her phone seems to be out of order.'

'Temp'ry fault. Be all right tomorrow. Rose has gone for good. Best tell your aunt that and tell her I'll be round tomorrow to have a word with her about moving in, right?'

'Very well,' said Ellie, now only anxious to leave. 'I'll tell her. Now I'd best be going. My friends are waiting for me downstairs.'

'They've gone,' said Tracy. 'I told the lads to tell them Rose had been taken ill — vomiting and the like — and that you're staying on a bit to look after her. So they went.'

'Yeah, they gone, man!' echoed Jogger, back on his mobile. 'They argued a bit, so us lot give the car a rocking and they got the hell out.'

'I see,' said Ellie. 'Very well, then. I'll call a cab.' She delved for her mobile in her bag, but was not particularly surprised when Jogger reached out a long arm and took it from her.

'Oops!' said Jogger, and dropped it on the floor. He then trod on it. 'Oh dear, look at that. Clumsy old me.'

Ellie sat down in the nearest chair. 'So what is it you want to speak to me about?'

Tracy heaved herself to her feet and stretched out one huge arm for another tin of beer. Having popped it open, she drank deeply. 'You lost me my job. You owe me one.'

'You lost yourself your job, if you're referring to what happened yesterday afternoon at the wedding. You can't blame that on me.'

'You owe me.' The woman swayed from one massive leg to the other. Her feet were incongruously tiny, but the ankles were swollen.

'Look, it's getting late. What is it you want?'

'I'm going to be your aunt's new carer. Me and my boy are going to live in that big house and you're going to help me get there.'

'Miss Quicke wouldn't have you, I'm afraid.'

'Oh yes, she will, if you tell her to. I've noticed you coming and going and I keep me ears pricked. You bloody own that house, don't you? You could bloody well turn her out if you wanted to? Right. So you tell her who her carer's going to be and she'll have to put up with it.'

'Is that what all this has been about? Electrocuting your aunt? Frightening Rose? Fixing my kettle?'

'It were an accident. How did I know the old cow had a heart?'

'Did you consider that my aunt might have a heart condition, too? Or Rose? You didn't care which of them got the shock?'

'It were an accident. Ask my friend Jase.'

Her 'friend' Jase spoke up for the first time. 'It were an accident. Only meant to give her a shock. Or one of the others. Din't matter which. Scare the old cow off, that's all it was for.'

'My daughter has been arrested for your aunt's murder.'

Tracy, Jase and Jogger rolled about laughing. 'Serve her bloody well right, acting like she's something from the ayleet, and us like scum.'

'And Rose? Did she treat you like scum?'

Tracy sneered. 'She's past it. And that daughter of hers, always looking down on us, making me serve food at her wedding, all lace and no knickers. Rose shouldna tried taking a job that's mine by rights. I worked for it, din't I? Put up with Lady Muck for months, do this, do that, you haven't done this right, you've got to do it over again. Living in that great big house with room for twenty people, but no, she wouldn't let me have even a little bit of it for me and my boy that's been unfairly excluded from school and treated like dirt. That job's mine and the sooner you realize it, the sooner you can go.'

Ellie thought, This woman's barking mad!

'However long do you think you could keep me here? Overnight? People will come asking for me, you know.'

Jase shifted uneasily. 'Come on, Trace. I gotta work tomorrow.'

'It won't take long. She won't last as long as Rose did. Will you, dearie?'

Ellie asked, with a feeling of dread, 'What did you do to Rose?'

'She did it to herself. We just made a bit of a mess with her flat, and then left her there with a few little surprises. Booby traps, you might say. She brought it on herself, right?'

Ellie felt faint. 'Brought what on herself?'

'You'll see.' Tracy took Ellie's arm and whirled her up and out of the door of her flat and along the walkway to Rose's front door.

'Let us in, Jase. Then fix it back the way you did it for Rose.'

Jase shambled up and did something to the door handle. He opened the door and stood back to let them in. Tracy shoved Ellie inside and switched on the lights, while Jase stood in the doorway, grinning.

The flat had been trashed. There wasn't a piece of furniture which hadn't been thrown around. Rose's cherished pot plants had been thrown at the wall and lay smashed on the carpet. Glassware, china . . . all in pieces. Rose had only had two pictures on the walls and they were now on the floor, the frames and glass in shards.

Rose had kept a collection of family photos on the mantelpiece: portraits of her parents, her long-dead husband, and of her daughter Joyce at different stages. These had been thrown around the place, some having been ripped up, others trodden on.

'Oh, how could you!' exclaimed Ellie.

'I never touched it. Boys will be boys, you know.'

Ellie looked in the bedroom. Here there was the same evidence of destruction. The bed had been overturned, the mattress flung off against the wall. The curtains had been torn down and thrown over it. The built-in cupboard had been ransacked, most of the clothing lying in a stir-fry on the floor. Ellie recognized the royal-blue suit Rose had worn for her daughter's wedding, and the good-quality hat and good coat which Miss Quicke had bought Rose the other day.

Ellie put her head round the door of the second bedroom. This had received the same treatment. Some of Joyce's wedding presents and her wedding dress had been savagely attacked. Joyce would be furious! In the kitchen everything had been taken out of the cupboards, the fridge and the tiny freezer, and piled into the middle of the floor. Tomato sauce and flour mixed with eggs decorated everything from the ceiling to the floors.

Strangely enough, none of the electrical equipment had been smashed. 'We might swop the microwave and the fridge in a coupla days,' said Tracy.

'This is appalling. Suppose this had been done to your flat?'

Tracy shrugged. 'No one's going to touch our place, are they? They wouldn't dare!'

'Where's Rose?'

'In her bedroom. She made the mistake of touching something she shouldn't, right? And if you're not very careful, you'll go the same way. Then it'll be "Two women found in tragic circumstances, faulty wiring to blame". As soon as you've had enough, bang on the wall. Three long, three short. Go on doing it till we hear you, right, and then we'll turn off the current and get you out. Don't bother trying to shout out of the window. Nobody takes no notice of shouting round here. Or breaking glass. Right?'

Tracy gave Ellie a push back into the kitchen and with her rolling gait made for the front door, where Jase was standing, holding a piece of wire in gloved hands.

'I wouldn't try to get out, if I were you. The handle on the front door's going to be wired up to the mains again. Other things, too, so be careful what you touch! Ha! Ha!'

The front door slammed shut.

Ellie was alone in a booby-trapped flat with the body of her dearest friend. Where was Rose? In the bedroom?

Ellie picked her way carefully through the debris to the main bedroom. The discarded mattress appeared to be moving — or was that an illusion?

Ellie leaped forward and pulled the curtains and the mattress away from the wall.

'Don't touch the lamp!' Rose was lying in a huddle in the small space between the bedside table and the wall.

She was dishevelled and looked as if she'd collected a black eye, but she was alive.

Ellie tried to help Rose to her feet, but failed.

'It's my knee,' said Rose. 'I must have twisted it when I fell. Don't touch anything. Ellie.' She collapsed on to the floor, nursing her knee, which had indeed swollen to twice its usual size.

'What happened, Rose?'

'I was just packing up this morning to come back to you when they burst in and started trashing the place, screaming at me that I wasn't going anywhere. I didn't understand at first, I really didn't.'

'Don't try to talk yet. You're trembling. Lean back on the mattress. I think that's safe enough.'

'You must warn your aunt, dear. I don't like to speak ill of anyone, but Tracy and Jase are not very nice people. There's been nothing but trouble in the flats since they came, not to mention the noise, but no one dares complain because if they do they get beaten up or their flats get trashed . . .'

'Why didn't you warn my aunt when Tracy first turned up to work for her?'

'I didn't know she worked for your aunt till after I moved in, and I didn't want to give her a bad character when she needed the job so badly, with her son out of school and everything, so it wouldn't have been right to warn your aunt then, when Tracy was really trying so hard. Well, at first she was, anyway. When Mo died, I thought how dreadful for poor Tracy, even though I knew they weren't on good terms. Something to do with a carpet that should have been Tracy's after her mother died, but Mo took it? Such silly little things can turn into a feud if you let them, can't they?'

'Dear Rose, you saw no evil.'

'Not till they burst in on me like that and started shouting. I couldn't believe it, even then. Tracy knocked me down and, oh dear, my poor eye, is it quite closed up yet? I have such a head, but I don't think we'd better look for the aspirins dear, do you? Then they started trashing the flat though I tried to stop them, and they said they'd stop as soon as I stopped working for your aunt but of course I couldn't agree to that, could I? Then they pushed me in the cupboard here in the bedroom and left me for ages, and I thought that I must be brave and really what an adventure it all was and I'd never imagined such a thing could happen to me, and my bits and pieces could all be replaced and weren't worth that much anyway. Only I couldn't get out and I thought of you and your aunt and how you were getting on, and I missed the service at the church, didn't I? Though I must say that Tum-Tum seems very nice . . .'

'Yes, he is. But Rose, do be quiet and let me think for a minute.'

'. . . and I could hear them moving around the flat and I couldn't think what they were doing, but then they let me out and said was I prepared to do what they asked and I said no. So they said I could try to right the mess if I wanted to, so naturally I started in the bedroom and went to pick up the bedside lamp and got such a shock I must have passed out. Then when I came to, I was under the mattress and they were throwing more things on top of me. So I played dead. Am I glad to see you, Ellie. I heard everything they said to you. How are we going to get out if the handle on the front door is electrified?'

'I don't know,' said Ellie. 'Do you think they were bluffing and we could just walk out?'

'I wouldn't like to chance it, dear.'

'Come to think of it, how are you still alive, if you got electrocuted?'

'I was wearing these heavy walking shoes, dear. I wasn't going to pack them because they're too heavy, so I thought I'd change into them. Rubber soles, you see. I suppose that's what saved my life.'

Ellie nodded. Rose had always liked good solid shoes, which she bought from the charity shop. Ellie looked down at her own shoes. They were simulated leather brogues, with a synthetic sole. They wouldn't prevent an electrical charge going through her. No, they couldn't chance the front door. Tracy had used Jase to rig the electrics at Aunt Drusilla's, and the kettle at Ellie's. He knew how to do it, all right.

Tracy was, of course, quite mad.

Tracy really believed she had a right to do whatever was needed so that she could get her own way. In a way, she was like Diana in that. Tracy didn't care that Diana was going to jail. She didn't care about anything except getting her own way.

Two women found in tragic circumstances. Faulty wiring to blame . . .

CHAPTER TWENTY

Ellie put her hands down at her sides, and looked around her. She wouldn't touch anything — no, not anything — till she was sure of it. The mess was indescribable, but she mustn't try to clear it up. In any case, Rose would never come back here again . . . poor Rose, forced to watch the destruction of her home . . .

Armand and Kate had been fooled into going away and leaving them. Roy was at the golf club. She had no mobile phone to contact anyone who might be able to help her.

'You stay here, Rose, and rest that knee. I'm just going to see if your phone's working again.' She picked her way back into the living room and located Rose's phone by the upturned table — which had lost a leg. The phone was off the hook, but there was no buzz indicating that the line was alive.

Dare she try it?

Anything they'd tampered with was liable to kill her.

'That poor woman came round looking for her friend,' they'd say. 'What a shame. Rose's flat was trashed? What a pity. But some of the boys around here . . . you know? And they were both electrocuted? How dreadful!'

Think, Ellie. What do you know about electricity?

Not nearly enough.

It's carried along wires. So if she could see wires trailing along the carpet, perhaps she'd know which items of furniture carried a lethal charge.

She seemed to remember that wood didn't conduct electricity very well, if at all. Nor paper. Nor material — unless it had metal in it.

So if she picked up the broken wooden table leg and poked around with it, she ought to be able to test out her theory.

She picked up the wooden table leg, and it didn't give her a shock. So far, so good. She poked at the telephone on the floor. Still no jolt. She would risk it. She picked up the receiver and found the line was dead. The wire leading from the main body of the phone had been cut. It lay in shards of glass, looking for all the world as if the wire had been cut accidentally.

So that was out.

She could break the window with the table leg and shout for help. But nobody in this area would take any notice of that.

A metal tray on which Rose had been accustomed to serve tea lay on its side. Ellie touched it with the tip of the table leg and jumped as she felt a jolt go up through her elbow. So the tray had been wired. Where were the connecting wires?

Ellie carefully teased broken china and glass away from the tray and spotted a wire which had been attached to the tray with a tiny clamp.

It would be a good idea to pray for protection before she made another movement. Stand still. Pray.

Be with me, Lord. You know my situation. If it is your will that I survive then help me, guide me.

The noise from next door was deafening. It made it very hard to think straight.

It would be a good idea to trace the wire from the tray back to . . . wherever it came from. Perhaps a plug that she could pull out of its socket?

She traced it under a rug. She lifted the rug and found a dozen more wires leading in different directions away from the door. The wires all joined together near the door and went under it.

She couldn't pull the plug out of the socket because the socket was outside the flat.

At least she'd still got electric light. Thank the Lord that she could see what she was doing.

She traced three of the wires to their destinations. The television set was one. The oven and kettle in the kitchen. Ellie wasn't too sure about the microwave, either.

The bathroom. There was a wire leading to the hot-water tap in the washbasin. Turn that on, and meet your Maker.

Stewart had used the rubber bath mat when he neutralized the kettle at Ellie's. No rubber bath mat. Just something in cotton, rather thin and worn.

Rubber. Gloves? Shoes? Where might something like that be?

Ellie went into the bedroom, her senses assaulted once again by the noise and the mess . . . torn duvet, pillows, sheets . . . smashed clock, smashed mirror. Smashed china figurines. Ellie had given Rose one of those for her last birthday. Don't think about that. Rose seemed to be dozing, reclining on the mattress. It would probably be the best thing for her, to have a little rest.

Most of Rose's clothing had been pulled out of the built-in cupboard and left on the floor, but her shoes were still inside. Ellie pulled them out. Heavy brogues, and lace-ups. Some silver sandals. Some plastic overshoes and a pair of wellington boots that Rose had bought from the charity shop one day when they'd had a sudden downpour. Ellie had offered to send Rose home in a taxi, but dear Rose had wanted to be independent and had bought the boots to walk home in.

Wellington boots. Good quality. Rubber soles?

Yes!

Ellie took off her own neat shoes, and pulled on the boots. They were too big for her, but she didn't care about that.

Now for some rubber gloves . . . anything rubber that she could use to protect herself with. There were only plastic gloves in the kitchen. Not much good for this sort of work but they might do.

She remembered seeing something, somewhere . . .

Ah. Rose had very wisely bought some large rubber shapes cut to look like feet, which she'd applied to the bottom of the bath, so that she didn't slip in the water. They were definitely made of rubber.

Now, if Ellie could only get a couple of them unstuck . . . ugh! They'd very firmly glued themselves to the bottom of the bath. She needed something to prise them up with. A knife from the kitchen? Ah, but be careful which one you choose. Standing in wellington boots may help, but may not protect you entirely.

A plastic spatula on the floor. Try that. The edge is reasonably sharp and yes, it was working . . . but . . . bother! That piece tore right across. Try another. Carefully, now. You've got all night to do this. Only, once you get out of the door, you'll still have to run the gauntlet of that gang of louts outside. Don't think about them. One step at a time.

Ellie stood up, holding two giant red rubber feet.

Rose moaned and shifted when Ellie shook her. 'Come on, dear Rose. One last effort and we'll be out of here. Put on your new coat and hat. It's probably raining again . . . there. And where's your handbag?' Rose blinked and covered her black eye with her hand.

Ellie helped her into her new coat and hat, and assisted her into the sitting room, where they retrieved her handbag. Rose gave a little cry and bent to retrieve one of her cherished family photographs.

'Never mind that now,' said Ellie. 'I'll come back and get those later and have them restored for you. Perhaps we'll set you up with a wall of photos in your new home? You need never come back here. Your home is with us now.'

Rose looked around her, her lips trembling. Then she nodded. 'Do you know, I used to pray that someone would have the courage to deal with those people next door? I didn't realize it would be me who'd bring them down. Shall we go straight to the police?'

'After you've seen a doctor,' said Ellie, who thought Rose really ought to be in hospital. 'Stand quite still till I get my own shoes.'

She found a plastic bag in the kitchen and put her own shoes and her handbag into it, to carry more easily. Then she faced the front door.

'Well, here goes!'

Wrapping the red rubber feet round her hands for protection, Ellie grasped the door handle and turned it. No shock. The relief! But the door still didn't open.

'Let me,' said Rose, unthinkingly stepping forward to help. 'You've to give it a tug in wet weather before it opens. Or perhaps they've double-locked it?'

'Don't touch it!' Ellie dug Rose unceremoniously in the ribs to prevent her touching the door. 'Sorry, but . . .' She looked closely at the lock. It had come away from the door jamb, no doubt broken open when the louts barged in.

Ellie tugged at the door with all her might and, Glory Be, it opened. She looked quickly up and down the walkway but there was no one in sight. It was raining heavily, which might keep the gang indoors. Also they wouldn't be expecting her to escape.

She looked down. A wire led from the handle down to the floor, snaking along the walkway to Tracy's flat. A larger coil of wires emerged from the rug by the door of the flat, and also led along to Tracy's flat.

'We'd better leave all that in place,' said Ellie, keeping her voice low. 'Keep your voice down. We don't want them coming out to stop us leaving . . . not that they'd probably hear us with all that noise going on. Come on, courage! We'd best not try to go down by the lift. Jogger said it wasn't working, anyway. So where's the other stairs?'

'This way.' Rose pointed to the right. 'But I don't think I can make it, Ellie. You go on and get help.'

'I'm not leaving you here. If necessary, we'll hop all the way to the chemist's. Come along, now. Lean on me.'

Ellie was sweating by the time they reached the corner, and Rose groaned every time she tried to put her foot to the ground. Once they reached the end of the walkway, Rose gestured to a door which led them into another corridor at right angles to the first one. Ellie opened the door and looked along the walkway, but there was still no one in sight.

Not surprising on such a foul night. They reached a door marked 'Emergency Exit'. 'I can't possibly do it,' gasped Rose.

'Oh yes, you can. Think of my aunt, and what she'd do in the circumstances. Would she let a sprained knee defeat her?'

Rose tried to laugh, though it came out as more of a sob. But she did start down the stairs, putting her good leg down first, then swinging the other leg round and down. Still they met no one.

Ellie couldn't think what they were going to do when they reached the bottom of the stairs. The rain might be keeping the gang inside. With luck. It was some way to the nearest bus stop, she hadn't a mobile phone to summon help with, and Rose certainly couldn't walk any distance.

On the third landing, Ellie had to catch Rose as she was about to fall.

'Just a bit faint. Be all right in a moment. Can't think what's the matter with me.'

Ellie held Rose up, wondering if it would be possible to knock on the door of another flat and ask for protection. Decided she couldn't risk it. Everyone here seemed to live in fear of the gang, and the people in the flats would probably send for the gang and not the police.

She prayed a bit. And then a bit more. Lord, help us, we're worn out and in pain and can't do this in our own strength. She realized she was still wearing wellington boots, which were hampering her own movements. She slid them off and put on her own shoes.

Ellie's ears stretched, expecting at any minute that someone would see them on that brightly lit staircase, and call up the gang.

'All right now,' sighed Rose. 'I keep thinking of dear Miss Quicke. How on earth is she managing without me?'

'She's dead worried about you. Can't get Channel Five without you fiddling with the set.'

'You should get a new set. We saw some splendid ones the other day.' Rose was being very brave, but her voice faded out on her.

Ellie had to almost carry her down the next flight of steps. Another rest. Ellie looked at her watch. Aunt Drusilla must be getting herself off to bed now. Roy might be having a last drink at the bar. Armand and Kate would be chasing one another round the bedroom.

They stumbled down the last flight of stairs. Rose's eye was completely shut and tears were running down her cheeks.

'Where are we?' Ellie asked. 'Is this the back entrance? Is there a public phone box nearby? No, silly question. Of course there isn't. Or if there is, it'll be out of order. Rose, don't give up yet. Which way to the nearest road?' They were in the brightly lit foyer of the staircase. Anyone passing by would be able to see them clearly, but they could hardly see what was happening outside in the darkness.

Was there anywhere they could go which would take them out of that bright light?

Rose slipped down the wall. 'Just . . . rest . . . a bit.'

'Not here, Rose! It's too dangerous! Look, there's a car coming. Perhaps if I flag it down, the driver might help us.'

Or not. Anyone driving a car into this part of the estate must live here and therefore acknowledge the supremacy of the gang.

One car, two cars . . . the driving rain made it difficult to see, but why was there a procession of cars driving around the block? Four . . . six cars?

Six cars in a row? There was nobody else in sight. No gang. No ordinary people going about their business. It was a foul night.

Could they be hunting for Ellie and Rose? No, because the gang didn't know they'd escaped yet, did they? And would those teenaged lads be able to rustle up so many cars?

The leading car was disappearing out of sight, but the last car was lagging behind. The rain was blinding, but Ellie thought she could see the driver peering out, looking for something . . . someone . . .

The last car stopped and the driver leaned on the horn. The car reversed. The driver wound down his window. Someone shouted out to them.

'Mrs Quicke! Here!'

Ellie knew that voice. She knelt down beside Rose and tried to pull her upright. 'Rose dear, it's that nice man from the minicab firm. Come along, we'll soon have you safely wrapped up in bed.'

The other cars were returning, circling around. Armand got out of the first car, followed by another minicab driver. Together they swooped on Ellie and Rose, and lifted them into the last minicab.

'About time, too,' said Aunt Drusilla, ensconced in the back. Hatted and gloved, Aunt Drusilla was wearing her most imposing tweed coat, and had her neatly furled umbrella with her. 'We've been round and round seven times, looking for some clue as to where you might be. Even then it took an old woman like me to spot you! Driver, dial nine–nine–nine!'

* * *

Aunt Drusilla explained how she'd organized the rescue party as soon as they'd got off the estate and could phone for the police and an ambulance. Armand and Kate had not believed the gang when they'd been told that Rose was ill and Ellie staying to take care of her. Only when the gang had started to rock their car did they realize they had to drive away for their own safety. As soon as they were off the estate they phoned Ellie's home number and managed to convince Aunt Drusilla that Ellie and Rose were in danger.

Aunt Drusilla had heard enough about the gang from Rose to realize that it was not a good idea to go down there without back-up — and in any case, would the police believe her story? Especially after they'd arrested Diana.

Not to be defeated, Aunt Drusilla mobilized her troops. Roy was summoned by mobile phone from the golf club. Aunt Drusilla knew which minicab firm Ellie used — the number was in Ellie's phone book, so she called them for help. Every single minicab driver not already out on a call was summoned to join in the manhunt. Only, no one knew precisely where Ellie had gone. Armand and Kate had left Ellie in front of the block in which Mo Tucker had lived, but Kate said that wasn't where Rose lived. So they'd all driven slowly round and round the three tower blocks till Aunt Drusilla had spotted Ellie and Rose at the bottom of the emergency stairs.

The police and the ambulance dead-heated. Rose was taken off to hospital, with Aunt Drusilla at her side. Only then did the other minicab drivers return to their usual duties. Ellie told her story, showing the police the red rubber feet which she still had in her pocket. When she led them up to Rose's flat, the wires were still in place to prove her story . . . the vandalism inside did the rest.

* * *

It rained on and off for the next fortnight and then when the hour went forward, the rain turned to April showers. The hours of daylight grew longer, and you could get out for a brisk walk if you took an umbrella with you.

Ellie took a turn round the park and came back via the church to see if it might be open. Tum-Tum was sometimes to be found, pottering around there before Evensong.

He was sitting on his favourite seat outside, hands clasped across capacious stomach, appreciating the scent coming from a bed of dark-red wallflowers nearby.

'Do you want to borrow the key again?'

She smiled and sat down beside him. 'What it is to have time to sit and stare.'

'I don't believe in rushing. Bad for the digestion. Got the house to yourself again at last?'

'Aunt Drusilla and Rose went off on a fortnight's cruise round the Mediterranean today. It seems very quiet without them. They did ask if I wanted to go with them, but our old friend Gilbert is hosting a cruise round the Bible lands in a couple of months' time and I said I'd go on that.'

'Have a banana? No? Are the baddies all safely rounded up?'

'Some on bail, some locked up. Tracy and Jase are being held on remand. Tracy's boy's been taken into care. A bad start in life and not much of a future, I'd say. The rest of the gang will probably just get their knuckles rapped.'

'Too young to know what they were doing?'

'So they say.'

Tum-Tum resettled himself on the bench so that he could see her face. 'And your daughter?'

Ellie shrugged. 'She's keeping her distance at the moment, and I'm not sorry that it should be so. As soon as she was released she moved back in with Derek Jolley and sees her son at weekends. She's busy redecorating a large house she's bought — ripping out all the old fireplaces, cornices, ceiling roses — all the original features. She says she's aiming for the young-professionals market. Perhaps she's right.'

'And how do you feel about her now?'

'A mixture. Sometimes I feel so cross about her selfishness that I could shake her. At other times I just ache for her, because I can't see much happiness for her in the life she's chosen. I do realize that she doesn't think of leaving Stewart as being wrong, but I still do, and that makes it difficult to talk to her about it. Children! When you bring them into the world, you have such dreams for them . . . and then they go their own way and you can't stop them making mistakes, can you?'

'What about your son-in-law Stewart? Has he moved in with his girlfriend?'

'No. He's scared to step out of line, in case the courts take Frank away from him when the divorce comes up. He sees a lot of Maria. I don't know what to hope for in that direction, and that's the truth.'

'So you're at a loose end?'

'Not exactly. Roy — my architect cousin — is drawing up the plans for the conversion of Aunt Drusilla's garage into two flats, and her old servants' quarters into a separate unit. It'll be like a small house. Rose can take her pick when they're finished. One of the units is to be let to a friendly soul who can help them out in the house — Maria says she knows just the right person. The conversions are a lot of work. New plumbing, wiring, everything. Then redecoration, keeping the old features, of course. It won't be finished by the time they return from their cruise, but Aunt Drusilla has agreed to move into one of her riverside flats till it's done.'

'I heard you were doing battle with the local Housing Association for someone?'

Ellie smiled. 'For Norm and old Mr Tucker. They really do need a ground-floor flat and he needs a new wheelchair. They're entitled to it, but neither of them is much good at dealing with authority and forms, so I said I'd help them out. Mr Tucker's looking forward to getting down the pub again, once he's got his new wheelchair.'

'I hear they're running a book on which of your suitors you'll take on a trip down the aisle.'

'Absurd!' said Ellie, going pink. 'Silly gossip. I've got far more serious things to worry about than that. Something's been eating my geraniums for a start, my guttering's not been mended, and the loo still doesn't flush properly.'

'Ah. There's always something, isn't there? Have a banana?'

THE END

THE JOFFE BOOKS STORY

We began in 2014 when Jasper agreed to publish his mum's much-rejected romance novel and it became a bestseller.

Since then we've grown into the largest independent publisher in the UK. We're extremely proud to publish some of the very best writers in the world, including Joy Ellis, Faith Martin, Caro Ramsay, Helen Forrester, Simon Brett and Robert Goddard. Everyone at Joffe Books loves reading and we never forget that it all begins with the magic of an author telling a story.

We are proud to publish talented first-time authors, as well as established writers whose books we love introducing to a new generation of readers.

We have been shortlisted for Independent Publisher of the Year at the British Book Awards three times, in 2020, 2021 and 2022, and for the Diversity and Inclusivity Award at the Independent Publishing Awards in 2022.

We built this company with your help, and we love to hear from you, so please email us about absolutely anything bookish at feedback@joffebooks.com

If you want to receive free books every Friday and hear about all our new releases, join our mailing list: www.joffebooks.com/contact

And when you tell your friends about us, just remember: it's pronounced Joffe as in coffee or toffee!

ALSO BY VERONICA HELEY

THE ELLIE QUICKE MYSTERIES

Book 1: MURDER AT THE ALTAR
Book 2: MURDER BY POISON PEN
Book 3: MURDER OF INNOCENCE
Book 4: MURDER BY ACCIDENT

THE BEA ABBOT AGENCY MYSTERIES

Book 1: A FALSE CHARITY
Book 2: A FALSE PICTURE
Book 3: A FALSE STEP
Book 4: A FALSE PRETENCE
Book 5: FALSE MONEY
Book 6: A FALSE REPORT
Book 7: A FALSE ALARM
Book 8: A FALSE DIAMOND
Book 9: A FALSE IMPRESSION
Book 10: A FALSE WALL
Book 11: A FALSE FIRE
Book 12: A FALSE PRIDE
Book 13: A FALSE ACCOUNT
Book 14: A FALSE CONCLUSION
Book 15: A FALSE FACE

Printed in Great Britain
by Amazon

42988896R00158